D1561574

THE
CAMBODIA FILE

Books by Jack Anderson

THE CAMBODIA FILE
CONFESSIONS OF A MUCKRAKER
THE CASE AGAINST CONGRESS

Books by Bill Pronzini

THE CAMBODIA FILE
LABYRINTH
BLOWBACK
GAMES
SNOWBOUND
UNDERCURRENT
THE VANISHED
PANIC!
THE SNATCH
THE STALKER

THE
CAMBODIA
FILE

Jack Anderson & Bill Pronzini

DOUBLEDAY & COMPANY, INC.
GARDEN CITY, NEW YORK
1981

ISBN: 0-385-14984-0
Library of Congress Catalog Card Number 80-5447

For our suffering fellowmen, the people of Cambodia

The good want power, but to weep barren tears.
The powerful goodness want; worse need for them.
The wise want love; and those who love want wisdom;
And all best things are thus confused to ill.
Many are strong and rich, and would be just,
But live among their suffering fellowmen
As if none felt; they know not what they do.

—Shelley
Prometheus Unbound

Prologue

Geographical and Historical Data (Updated Report, April 1970)

On a topographical map, Cambodia (or Kampuchea, as the country is known to its Khmer natives) may be seen as a great bowl, with heavily forested mountain ranges—the Dangrek, Cardamom, and Elephant—along three of its perimeters and a flat plain dominating two thirds of its central region. It is bordered on the west and north by Thailand, on the northeast by Laos, on the east and southeast by South Vietnam, and on the south and southwest by the Gulf of Thailand. Some 70,000 square miles in size, or approximately that of the state of Washington, it maintains a population estimated at seven million people. Its principal cities are Phnom Penh, the capital; Battambang City, Siem Reap, Kompong Som, and Kompong Cham.

A large portion of the central geographical zone is composed of water—the Tonle Sap, its tributaries (including the Tonle Sap River), and the Mekong River, which flows for five hundred miles through eastern Cambodia from Laos to South Vietnam. During the dry season, from October to May, the Tonle Sap shrinks to a swamp area of less than one thousand square miles with a depth of between three and ten feet; but in those months when the country is buffeted by monsoon rains (May to September), the Tonle Sap expands to cover twenty-five hundred square miles and attains a depth of from thirty to forty feet.

Influenced by the southeast monsoons, Cambodia's climate is tropical. Average annual rainfall is eighty-five inches, but the central plain receives less precipitation because of the sheltering mountains. The average annual temperature is eighty-two degrees Fahrenheit, with seasonal variations ranging from ninety-seven degrees in April and May to sixty-eight degrees in December and January.

The geographical location and climactic conditions combine to make the country rich in both vegetable and animal life. Forests cover 50 percent of the terrain; hardwoods such as teak predominate, along with rosewood, pitch pine, and a dense secondary growth of bamboo, rattan, banana, coconut and sugar palm, mango, orange, and kapok. The major crop is rice, with an average annual yield of more than two million metric tons; other important crops include latex (there are a number of thriving rubber plantations), tobacco, corn, cassava, millet, and sweet potatoes. Game beasts are prevalent in the mountainous areas, notably the wild ox (*koprei*), rhinoceros, leopard, panther, and tiger. Elephant and water buffalo also proliferate and are domesticated for use as draft animals.

There has been human settlement in the country since the Neolithic and Bronze Age periods, when the Somrongsen culture existed in the Tonle Sap region. Cambodia also appears in the writings of Chinese historians in the second century A.D. as part of the state of Funan. The earliest civilized inhabitants, however, were the Cham—a race which migrated to Indochina from southern India, bringing with them the Brahmin religion and the Pali script. The kingdoms of the Cham were well established in the sixth to eighth centuries A.D., when new immigrants, the Khmer, arrived from Laos.

The Khmers settled in the Tonle Sap area and soon became the country's dominant race. They brought not only the Buddhist religion but also a complex folklore comprised of a mixture of beliefs in pagan spirits and demons (*asuras*), and such Hindu mythical figures as crocodile and serpent gods. The fantastic and the supernatural held a great appeal for them, owing in part to the fact that they were ceaselessly harried by enemies—in the dry season by the Thais, in the rainy season by the Annamese (Vietnamese people who added a final mixing ingredient to produce the Cambodian race as we know it). It was the Khmers' constant state of misery and fear, caused by these aggressions, which stimulated their imaginations and encouraged the creation of legends and an established mythos.

At the height of their civilization, A.D. 850–900, the Khmers built the famed temple city of Angkor in the northern province of Siem Reap. It was completed under the rule of Jayavarman VII and flourished for more than two hundred years. It also represented the pinnacle of Khmer artistic achievement, an architectural wonder no less substantial than the Parthenon.

Although the Angkor empire collapsed in the thirteenth century, Angkor Wat remained the country's capital until 1434. In that year Khmer king Ponhea Yat established Phnom Penh—a settlement in the southeast-central sector where the Tonle Sap River, the Mekong River, and the Bassac River form a confluence known as the Quatre Bras (Four Arms) or Chakdomukh—as the new capital of Kampuchea. Angkor was ultimately abandoned to the jungle, not to be rediscovered until the 1800s.

After yet another century of bloody struggle for the crown, Cambodia was invaded by the Thais in 1593 and subsequently became a vassal state of Thailand. It continued to be a vassal state, except for short periods, until the intervention of the French in the middle nineteenth century.

The French, promising to protect Cambodia's independence from Thailand, half persuaded and half forced King Norodom I (1860–1904) to accept a French protectorate in 1864. They controlled Cambodia with no more compassion than the Thais had shown in previous centuries, however; their interest seemed to be more in increasing their Asian sphere of influence than in administering to the needs of the Cambodian people. The French governor generalship created a Grand Council of economic and financial interests; and under the council, consultative native assemblies were established in the individual provinces. But the assemblies had little function and no autonomy.

The twentieth century brought few immediate changes; the situation in Cambodia remained stable throughout World War I and the 1930s. It was not until the beginning of the Second World War in Europe that a major metamorphosis came about. The quick defeat of the French by Germany and the subsequent Vichy government gave the Cambodians a good deal of contempt for the French—the more so when Japan and Vichy concluded an agreement granting the Japanese full control of the country's ports, which in effect ceded over protectorate status to Japan. When, in March of 1945, Japan declared the French rule of Indochina at an end, King Norodom Sihanouk (the reigning monarch since 1941) declared independence.

The period of Cambodia's freedom was brief. The postwar French wanted their protectorate back; they offered a French union to Vietnam, Laos, and Cambodia. This act was considered one of betrayal by Cambodians and caused Sihanouk to leave the throne in protest and to go into voluntary exile. Once again there was revolt against French rule, with the resulting Indochina War bringing, after eight years, a final and catastrophic defeat of the French. This led to the Geneva Accords of July 21, 1954, which ensured the withdrawal of the French and the neutrality of Cambodia and Laos.

Sihanouk returned from exile to assume leadership once again, under an avowed posture of neutrality. Cambodia's significant leader of the twentieth century, Sihanouk was an intelligent but vain and arrogant monarchist who hated the United States and its freedom of the press, and who, like many nationalist figures of his type, believed that the people's will and his own were synonymous; i.e., that his conduct needed little justification. (During this period he produced, directed, and starred in several amateur suspense films of low artistic merit. Not only did he play the romantic lead in these films, but often cast in major roles other members of his family and court; his wife, in fact, in a film entitled *Joy of Living,* was one of a number of women with whom Sihanouk's flamboyant American character enjoyed the "rewards of dissipation.")

Sihanouk's policy of neutrality enabled the country to obtain substantial aid from those competing powers who were contesting for the neighboring state of Vietnam. American aid, however, was given under conditions which would have violated Cambodian neutrality and allowed American military occupation, and therefore Sihanouk rebelled. His swing to the left, under way from at least 1961 when he grew convinced that the Viet Cong were going to triumph in South Vietnam, became pronounced in 1963; when Washington would not support negotiations with the communists, he severed relations with the United States in that year. (See CIA INTELLIGENCE MEMORANDUM SC NO. 10527/65.)

It was a dozen years earlier than this, in late 1951, that the communists established their first foothold in the country with the formation of the Khmer People's Party. After the Geneva Accords, when guerrilla activities began to gain momentum through alliances with Vietnamese and Chinese insurgents, the Front Uni National du Kampuchea (FUNK), or National Liberation Front of Cambodia, was born. And in late September of 1960, the first nationwide Party Congress was held to formally constitute the Khmer Communist Party by adopting a set of party statutes and electing a Central Committee. As the war in Vietnam escalated through the 1960s, so did communist activity in Cambodia. By the end of the decade, FUNK had become a strong and unified force, particularly among the dissatisfied and poorly educated peasant population.

The escalation of the Vietnam War also served to make Cambodia of increasing interest to the United States (and to the communist countries as well), inasmuch as its geographical location meant that arms and troops could be moved from southern Cambodia into Vietnam. With the increase of American influence upon the economic and social structure of Cambodian life, the government's avowed neutrality became untenable; and in the eyes of many political figures, Sihanouk himself became an unacceptable leader. Thus, in the coup of March 18, 1970, Sihanouk was dismissed as chief of state by the National Assembly (the lower house) and the Council of the Kingdom (the upper house), and subsequently fled to Red China. The President of the National Assembly, Cheng Heng, was confirmed in his place, and Commander in Chief of the Khmer Armed Forces, Lon Nol, was named Prime Minister of the Salvation Government.

Despite internal difficulties and continuing communist activity in the provinces, it is the belief of most observers that the new regime will, with American assistance, soon bring an end to the country's centuries-long history of bloody strife and civil chaos.

Excerpts from a Public Address by President Richard M. Nixon, May 1, 1970

For the past five years . . . North Vietnam has occupied military sanctuaries all along the Cambodian frontier with South Vietnam. Some of these extend up to twenty miles into Cambodia. They are used for hit-and-run attacks on American and South Vietnamese forces in South Vietnam.

These communist-occupied territories contain major base camps, training sites, logistics facilities, weapons and ammunition factories, airstrips, and prisoner-of-war compounds.

For five years, neither the United States nor South Vietnam moved against those enemy sanctuaries because we did not wish to violate the territory of a neutral nation. Even after the Vietnamese communists began to expand these sanctuaries four weeks ago, we counseled patience to our South Vietnamese allies and imposed restraints on our commanders. . . .

North Vietnam in the last two weeks has stripped away all pretense of respecting the sovereignty or neutrality of Cambodia. Thousands of their soldiers are invading the country from the sanctuaries; they are encircling the capital of Phnom Penh. Cambodia has sent out a call to the United States and a number of other nations for assistance.

If this effort succeeds, Cambodia would become a vast enemy staging area and springboard for attacks on South Vietnam along six hundred miles of frontier—and a refuge where enemy troops could return from combat without fear of retaliation.

North Vietnamese men and supplies could then be poured into that country, jeopardizing not only the lives of our own men but the people of South Vietnam as well. . . .

This is my decision:

In cooperation with the armed forces of South Vietnam, attacks are being launched this week to clean out major enemy sanctuaries on the Cambodian-Vietnam border.

A major responsibility for the ground operations is being assumed by South Vietnamese forces. For example, the attacks in several areas . . . are exclusively South Vietnamese ground operations under South Vietnamese command with the United States providing air and logistical support. . . .

This is not an invasion of Cambodia. The areas in which these attacks will be launched are completely occupied and controlled by North Vietnamese forces. Our purpose is not to occupy these areas. Once enemy forces are driven out of these sanctuaries and their military supplies destroyed, we will withdraw.

These actions are in no way directed at the security interests of any nation. Any government that chooses to use these actions as a pretext for harming relations with the United States will be doing so on its own responsibility and at its own initiative and we will draw the appropriate conclusions. . . .

We take this action not for the purpose of expanding the war into Cambodia but for the purpose of ending the war in Vietnam and winning the just peace we all desire. . . .

Column by Jack Anderson, July 4, 1970

Washington—The lessons of Cambodia, now that U.S. troops are back on the Vietnam side of the border, are being reviewed at the highest levels. Out of this agonizing analysis have already come two conclusions:

Lesson No. 1—President Nixon will send Cambodia all the military aid he can wangle out of Congress. He will also support the South Vietnamese forces that continue to fight in Cambodia. But he has emphasized to subordinates: "We have no intention of going back."

Lesson No. 2—Never again will the President commit American armed forces without taking congressional leaders into his confidence. His failure to consult Capitol Hill has created the worst constitutional crisis since the congressional rebellion against President Woodrow Wilson after World War I.

The Nixon administration will continue, of course, to present the Cambodian operation as a glorious success. But in the deepest of privacy, some top officials are calling it Richard Nixon's Bay of Pigs.

Excerpts from a White House Press Statement on the End of U.S. Bombing in Cambodia, August16, 1973

As the President indicated in his letter to congressional leaders on August 2, this administration is terminating combat activity in Cambodia in compliance with the specific, direct, and binding instructions from the Congress. The President continues to hold grave reservations about the wisdom of this legislative action. He is concerned that by its action, the Congress has eliminated an important incentive for a negotiated settlement in Cambodia and weakened the security of Cambodia's neighbors in Southeast Asia and has eroded the structure of peace in Indochina laid down in the [Paris cease-fire] agreements of January 27. . . .

We continue strongly to support a cease-fire through negotiations among the Khmer parties. An end to the fighting and respect for Cambodia's sovereignty and neutrality are our principal goals there. . . .

Excerpt from U.S. Department of State Post Report (Khmer Republic), January 1975

Phnom Penh has long been considered one of Southeast Asia's most charming and beautiful capitals. The products of Khmer culture and tradition, as well as the influence of the French, can be seen throughout this attractive and exceptionally clean city.

Recent events have created inconveniences and curtailed travel but have also added an atmosphere of challenge and interest to the post. Personnel assigned to Phnom Penh are participating in the activities of a post of critical importance in international affairs.

May Heaven protect our King
And give him happiness and glory;
May he reign over our hearts and our destinies.
He who—heir to the builder Monarchs—
Governs the proud and old Kingdom.

The temples sleep in the forest
Recalling the grandeur of the Moha Nokar.
The Khmer race is as eternal as the rocks.
Let us have confidence in the faith of Kampuchea
The empire which defies the years.

Songs rise in the pagodas
To the glory of the holy Buddhist faith.
Let us be faithful to the creed of our ancestors
So that Heaven may reward us
Of the old Khmer country of the Moha Nokar.

—Cambodian national anthem
prior to March 1970

The Khmers are recognized in the world as issued
    from a warrior nation,
Winning resounding victories and erecting monuments.
The old artistic monuments in abundance are the
    reflections
Of the flourishing civilization of our ancestors.
Khmers, stand up! Khmers, stand up!
Khmers, stand up to fight and to glorify the Republic!

—Cambodian national anthem
spring 1970 to April 17, 1975

The red, red blood splatters the cities and plains
  of the Cambodian fatherland,
The sublime blood of the workers and peasants,
The blood of revolutionary combatants of both sexes.
That blood spills out into great indignation and a
  resolute urge to fight.
17 April, that day under the revolutionary flag
The blood liberates us from slavery.

—National anthem of
Democratic Kampuchea

PART ONE

Mid-February to April 12, 1975

Foxworth

Parasols.

There were scores of them in Le Phnom Park—white, yellow, blue, varying shades of red; bobbing, sometimes spinning in slender brown fingers. The park seemed abloom with parasols, as bright and cheerful as tropical flora.

Than Kim, David Foxworth's Khmer mistress, had one: large, white, frilly, which she had bought in one of the French shops near the Marché Central. She carried it in her left hand, the one closest to him, so that it shaded both of them as they walked. She spun it continually, like a child playing with a pinwheel, and on her delicate face there was an expression of pleasure.

Around them, the usual Sunday morning crowd ebbed and flowed. Khmer male civilians in Western clothing or, here and there, in peasant pajamas; Khmer women in light summer dresses or native *sampots*. Republican Army officers in green khaki. An occasional war correspondent or official from one of the embassies, eyes hidden behind dark glasses. Saffron-robed monks with shaved heads, carrying brass begging bowls in one hand and parasols in the other. Vendors selling fried bananas, pieces of sugared mango. Fortune-tellers working the stupa-ringed *wat* atop Le Phnom, the ninety-foot man-made hill built to commemorate the founding of the city in 1434.

The air was thick with sultry dry-season heat. Sunlight reflected in dancing barbs off the water in the fountains, made the mossy gray stone of the pagoda glisten with a sweaty sheen. Sugar palms and scarlet jacaranda trees offered some shade, but most of the strolling women and all of the bonzes carried parasols. And many of them wore the same expression of pleasure as Kim.

Parasols, smiling faces, an atmosphere of gaiety and well-being. Paris in the spring, strollers in the Tuileries.

Phnom Penh under siege in war-torn Cambodia.

Foxworth could hear the far-off sounds of the morning shelling—the low-pitched whine of B-40, B-41, and 107-mm. rockets coming out of the communist rocket belt in the swamplands of the lower Mekong, near the ferry town of Neak Luong thirty-eight miles to the southeast. It had been six weeks since the Khmer Rouge launched, on New Year's Day, their full-scale offensive against Phnom Penh; six weeks since they had cut all roads into the city, sealed off the sixty miles of river between Phnom Penh and South Vietnam that had provided the capital with over 90 percent of its vital food and military supplies; six weeks since large numbers of refugees began pouring into the city, carrying tales of enemy atrocities in the surrounding provinces. And yet most of the Khmers did not seem to act or react any differently than they had in the past. Even among the well-educated with whom he worked at the embassy, there was almost no display of anxiety.

It was bizarre. People went about their weekday business with an air of subdued normalcy, and on Sundays they clogged Norodom and Monivong Boulevards and the quay along the Tonle Sap, walking hand in hand, smiling in the sun. And the parasols bloomed again, gay as ever among the greenery in Le Phnom Park.

Foxworth had been in Phnom Penh for well over a year now, but the Khmer attitude still baffled him. "You think us unfeeling," Kim had said to him not long ago. "We are not. It is only that we have suffered many years now and we are weary of war; there has been too much tragedy in our lives. If we cannot have peace and happiness, then we must pretend we have them. We must ignore the ugliness and embrace the goodness. That is the only way we can survive."

It sounded naïve and self-defeating to Foxworth. You didn't win wars and solve internal problems by pretending they didn't exist. So it was no explanation at all, as far as he was concerned. Maybe there *wasn't* an explanation, or at least none which the Western mind could fathom. More and more of late his intellectual grasp of the country, like the country itself, seemed to be collapsing. Or perhaps shifting toward a different perspective, one he hadn't yet realized.

He wished he had not allowed Kim to talk him into coming here today. The heat, the sporadic sounds of war, the false gaiety and the damned parasols—all of these had combined to make him feel irritable and frustrated. Not to mention the looks of contempt and occasional jeers directed at Kim because she was in the company of an American. In the matriarchal Cambodian society, in which the woman's role of manager, master of common sense, and organization was as rigidly defined as that of homemaker in the States, any Khmer woman involved with an American was thought either foolish because she was being used as a plaything by a foreigner or an outright whore. The prejudice at the upper levels of society was veiled, but out here in the streets, among the lower classes, it was open and sometimes ugly. It would have been much more comfortable for both of them if they had spent the morning at his villa, or swimming and playing tennis at the Cercle Sportif Khmer.

More sharply than he meant to, he said to her, "Do you have to keep twirling that thing?"

"My parasol?"

"Yes."

"It bothers you?"

"Yes," he said, "it bothers me."

"Why?"

"Because it does, that's all."

Obligingly, she stopped spinning the umbrella and smiled up at him. Her features were not only delicate but sensual, flawless: prominent cheekbones, small round mouth, oval brown eyes that were large and open—the kind Khmers considered to be an indication of intelligence. Thick wavy hair, midnight-black, worn long down the curve of her back. Slender supple body, small-breasted, with skin as smooth and burnished as a bronze statuette. He had thought her strikingly attractive the first time he'd seen her at a chancery reception; now he thought her beautiful. But did he know her any better now than he had at that first meeting?

They had made a half circle of the park, from southwest to northeast, and were a block away from the Tonle Sap. Kim asked, "Shall we walk along the river for a while?"

"I'd rather go to my villa."

"Only for a short while, *dekkun*?" She used the Khmer word playfully; it meant "power and favor" and was employed by the lower classes when begging courtesy from a member of the upper class. "We will have the afternoon and evening alone together."

He could not refuse her. She asked little of him and refused him nothing. "All right," he said.

They left the park and walked down a side street to the Boulevard 9th Tola. The radio clipped to Foxworth's belt gave off squelch and the voice of the control operator on radio watch at the embassy. But the call wasn't for him; it was for one of the other employees, who was on some sort of off-hours assignment. The radios were a nuisance sometimes, but they were also a vital communications link. There were few operational telephones in Phnom Penh, and the embassy radio net was the only way for special orders, vehicle dispatches, and other information and instructions to be transmitted.

When they had crossed the wide boulevard, dodging through French automobiles and motorbikes and three-wheeled passenger cyclos, they walked out on the quay that sloped to the water's edge. More people here: more parasols. Under the sun the muddy brown surface of the river glistened with quicksilver highlights. Sampans and canoelike pirogues dotted it; a flat-bottomed, paddle-powered ferry drifted past; downstream a GKR gunboat was visible, flying the rectangular blue-white-red flag of the republic.

Something else was drifting past, Foxworth saw, between the ferry and the quay, less than fifty meters from where he and Kim were. A pair of black logs, he thought at first. But when he stopped and peered out there he realized that they were two bloated bodies clad in peasant dress, floating face down and side by side like a parody of the lovers who strolled together on the quay.

One of the pirogues avoided the bodies' sluggish progress; the Khmer inside looked at them without curiosity. As did Kim. Her attention shifted to a young girl, dressed in a black *sampot* and a loose-fitting maroon blouse, who stood nearby. Balanced on the girl's head was a basket filled with pieces of sugared fruit. Kim gestured to her, gave her twenty riels for two pieces, and then turned back to Foxworth. Smiling, she extended one of the pieces.

"For you," she said.

He shook his head. "I don't want it."

"It's very good—"

"I'm not in the mood for sweets."

Kim's smile faded; she looked hurt. She opened her purse and put both pieces of fruit inside—carefully, as if saving her small gift for another time.

"There are two bodies out there," Foxworth said, gesturing at the river. "You saw them."

"Yes?"

"Dead men, Kim. Dead Khmers."

"Yes," she said.

"Well? Doesn't it bother you, for God's sake?"

She looked at him with her wonderful, unreadable eyes. "There are dead Khmers everywhere," she said gravely. "This is a country of dead Khmers."

Natalie

Natalie Rosen arrived in Phnom Penh—her first and last visit to Cambodia—on the last day of February.

She had had quite a bit of difficulty in obtaining a visa because of the gravity of the war situation. It had taken more than a week of applications and interviews at the U.S. embassy in Bangkok, and even at that she might not have gotten the visa except for her father. He was on sufficiently good terms with the New York State Democratic Committee to have had them lean on the State Department. Not that her father was anxious for her to enter Cambodia alone, but he had accepted the necessity of it. There was only so much the Refugee Relief Fund could do in New York and Thailand, through their own offices and through those of the International Red Cross, the Catholic Relief Service, and other refugee organizations. It was important for someone—for her, because she was already in Thailand for visits to the refugee camps along the Cambodian border—to view the situation firsthand, talk to American officials, relief workers, and refugees in Phnom Penh.

The Air Cambodge flight from Bangkok landed at Pochentong Airport a few minutes past nine, after diving at what seemed a suicidal angle to avoid rocket fire. By the time the plane jolted across the shell-pocked runway to the terminal, and she and the other few passengers had disembarked and made their way past flak-jacketed ground personnel and heavily armed soldiers, Natalie was shaken and drenched in perspiration. And aware that her five days in Cambodia was going to be an experience unlike any other in her life, one she was certain never to forget.

It was ten-thirty before she cleared Customs and picked up her bags. No one seemed to speak English; she would have been lost without her shaky French. But at least the people waiting to meet her, as had been arranged by cable, were both fluent in English. The man was a member of the GKR refugee service and the woman, an attractive Khmer named Than Kim, worked as an interpreter and refugee liaison for the U.S. embassy.

They escorted her out to a government-marked Fiat, the man talking all the while, asking the kind of polite questions natives in places like Spain might ask tourists. And then, when they were under way, offering the latest war news: the communists had ceased using the riel and adopted a barter system, according to a clandestine radio broadcast by Khmer Rouge leader

Khieu Samphan, and had also released a list of "seven trait-ors," including Lon Nol, Sirik Matak, and Cheng Heng, who were targeted for execution; increased military activity around Neak Luong had forced the evacuation of all Catholic Relief Service and GKR Red Cross teams, which meant that some thirty thousand people were short of food and medical supplies. The man's cheerfulness struck Natalie as remarkable under the circumstances, and after a while became a little off-putting.

The trip into the city was hot and depressing. All along the four-lane highway, amid the signs and billboards in squiggly Khmer lettering and the neat French-style landscaping, were the scars and festering wounds of war—burned-out buildings, crudely built refugee shacks, ugly spills of garbage and coils of barbed wire, young boys openly selling black-market gasoline in glass jars. She had seen squalor and devastation before, but here it was contrasted against lush tropical vegetation and sym-metrical city planning; here it seemed somehow even more ter-rible than in the refugee camps in Thailand.

"What did we do?" she said aloud. "What *can* we do?"

The woman, Than Kim, turned toward her with a sad smile. "There are many problems," she said. "So many refugees, so much need. Not even the Americans know what to do."

No, Natalie thought, not even the Americans know what to do. Least of all the Americans.

They reached the center of Phnom Penh and turned left past the railroad station, onto a wide avenue called Monivong Boul-evard that was lined with bright red jacaranda trees. It was also crowded with military vehicles, most of which carried the Re-publican Army insignia of the Black Cobra, and with pedicabs, bicycles, motor scooters. Natalie saw several armed soldiers, several civilians in peasant dress begging or selling wares on street corners. Otherwise the atmosphere seemed, pathetically, little different from the central district of Bangkok or any other large city in Southeast Asia.

Hotel Le Phnom, where she would be staying, was a white French Colonial building divided into a four-story main section and a three-story adjunct, set on landscaped grounds behind a low wrought-iron fence. The GKR driver parked in front of the main entrance. Kim led Natalie across the covered porchway and inside.

The lobby was dark and seemed to drip with heat. As they crossed to the reception desk, Kim explained that the hotel had been mostly without electricity for the past few weeks. It didn't matter that much to Natalie—she was used to the discomforts of hot weather—but Kim seemed to think it was necessary that she know why there was no air conditioning.

When Kim had left her with a promise to return after the midday rest period, and Natalie had finished signing the register, a male Caucasian in a rumpled tropical suit rose from one of the lobby chairs and approached her. He was tall and thin and dark-haired, a few years older than her twenty-six, with an unshaven Hapsburg jaw that made his lower teeth prominent and kept him from being particularly good-looking. He leaned a hand on the desk beside her and gave her an intense look of appraisal.

"Natalie Rosen, right?" he said.

"How did you know that?"

"Word's been around you were expected. My name's Deighan, Peter Deighan. Maybe you've heard of me."

She had heard of him, all right. He was a free-lance journalist whose work had appeared in a number of American magazines and so-called underground newspapers over the past ten years. He had begun by writing extensively and insightfully about the antiwar movement, the rise and fall of the SDS, the 1968 Democratic convention; then, on the basis of an article on the convention called "The Year of the Pig in the Pit of the Tiger," he had persuaded a major slick magazine to send him to Vietnam as a roving correspondent. His combat-zone dispatches had been published in that magazine over the next three years, attracted a good deal of critical attention, been compared to the war correspondence of Hemingway and Robert Ruark, and later gathered into a collection called *The Only War We Had* which had been nominated for a Pulitzer Prize.

For the past year or so, Deighan had been in Cambodia on a similar assignment. But this time he had stayed away from the front: almost all of his Cambodia dispatches had been written from and about Phnom Penh. And both Natalie and the critics felt they lacked the power and commitment of his earlier work and seemed gratuitously anti-American—the writings of a tired, disillusioned, and bitter man.

"Yes," she said, "I know who you are, Mr. Deighan."

"Call me Peter; I hate formality. When can we talk?"

"Talk?"

"An interview. On your work for the Refugee Relief Fund, that sort of thing."

Natalie hesitated. It occurred to her that he might want to use an interview to attack the refugee program as some kind of hypocritical undertaking, which would do the Fund no good at all. But then, if she refused him he might write a negative piece anyway, out of spite. There was an abrasiveness about him, a kind of seedy arrogance that she didn't care for; and yet his eyes had a pained and somehow vulnerable look that was appealing.

"Well, I have an appointment at two o'clock," she said, "and I'd like to get settled right now. How about this evening?"

"I don't work evenings. How long do you take to get settled?"

"Half an hour or so, I suppose."

"Hotel bar in forty-five minutes? We'll have an hour before your appointment."

"All right, Mr. Deighan. Forty-five minutes."

"Peter," he said. "For Christ's sake."

He gave her a nod that was almost curt and drifted across to the bar entrance. She looked after him for a moment, then shrugged and followed a Khmer room boy across to the stairs.

Her room, on the second floor, was dark and semielegant in a florid French manner; kerosene lamps were set around it to substitute for the nonfunctioning electric lights. A posted notice on the door to the adjoining bath, written in French, urged guests to conserve water. Heeding it, Natalie washed herself with a cloth dipped in cool water, instead of taking the shower she wanted, and dried off carefully to avoid heat rash and fungus infection—two constant threats in this sort of climate.

Then she put her black hair into a bun, changed into fresh clothes, and spent some time unpacking.

When she went downstairs again and entered the bar, she found Peter Deighan sitting alone at a table that overlooked a deserted swimming pool. His eyes followed her through a cloud of cigarette smoke as she approached him, but he didn't stand or say anything. She sat down across from him. Her breasts, which were good enough but hardly spectacular, seemed to interest him a great deal; he stared at them for a full ten seconds before lifting his gaze to her face. Terrific, Natalie thought. First an interview, then an invitation. And not a subtle invitation, either: "Want to go somewhere and screw?" or the equivalent thereof. The macho approach. Hemingway and Ruark, with a little Dos Passos thrown in.

Deighan said, "Drink?"

"No, thanks. It's a little too early for me."

"You wouldn't think so if you'd spent as much time in war zones as I have." He raised his glass—something clear that was probably vodka—and tossed it off Russian fashion, with a back flip of his wrist.

God, yes, Natalie thought. Hemingway *redux*.

"War zones," Deighan said again, as if he liked the sound of the phrase. "Gives people like me a chance to wallow in it."

"Wallow in what?"

"Death and destruction. Free fire zones and daily briefings and swarms of refugees and bodies in the streets. It isn't much of a war as the great ones go, but it's the only war we've got."

The only war we've got; *The Only War We Had*. He seemed to like that phrase, too. Natalie wondered how many drinks he'd had in the past forty-five minutes.

"About the Refugee Relief Fund," she said.

"What about it?"

"Mr. Deighan, I thought you—"

"Peter. *Peter,* damn it."

"I thought you wanted to interview me about the Fund."

"Refugee relief," Deighan said. He lighted a fresh cigarette. "Save what's left of the little brown folks in their little brown bombed-out country."

"Look, maybe we'd better postpone this until later—"

He leaned toward her, his eyes bright and suddenly furious. "You know what's been going on here, lady? You have any idea what I'm wallowing in? Well, I'll tell you. Between March 1969 and August 1973, U.S. planes dropped 539,129 tons of bombs on Cambodia; and since May 1970 the invasion by U.S. ground troops has been responsible for half a million Khmer deaths and over three million refugees. *That's* what I'm wallowing in."

"I know the statistics," she said.

"Do you? Do you really? I'm not talking about statistics, sweetheart; I'm talking about people. Americans, your countrymen and mine, coming over here and slaughtering half a million little brown people in the name of democracy. And it wasn't just Nixon and Kissinger, either—it was all of us because we all let it happen. You hear me? I say we're *all* guilty."

"I hear you," Natalie said levelly. "If you're looking for an outraged argument from me, you won't get it. It so happens I think you're right."

Cambodia File: Post Security Report — Foxworth, David (Top Secret)

White Anglo-Saxon male, born Cleveland (Shaker Heights) Ohio, January 31, 1944. Father: Benjamin Foxworth, Senior Vice-President for Development, American Motors Corporation. Mother: Dorothy (née Brown), President of Chapter, League of Women Voters. No other living relatives.

Educated in private schools, Cleveland area; B.S., Economics, University of Michigan, 1966; M.S., Economics, 1968. Member: Young Americans for Freedom; Young Republicans. Economics Instructor, Michigan State University, 1968-1972. State Vice-Chairman, Committee to Re-Elect the President,

1972. Researcher, Ford Foundation, 1970-1972. U.S. Diplomatic Corps, 1972.

Previous posts: Kuala Lumpur, Malaysia, 1972-1973. Assigned to chancery, Khmer Republic, January 1974.

Physical characteristics: Height 5'10"; weight 175 lbs; no physical deformities or identifying marks. (See attached photographs.) IQ: 123 (Stanford-Binet administered). Languages spoken: French (fluent); Khmer (rudimentary). Religious affiliation: Protestant. Marital status: unmarried.

Embassy duties: Political liaison with native community (Political Section); also engaged in coordinating interrogation of refugees and in overseeing newly augmented refugee program; also involved in special assignment work for the Central Intelligence Agency, regarding matters of low-level security.

Residence: No. 115 MV Mao Tse-tung, Chamcar Mon sector, Phnom Penh.

Comments: Subject has never evinced any manner of disloyalty to the United States; criminal associations not noted, political affiliations with suspect groups not noted. In 1969-1970 subject lived with one Andrea Vernon (deceased 12/19/74) off-campus at Michigan State University in evident out-of-wedlock relationship. No offspring; relationship terminated by mutual consent. Since arrival in Khmer Republic, has evinced no suspicious thoughts with regard to status quo. Established evident out-of-wedlock relationship with Khmer woman, Than Kim (See REPORT—THAN KIM), September 1974; but such relationships common among middle-echelon post employees, and as Than Kim is also employed at the chancery, it may be assumed that subject's involvement with her imposes no risk.

Security clearance: Level Five.

Foxworth

The U.S. embassy complex, located on the corner of Avenue 9th Tola and Avenue Suthearoth, was like a microcosm of

Phnom Penh itself: battle-scarred, protected by maximum security forces, but still functioning under a pretense of normalcy. Or so Foxworth thought when he arrived for work on the morning of February 28. The surrounding chain-link fence showed evidence of shell damage, as did the main embassy building within; and the rocket netting atop other surmounts of barbed wire and wooden slatting gave it all a grim, fortresslike aspect. The Cambodian soldiers stationed at the guardhouse and on the gates, the marines patrolling the grounds, completed the impression.

Foxworth stopped his Fiat in front of the barrier at the right-side gate, waited through a standard bomb check on the car—mirrors attached to broom handles, to scan the undercarriage—and was admitted to the compound. He drove past the two-story concrete slab of the main building, past the motor pool, the bunkers, and the basketball court, the remaining single-story frame buildings with their sheet metal roofs, into the parking lot at the rear. He parked opposite the document incinerator, crossed around behind the building where the military delivery team and military attachés worked, and entered the embassy through the thick iron door on the east side.

In the mausoleumlike lobby a lone young woman, three quarters Vietnamese and one quarter Cambodian, sat behind a square reception desk. She liked to flirt with Americans and winked broadly at Foxworth as he passed. He smiled back at her—and then stopped smiling when he remembered the comment one of his coworkers had made not long ago: "If a rocket gets across the netting and hits the front entrance, old Theda Bara will be the only casualty. All of *us* are protected, thank God."

To the left and right of the reception desk, against the side walls, were two heavy plexiglass doors behind which marine guards stood at attention. Foxworth went to the door on the left, spoke to the guard there through an intercom unit. After he was admitted he went up the stairway beyond, punched his code number at the metal door on the second-floor landing, then followed the long corridor inside to his office.

The first thing he did when he stepped inside was to turn on the air conditioner. As early as it was, the air in there was sticky with heat. He thought again that it was a good thing the embassy had its own electrical generator. Sleeping almost every night lately without air conditioning was bad enough; working without it would have been intolerable.

On the gray-metal surface of his desk, he noticed, was an envelope marked with his name and the words "Eyes Only." He knew what it was, of course: another communiqué from CIA headquarters in McLean, Virginia, delivered in the latest diplomatic pouch from Washington and passed through POLMIL 3, the resident CIA office. Now what? he thought. But instead of opening it or sitting down, he crossed to the window and stood looking out. He had worked for the CIA ever since coming to Phnom Penh, but his connection was minor, mostly the gathering of military data from refugees and other sources. There were some who claimed that the Central Intelligence Agency had masterminded the 1970 coup which toppled Sihanouk from power and installed Lon Nol in his place, but while Foxworth was not privileged to upper-level policy decisions, he discredited the possibility. In his mind the CIA was an honorable organization, and serving it was just another way in which he could serve his country; he was proud of his status with the Company. Still and all, the way things were being handled these days—increasing demands for information, heavy emphasis on secrecy and cloak-and-dagger intrigue—was vaguely annoying. He had enough work and enough headaches without almost daily communiqués from McLean.

Past the curved iron railing of his balcony, beyond the compound fence, he could see Chamcar Mon, where Lon Nol lived and held court, a block distant. Sunlight glinted off the shards of broken glass that, with barbed wire and rocket netting, topped its outer walls. But Lon Nol's security was not as good as that of the embassy; it tended to be weak and vulnerable. Not unlike the government itself . . .

Behind him he heard the door open; he turned from the window. Tom Boyd. Boyd shut the door, said "Morning, Dave," and came forward to the desk. He was a big thick-necked man, Foxworth's age, with a pencil mustache that might have once been grown to make him look older but that now only made him look callow. Foxworth didn't consider him a close friend among the two hundred Americans on the embassy staff, but they got along well enough to play tennis at the Cercle Sportif Khmer or to socialize once in a while.

Boyd reached out and tapped the envelope with a blunt forefinger. He was CIA-connected too, Foxworth knew. "You read this yet?" he asked.

"No, not yet."

"You're going to love it," Boyd said. "All about the screening of potential Khmer evacuees."

"Already?"

"Sure already. Time's getting short, son."

"How long do you think we've got?"

"Three months, maximum. Hell, we've already begun a general phasing out of staff—all nonessential personnel by twos and threes on the commercial flights."

"You and I won't be leaving that way," Foxworth said.

"Not much chance. Lucky buggers, aren't we."

"You want to evacuate that badly, Tom?"

"I don't want my ass shot off, that's for sure."

"It's not going to come to that."

"Let's hope not."

Foxworth shook his head, sat down and brooded at the calendar on his desk. Emergency evacuation of the embassy had been in the planning for more than ten months, when it first began to appear that American funds might run out and that, even if they didn't, Lon Nol's forces would not be able to keep the Khmer communists from taking Phnom Penh. But the plans had not been worked out in detail until November, after the beginning of the KC's new dry-season offensive and the sudden exodus of many of the other Western and pro-Western diplomatic missions, who feared for their safety. And the first steps hadn't been taken until the December report of a major meeting in KC Area 304, Kompong Cham at Stung Treng, between the Khmer Rouge and the North Vietnamese military authority, at which the assault on Phnom Penh had been mapped out. Now evacuation was no longer either a possibility or a probability. It was an imminent actuality. Embassy staff being phased out; U. S. Marines, helicopters, and warships on standby alert. Admission that defeat was inevitable: the capital was going to fall, the country was going to topple, and then the communists would control one more critical chunk of Southeast Asia.

"Bastards," Boyd said abruptly.

Foxworth looked up. "Who? The Reds?"

Boyd waved a hand and said, "All of them. The Reds, Lon Nol and his parasites, Sihanouk—*all* of them. The world press is going to have a field day when we pull out. Not to mention those elitist pseudo-liberal sons of bitches back home. You know that as well as I do."

"I know it," Foxworth agreed. He paused. "How closely are we supposed to screen the Cambodians?"

"Pretty closely if they're nonstatus civilians or lower-echelon military personnel. Embassy and government people have priority, and security clearance already, so we won't have to worry too much about them. There just isn't that much room on the commercial and military flights, that's the problem. Or on the helicopters when the time comes for Operation Eagle Pull."

"A lot of them won't want to go in any case."

"True enough," Boyd said, and made a gesture that expressed contempt. "It's that damned Asian attitude again. They think they can sit down with the Reds, work with them, and they can't be told any different. They don't even pay attention to the atrocity reports. Or if they do, they think it won't happen here after we're gone."

"How does Samthan feel?"

"Who knows?" Boyd said. Samthan was the Khmer woman with whom he had been having an affair for some months, his third Cambodian mistress in his three-year tour of duty at the post. "I can't talk to her. I can't talk to any of these people." He smiled like a Harvard undergraduate, which was what he had once been, and said, "In the sack, thank Christ, it's an international language."

"Are you taking her with you when you go?"

Boyd lit one of the French cigarettes he liked. "I don't think so. You taking yours?"

"Kim?"

"Unless you've got another one on the string."

"I want to take her," Foxworth said. "But she's suspected for some time that we're going to pull out and she doesn't like the idea."

"The old crap about us being responsible for the war, I suppose, and then running out on them." Boyd exhaled noisily; smoke drifted across the room, fluttering in the draft from the air conditioner. "Tell me something, Dave."

"If I can."

"You serious about Kim?"

Foxworth hesitated. "In a way," he said at length.

"It's a mistake, getting too involved with them. I'm not with mine and it's going to save me all kinds of grief. There's a whole country of women back home, don't forget that."

A sudden small anger flared inside Foxworth. "And Kim's just another little brown native, right?"

"Hey," Boyd said, "take it easy. Don't jump on me. I care about these people too, you know. I've put three years of my life into this godforsaken country and it's not my fault it came out this way."

From outside, faintly, there was the booming thud of an explosion—not just a bursting shell but the kind of concussion that meant a fuel storage tank, or maybe a factory building, had gone up. Communist rockets had been finding more and more targets within the city limits in recent days; by day the hot sky was smeared with billows and tracers of smoke, and by night you could see the pulsing glow of fires against the skyline.

Boyd jabbed out his cigarette in the desk ashtray. "I mean, I worry about what's going to happen after the Reds take over. It's going to be bad, my friend."

Foxworth was silent.

"And I mean *bad,*" Boyd said. "Pure screaming hell."

Chey Han

At 0800 hours on the first day of March, Field Commander Chey Han and the FUNK battalion he led captured the village of Cheom Pram in Kompong Chhnang Province. They took it as they had taken other progovernment villages on their push southward to Phnom Penh—swiftly, mercilessly, in the glorious name of the revolutionary Angkar.

Resistance was minimal, as reports had led Chey to believe it would be. There had been heavy fighting in the area for the past few days, but he and his soldiers had driven the government troops steadily backward until the village became vulnerable; once again the T-28 bombers and American-made Cobra gunships of the Forces Armées Nationales Khmer had not been able to halt or even slow the advance. Most of the people of Cheom Pram had fled during the night. Fewer than two hundred of the foolish village militia and but a handful of FANK soldiers had stayed to face the wrath of the People's liberation forces.

The soldiers broke through the flimsy line of defense on the northern perimeter of Cheom Pram within an hour after the fire fight began, using mortar fire at first and then grenades and automatic weapons. When they reached the dusty shell-pitted main street, stopping only long enough to seize more American weapons from the bodies of the fallen, the village was theirs. There remained only the tasks of searching and securing each of the *paillotes* and of crushing a last small pocket of the enemy near the *wat* at the southern end.

Chey Han's men, and the *neary* who fought beside them, fanned out through the village: silent soldiers of the revolution, clad in ragged military and civilian dress—black pajamas, the green khaki uniforms of the enemy, *sampots,* Western-style shirts and jeans, Ho Chi Minh sandals, bandoliers of ammunition for their assault guns. The front ranks converged on the wing-roofed *wat,* the rest went to the nearest rows of stilt houses. There had been no need for Chey to issue orders; the soldiers were well disciplined and had had much experience in the securing of captured territory.

He stood alone in the middle of the street and surveyed the area, his .45 caliber American M1 pointing like a finger toward Phnom Penh to the south. A row of three *paillotes,* and the sugar palms and banana trees flanking them, had been burned by artillery fire; they smoldered like charred skeletons in the morning sun. Here and there were red-streaked corpses, the carcasses of oxen and water buffalo.

Most of the storage areas beneath the stilt houses were cluttered with rickety oxcarts, tireless bicycles, plows, hand tools, personal possessions; a live goat bawled madly in one nearby. This told Chey that Cheom Pram had been abandoned in great haste, and he nodded with satisfaction. Perhaps they had not bothered to take all their rice stores with them, as had been the case in other liberated villages. If not, the Angkar would be pleased. More food for the People's army; the soldiers fought even more fiercely when their stomachs were full.

A brief flurry of activity at a *paillote* fifty meters distant drew Chey's attention. An old man had been hiding in the litter beneath it and had been flushed by one of the cadre. Chey heard a shout, saw the old man stagger out and run away, bawling as madly as the goat, toward the jungle that stretched behind the village to the east. The soldier leveled the Chinese AK-47 he carried and ended the old man's flight with a single burst.

Chey looked toward the *wat* again. The firing there had become sporadic, and now it ceased altogether: the final pocket of resistance had been eliminated. A heavy silence descended on the village, one thick with heat and the mingled odors of dust and blood and excrement.

He lowered his M1, and with his uniform sleeve wiped gritty sweat from his light-tan face. He was a muscular, wide-shouldered man in his early thirties, a few inches taller than the average Khmer, with a flattened nose and short cowlicked hair that gave him a somewhat brutish appearance. His wife, whom he had seen only twice since joining FUNK in 1969, had called him her Great Ox. He considered this a compliment, an indication of strength. In his native Preah Vihear Province, he had been a menial for all his strength, but that had been a long time ago, in another life.

Men and *neary* were beginning to emerge from the stilt houses, some of them carrying sacks of rice and other abandoned foodstuffs. These were placed in the center of the street, in rows and piles for swift loading onto trucks and subsequent transportation to the support base near the Krang Ponlei. Yes: the Angkar Leu would be pleased.

Chey moved among them, toward the *wat*. One of his lieutenants, Prak Sreng, approached him with a report that three abandoned FANK vehicles had been found near the road leading south from the village—two American GMC trucks and an M-113 personnel carrier.

"Damaged?" Chey asked.

"Yes. But perhaps they can be repaired."

"Show me where they are."

Prak Sreng led him southward. Near the *wat* and in the trees beyond were a dozen scattered bodies, some of them in FANK uniforms, others in peasant dress; soldiers clustered around them like tigers around fallen prey, liberating weapons and ammunition and other usable possessions. The pagoda's stucco walls were bullet-scarred, splattered in places with bright spills of blood. Another soldier came out through its doorway as Chey and Prak passed, carrying three clay statues of Buddha. He hurled each of them to the ground and kicked dust over the broken shards.

Twenty meters beyond, the village street curled away to the east and became a road. It was narrow, deeply rutted from the passage of oxcarts, overlain with reddish dust that showed the tire marks of other evacuation vehicles; two more corpses lay sprawled at the edges. From there Chey could see several soldiers, most of them *neary,* spreading out toward the jungle to search for hidden stragglers.

The abandoned GMC trucks, doors gaping open, and the personnel carrier were pulled off to the sides in different locations. There were three flat tires on the first truck, and a black puddle of oil from a punctured pan beneath the second; the hood of the M-113 was upraised. All three vehicles showed heavy wear, but the trucks were in much better condition than the Chinese Molotovas and Czech Skodas under Chey's command.

Prak at his side, Chey moved toward the nearest of the trucks. As they reached it, the piercing scream of a woman erupted from the jungle directly across from them. It went on for a full five seconds, climbing in pitch, and then broke off into silence. Both men reacted to it: it might have come from one of the *neary*. They ran forward through the high brown savanna grass, weapons at the ready, Chey a few steps in the lead.

The scream came again when they reached the jungle's perimeter; but this time, as they plunged ahead into a dense tangle of betel vines, underbrush, and evergreen and fruit trees, it was lost in a short stuttering burst from an automatic weapon. Chey veered to his left, dodged over and around the gnarled roots of a *sralao* tree, and came to the edge of a small clearing.

When he saw what was in the clearing he slowed to a halt and allowed his hands to relax their tight grip on the M1. On the far side, at the base of a pitch pine, the remains of a peasant woman lay bullet-torn and bloody. Triangularly to Chey's left, kneeling on the ground in an attitude of prayer, was a bonze in a tattered saffron robe; and over the monk, an expression of triumph on her lined face, stood the middle-aged *neary* called Ly Sokhon.

"Look!" she cried. "Look, I've found a bonze!"

Chey did not like Ly Sokhon. She was a bitter humorless woman who seemed to take pleasure in the spilling of blood, and he suspected her of being a little mad. But he had never had words with her, never spoken aloud of his dislike. She was the wife of Im Chung, who was reputed to be a member of Angkar Leu, and claimed acquaintance with Pol Pot, Khieu Samphan, Ieng Sary, and other leaders of the revolution. Even an officer of Chey's rank did not dare speak out against such a person.

"See how he begs for his life?" she said. She jabbed the muzzle of her AK-47 against the bonze's spine, bending him forward so that his young-old face was but half a meter above the ground. "One day soon all our enemies will beg this way at the feet of Angka."

"One day soon," Chey agreed solemnly.

Ly Sokhon drew the short thick Vietnamese sword she carried in a sheath at her waist. "The bonzes are as corrupt as any of Lon Nol's officials. They are symbols of all that the People despise." Her eyes glowed like candle flames. "What is infected must be cut out," she said.

And with two quick strokes of the sword she cut off the holy man's head.

"Look, Comrade!" she shouted then. "Look at how the blood of the enemy stains the earth!"

Chey did not look. He had renounced all religious teachings after joining the revolution and he no longer believed in the wisdom of Buddha or the sanctity of bonzes; yet, strangely, he felt an inward wincing. In curt tones he said, "There is work to be done, Mit Ly. The blood of one bonze is of small consequence. Only the blood of the traitors in Phnom Penh will mean victory."

Ly Sokhon's smile faded; calculation changed the shape of her expression. But she said nothing. Turning, she bent to cleanse the blade of her sword on the monk's robe.

Chey motioned to Prak Sreng and led the way back through the jungle. When they emerged into the savanna grass he heard the sound of approaching trucks and saw flames and clots of smoke rising from the pagoda. The food supplies would soon be removed to the support base; the burning of the village had already begun. Now there was only the task of repairing and removing the FANK vehicles—and quickly, in the event government planes and helicopters made another foray into this sector.

He made a rapid examination of the GMC trucks and the M-113, issued instructions to Prak, and reentered the village past the burning *wat*. Most of the battered Molotovas and Skodas were loaded; soldiers were beginning to clamber in on top of the rice sacks. Two other soldiers moved among the empty *paillotes,* setting them ablaze with gasoline-soaked fire-brands.

Ly Sokhon stood alongside one of the trucks, her arms cradled around her AK-47, watching him stoically as he approached. There were streaks of drying blood on the right sleeve of her pajamas. Chey went past her, to where the rearmost truck was just starting to reverse into a turn, and jumped onto the running board.

The eyes of Ly Sokhon, he saw as the truck completed its turn, still clung to him like those of a jackal.

Kim

In the lantern-lit garden of David Foxworth's villa, as she had on other evenings when they were alone together, Kim performed the traditional *lamtong.* Her body moved with slow swaying grace, hands and arms and fingers all creating undulant patterns. The fluid movements of the dance soothed her, even without the music which should properly accompany it.

But it was not so for David on this evening, she felt. He sat at the garden table, watching her, a gin-and-quinine at his elbow; yet he seemed to take no pleasure in her performance. There was a restlessness in him tonight, a moodiness, and his eyes, half shadowed in the pale light from the table lantern, seemed troubled and remote. He had said little to her when she arrived, little during the meal his cook, Nong Yeth, had prepared; and he had eaten only small portions of the *samlor mochou* and the *chhar*—the chicken sour soup and the vegetables fried with pork—which ordinarily he liked.

Perhaps he was brooding again, as he had during the Christian holidays, over the accidental death of the woman Andrea Vernon with whom he had once lived in the United States. Even though he had not seen this woman for almost five years, her death had caused him great sorrow and pain. Kim had said to him then, "You must have loved her very deeply," and he had looked at her with an expression of surprise and said, "No, I didn't love her. Why do you think I loved her?" Americans were very strange sometimes. She did not understand Americans at all.

And she did not really believe he was brooding again over Andrea Vernon. There were other matters on his mind tonight. Possibly he would tell her what they were; possibly she did not wish to hear what they were. Meanwhile, there was the *lamtong,* and the two of them alone in the garden, and, if it was to be, a night of lovemaking before them.

After a time she brought the *lamtong* to its completion. David smiled up at her as she stood before him—a detached smile, one without gladness. Kim half bowed, her hands placed together and postured at lip level. Then she went to seat herself across from him.

She waited for him to speak but he remained silent. His gaze, instead of meeting hers, rested on the wet marks made by his glass. He was not a handsome man compared to other Westerners she had met, but there was strength and gentleness in his features; and his eyes and his hair had fascinated her from their first meeting, the eyes because they were such a deep blue-green, the hair because it was golden brown and as fine and soft as silk. It was extraordinary that she should have accepted an American as her lover, when her feelings about the Americans were mixed and had been for a long while. But in a time of war many things were extraordinary. And the human heart had no answers to give to the human mind.

Kim watched him, watched giant moths flitting in the glow of the lantern. It was still in the garden, without the sound of their voices; there was even a lull in the Khmer Rouge shelling, so that the night itself seemed hushed. The sultry air was sweet with the scents of hibiscus and frangipani that grew around the stucco walls.

At length David leaned back in his chair, passed a hand wearily over his face. "Kim . . . look, there's something I have to tell you."

"Yes?"

"Please try to understand." He drew a breath, released it as he spoke again. "A decision has been made by President Ford and his advisers in Washington. I wish it hadn't had to be made, but there was just no other alternative. Not with things the way they are now."

He paused, seemed to want to reach out to touch her. Instead he locked his fingers together in front of him in an unintentional posture of prayer.

"Part of the embassy staff is being withdrawn," he said. "Unless things change drastically in the next few weeks, the embassy will be shut down and the rest of us evacuated before the end of the dry season."

Kim sat without moving or speaking.

"I'm going to make arrangements for you to leave for Thailand before that happens," he went on. "The chances are good that I'll be granted reassignment to the embassy in Bangkok; we can be together again there."

"Can we?" she said.

"Yes. Of course we can."

She thought in that moment of her husband, Charoun, who had been killed in action three years before. Of her mother who had died in childbirth, and her father and stepmother who had died of cholera. Of her half-brother, Chey Han, whom she had not seen in ten years and who, it was said, had joined the Khmer Rouge. There was a great sadness inside her—and in the center of it, a small flame of anger.

"Perhaps I don't wish to go to Bangkok," she said.

"Kim—"

"Perhaps I don't wish to join the Americans in abandoning my country."

"We're not abandoning Cambodia," he said. "Washington will continue to send military aid. We'll do everything we can to restore peace—"

"Peace for whom? For us, or for yourselves? To the Khmer Rouge, peace means victory. To the Americans, it means withdrawal to the safety of your own land."

"What would you have us do? Bring in troops and planes and fight Lon Nol's battles for him?"

"It was what you did in 1970."

"The circumstances were different then."

"Oh yes. The circumstances were very different then."

"Kim, you're not being reasonable. We can't take an active role in the war, not after what's happened in Vietnam. The American people wouldn't stand for it."

"And what of my people? They have been forced to accept the bringing of war, and now they must accept desertion and certain defeat."

Anger glowed in David's eyes. "Damn it, I don't want to hear that kind of talk."

"Then hear your own talk," Kim said. She stood. "Hear the voice of the wind."

She turned from the table, crossed the garden in rigid steps, entered the villa. It was not cool inside; without electricity, the air-conditioning unit was useless. Such a pity for David, she thought. The unit had been provided by the embassy, she knew, along with most of the furnishings. Comfort meant much to the Americans, was highly valued, as if life could not be endured without it. They had brought it with them as they had brought the war, and kept it for themselves as they kept the promise of peace, and would take it away with them as they would take away the last hope for a free Kampuchea. Their comfort and their peace would be preserved.

But what of their victims? Did the men in power in the American government care what happened to the Khmers? Did anyone in that place of luxury truly care?

She sat on the teakwood couch, the fingers of her right hand touching the small ivory Buddha she wore on a chain around her neck. On the wall across from her there was a painting of Naga, the divine serpent, which the peasants of the Mekong lowlands believed had created Kampuchea. She stared at it until the serpent's painted image began to blur in her vision.

David came in from the garden. She did not look at him as he crossed the room, but when he sat beside her and put his hand gently on her shoulder, she turned her face to him. His eyes were grave.

"I don't want to fight with you, Kim," he said. "No more angry words. They only hurt both of us."

She nodded.

"I care for you a great deal, you know that."

Again she nodded.

"You care for me too, don't you?"

"Yes. I care for you."

"And you want us to be together?"

"In Bangkok?"

"Or anywhere else."

"Cambodia is my country," she said.

"But you *can't* stay here, not if the KC takes over."

"Perhaps it will not be so bad as you believe. At least the war will be over and there will be peace. We will have lost our freedom, but perhaps we will be able to join with the Khmer Rouge to rebuild our nation."

"Join with them? Kim, they're communist fanatics!"

"They are Khmers. As I am."

"Yes, but above all they're hard-core communists. Victory isn't enough for them; there's no such things in the Marxist or Maoist doctrines as compassion and compromise. Look at what they've already done in the provinces: mass executions, wanton butchery—"

"War is a time of atrocities," she said. "Are those of the Khmer Rouge any worse than those of FANK? Are they any worse than those of the American bombing planes?"

"You're wrong," he said. "Wrong. The same thing that's happening in the provinces will happen in Phnom Penh. And I won't let you be here when it does."

She looked again at the painting of Naga. My country, she thought. My Kampuchea.

"Kim?" David said. "You *will* go when the time comes?"

She said nothing.

She had no answer yet to give him.

Cambodia File: Post Report on the Khmer People (Staff Eyes Only)

Positive character traits: The Khmers possess a gentle temperament and a sensitive, emotional nature. Their personality is also amazingly mobile, in that they are capable of instantaneous changes from sadness to exuberance, from extreme lethargy to bursts of great energy. Variously they have been described as cheerful, formalistic, curious, patient, placid, and naïve in a way that is almost childlike.

Social customs and mannerisms: In the traditional Cambodian salutation, the hands are placed together and balanced at lip level while a half-bow is executed. The higher the placement of the hands, the greater the expression of deference. Ritual bows may be used for ironic effect, and also may mimic deference while actually implying and containing a hostile response. Although the Khmers maintain a controlled demeanor, it is not considered shameful to display outward emotion by means of facial expression and/or vocal inflection. Any exaggeration of emotional response, however, outside of the immediate context, is considered capricious. Witticisms and humorous retorts are thought to be conversational gems. Body contact in social situations is avoided as a crudity, and use of hands to gesticulate seldom occurs. Also, mention of an individual's given name is uncommon in ordinary speech.

(Note: Family names always precede given names, as opposed to Western custom; e.g., Lon [family name] Nol [given name]. It should also be remembered that married women do not generally take the family name of their husband, but retain their own. Offspring, on the other hand, whether male or female, take the family name of the father.)

Religious influence: The teachings of Buddha, the supreme Indian sage of 2,500 years ago, are noted in all aspects of cultural and social existence. Eighty-five percent of Cambodia's non-communist population are followers of Buddhism. All Khmer males are required to serve for two years, during their young adulthood, as a bonze (monk) in order to learn humility and to serve the religion.

Vices and addictions: Khmers place a considerable emphasis on sexual expression within marital bounds. Extramarital sex is tolerated at certain levels, but promiscuity is frowned upon and may be grounds for social ostracization. Prostitutes are regarded as a necessary evil. In another area, addiction to tobacco is almost universal, with American and French cigarettes preferred to the homemade variety. Intoxicants such as rice wine and marijuana (usually in the form of cigars wrapped in banana or palm leaves) are also held in substantial favor. Other curious habits include the chewing of betel leaves, and the ingestion of such items as dog meat, which is considered a delicacy, fried tarantulas, locusts, and beetles.

Negative character traits: Vanity, fickleness, indolence. And, most importantly, a capacity for violence and gore which far exceeds that of any Western race. Cambodia's long history of subjugation and docility, with alternating periods of savagery and revolution, is no doubt responsible for the Khmers' ambivalent reactions to external stimuli. Thus, despite their gentleness and emotional range, and despite their religious beliefs, they can be treacherous and are capable of acts of extreme brutality when provoked.

Comments: The alternation of the gentle and the violent, the religious and the militaristic, make the Khmers a complex and highly volatile race, relations with which—on the individual as well as on the collective level—must be handled with caution. It is recommended that employees limit their relationships with all Khmers to those which are strictly necessary, and that such relationships do not extend beyond the boundaries of said necessity.

Natalie

The first refugee sector to which Than Kim and the GKR Red Cross team took Natalie was west of Olympic Stadium, near the city's perimeter. Jerry-built structures had sprouted there in patternless clusters, like brown weeds around and among lower-class housing: shacks and long rectangular "apartments," all made of wood and roofed in sheet metal. Raggedly dressed, malnourished adults and children moved in aimless groups, like souls from Dante's Seventh Ring. Most were displaced peasants, Natalie knew, who had lost everything to the KC and who were waiting with little hope for someone—Lon Nol and his troops, the Americans, even the Khmer Rouge themselves—to give it back to them. And their faces—

God, she thought, their *faces*.

She had seen ones like these only once before in her life, not in the refugee camps in Thailand, not even in person: they had peered up at her out of old photographs. They had been the faces of the people in the Nazi concentration camps, the photographs of the survivors that had been confiscated or kept among personal possessions when the Russian and American armies swept through Auschwitz, Dachau, Buchenwald. Faces beyond oppression, beyond even pain; faces smoothed into a kind of empty and transcendent peace, like those of the already dead: features drawn in upon themselves, eyes—even those of the children—enormous and wistful and old.

Her father had a scrapbook of those photographs, and on her thirteenth birthday he had shown it to her. In Berlin, where Abraham Rosen had been born, he had once been a doctor of philosophy and a professor of English before the rise of Hitler; later he had been stripped of everything except his sanity and sent to Treblinka. His first wife had gone with him, as had his sister and two brothers; he had been the only survivor. And a survivor of Buchenwald after that. He had come to New York

City in 1947, but had not taught again until undertaking a weekly class at Columbia a few years ago. Instead he had re-married—another survivor of Buchenwald, Natalie's mother—and then dedicated his life to refugee work, first joining the HIBS and then founding the Refugee Relief Fund.

Before 1962, when he had shown her the scrapbook, he had never spoken to Natalie of the Nazi camps; and he didn't speak of them after that day. When she had graduated from NYU in 1970 and told him of her decision to join in his work, instead of pursuing a law career as she had first planned, he hadn't been surprised; nor had he been pleased or displeased. He seemed to take no position at all. And maybe, Natalie thought, that was the key to the Abraham Rosen she knew: he took no position on anything, he just did what he felt was necessary. A long time ago, in the early 1930s, he might have been a man who took all sorts of positions; but now he was a different man, one who had known total devastation, absolute loss, and who was unable to take anything seriously except those who, like himself, had managed to survive.

Well, that wasn't her problem, Natalie thought. Not yet, any-way. If anything, she was the exact opposite of her father: she took everything too seriously, as he was fond of pointing out to her. And her responses to human pain and suffering were not those of Abraham Rosen's professionalism. She might end up like him, focusing on fund drives and political necessities, but now, at twenty-six, she could react only in terms of feeling. And that feeling was empathy . . .

The car slowed and stopped before a GKR supply house and infirmary. They got out into thick waves of heat, entered the building. Natalie was introduced to two other refugee workers, neither of whom spoke English; then she was shown around the facility.

Supplies, she discovered, were frighteningly sparse. There were few medical and hygienic provisions, and barely enough rice and canned goods to feed the refugees in this sector; the supply of rice and produce had dwindled at a steady pace since December, Kim said, when the Khmer Rouge had taken the Mekong and cut off the city's agricultural pipeline. American

DC-8s had been shifted from carrying daily cargoes of military supplies to carrying daily cargoes of rice in order to provide food for the capital. But how much of it would reach the refugees? Foodstuffs earmarked for refugee distribution, as Natalie had learned already, were regularly stolen and later sold on the black market. And those goods which were distributed were often enough of poor quality. Like the shipment of American-made vitamins to Cambodia in 1974, which she and her father had found out about several months ago: the vitamins had been voluntarily withdrawn from the U.S. market by the manufacturer because they contained cyclamates. It was one thing to protect American consumers from products which might cause cancer; but when it came to an obscure Asian race half a world away, who the hell cared?

But these things were only part of the problems faced by the refugees and the volunteer workers. There was not enough water because of the dry season and the number of people who had poured into Phnom Penh in the past few months, swelling the population to well over a million. Garbage could not be burned fast enough; it littered the streets and attracted hordes of rats and flies, and the incidence of cholera cases had reached epidemic proportions. The military was running out of manpower and had taken to conscripting youths barely in their teens from among the refugees. And bureaucratic red tape, both American and Cambodian, was being ludicrously maintained as an apparent symbol of organization and order.

From the supply house and infirmary, Natalie was taken to look at some of the residence facilities. As they neared the first of the buildings, she saw a young Khmer with a disfigured face sitting in the shade along its side wall. Clenched in both hands, as though he were afraid someone would try to steal it, was a cheap transistor radio. The words and music of a Khmer song carried to Natalie and she recognized it as one she had heard several times already, on the car radio and at the GKR refugee center. She asked Kim what it was.

"A patriotic song called 'Samaki,'" Kim told her. "The government broadcasts it many times each day on Radio Phnom Penh."

"What does *samaki* mean?"

"Unity," Kim said. "Against the Khmer Rouge, you see."

"Yes. I see."

They entered the nearest building. Most of the makeshift "apartments" were paneled in tin and floored with dirt, and contained little more than sleeping mats and the piteously few possessions of the refugees. The tin walls seemed to lock in the heat, so that the cubicles were as damp and stifling as saunas. And the air was foul with the mingled stenches of rotting garbage and human waste.

Natalie remembered the statistics Peter Deighan had quoted to her yesterday, at the start of his abortive "interview" with her: 539,129 tons of American bombs dropped on Cambodia; half a million Khmer deaths and over three million refugees. And yet refugee care had not even been part of the U.S. program until recent months. Before 1973 there hadn't been any refugee program at all. The United States had barely acknowledged that there *was* a refugee problem, because that would have involved an admission of culpability. It was only pressure from relief organizations like the Fund, and investigations by the World Health Organization and the Senate Refugee Subcommittee, that had forced them into it, and then in a token way and more as a means of saving face than from any genuine concern for the plight of the Cambodian people.

Nothing was being *done*. Last month the office of Inspector General of Foreign Assistance at the State Department had issued a statement that the children of Cambodia were starving to death—admitting it in public, for all to hear—and yet there was still no administrative action, no U.S. attempt to coordinate either the volunteer workers or the relief groups themselves. Workers had no specific duties to perform; they helped to build shelters, explained sanitation procedures, worked with the sick, tracked down doctors, traced missing shipments of food and medical supplies, did a hundred other small jobs. But all they really accomplished, all anybody *could* accomplish without a strong U.S. government program, was a sweeping around of the debris of chaos.

Knots of refugees watched silently as Natalie and the others passed among them—children with swollen stomachs and limbs, with stick-thin arms and no muscular control, with hair falling out and skin hanging in scabrous folds, with amebic and bacillary dysentery, malaria, tuberculosis. She could feel their pain flowing into her, and it was unbearable. She would have to get away from here soon or the pain would break her down, make her hysterical.

What are they thinking? she wondered. What *can* they think of me, an American woman, well dressed and well fed, inspecting them like so many cattle in a pen?

Impulsively she stopped before one of the refugees—a middle-aged woman wearing a black *sampot,* with lips and teeth stained by betel juice. "Does she know who I am?" Natalie asked Kim. "Does she know why I'm here?"

Kim spoke to the woman in Khmer, received a hesitant and just-audible reply. "Yes. She knows."

"How old is she? How long has she been here?"

"She is thirty-two," Kim said after another exchange, "and she is from a village in Kompong Speu Province. She has been here for six months. Her husband and her two children were killed in the fighting."

Thirty-two, Natalie thought, and I took her for middle-aged. "Ask her what she needs—food, medicine, clothing, anything at all. Tell her I'll get it for her, whatever it is."

Kim spoke again in Khmer. There was a long pause this time before the woman answered. And when she did Kim shook her head sadly and translated. "She says that what she needs you cannot give her."

"Maybe I can try—"

"No. You can't help her."

"Why not? What is it she wants?"

"Her husband and her two children," Kim said.

Cambodia File: Post Report on Civil, Military, and Government Corruption, March 1975 (Top Secret)

The Lon Nol regime is remarkably corrupt. FANK soldiers ransack and loot captured villages, even dismantle entire houses, and sell the spoils on the streets of Phnom Penh. Logistics officers sell army supplies, most of them of U.S. manufacture, on the open market—not only in the city, where uniforms, glass jars of gasoline, even ammunition and weapons are available in the Central Market, but to the Khmer Rouge themselves; there is documented evidence (appended) that in the 1973 battle for Kompong Cham, the first battalion of communist soldiers wore FANK uniforms. Army field commanders create phantom soldiers in order to pay bribes for necessary supplies. Air Force pilots transport contraband from Sino-Vietnamese merchants who deal with the enemy, demand exorbitant bribes for air transport of ground troops, and charge wounded soldiers fees to be flown out of war zones to hospitals in the capital.

Everywhere there is open smuggling, black-marketeering, graft demanded and given for every type of public and government service; even teachers take bribes from students on exams. Not only merchants and soldiers collaborate with the KC, but upper-echelon GKR officials as well. Following, as one example, is a communiqué (retranslated from French) between communist agents in the north and Chief of Staff Sosthene Fernandez, which concerns an exchange of exportable latex from communist-held rubber plantations for medicine, salt, sugar, rice—*and, concealed under the salt, weapons and ammunition.*

ORIGIN: HDQTRS OF FANK
1/17/74

14206

DESTINATION: COMMANDER IN CHIEF OF
HDQTRS OF MARINE CORPS COMMANDER
IN CHIEF OF HDQTRS OF AIR FORCE AND
COMMANDER IN CHIEF OF HDQTRS OF
FIRST MILITARY REGION

Promise CIE Cambodians to transport rubber from
Prek Ka to Kompong Cham on the following conditions STOP.

1. Transport by land from 6 to 17 hours by five
trucks which have the sign white flag one meter by
two meters with the letters CC in black, yellow flag
one meter by two meters on the hood with the letters
CC in black, from depot at Stung Treng.

2. Transport by water from Stung Treng to
Kompong Cham by following boats No. 10.452,
10.453C, 10.451C, and HF.4321. All of these boats
must have on the roofs one yellow blanket two meters by one meter with the letters CC in black. And at
the rear one white flag two meters by one meter with
the letters CC in black. The trip must be made only
from 6-17 hours. Recipient destination of the present
message must do this necessary work to avoid firing
at the boats.

This civilian and military corruption is not so much the result of character flaws in most Khmers, as of staggering
inflation and minuscule salaries: seven dollars per month for
soldiers, not much more than that for teachers, tradesmen, civil
employees. A top-to-bottom domino effect has been created;
people demand bribes of others on every level, most of them
simply in order to survive. The Khmers have a phrase for this
rampant corruption: *Tauch sy doy tauch thom sy doy thom.*
Which translates to mean that the rich and powerful take much,
while the poor and humble take less—but *everybody* takes.

Some of those Cambodians who remain incorrupt blame the wholesale degeneracy on U.S. aid, bureaucracy, and insensitivity. A great deal of American money has been funneled into Cambodia but little has filtered out of the power structure. Supplies and goods, they claim, are not being distributed to the people or to the fighting forces, but are being hoarded or sold on the black market; and they charge that Americans condone the corruption, as long as it is limited, because ignoring it is easier than trying to cope with it. If greater pains had been taken in the first place, these Khmers say, to oversee and regulate the distribution of aid and supplies, inflation could yet be controlled and corruption minimized.

These claims, however, have no official foundation and should not be considered valid. Corruption is and must remain a Khmer problem.

Foxworth

When he finished typing the report on corruption Foxworth signed it, stapled the original and the appendices together, and put everything into a folder. Then he rubbed at his gritty eyes, looked at his watch. Five-fifteen. It had been a long wearying day, and what he wanted more than anything right now, he thought, was to climb into a nice cool bath and soak off some of the tension, some of the prickly sweat that chafed at his armpits and thighs. But of course that was out of the question in water-poor Phnom Penh. He would have to settle instead for sitting naked in his villa with a tall gin-and-quinine and whatever breeze he could coax out of his battery-powered fan.

He thought of the bathtub in the East Lansing flat he and Andrea had shared, back in the days when they were living together and teaching at Michigan State. It had been one of those old-fashioned standing tubs with claw feet, very deep and wide, so that you could slide all the way down inside it until you were completely submerged except for nose and mouth. God, how he had loved that tub in the heat of a Michigan summer. He and Andrea would get into it together sometimes, it was that big, and once they had made love because she wanted to know what it was like to do it underwater—

He shook himself. Andrea. Memories of Andrea. And he didn't want to think about her anymore; he had thought about her too much already. She was dead, she had been dead for two months now. She had been leading a group of French students on a chartered bus tour of the Midwest, something she had always wanted to do, show the people of other nations what America's heartland was really like, and the driver had lost control on an icy road near the Iowa state line, the bus had skidded down an embankment into a half-frozen river; Andrea and the driver and six of the students had been killed, and two dozen others seriously injured.

He knew all of that because his mother had sent him a newspaper clipping about the accident, along with a letter that said it was best if he heard the news from her instead of a stranger or Andrea's family. Which meant that his mother, simple woman, was trying to protect him from any guilt Andrea's people might try to heap on him, because if he had married her she would not have been on that bus. But it hadn't worked. He had never heard from any of Andrea's relatives, but his mother's letter had arrived two days before Christmas and he had done all the heaping of guilt on himself, creating a depression that lasted throughout the holidays.

He didn't know why he should have felt—should still feel—so guilty. It was Andrea, not him, who had made the decision to end their relationship. He remembered the last night they were together, the argument triggered by his refusal to commit himself to marriage, to any of her arbitrary emotional demands. And he also remembered, clearly, almost verbatim, the last words she had said to him before she walked out of his life.

"It's no good, David," she had said, "it's all over between us. You just don't care enough. Inside you there's something that's removed from reality. You're pleasant, you're bright, you're dedicated, you make reasonable arguments for what you think you believe in, but the truth is you've never believed in anything that wasn't handed to you straight out of Grosse Pointe or a college textbook. There's a part of you that can't be touched, that hasn't learned how to give a damn, and I doubt if you're even aware of it. You think you're a feeling person, you always talk about your concerns; those middle-class superstitions and traditions you call beliefs incite the same passion in you that other beliefs might in the kids who resist the draft, and you just don't know the difference. You're a little pathetic, David. I can handle that when it's ideological, but this isn't ideology, this is *humanity;* you don't care about me because you can't even care about yourself. That's the truth of it. And the truth of it, too, is that you won't even remember me in a few years. I'm saying things now that go against your grain, that don't remind you of what you think of yourself; the only way you'll be able to deal with them is to block out the source, forget the person who said them."

He had told her she didn't know what she was talking about, and she had walked out, and except for glimpses on campus his life had never intersected with hers again. The remarkable thing was, after only five years he *did* find it difficult, just as she had predicted, to remember exactly what she was like. She had been tall, almost as tall as he was, with long, well-formed, and powerful legs and round breasts; a high voice oddly out of alignment with her dark solemn eyes; blue-black hair, high cheekbones, tiny ears. But all of these facts he might have read in an embassy dossier on a stranger named Andrea Vernon. He had retained no impression of the real Andrea, the woman who lived inside the corporeal shell.

She had been right about that much. Had she been right, then, about the rest of it too? No. He refused to accept that. He had loved her, his first love, and he mourned her death as he had mourned the death of their affair, and if he couldn't recall her it was because of too much feeling, not too little. And yet the guilt, the damned guilt, stayed with him and kept eating at him, and if she'd been wrong about him—and she had been, she must have been—he simply did not know why he should feel guilty at all.

Thinking of Andrea on top of the report on Khmer corruption, and that on top of the argument with Kim last night, made him feel depressed. He wanted that gin-and-quinine more than a bath or anything else right now; maybe several gin-and-quinines. The need drove him out of his chair, out of the office without bothering to straighten his desk. And then out through the side lobby entrance, into the thick blasting heat of late afternoon.

The first things he saw when he emerged were the limousines carrying Ambassador Dean and the six U.S. congressmen who had come to Phnom Penh on an eight-hour fact-finding mission, as they went around the oval drive from the front of the embassy and out through the left-side, "official departures" gate. Foxworth stopped and stood watching until the last of the cars had turned onto Avenue 9th Tola and the Khmer guards reshut the gate. Then he put on his dark glasses, opened the top two buttons of his shirt, and started back toward the parking lot.

Eight hours, he was thinking then. How could six politicians on a fact-finding mission find any facts in eight hours? How could they learn enough to make an honest report on the advisability of continuing American military and economic aid? For that matter, how could they learn enough in eighty hours, or eight hundred, if their observations were being controlled and shaped under the auspices of that massive fraud, the Lon Nol government?

Lon Nol didn't *have* a government, he had a contrivance. It was conducted in fantasy and maintained by delusion; it was as much a government as a painting of the White House was the White House. Lon Nol and his band had no connection whatsoever to the needs of the people, could never rally them against the Khmer Rouge. The Khmers in the streets of Phnom Penh and Battambang City had known the truth of this for years, and so had everyone connected with the embassy. But the delusion had kept right on being maintained, here and in Washington, for reasons of political expediency which no longer seemed clear to Foxworth.

The Prime Minister, the great Marshal, was a brutal and unbelievably stupid man—*that* was the truth. And those two traits had only been worsened by the stroke he had suffered and that had paralyzed half of his face in December of 1971. He didn't trust any of his advisers, had several times ordered FANK troops to butcher KC soldiers and sympathizers, and had once issued a public order not to sell frogs because "they hopped into lights and exploded." He professed to be an antimonarchist and virtually abandoned the Royal Palace except for the use of the practice theater for ballet; but he held ceremonial court in a palatial room near his house in Chamcar Mon—a room made of concrete and decorated with potted palms, with a raised chair like a throne which he would occupy during banquets and such functions as visits from U.S. congressmen. His own house in the twenty-five-acre compound was filled with tawdry, tourist-style reproductions from Angkor Wat, one of which depicted a number of Cambodian bathing beauties on the shore of the Mekong, water glistening on their naked breasts. He drew his strength from American sanction, like Thieu in Vietnam, and would last in power just so long as the Americans lasted in the country, not one minute more.

Lon Nol, the exploding frog.

The rest of the inner circle of leaders were just as bad in their own ways, just as ill prepared to cope with a big-time power conflict. Cheng Heng—quiet, reserved, with an aura of religious formality, who spent more time cultivating his orchid garden than attending to political matters and who seemed more interested in his own position within the hierarchy than in the republic itself. Sirik Matak—hyperactive, ingratiating to Americans and snotty to his own people; an elitist who seldom gave straight answers but who was forever coming up with outlandish "solutions" to ending social problems and winning the war. Sosthene Fernandez—part Cambodian and part Filipino, all corrupt and all inept; popularly characterized as "a rooster crowing at the sun." Lon Non, the Marshal's brother—deceitful, widely hated, who had pretended to organize Phnom Penh's intellectuals in well-publicized "summits" but who had instead been instrumental in crushing teachers' organizations and in jailing dissident students.

Most of the subcabinet people were all right, particularly

those who were Western-educated under American grants; they had long seen Lon Nol as an evil force, a vestige of the old political corruption and elitism under Sihanouk. But they were afraid of him and refused to mount an opposition for fear of arrest, imprisonment, or even death. The only man in the inner circle worth anything at all was In Thom—sincere, scrupulously honest, less power-seeking than any of the others, popular and well respected among the people. Yet he lacked the administrative ability to be the kind of strong leader the country needed, even if he had been able and willing to challenge the Marshal's authority.

The republic had been stuck with Lon Nol and the U.S. was still committed to him because of the lack of alternatives. And everything had degenerated into chaos as a result.

So why worry that the six congressmen were here only eight hours? Foxworth thought with some bitterness. Eight or eighty or eight hundred—with Lon Nol at the helm, it just didn't matter anymore. If Congress voted to continue sending military and economic aid, it would only prolong the inevitable. The writing was on the wall; U.S. evacuation and abandonment were imminent, the fall of the country was imminent, and the report of a fact-finding mission wasn't going to change any of that one little bit—

"Dave! *Hey!*"

Foxworth had reached his Fiat when he heard the shout behind him. He turned to see Tom Boyd approaching, carrying his attaché case in one hand and a paper-wrapped parcel in the other that was obviously a bottle from the embassy-maintained liquor store.

"You losing your hearing?" Boyd said as he came up. "Or are you just ignoring me for some reason?"

"What?"

"I called to you three times."

"Sorry. I was brooding, I guess."

"About what?"

Foxworth shook his head; he didn't want to go into his thoughts and feelings with Boyd, not now and not at the best of times. For some reason, he found himself less and less willing to put up with Boyd and the man's dogmatic, Kiplingesque attitudes toward the Cambodians.

"I know what you need," Boyd said. He held up the paper-wrapped bottle. "Let's go over to my place and hoist a couple of tall ones."

"I don't feel like driving that far, Tom. I don't feel like shuttling around all the time like a lunatic in an asylum. Why couldn't they at least have a PX and bar here the way they do at any other damned post?"

Boyd frowned. "What's eating at you, Dave?"

"The lies and the pretense," Foxworth said, "that's what's eating at me. Cambodia's going to go down the tubes before the dry season is over and we all know it—you, me, Dean, the Joint Chiefs, the Council of Military Advisers, Kissinger, President Ford. Why don't we just admit it and get the hell out with some dignity?"

Now Boyd was staring at him. "You hear what you're saying, man? That sounds like the kind of crap the KC is pumping out up north."

Foxworth was surprised at the depth of his own anger. It was Andrea Vernon, and Kim, and the imminent evacuation, and the futility and corruption and incompetence—all of that and more working on nascent feelings of what might have been remorse. He shook his head and squinted up at the sun glaring through the rocket netting atop the fence.

"Maybe you're right," he said. "I guess I shouldn't have popped off like that."

"If you can't deal with it anymore, Dave, you'd better request an immediate transfer."

"Yeah. Maybe I should."

But he knew that he wouldn't. For better or worse, no matter what his feelings, he was going to stick until the very end.

Ly Sokhon

Near dusk, in the jungle where her FUNK guerrilla battalion was camped for the night, Ly Sokhon sat alone with her ration of rice and the fish paste called *prahoc*. She always ate alone. All of the other *neary* were afraid of her, as were most of the male soldiers, and none sought her out for companionship or dialogue. But the choice was hers, not theirs. She preferred solitude, demanded it; if that was not her preference she would have told them so and they would have flocked around her like birds.

They were such fools, these young soldiers. There were times when she wanted to say to them, "Don't you understand that this fear you have of me is meaningless? By myself I am nothing, just as you by yourselves are nothing. We are only cells in the great body of Angka. The revolution is all, and Angka is the revolution, and we are Angka."

But they would not have understood. There was no fashion in which simple uneducated peasants such as these could begin to understand. In their own way they were as ignorant and worthless as the traitors who embraced the American puppet Lon Nol. They were necessary cells now, to be used and shaped for the purpose of the revolution, but if they no longer served the body well, they too would be cut out like a cancerous growth.

Only the strong and healthy can serve the body of Angka, she thought.

When she finished eating she stood and walked slowly across the camp. It was quiet now, except for the low murmur of voices and the rustling of animals in the tangle of trees and vines and underbrush. The jungle was dense in this area, west of the Krang Ponlei rice fields; with the coming of night and the thick canopy of branches overhead, shadows were deep and purple-hued within it. Firelight and the coal ends of cigarettes flickered redly against the pockets of darkness, and what could be seen of the sky showed more redness, like a bleeding wound.

Another day almost done. Another day closer to victory. There would not be many more sunsets before the one she would see from the capital itself, from the center of Phnom Penh. Then the red would not be mere flickers against the darkness; then the blood would be spread across the land instead of the sky. And instead of quiet in the camps and support bases of the People's army, there would be great rejoicing and the name of Angka sung loud from every throat.

These were good thoughts, and Ly Sokhon smiled to herself as she crossed toward the shallow ditches that had been dug for the elimination of body waste. But then she noticed Chey Han nearby, talking to Prak Sreng and another of his lieutenants, and the smile faded. She touched the hilt of her Vietnamese sword. Some fatten on blood, she thought then, while others are sickened by it. Some take strength; some lose strength and soon waste away.

Which was Chey Han?

During the six months she had been with his battalion, he had seemed a competent commander—courageous, loyal, more intelligent than most soldiers even of his rank. Yet she was not sure of him. She recalled the look on his face at Cheom Pram, when she had cut off the bonze's head; she heard again his snappish words to her. If he did not approve the execution of a bonze, perhaps he was not so strong and loyal as he seemed. Perhaps he lacked the absolute understanding of the nature of the revolution.

She shrugged. It was not a matter of concern to her, not unless Chey Han faltered in the performance of his duties. If it developed later that he was an unhealthy cell, Angka would see to it that he was removed. Angka would have his head as she had had the bonze's.

Ly Sokhon relieved herself in one of the ditches, then returned to where she had left her knapsack. From inside she took out her nylon hammock and slung it between two of the trees, draped it with the green nylon mosquito netting. It was almost dark now; some of the soldiers were already asleep in their hammocks. But she was not ready for sleep yet. Not just yet.

There were three marijuana cigars wrapped in banana leaves inside her knapsack; she removed one, sitting cross-legged in her hammock, and fired it with the American Zippo lighter she carried. She did not often allow herself to be carried away on the smoke of dreams. But the day had been a productive one, and she felt a need to drift backward into the long-dead past. To the year 1949, to the French city of Paris, to the hotel for Khmer students at 17 Rue la Cepede, Place Mouffetard.

To the leader of the revolution: the man known as Pol Pot.

His name then had been Saloth Sar and he had come to France on a scholarship, as had she and Ieng Sary and many others. And as had she and the others, Saloth Sar had discovered the great truths of Marxism. Outwardly he had been shy, reserved, quiet, and had seemed more interested in social activities than in studying at the École Française de Radio-Electricité; but this had only been a false face presented for the blind eyes of the French and the resident Khmers, who supported Sihanouk and his corrupt monarchy. During private organizational meetings and night-long discussions, Saloth Sar had spoken eloquently on the subject of his new ideology—and excited her and the others with his plans for a People's revolution in Kampuchea.

How many among them then, she wondered, had truly believed these plans would one day be carried out? That Saloth Sar himself would lead the revolution? Not many, perhaps. But *he* had believed. And so had she.

She had been drawn to him at once. He had not preferred any one woman, not even Khieu Ponnary, whom he later married, when that one arrived at 17 Rue la Cepede; their social life had been an active one and there had been much desire for experiment. Yet there had been times when the passion of his and Ly Sokhon's beliefs led to passions of another kind, and she had chosen to feel that he thought of her often, preferred her to Khieu Ponnary or any of the other women.

Of course, that did not matter now. It had all been a long time ago, when desire still burned in her flesh and personal feelings still carried meaning for her. A dozen years had passed since she had last seen him, though in spirit they had never been far apart. Her only regret was that Saloth Sar had left Paris before her and that she had not sought him out after her own return, joined him in January of 1953 when he adopted his revolutionary name of Pol Pot and entered into guerrilla activities in the northern provinces. This was what Ieng Sary, Son Sen, Khieu Ponnary, and others in the Angkar Leu had done—gone underground with Saloth Sar. But she, foolishly, had chosen the course of Khieu Samphan and Hou Yuon, and entered the anonymous ranks of Sihanouk's lackeys in an effort to effect change from within. She had become a part of Hou Yuon's Kampucheabut, where she taught communist dialectic to other revolutionaries; it was only much later that she had carried the banner of the revolution among the peasants in the western provinces, and taken to the jungle herself to spill the blood of the enemy.

Would things be different for her today if she had joined Saloth Sar that long-ago January? Would it be she and not Khieu Ponnary who stood at his side in the inner circle of the Angkar Leu? Perhaps. But she had no way of knowing, no way to be certain. Outside of the revolution itself, there were no certainties in her life.

She drank deeply of the acrid smoke from her cigar. And in the mists that formed in her mind, an image of Saloth Sar as she had last seen him appeared. That had been at the second National Party Congress in 1963, when Pol Pot was officially elected to the position of Party Secretary—a boon to his career. He had been acting Party Secretary for a year prior to that, ever since the assassination of Touch Samouth, and there had been rumors that he had been responsible for Touch Samouth's death. But Ly Sokhon neither knew nor cared if these rumors were true. He was the leader, and in her eyes he would always be the leader. Touch Samouth could not have led the people to victory; the death of Touch Samouth mattered no more than her own girlish desires.

Nothing matters, she thought, drifting, gazing at the bright face of Saloth Sar, nothing matters except the revolution.

Ah, but when the primary struggle was ended, when victory had been claimed, would she and Pol Pot meet again? Would they touch hands and drink a rice-wine toast to liberation, as they had in Paris a quarter of a century ago?

Possibly. It was a moment to be wished for, a reunion far more meaningful to contemplate than one with her husband, Im Chung, whose loyalty to Angka could not be questioned but who was a cell of no importance within its body. But it was not something to dwell upon. Not now, not yet.

Only the revolution.

Only victory.

Ly Sokhon finished her cigar, lay down in the hammock beneath the mosquito netting, and drifted with the image of Saloth Sar toward sleep. And when sleep came, the dreams that followed were good dreams, almost as good as those the marijuana had opened up from her past. For in them the heads of bonzes and the heads of Lon Nol and his puppets rolled and rolled through the empty streets of Phnom Penh, laying down bright trails of blood that leaped and burned like fires to light the future of all Kampuchea . . .

Cambodia File: Post Security Report— Than Kim (Secret)

Khmer female, born Rovieng (Preah Vihear Province), May 16, 1947. Father: Than Long, farmer (deceased). Mother: Heng Samoeun (deceased). Stepmother: Kheng Ponnary (deceased). Half-brother: Chey Han (believed deceased). Aunt: Heng Thirith, seamstress (residence: No. 218 MV Samdach Phoung, Toek Loak sector, Phnom Penh). No other living relatives.

Educated local primary schools (six years) and secondary schools (six years); graduate University of Phnom Penh, 1969, with degree in Linguistics. Joined embassy staff as civilian interpreter, August 1970. No other positions held.

Physical characteristics: Height 5'1"; weight 100 lbs; distinctive strawberry-shaped birthmark on left shoulder, otherwise no physical deformities or identifying marks. (See attached photographs.) Languages spoken: English (fluent); French (fluent); Thai (conversational); Vietnamese (rudimentary). Religious affiliation: Buddhist. Marital status: widowed (husband Chea Charoun, colonel, Republican Air Force, killed in action Ratanakiri Province, Feb. 15, 1972).

Present embassy duties: Interpreter; refugee liaison; translator of captured enemy documents.

Residence: No. 46 MV Phum Chup, Tuol Tompoung sector, Phnom Penh.

Comments: Subject has never evinced any manner of disloyalty to the United States of America; criminal associations not noted, political affiliations with suspect groups not noted. Established evident out-of-wedlock relationship with post employee David Foxworth (See REPORT—FOXWORTH, DAVID), September 1974; but such relationships common among middle-echelon post employees, and it may be assumed that this relationship imposes no security risk. Also, in the absence of contraindicating data, it may be assumed that the death of subject's husband (and of subject's parents in war-related manner) indicates strong pro-U.S. and anticommunist sentiments.

Security clearance: Level Ten.

Kim

Le Royal Restaurant, behind Hotel Le Phnom, was two thirds full when Kim and David entered a few minutes past eight o'clock. It was also dark and somber-looking, with its candles and kerosene lamps serving in place of electric lights and its too-elegant French Colonial decor. Once she had enjoyed dining here, because it was one of the city's most expensive restaurants. Tonight, after a day among the starving refugees, its false luxury seemed only depressing.

Where she had wanted to go, on this evening, was to one of the lively Khmer restaurants—Bopha Nakry, Pic Dara, the Angkor—and then either to a funny cinema or to the Apsara bar on Sok Traing Avenue, where the band was perhaps the best in Phnom Penh and there were *ramrong* and *saravani* circle dances to be performed. Gaiety was what she yearned for on this evening, a few brief hours of merrymaking: drugs for the pain and salve for the raw wounds inside her. The pain would never go away, she knew now, and the wounds would never heal; but temporary relief, the pretense of joy, was so much better than none at all.

David did not understand this. No American did, it seemed, nor ever would. They could not go to a cinema, he said, because she knew as well as he that the cinemas had been declared off limits to American embassy personnel, for security reasons. So had some of the dancing and drinking bars, and even though the Apsara was not one of them, there was no sense in tempting fate; KC assassins and saboteurs were known to be loose in the city, weren't they? Besides, he said, he didn't feel like dancing. He had never cared for the idea of a wake, he said, and he wasn't about to join one before the fact.

Kim did not know what a wake was and had asked him to explain his meaning. But he had only shaken his head, and then said he would take her to Le Royal for dinner and perhaps to the Monorom Hotel bar for a brandy afterward. That was all. That was as much of a compromise, he said, as he was willing to make.

No, he did not understand at all.

As they stood waiting for the *maître d'hôtel,* and despite the dim lighting Kim recognized several of the diners. Two sub-cabinet officials, an army general in his much-decorated khaki uniform, the mistress of a war profiteer who had been found murdered three months ago in his villa on Mao Tse-tung Boulevard. A member of the French consul's staff dining with a member of the Japanese diplomatic mission. Three journalists, two Americans and one Australian, talking in loud voices as a certain type of war correspondent seemed always to do.

And sitting alone at a corner table, the American woman called Natalie Rosen.

Kim said, "That is the woman who arrived yesterday from Bangkok—the refugee worker from your New York City."

"It's not my New York City," David said. He followed her gaze across the room. "She's pretty young to be in Phnom Penh by herself."

"Perhaps. Would you like to join her?"

"I've got an appointment with her tomorrow morning. I can meet her then."

"But she is alone tonight," Kim said, "and she is also an American. It would be a courteous thing to do."

David hesitated. Then he sighed and said, "I suppose so."

He spoke to the *maître d'hôtel* in French, sent him to ask Natalie Rosen if they would be welcome to sit with her. They would not have been welcome to sit with the subcabinet officials, the army general, or even the mistress of the war profiteer; the looks each of these gave Kim made that fact plain to her. It was because she was with David, of course, and they thought of her as a whore. But this did not bother her. Let them think what they would. The prejudice and the impure thoughts were theirs, not hers.

David seemed to stare around the room as they waited, as if it were unfamiliar to him; as if they had not come here three times in the past. He looked tired tonight, drawn deep within himself. Not once had he spoken of the Americans abandoning Kampuchea, of his plan for her to flee to Thailand. Yet Kim sensed that there was little else on his mind.

The *maître d'hôtel* returned and said that Natalie would be pleased to have them join her. He led them to her table.

Natalie smiled at Kim and seemed glad to see her, glad for the company. But an expression of surprise registered on her face when David introduced himself. "I've been looking forward to meeting you, Mr. Foxworth," she said. "I didn't know you and Kim were . . . friends."

"We're all friends at the embassy," David said. "Just one big happy family."

There was a silence. Natalie and David seemed to study each other in the bold fashion of Americans meeting for the first time, as though each wished to learn immediately the most intimate secrets of the other. This curious behavior had always puzzled Kim, but she had never tried to analyze it. It was simply the way of their race.

A white-jacketed waiter appeared, took David's order for two demis of whiskey, and presented them with menus. Natalie had arrived only minutes ago, she said, and had not had time to order anything but a drink.

When the waiter had gone Natalie looked at David again in the same probing fashion. "Difficult day, Mr. Foxworth?"

"Why do you ask that?"

"Your comments about the embassy. It sounded as though you were upset about something."

"No. Just tired and a little tense, that's all."

"I can understand that," Natalie said. "How long have you been in Phnom Penh, if you don't mind my asking?"

"Fourteen months."

"God. I've only been here two days and my nerves are already frayed. How do you stand it, day after day?"

"Living in a war zone is like anything else, Miss Rosen," David said. "You get used to it."

"I doubt if I could. This afternoon, for example. There was a woman in one of the refugee sections Kim and I visited—a thirty-two-year-old woman who looked middle-aged and who'd lost her husband and two children in the fighting. I wanted to do something for her, give her something, but what she said she wanted I couldn't give her. Could I, Kim?"

"No. No one could."

David said, "I suppose she wanted peace."

"Not just so," Kim said. "It was her husband and children she wished for. That they were still alive, you see."

Natalie was frowning. "Why did you say it like that, Mr. Foxworth? Why *shouldn't* she have wanted peace?"

"Everybody wants peace."

"Some of us seem to want it more than others."

"Yes? Meaning what?"

"The official U.S. position is victory first, peace second. Isn't that right?"

"No, it isn't. Look, I'm in no mood tonight to argue politics or discuss the refugee situation. I came here to have a quiet dinner—"

"Oh, I see," Natalie said. "Things like the war and the refugees only interest you during business hours."

A muscle jumped on David's cheek. "I don't care for your insinuations, Miss Rosen."

"How about the Cambodians? Do you care for them?"

"Of course I care for them."

"You don't act like it."

"That's for damn sure," a new voice said. "None of these embassy spooks gives a good goddamn about anybody in this country."

They all looked up, startled, at the man who had approached silently and who now stood just behind Natalie's chair. Kim felt a ripple of dislike. It was the man Peter Deighan —another of the journalists, like the ones at the table across the room, who spent their days in Hotel Le Phnom and their nights in restaurants and the arms of *taipan* from the cheaper bars. She had no respect for them, as she had for those who wrote their words from the front; and her distaste for Deighan was greater than most, because he had once made an obscene suggestion to her at the Festival of Ancestors celebration and then drunkenly touched her in an intimate place.

David's face was pinched with anger. "What do you want here, Deighan?"

"A little drink, a little stimulating conversation." Deighan seemed to sway as he turned his head toward Natalie; his eyes were very bright in the dark room. "Hello, Natalie. Mind if I join you?"

"Yes," she said coldly.

"Harboring resentment about yesterday? Can't say as I blame you. But what the hell—another night, another party in honor of the dead."

56

David said, "Why don't you go back to the hotel and sleep it off."

"Why don't you and the rest of your CIA buddies go find another country to destroy."

"Now listen, Deighan—"

"Call me Peter."

"You're not wanted here, can't you see that?"

Deighan laughed suddenly, a booming sound like the trumpet of an elephant. Everyone turned to look at him; the low murmur of other voices ceased throughout the room.

"*I'm* not wanted here?" he said. "You think you are? You think any of us from the good old U.S. of A. are?"

Natalie put her hands flat on the table. She looked annoyed, nervous, and uncomfortable. "Please, Mr. Deighan—"

"Call me Peter."

"You're making a scene."

"Don't be standoffish," Deighan said. "The name's Peter. Scene, eh?" He looked at Kim for the first time. "You think so, too, Mrs. Than? Kim?"

Kim said nothing. This was another thing about Americans—perhaps one of the primary things—which troubled her. They were so quick to judge each other, so quick to form allegiances, to switch allegiances, to create enemies, to make fools of themselves. Each of them appeared to believe he knew more, or felt more deeply, or was in a position more right or more just than the other. And if one was not an American, one did not dare to intervene. Because then, as David and Natalie had turned from harsh words for each other to harsh words for Peter Deighan, they would turn on you, ally themselves against the outsider.

"Well," Deighan said, "that seems to make it unanimous. I appreciate unanimity; there's damned little concensus in this world. But appreciating it doesn't mean I have to go along with the will of the majority, right?"

He turned to another table, pulled a chair from under it, and set the chair between Kim and Natalie. "There," he said as he seated himself. "Isn't this nice? Just the three of us. Four. Sorry, Kim. But you're a Khmer and you don't really count. Not to the boys back home, anyway. Right, Foxie?"

David glared at him. He appeared to be making an effort to control himself; the muscle on his cheek fluttered like the wing of a butterfly. "I've lost my appetite," he said to Natalie. "Kim and I'll be leaving now. You're welcome to come with us if you want."

"Yes, I think I—"

"Running away?" Deighan asked. "Sure, that figures. Run away from trouble, run away from commitments, run away from responsibility. Tell me something, Dave. How do people like you sleep at night? How do you *get* to sleep in the first place? Booze? Sleeping pills?" He leered sideways at Kim. "Or do you get the little woman here to use some erotic Khmer method?"

David stood with such suddenness and such violence that his chair toppled over backward and his right shoulder struck the waiter, who was returning with their drinks. The tray erupted from the waiter's hands; liquid splashed him, glasses and tray clattered to the floor. The waiter stumbled, fell to one knee, knelt there with widened eyes. David barely glanced at him. His attention was centered on Deighan, who had also gotten to his feet; and his hands were clenched in the manner of actors in the American cinema.

Kim watched them glare at each other. It was very quiet in the room now. All of the other diners were sitting motionless, waiting, like the carved figures in the great temples at Angkor Wat.

So strong, the Americans, Kim thought, and yet so weak. She had trusted and believed in them once, when Charoun was alive, because he considered them to be the saviors of freedom in Kampuchea. That was why she had gone to work at their embassy, why she had remained there after Charoun's death. Had he been so wrong in his feelings? Had she? She still could not quite reach a decision. The Americans' great strength held her, as David's strength held her in the night; their weakness repelled her, as David's weakness repelled her at moments such as this.

"Well, Deighan?" David said.

"Well what? And call me Peter."

Across the table, Natalie appealed to Kim with her eyes. Kim shook her head, counseling passivity. There was nothing to be done. David and the man Deighan would do as they wished; the Americans always did as they wished.

"I've had about all I can take from you, mister."

"That so? What are you going to do? Stick me with a poison dart? That's the weapon your spook assassins use these days, isn't it?"

David's hands clenched more tightly. He took a step forward.

And from outside, not so far away, there was the sudden shrieking of a rocket—then an explosion both loud and of such force that Le Royal's chandeliers danced and made musical tinkling sounds.

All heads and eyes, even those of David and the journalist, turned in that direction. Everyone sat as statues again, listening, poised at the edge of flight. Natalie's hands, Kim saw, were folded under her chin as if she were making prayers; there was a frozen look of awe on her pale-skinned face.

Many seconds passed. The chandeliers were still again. What could be heard of the night was still again.

Deighan was the first to move. The shape of his expression changed and he blinked several times, as if awakening from sleep. He passed a hand over his face, over his slack mouth. Then his eyes roamed the room, flicked over Natalie and Kim, settled on David once more. And slid away.

He turned as a soldier turns and walked swiftly toward the entrance.

David's hands relaxed. He watched Deighan until the journalist was gone; then he sat down again.

"Bastard," he said to no one.

Another rocket whined, farther away this time, and burst with a dull echoing thud. The chandeliers did not dance or tinkle, but the diners reacted as before—listening, waiting, poised.

On and on, Kim thought. It goes on and on and on.

Deighan

When he walked out of Le Royal Peter Deighan went straight back to Hotel Le Phnom and up to his small corner room on the third floor. It was hot and stuffy in there; he opened the window facing Monivong Boulevard, just far enough to let in some of the dry night air and the sound of the KC shelling. Then he lit a kerosene lamp, put it on the desk between his old Underwood portable and the half-empty bottle of vodka, and sat down.

For a time he did nothing except stare mothlike at the lamp flame. The inside of his mouth began to feel crusty; he picked up the bottle and poured himself three fingers and drank them off in one long swallow.

More shells burst somewhere in the night, none of them close. Across the street, above the cathedral and the Descartes *lycée,* the sky looked as though it were burning.

Lighting a cigarette, Deighan inserted a sheet of paper into the typewriter and began to type.

> Dear Carol,
>
> Here I am again, drunk and disorderly at the old machine. Time is eight p.m. and I've just returned from Le Royal Restaurant, where I disrupted the dinner of about 30 people, made several inflammatory remarks to Natalie Rosen and a Khmer woman named Than Kim, and almost got into a fistfight with my old embassy buddy, Dave Foxworth. A fine evening's work, you must admit.
>
> Did I tell you about Natalie Rosen? No, I don't think I did. She's a young American refugee worker who showed up in PP yesterday. Very dedicated. Very liberal, too; can't get under her skin with anti-U.S. sentiments like you can with the embassy boys.

Nice eyes, nice breasts. Not quite as nice as yours, as I recall, but since it's been almost a year since I've seen either pair, I can't really be sure.

Anyhow, I thought I'd interview Natalie. Thought I'd take her to bed, too. Interview didn't work out too well. Neither did taking her to bed. But then, not too many things seem to be working out for any of us these days.

You'll forgive me, I trust, if I say that this isn't what I want to be doing right now. Writing to you, I mean. There's one other thing I'd much rather and may yet do. And no, it's not climbing into the rack with Natalie Rosen.

Do I seem obsessed with sex these days? I'm not. Getting laid is no problem in PP. All you have to do, you go to one of the bars, you sit down at a table, you pick out a girl you like, and you buy her maybe a dozen glasses of Seven-Up or Coke at 50 riels a glass. Then you can take her home with you, if you've got a home, or you can go home with her, or you can go to what passes for a hotsheet hotel. Whole evening of slap-and-tickle, as the limeys say, for 500-600 riels which, at the latest exchange rate of 1500 riels to one U.S. dollar, works out to about 33 cents.

Where else in this lousy world can you get laid for 33 cents?

But getting laid isn't what I want to do either. Or what I've wanted to do for the past few weeks. So why don't I just go ahead and do it, whatever it is, you may well ask? Why the procrastination?

No *cojones,* as Hemingway said.

Hemingway. I've always hated him, Carol, you know that. Hated everything he was—coward, poseur —and everything he stood for. Hated being compared to him as a writer or a human being. Funny thing is, though, I seem more and more of late to be turning into a mirror-image of the old man. Booze, sex, machismo, deliberate boorishness—the whole Papa shtick. I'd probably be writing in his damned style by now if I was writing anything at all these days.

Why emulate a man I hate? Answer to that one's easy, babe. Elementary psychology.

Fact of the matter is, I've been at war too long. Seen too much, written too much, felt too much. My life has been built around death too long—that's the crux of it.

Be nice if I could go someplace without a war for a change. Do something new and different and clean. But where could I go? What could I do?

Paris to write a novel? No novels in me, kid. War is the only thing I write well about, and I can't write about war any more.

Home to you? Tom Wolfe (now there was a writer) said it all on that subject: "You can't go home again." Nothing waiting for me back there in California, we both know that. No job, no friends, no future.

No wife and no marriage.

It's been over for a long time, Carol; we both know that, too. Which is part of the reason I asked for this assignment in the first place, you know. Of course you know. Easier to go to war than to face the truth about us, face the break-up and the divorce and the recriminations. I thought it was a good way to keep you, at least for a while; I knew you wouldn't divorce me while I was over here, facing danger, risking my ass, all that heroic crap. But that's not being fair to you or me. Hanging on just won't make it. Neither will pretense.

It's all over, all kaput.

All nada.

"Our Father who art in nada, nada be thy name. Thy nada come, thy will be done, on earth as it is in nada." Papa was right about that much, anyway.

So enough. Maybe now, finally, I can do the one

and only sensible thing I've got left to do. For your sake and mine, babe, let's hope so.

Deighan rolled the page out of his typewriter, laid it on top of the first page of the letter, and carefully signed it. He poured two more fingers of vodka and drank them. He looked out at the tracer-streaked sky and listened to the rockets.

He opened the desk drawer and took out the American-made .45 caliber military automatic he had bought on the black market a month ago.

For a long while he sat holding the gun in his hand, staring at it in the flickering lamplight, his finger curled around the trigger. Thinking of Hemingway in Ketchum, Idaho, in 1962, seated at the kitchen table with the shotgun muzzle pressed inside his mouth and his finger curled around the trigger.

Sweat broke out on Deighan's forehead; he could feel it begin to trickle down into his eyes. The hand and the gun blurred and then started to shake. Finally he made a sound deep in his throat, and threw the weapon back into the drawer, and slammed the drawer shut.

No *cojones,* he thought. No *cojones.*

Then he picked up the letter to his wife, tore it into shreds over the wastebasket. And poured himself another drink.

Foxworth

It was just ten o'clock when Foxworth, with Kim beside him, turned his Fiat onto Norodom Boulevard and headed it south between the symmetrical lines of jacaranda trees.

Traffic was sparse: a few military vehicles, a few private automobiles with official plates, but none of the motorbikes and cyclos that clogged the central district by day. Lon Nol's general curfew order, although little enforced so far, kept most of the population indoors after 9 P.M. The only ones who seemed to go out for the evening—more pretense at normal activity,

Foxworth thought—were high-ranking Khmer officials and Westerners like himself.

Most of the stucco-and-cinder-block government buildings, banks, and private villas they passed were dark and fortressed against rocket attacks. To the east, the whimsical curving roofs and cornices, the gilded spires of the Royal Palace looked like shadow shapes cut from cardboard and pasted on the backdrop of a starlit sky. There was a strangeness to it all, an aura of desolation that was almost spectral—as if the city were a shell already abandoned, already dead.

Driving through it gave him an eerie and vaguely unsettled feeling and put him in an even more cheerless mood. He glanced over at Kim, sitting with her hands folded and her body in a rigid posture, looking straight ahead as she had since they left the parking area at Hotel Le Phnom. In the semidarkness of the car her face had a sculpted Oriental cast. The inscrutable Oriental, he thought, and wondered what *she* was thinking just now. What she had thought of the incident at Le Royal.

She wasn't indifferent to it, that was certain. She had not said ten polite words to him since Natalie Rosen excused herself, less than a minute after Deighan walked out, and left them alone together. He hadn't wanted to stay either, but Kim had said three of her ten words when he suggested leaving: "I'm hungry please," and so he had given in and forced himself to swallow part of an order of sweetbreads. She had eaten a steak and several other things with apparent relish, but she had kept her eyes on her plate the entire time.

Well, he could hardly blame her for being upset. He knew he had acted like a damned fool. First with his reaction to the overzealousness of Natalie Rosen, who was a little naïve and probably too emotional but who at least cared; then, in spades, with his reaction to the nasty goading of Deighan. The near-fight had been as much his fault as Deighan's. He should have known better than to let a drunk—and a flaming left-wing drunk, at that—provoke him into losing his temper. That was exactly what Deighan had wanted, for whatever perverse reasons of his own. Now, at least one of the other journalists who had witnessed the incident, and maybe even Deighan himself, would be sure to file a dispatch blowing it all out of proportion.

The pink-limestone statuary of Independence Monument loomed up ahead. The embassy and Lon Nol's Chamcar Mon fortress and his own villa on Mao Tse-tung Boulevard were only a few blocks away; but Kim lived farther south, in a residential sector between the Boueng Trabek and the Bassac River. He would have her home in another ten minutes, and be home himself ten minutes after that.

It wasn't the way he wanted things to end tonight—both of them alone, Kim upset and brooding—but he knew that was the way it would turn out. He had tried apologizing to her at the restaurant, when he'd finally come out of his funk, but if she accepted it she had given no sign. Tomorrow she might come to him smiling and cheerful, with all of tonight forgiven if not forgotten. But only tomorrow, only after a period of time and distance between them.

Still, he ought to make one more effort to break her silence. If nothing else, he would at least have the sound of his own voice to listen to; the stillness inside the car, the eerie emptiness outside, kept intruding on his mind and making him feel edgier by the second.

"Kim?" he said.

No answer.

"I'm sorry for the way I acted tonight. I mean that. The last thing I wanted to do was spoil the evening for you."

No answer.

They were passing near the embassy now. There was no activity anywhere in the area, no lights of any kind on Avenue 9th Tola.

"I won't let it happen again," he said. "I promise you that."

She moved for the first time, turning her head out of profile to look at him. A dozen seconds passed. Just ahead was the intersection of the street she lived on, Avenue Phum Chup; he slowed and made the turn, and as he did she finally spoke.

"It will happen again," she said.

"No. It won't."

"It will. It must."

"Why must it?"

She looked away from him again, through the windshield. The district was on the fringe of the lower middle-class Khmer neighborhoods: traditional Cambodian houses built on stilts with wooden walls and thatched roofs, most of them fronted by jacaranda and palm and banana trees, all of them just barely served by the main power lines. Kim could have afforded to live in one of the upper-middle-class villas in the Tuol Kauk district, where the Chinese merchants and other embassy Khmers lived; but for some reason she preferred to stay here on Avenue Phum Chup, where she had lived from the time of her graduation from the university. Maybe it was because she had shared the house with her late husband; maybe it held memories for her. He had never asked her and she had never volunteered the information.

The houses were all dark and silent now as he drove past. The street, pocked here and there from a lack of maintenance, was also dark and silent—but on the upcoming cross-street headlights made a widening shimmer to the south, beyond the corner house, coming fast toward the intersection. The faint accelerating roar of a large-horsepower engine became audible above the hum of the Fiat's air conditioner.

"Kim?" Foxworth said. "Why must it?"

"Because you're an American," she said.

"Now what does that—"

He didn't finish the sentence because in that moment the engine noise on the cross street increased to a howl and a big canvas-covered military truck came hurtling into view; and as it reached the corner there was the sudden screech of tires on pavement, and the lights and the truck swung around toward the Fiat in a sharp arc. Kept on coming in a sliding, wobbling rush, the light-glare dancing across the Fiat's windshield, half-blinding him. And he realized all at once that the driver had taken the turn too fast, that the truck was out of control and plunging toward them on a collision course.

He thought: Oh my God! and jammed on the brakes, wrenching the wheel hard right with one hand, throwing out his other arm in front of Kim to keep her from being jerked forward into the dashboard and the window glass. The Fiat bucked, slewed sideways. At the same time, with thirty or forty yards separating them, one of the truck's oversized front tires hit a chuckhole; the machine shuddered, lifted off the ground on its left-side tires at a skidding angle. The lights slid away from the Fiat's windshield, making jagged yellow slash marks on the wall of darkness. Then there was an explosion of sound as the truck fell over onto its left side, rolled and skidded onto its top, flopped onto its right side.

The Fiat ground to a stop with its front bumper buried in a clump of frangipani; the engine coughed once and stalled. Less than a dozen yards away, trailing strips of canvas like flayed skin, the truck caromed up over the curbing and seemed to wrap itself around the bole of a palm tree. Shuddered again under a shower of dislodged bark and fronds and then was motionless, both headlights still burning and angled in a frozen glare toward one of the stilt houses. The noise faded into dying echoes, into the faint clatter of something metallic bouncing along the pavement. Into a kind of electric silence.

Foxworth's stiffened right arm was still flung across Kim's chest, holding her back against the seat. She hadn't made a sound the whole time, but he could hear the rapid and irregular tempo of her breathing. His own breath seemed to rattle in his throat; wetness flowed down from under his arms, hot and clammy at the same time.

But things kept on happening outside. More headlights shimmered closer on the cross street, coming from the same direction as the truck; more engine noise cut away at the crackling stillness. Both cab doors on the wrecked truck wedged open and a pair of dark shapes staggered out. The one from the passenger side stood looking dazedly toward the intersection, at the brightening glow of light there; he had something long and blackish cradled across his chest. The driver came lurching around behind the truck and up next to him. Both of them were Khmers and both wore peasant outfits; the driver was the heavier and taller of the two. He reached out and pulled the blackish something out of the other one's hands—and when he did that, light from the corner outlined it and let Foxworth identify what it was.

Automatic weapon. Submachine gun.

Time and motion seemed to slow down, to tilt off center in Foxworth's perception. Yet all of his senses appeared to sharpen at once. He smelled the cloying sweetness of the frangipani, the sharp odors of spilled oil and gasoline, the stench of his own sweat. He heard Kim's hissing intake of breath, the wild stutter of his heart above the oncoming engines. He saw clearly the two jeeps, one on the tail of the other, come barreling up to the intersection; saw their drivers veer the machines to abrupt halts at sight of the truck and the two men alongside it; saw half a dozen armed FANK soldiers, all of them dressed in khaki uniforms, pile out and scatter left and right.

Saw the heavy-set Khmer drop to one knee and open fire with the submachine gun.

The night erupted again, this time in orange streaks and chattering bursts and the whine of ricocheting bullets. Some of the soldiers had automatic weapons of their own, and one, inside the lead jeep, began to fire a monopod-mounted machine gun. In the first savage cross fire the smaller Khmer at the truck went down and so did two of Lon Nol's troops—one of them with a thin piercing cry that keened the night like a 107-mm. rocket.

Foxworth sat paralyzed, watching it happen.

Thinking: This isn't happening, this can't be happening.

Kim clutched at his arm, beat at his arm, saying something in Khmer that he couldn't understand. He still didn't move, couldn't make himself move. Outside, the heavy-set Khmer was down on his belly at the truck's rear, pumping another fusillade at the lead jeep. Except for the one on the machine gun, all of the soldiers were hidden behind the jeeps or behind the trees in the corner lot; each of their positions was marked by muzzle flashes as they returned the fire.

Kim leaned forward and up and hit Foxworth in the face with her closed fist.

The blow, the sudden sharp pain on his cheekbone, brought him out of it. His perception lurched again, slid back on track; urgency filled him and let him function. He shoved the clutch in, reached down for the ignition key and twisted it. The starter whirred, caught for an instant, died away. Ahead at the truck, the heavy-set Khmer swiveled his head and his weapon toward the sound. Foxworth twisted the key again, savagely, and this time the engine coughed to life and held, barking through the exhaust. He slammed the gearshift into reverse and released the clutch, reaching out to grab hold of Kim's head and shove her down on the seat beside him. The Fiat began to yaw backward out of the frangipani shrub, spraying light over the wrecked truck and across the nearest of the two army jeeps.

A soldier stood up behind the jeep and hurled something in an overhand arc at the truck.

The heavy-set Khmer had lifted onto one knee; he leveled the submachine gun at the Fiat and squeezed off a short burst.

Foxworth made an involuntary sound and ducked his head, hanging on to the wheel with his left hand, still pushing Kim down with his right. The far corner of the windshield spider-webbed. Two or three bullets came whistling through and spattered the air above them with fragments of glass. The Fiat had already begun to fishtail; he couldn't hold the wheel steady, twisted down the way he was. He lifted his foot off the accelerator, started to bring it down on the brake—

And that was when the truck blew up.

A ball of flame burst upward, turned the sky dawn-bright for an instant. The force of the blast shook the Fiat, made Foxworth do two things in reflex: snap his head up and jab his foot down so hard on the brake pedal that the front end lifted up, slammed him and Kim hard against the seat back. The force of the blast also threw the heavy-set Khmer up into the air, arms and legs spread out at loose angles like a dummy made out of cloth and sand. He was silhouetted briefly against the bright orange flare; then he fell and became a black shapeless blob on the black street.

The Fiat, engine dying again, had come to a diagonal stop forty yards away. Shrapnel peppered it like a metallic rain for three or four seconds. Beyond the side window Foxworth watched tongues of flame and thick belches of black smoke pour up out of the shell of the truck.

He began to tremble. Kim sat up beside him, panting, and

caught hold of his arm and clung to it. But he couldn't stop trembling. He had been in Phnom Penh, in the middle of a combat zone, for fourteen months now; he had seen the fearful effects of war every day. Yet it had never touched him in all that time, never threatened *him*. Until tonight. Until right now.

The remaining FANK soldiers were running across to the burning truck, weapons held in firing position. None of them glanced at the stalled Fiat. None of them, Foxworth realized, had paid even the slightest attention to it at any time during the skirmish.

"What's the matter with them?" he heard himself say aloud, in a voice that rattled and shook as badly as his hands. "Don't they know we're here? Don't they give a damn about us?"

Kim made no reply.

And out on the street, one of the soldiers put the muzzle of his automatic weapon against the head of the heavy-set Khmer and blew it to bloody tatters with a short burst. Then he and another of the troops picked up what was left of the corpse and slung it inside the flaming truck and stood there watching it burn.

Natalie

She sat waiting for David Foxworth in the empty press room off the embassy's reception lobby. It was the morning of March 3 and already a quarter past ten, which made him fifteen minutes late; she had been sitting there alone for twenty-five damn minutes. She was beginning to wonder if she was being given a version of the old bureaucratic runaround.

When she'd arrived yesterday morning for her first scheduled meeting with Foxworth, another staff member named Tom Boyd had met her with a message: Foxworth was ill and wouldn't be in. So the meeting was rescheduled for today—and here she was, but where was he? She half expected Boyd or one of the other embassy people to walk in any second, all politeness and apology, and tell her the appointment had to be canceled again.

Well, she wouldn't put it past Foxworth to duck her altogether. After that awkward little scene in Le Royal the other night, he might not want to face either her or the kinds of questions she would ask. And there wasn't anything she could do about it; she was booked on a return flight to Bangkok first thing tomorrow, and if she made noises about wanting to stay longer, they could simply refuse to extend her visa.

She did some more thinking about David Foxworth. Her impression of him in Le Royal had been about what she'd expected: a typical foreign-service functionary; loyal, stubborn, intelligent enough but lacking in human compassion, and possessed of an acute case of tunnel vision where the war and the U.S. role in it was concerned. He may have had hidden qualities, of course; he had attracted Than Kim, after all, and Natalie had come to like and respect her. And he did have enough sensitivity to be enraged by what Peter Deighan had said to him. He wasn't the worst of the embassy officials she'd met, but the fact that he was probably one of the best was a terrible indictment of the situation in Cambodia and of the government which had sent him here.

A small wry smile lifted one corner of her mouth. No, Foxworth wasn't the worst. There was the senior official who had made an obscene suggestion to her as she was leaving the embassy yesterday. And Boyd, with his unctuous smile and his white-man's-burden condescension dripping at every mention of Cambodia or Cambodians. And the military attaché sopping up gin with a wire-service correspondent in the bar at Hotel Le Phnom, saying in answer to the reporter's question about what he felt would happen if and when the Khmer Rouge took the country, "They'll do the same lousy screwed-up job of running it Lon Nol's boys have. Hell, they're Cambodians, aren't they?"

The Ugly American, Natalie thought. God, the city was full of them. Arrogant, ethnocentric. Uncaring. Self-serving. Newspeople pouring in daily, hoping to be on hand for the final U.S. pull-out, like the ghoulish witnesses at an execution. Men such as Peter Deighan, the macho cynics and the so-called soldiers of fortune, who found war exciting and death and horror a good way to make a buck. The cheerful, friendly Frenchman at the hotel who she had been told was a dealer in hard drugs, supplying not only members of the press corps but certain members of the embassy staff as well. The fat little photographer with his color glossies of mutilated bodies, licking his lips as he passed them around, his eyes bright and full of heat. General Theodore Mataxis, former head of the U.S. Military Equipment Delivery Team, who had returned to Phnom Penh as a private citizen to openly buy American weapons from Cambodian army officers, for resale to a Singapore arms dealer. And she had only been here a few days; there were no doubt a lot more she hadn't met or didn't know about.

Did all war zones attract these kinds of people, the way Southern California was supposed to attract the lunatic fringe back home? Probably. But war also created its own lunatic fringe. Constant exposure to savagery, to one brutal shock after another, had to take its toll eventually; you either got out before it was too late or you became brutalized yourself. Apathy, alcoholism, abnormality—these and a hundred variations were the prices Foxworth and Deighan and the rest of them paid.

It was the price her father had paid too, Natalie realized abruptly. He had survived the concentration camps of Nazi Germany by making himself not care anymore, because the only other alternative was madness; but it had scarred him for life and he had never quite recovered. Maybe that was why he had thrown himself so deeply into refugee work: he was trying to keep others from suffering all that he had suffered and at the same time he was trying to learn how to care again . . .

The sound of the press room door opening made her blink, look up, then get to her feet. David Foxworth shut the door behind him and said, "Good morning, Miss Rosen," in the kind of voice people use when they wish they were somewhere else.

Natalie felt annoyance rise inside her. And an impulse toward bitchiness, even though that was a tendency in herself she hated. The atmosphere in Phnom Penh was starting to take its toll on her, too. "You're twenty minutes late, Mr. Foxworth," she said. "Or don't you believe in being on time for your appointments?"

"Sorry. I was at a meeting."

"I thought maybe you were going to be ill again."

"Ill? Oh," he said, "yesterday."

"Yesterday. You *were* ill, weren't you?"

"Not exactly."

"Then why didn't you keep our appointment?"

"It's something I'd rather not talk about, if you don't mind."

He moved past her to one of the tables, laid his briefcase on it, and stood waiting for her to join him. There was an air of preoccupation about him, as if part of him was somewhere else, focused on other things. When she sat down across from him he took a chair for himself, opened his briefcase, and shuffled through a sheaf of papers. It was quiet in the room, except for the hum and whirr of the air conditioner; but it was the kind of quiet that seemed to pervade the rest of the embassy, a hushed uneasy stillness that made you feel tense instead of comfortable.

"I have a communication here from Washington," Foxworth said at length. "The White House has agreed to ship free rice under Title II of the Public Law 480 program. Starting on the fifth, seven hundred metric tons of rice per day will be flown in from Thailand."

Natalie considered that for a moment. "Well, it's something, anyway," she said.

"You don't seem very pleased at the news."

"The only news that would really please me, Mr. Foxworth, is that there won't be any more refugees to feed. That the war is over and we won't be helping to kill any more Cambodians."

She thought he might flare up again at that, the way he had at Le Royal, and the mood she was in, she would have welcomed another confrontation. But his expression didn't change and he said nothing; his eyes shifted to the window, beyond which an armed group of marines were moving toward the front of the compound. Sunlight blazed around them, glinting off metallic surfaces. Everywhere you looked, she thought, everything you did or heard or saw, was a reminder of war. And death. *Memento mori.* Reminder of death.

When Foxworth looked back at her there was a flicker of something in his eyes that might have been pain. But it was gone so quickly that she couldn't be sure. From behind the flat mask of the bureaucrat he said, "Do you want to discuss the refugee situation, Miss Rosen, or do you want to keep on playing devil's advocate? If all you're interested in is sniping at me, then we're both wasting our time."

There was a sharp answer to that on her tongue, but she didn't give voice to it. He seemed tired, drained of antagonism, and all at once she felt the same way. What was the sense in two Americans fighting a meaningless battle when millions of Khmers were involved in a life-and-death struggle all around them? Too much conflict, not enough compassion. It was the Cambodian people, for God's sake, who mattered.

"All right," she said. "Suppose we discuss the refugees."

But Foxworth had little to tell her that she did not already know. The PL-480 Title II program was one she had expected President Ford, under pressure from Congress, to eventually agree to implement; only Title I rice had been shipped until now, making it necessary for the Cambodian government to buy it and then resell it to those who could afford the inflated price. But even an increase to seven hundred metric tons per day was not nearly enough to feed the starving population. In 1973, when Phnom Penh contained half as many people as it did today, the government estimate of daily needs had been close to eight hundred metric tons.

And there were still no new provisions for medical supplies or blood and plasma to replace the near-empty blood banks. No provisions for qualified doctors and surgeons to treat the wounded, the diseased, the malnourished. No provisions to funnel available money direct to relief groups rather than through the Lon Nol government, where most of it always disappeared before it could benefit any of the refugees.

It was a hopeless situation. Foxworth knew that as well as she did; she could see it in his eyes, feel it in the pauses when he spoke. The people were doomed. A small number of them might be able to flee the country before it toppled, but the majority would either die of privation or illness or be left to the mercies of the Khmer Rouge. What good would Title II rice be then? What good would any of their efforts be when it was too late and freedom was something lost in the wreckage?

When it was too late, Natalie thought bitterly. It was already too late; it had been too late when those first bombs were dropped on Cambodia in the name of peace. It was the people who mattered, but few had ever thought of the people and few ever would. Countries, ideologies, political gamesmanship—those were what the heads of governments thought about. But the people? Look at Kissinger, Nixon, Lon Nol, the Khmer Rouge leaders, any of the world statesmen East or West, communist or capitalist or opportunist: the people never mattered at all.

The meeting with Foxworth lasted less than an hour; there was nothing to be decided, nothing to be gained in further discussion, and neither of them cared to prolong what amounted to an exercise in futility. He went with her out of the press room and across the dark lobby to the main entrance.

"You're flying back to Bangkok tomorrow?" he asked then.

"Yes."

"And then?"

"There's a lot to be done, Mr. Foxworth. Arrangement for special medical supplies, if I can manage it. Resettlement of refugees from here and the Thai camps. Back to New York in a couple of weeks to help raise more funds."

Pain flickered in his eyes again; this time she was sure of it. "You really care, don't you, Miss Rosen?"

"Yes," she said, "I really care. Don't you?"

"I always believed I did."

"But now you're not so sure?"

"Now maybe I'm starting to learn how." He put out his hand, gripped hers. "Goodbye, Miss Rosen."

"Goodbye, Mr. Foxworth."

He gave her a solemn nod, turned, and went away toward the heavy plexiglass doors across the lobby. Watching him, Natalie felt something stir inside her, a kind of softening and shifting of her feelings. *Now maybe I'm starting to learn how.* Like her father? she thought. Trying to learn how to care?

On the way to her next appointment at the Preah Ket Melea Hospital, she wondered again if there was more to David Foxworth than she had first thought. In a different time, in a different place, she might have liked to find out. It was just possible that he might fascinate her if she got to know him.

But then, she *wasn't* going to get to know him. The chances were she would never even see him again. And maybe that was just as well. Kim seemed to care for him, and if he was any kind of man at all he would care for her in return, take her out of Cambodia before the end came. Besides which, the last person in the world she would want to get herself involved with was a member of Kissinger's diplomatic corps: hawks and doves, like East and West, were twain that probably could never meet.

She stopped thinking about Foxworth altogether when they arrived at the hospital. What she thought then, as she walked among boys barely into their teens lying two and three to a bed, wounds festering for lack of antibiotics and competent physicians, and wasted babies dying of malnutrition, the five-year-olds with toothpick limbs and distended stomachs, the ten-year-olds dehydrated and shrunken to the size of the five-year-olds, was what she had thought many times in the past few days, and would think many times again for as long as she lived.

She thought: Dear God, the children.
What have we done to the children?

Cambodia File: War Calendar

March 11—Prince Sihanouk, from his exile in Peking, issues another statement promising a reconciliation with the U.S. if he is returned to power and Lon Nol and his "traitors" are driven from Phnom Penh. He also discredits U.S. claims that Cambodia faces a retaliatory bloodbath if the Khmer Rouge seize power.

March 17–18—The GKR navy abandons its naval support base at Neak Luong, owing to heavy damage and casualties. Four naval supply convoy ships to Neak Luong are later destroyed by the Khmer Rouge at a barricade built across the Dei Dos chokepoint.

March 25—General Lon Non, the Marshal's brother, resigns from the Army. Commander in Chief and Chief of Staff Sosthene Fernandez had previously resigned under pressure from the Cabinet.

March 28—Radical university students join the mounting popular demand for the resignation of Lon Nol; they also demand an end to American aid. The GKR subsequently closes all schools in Phnom Penh as a security measure.

April 1—Neak Luong falls in bloody hand-to-hand combat, with heavy loss of life and matériel. Some 5,000 KC troops begin to move north toward Phnom Penh with more than a dozen captured howitzers and thousands of rounds of ammunition.

April 1—Khmer Rouge leader Khieu Samphan broadcasts live on clandestine radio, proclaiming the legitimacy of the revolutionary government and calling once more for the execution of the "seven traitors": Lon Nol, Sirik Matak, Long Boret, Sosthene Fernandez, Cheng Heng, Son Ngoc Than, and In Thom. He appeals to all FANK troops to lay down their arms immediately and join the KC.

April 1—President Lon Nol, his family, and a large entourage leave Cambodia for Indonesia and subsequent resettlement in Hawaii. General Saukham Khoy, President of the Senate, is appointed acting Chief of State in accordance with the constitution.

April 3—In the wake of diplomatic departures by the Indonesians, Malaysians, and all other pro-Western missions, the U.S. embassy, publicly claiming reduced work load, begins evacuating two thirds of its remaining staff.

Foxworth

"Kim," he said, "will you please listen to me? It's only a matter of time now; the Khmer Rouge are closing in on the north and south perimeters. You've got to leave and you've got to do it right away, before they get close enough to shut down the airport. I can arrange to get you a seat on one of the planes to Bangkok—"

"No," she said.

He stood looking down at her, sitting on one of the chairs in his lamplit villa, the flickering play of light and shadow accenting her features and yet hiding her expression. The taste of frustration and anxiety was bitter in his mouth. He had said those words a hundred times in the past month, but for all the effect they had he might always have been alone and talking to himself. But he had to keep on saying them and he said them again now: "You've got to leave before it's too late, you've got to let me get you to Thailand. Why won't you accept that?"

"I don't wish to leave my country."

"The Khmer Rouge—"

"I am not afraid of the Khmer Rouge."

She had been like this for more than a month, ever since the nightmare on Avenue Phum Chup—cool, distant, calmly defying him whenever he brought up the subject of her leaving Phnom Penh, and yet acquiescing to him on every other level. If he wanted to spend time with her, here at his villa or at her house, she was always willing to accommodate him. But she seemed to take none of her earlier pleasure in being with him; and she didn't suggest things that she liked to do, as she had before. If he wanted her to sleep with him, she always agreed without question. But each of the two times he had made love to her, she only lay motionless, looking away from him, not touching him with her hands or her eyes, so that he felt ashamed afterward, as if he had committed a kind of rape.

At first he'd been afraid it was because of the way he had frozen up that night on Phum Chup, nearly getting both of them killed in the cross fire between the FANK soldiers and the KC saboteurs; that she might consider him a coward. The question of cowardice was one he had asked himself, lying sleepless and feverish that night, all the next day. There was no denying the incident had had a profound effect on him, that it had made him reexamine himself and his role in this war. But he was not a coward. Once you began admitting truths to and about yourself, something as basic as cowardice wouldn't stay unrevealed for long. No, it had been surprise and shock and the enormity of the situation, the sudden jarring *personal* threat of war rather than war as a kind of abstraction, that had kept him from reacting immediately.

Still, it worried him what Kim thought. He didn't want to be diminished in her eyes, to be an object of her contempt. Yet when he asked her if that was what was wrong, the matter of cowardice, she said no. And he believed her.

There was only one other possible answer: it was nothing he had done, it was the fact that he was an American, an embassy official, a part of the government that had helped to tear her own country apart in the past half dozen years. Her position on the war had begun to shift before that night; and the incident must have had a profound effect on her too. Like so many other Cambodians in recent days, her trust and faith in the

United States had been eroded to the point now where she no longer had trust and faith even in him.

And there seemed to be nothing he could do to reestablish it. He couldn't reach her anymore, not with logic and not with emotional pleas; she had walled herself off from him, retreated behind a bamboo curtain that no Caucasian could penetrate.

Foxworth turned away from her, licking at the dry bitter taste that caked the roof of his mouth, and went to the teak sideboard. There was a bottle of Beefeater gin standing on top of it, along with a liter of quinine water and the empty glass he had been using. He poured equal amounts of gin and mix into the glass, drank it off. Good quick stream of fire down into his stomach—but it didn't burn away the bitter taste.

Behind him Kim said, "You should not drink so much liquor." No reproach in the words; just a flat neutral statement.

"Why not?" he said, turning. "What difference does it make?"

"It is not good for your health."

"What *is* good for my health? Letting you stay here and face the Khmer Rouge when they overrun the city?"

"I will not run away."

"It's not running away."

"Not if you are a pig like Lon Nol. Or an American."

"Call it what you want, but it's the only choice that makes sense. If things had been handled differently, if some decisions hadn't been made and others had been, then maybe we could stay and help turn back the Khmer Rouge. But not now; now it's too late."

"Yes," Kim said. "Too late."

"I don't know how much longer it'll be before evacuation orders come through. Can't you understand that?"

"I understand."

"They won't give me much warning. A few hours, not much more. Dean wanted to shut down the embassy by April fifth; Kissinger cabled him no, he's still trying to get Sihanouk to come back here from China as a negotiator, but he could change his mind and it could still happen by then. Even if it doesn't and we stay for another week or two, the airport is liable to be closed and we'll have to go out by helicopter. I may not be able to arrange a seat for you unless—"

"There is no need for you to arrange anything," she said, "except your own departure."

It was no use, she just wouldn't listen. What was he going to do? He couldn't force her to leave against her will, and he couldn't leave her here to die at the hands of the communists. Christ, what was he going to *do?*

Pour another drink, that was what he'd do right now. Reflex action: every time the tension mounted lately, reach for the gin, reach for the safety valve to relieve the pressure and keep himself from blowing under the strain. Kim was right—it wasn't good for his health. But he had nothing else, and he needed something with her defying him, conditions worsening by the hour, the end and the Khmer Rouge both drawing near.

Neak Luong, FANK's last line of defense on the Mekong, in the hands of the KC. The government's 1st and 2nd Divisions, protecting Phnom Penh's southern approaches, beginning to crumble as soldiers deserted in droves and fled into the city. The same thing happening on the northwest, with the 7th Division, in the face of the KC offensive to close Pochentong Airport. And in the city itself there was chaos. The government in ruins while Lon Nol, publicly labeled a national hero by his Socio-Republican Party, was on his way to Hawaii with God only knew how much stolen money. No water, no electricity, no sanitation. Almost no food, and the daily airlift of rice from Saigon, all that stood between the population and complete starvation, in danger of being halted because of the heavy artillery fire on the airport. Bodies littering the streets, left to decay or to be stripped of flesh by the rats. More and more shells finding targets in what was now a ceaseless barrage, starting fires that were never fought, leaving more dead among the garbage and the rubble. A more strictly enforced curfew that kept most people off the streets, kept Foxworth and what remained of the embassy staff confined to residences when they weren't putting in twelve- to fourteen-hour days inside the embassy compound.

Conditions there were just as bad. Fewer than 125 American military and diplomatic officers remained, and some of those would be gone by tomorrow night; the rest, those in what were considered important positions or had CIA ties like himself, would stay until Kissinger and Ford finally relented—but none of them were doing anything, could do anything, except waiting to be evacuated by charter flight or helicopter, if it came to that, in what had been labeled Operation Eagle Pull. Confusion, dissension, dismay, were rampant. Congress was at fault because of their restrictions on the White House war effort; the White House was at fault for not implementing stronger programs to cut corruption and unify the Cambodian fighting forces; Kissinger was at fault for his drastic and criminally misguided Asian policies; the Cambodians were at fault, all of them, regardless of which side they were on, because of the kind of race they were. Ambassador Dean was suffering from high blood pressure and nervous exhaustion. The AID program head, Thomas Olmsted, had died at his post, and another official had had a heart attack. Dean's deputy, Robert Keeley, was undergoing treatment for bleeding ulcers. There were unconfirmed reports that some members of staff were using drugs; confirmed reports that others, Foxworth among them, were drinking to excess. Even Boyd, whom nothing had seemed to affect up until a few weeks ago, showed signs of cracking under the stress.

None of them had escaped the effects of the coming collapse; whether Kim thought so or not, none of them wanted to run or to have it end this way. It was only the Khmers, some of them—Kim—who were aloof from the tension, waiting patiently for whatever would happen when the war was over and the enemy owned the land.

I don't understand her, I never did.

Kim watched him drain his third drink; he could feel her eyes on him, rich dark lustrous eyes staring at him from behind her bamboo curtain. He put the glass down, turned to face her.

"Isn't there anything I can say to you?" he said. "Isn't there any way I can make you listen to me?"

"No, *dekkun.*"

"Don't call me *dekkun.*"

"I'm sorry. Do you wish me to stay with you tonight?"

"Do you want to stay?"

"If it is what you wish."

"Do you want to sleep with me? Be with me?"

"If it is what you wish."

It was stifling in there. He felt it all at once—the gin fire combining with the thick dry season heat, making it hard for him to breathe, as if his lungs were swaddled in cotton and he was inhaling tiny clogging fibers of it. "If you want to stay, stay," he said to her. "Do what you want, not what I want." And he went over to the garden door, not looking at her, a little unsteady on his feet, and stepped outside.

The night was full of tracers and fireglow and the echoing thunder of heavy artillery. And the sweet smell of hibiscus and frangipani too, like incense burning for the dead. He opened his mouth and took several deep breaths, trying to clear his lungs, trying not to smell the flowers or listen to any more of the war. The feeling of suffocation passed, left him limp and sweating cold and hot at the same time, as if with fever.

He went back inside. Kim was no longer sitting in the chair; the room was empty except for the darting shadows thrown against the walls by the kerosene lamp. He stood in the semi-darkness, still sweating hot and cold, thinking, What am I going to *do?* and calling her name and hearing it echo hollowly beneath the louder echoes of the guns.

"Kim! Kim!"

But she was no longer there.

Cambodia File: Excerpts from an Address Before a Joint Session of Congress by President Gerald R. Ford, 9:04 P.M., April 10, 1975

. . . A vast human tragedy has befallen our friends in Vietnam and Cambodia. Tonight I shall not talk only of obligations arising from legal documents. Who can forget the enormous sacrifices of blood, dedication, and treasure that we made in Vietnam? . . .

In Cambodia the situation is tragic. The United States and the Cambodian government have each made major efforts, over a long period and through many channels, to end that conflict. But because of their military successes, steady external support, and their awareness of American legal restrictions, the communist side has shown no interest in negotiation, compromise, or a political solution. And yet, for the past three months, the beleaguered people of Phnom Penh have fought on, hoping against hope that the United States would not desert them, but instead provide the arms and ammunition they so badly needed.

I have received a moving letter from the new acting President of Cambodia, Saukham Khoy, and let me quote it to you:

"Dear Mr. President," he wrote. "As the American Congress reconvenes to reconsider your urgent request for supplemental assistance for the Khmer Republic, I appeal to you to convey to the American legislators our plea not to deny these vital resources to us, if a nonmilitary solution is to emerge from this tragic five-year-old conflict.

"To find a peaceful end to the conflict we need time. I do not know how much time, but we all fully realize that the agony of the Khmer people cannot and must not go on much longer. However, for the immediate future, we need the rice to feed the hungry and the ammunition and the weapons to defend ourselves against those who want to impose their will by force [of arms]. A denial by the American people of the means for us to carry on will leave us no alternative but inevitably abandoning our search for a solution which will give our citizens some freedom of choice as to their future. For a number of years now this confidence was misplaced and suddenly America will deny us the means which might give us a chance to find an acceptable solution to our conflict."

This letter speaks for itself. In January, I requested food and ammunition for the brave Cambodians, and I regret to say that as of this evening, it may soon be too late.

Members of the Congress, my fellow Americans, this moment of tragedy for Indochina is a time of trial for us. It is a time for national resolve.

It has been said that the United States is over-extended, that we have too many commitments too far from home, that we must re-examine what our truly vital interests are and shape our strategy to conform to them. I find no fault with this as a theory, but in the real world such a course must be pursued carefully and in close coordination with solid progress toward overall reduction in world-wide tensions.

We cannot, in the meantime, abandon our friends while our adversaries support and encourage theirs. We cannot dismantle our defenses, our diplomacy, or our intelligence capability while others increase and strengthen theirs. . . .

Above all, let's keep events in Southeast Asia in their proper perspective. The security and the progress of hundreds of millions of people everywhere depend importantly on us.

Let no potential adversary believe that our difficulties or our debates mean a slackening of our national will. We will stand by our friends, we will honor our commitments, and we will uphold our country's principles. . . .

Kim

The speech of the American President was broadcast live over Radio Phnom Penh at eleven o'clock on the morning of April 11. She listened to it in the front room of her house, sitting quietly, hands folded together in her lap. She was supposed to be at the embassy, working with other translators on a series of intercepted Khmer Rouge documents, but she had stayed away the past two days and there was no reason why she should not stay away a third. The embassy was no longer important; the documents were no longer important. The American President's speech was not important, either. Unless it was one of mercy and hope, and of course she knew it would not be. And it was not. It was the end of all mercy and all hope, as she had expected it would be.

His words were the easy ones of the powerful, sure of his strength and convinced of his purpose even as he faced defeat, because it was not *his* defeat but that of the already conquered. They were words she had heard from the Americans all her life. And they were the words of the French in 1954, to rationalize another retreat across another generation of Khmer corpses; they were the words, she was sure, which had been spoken to her ancestors by the Thais and the Annamese and all the other conquerors of Kampuchea across the mists of time.

When the words had ended she shut off the radio and sat for a while longer in silence. There seemed to be nothing inside her except a great sadness and a great emptiness. And yet, oddly, she found herself thinking of her dead husband, Chea Charoun.

Charoun had been a colonel in the air force and the Vietnamese had shot down his plane near the border in Ratanakiri Province more than three years ago. It had been a routine mission, one of several for which he had been scheduled that month, one of a hundred which he had flown in the months before; but he had taken his T-28 bomber too close to a KC artillery emplacement and the flak had severed one wing and he had died in the crash. The news of his death had come to her three weeks later, by messenger from Kompong Cham, where he had been stationed. By then the earth had swallowed him as mysteriously as, thirty years before, it had brought him forth.

She could not remember him very well; the news of his death seemed to have closed off her memory, sealed over the part of her which had been invaded by Charoun and was reserved for him. If she had dwelt on him in the past three years, it must have been below the edge of consciousness; it must have been in dreams. But now he was in her mind, shimmering there like a spirit—a rather tall and handsome man who had courted her only briefly before their marriage and who had lived with her in this house more briefly yet between his bombing missions and his military ground duties. She could almost hear his voice, intense, whispering to her of his dreams and his hopes, of his po-

sition and hers and that of the Americans in a free and democratic Kampuchea.

"The end of this war must be victory," Charoun had said in
the first weeks of their marriage, "because victory means freedom, and only when we have freedom will we truly have control
of our destiny. The Americans will help us to victory; they will
help us regain our land. This I believe with all my soul."

And these words had stayed with her, become her own words
and her own beliefs, and led her to work for the Americans and
to continue working for them after Charoun's death. But they
were no longer her words or her beliefs. Charoun was dead,
and so were the things he believed with all his soul.

She stood and went to the window, looked out past the car
the Americans had arranged for her, past the garden and MV
Phum Chup and Norodom Boulevard to the heat haze and the
smoke above the Quatre Bras. The noise of the heavy artillery
from there was like a constant drumbeat; it never stopped for
more than a few seconds now, throughout the day and throughout the night. Khmer Rouge forces ringed the city now, were
reportedly within a mile of Pochentong Airport. The daily airlift of rice had been halted. Soon the Americans would be gone
—perhaps today, perhaps tomorrow. And the Khmer Rouge
would come. And the guns would stop.

Or would they?

Were the communists saviors, as Prince Sihanouk claimed,
bringing unity and peace at last? Or were they only a new wave
of conquerors, invaders from within, bringing not an end to war
but more bloodshed and death to their own kind? She did not
know. But at least they were Khmers. She had believed in the
Americans and the French, and all they had offered was deceit;
there was no one left to believe in now except other Khmers.

Kim turned from the window. Past the bamboo partition separating this room from the bedroom, she could see the bed with
its shawl of mosquito netting; it held her gaze for a moment.
The bed had been hers for five years, just as the house had been
hers for five years, and in it she had lain with Charoun and lain
with two others in the military and lain finally with David Foxworth. The lovemaking had been good with Charoun, because

he was the first man to enter her body and take possession of it, but it had been even better with David. Not recently; before, when she still shared Charoun's beliefs about the Americans. As her belief shriveled, so it seemed her passion for David shriveled. It was not something she would have wished for. It was only something that had happened.

Would he come here tonight? Yes, she thought, he would come. He would know of the American President's speech, of course, and he would surely come to plead with her again. Perhaps, if the orders had come for their evacuation, he would be desperate enough to tie her hands and her feet and carry her off to a waiting helicopter. Would he do something such as that? Possibly. It was difficult to tell what Americans would do in moments of crisis; they did not themselves ever seem to know what they would do until they did it.

But it would make no difference if he came. She had already decided, even before listening to the empty words of the American President, what she herself must do. And she must also promise herself that she would not think of David anymore, not let the image of him in her thoughts. She must keep him below the edge of her consciousness, as she had done with Charoun; she must confine him to her dreams. That way, as with Charoun, her memory of him would also close off, and that part of her which he had invaded and which had been reserved for him would be forever sealed away.

She went into the bedroom, took her bag from beneath the bed. And began to pack into it those few personal belongings—some clothing, a statue of Buddha, a hammered-silver bracelet given to her by her half-brother Chey Han when they were children—which she would take with her when she went away.

Chey Han

The battalion commanded by Chey Han, together with other battalions in FUNK's 1st Division, had broken through the government's northwest line of defense at the village of Khmounh, on the outskirts of Phnom Penh, and were now within two kilometers of Pochentong Airport. The enemy had been forced to fall back more than a mile, near Phnom Sampeo and the North Dike Road perimeter; it was only a matter of time before they would be cut off at the rear flank and surrounded. Then the airport would belong to Angka—and soon after that, the city itself.

The fighting had been merciless and bloody for the past few weeks, and the cost great to the People's liberation forces. More than half of the eight hundred soldiers under Chey's command had been killed or too seriously wounded to continue fighting. His most valued lieutenant, Prak Sreng, had been blown apart by a grenade, the *neary* leader Ly Sokhon had been shot in the leg, and he himself had suffered burns and shrapnel wounds from an exploding 105-mm. shell at Khmounh. The remaining soldiers were weakened by malaria, dysentery, fatigue, and hunger. Morale had been poor until recent days and the promise of ultimate victory for the revolution; everyone was weary of fighting, weary of their meager guerrilla existence in the jungles.

Chey could understand this. He was no less weary than any of the soldiers—more so because of the responsibility of leadership Angka had seen fit to bestow upon him. The taste of victory would be sweet, but sweeter still would be a full belly every day of the year, the warmth of his wife Doremy's body, the murmur of laughter instead of the roar of guns in his ears.

He thought of these things as the liberated FANK jeep brought him back to the temporary support base, and they helped to ease his pain. He had fought at the front throughout the day, but the fire in his left side had become intolerable; some of the shrapnel wounds had opened again and begun to bleed, and huge blisters had formed and popped and drained yellow fluid where the skin was burned. He had almost collapsed when the sun reached the western horizon and the evening shadows lengthened; one of his remaining lieutenants had had to help him into the jeep.

He was not sure yet what he would do when the war was over. If it was the will of the Angkar Leu, he would remain a

soldier and continue to serve as he was bidden; but his desire
was to return to Preah Vihear Province, to take his wife onto a
few hectares of good land near Rovieng where he could grow
rice and beans. Where he could sit in the evening shade and
chew on shiny green betel leaves coated with lime and filled
with areca nut, tobacco, cloves, cardamom. Where he could
watch one of the coppery dry-season sunsets without thinking
of blood, and there would be no headless bonzes to turn his
dreams into nightmares.

The jeep jolted to a stop, jarring him, and he realized that
they had reached the jungle base of the quartermaster troops.
His head ached and his eyes were gritty; he must have slept for
a time. Yes, because the sleep image of the bonze lingered at
the edge of his mind: dancing, juggling a brass begging bowl
and his severed head while blood painted his hands in gouts of
bright crimson . . .

Chey shook himself. It was strange that the death of the
bonze at Cheom Pram should haunt him this way. He had
killed many men, many women, even two other bonzes himself
with his automatic weapon—and yet it had been Ly Sokhon
who slaughtered this bonze. What did the nightmare images
mean? He was no longer a Buddhist, no longer a believer in the
religion of the oppressors; he felt no remorse at the death of any
holy man, no guilt. Yet the nightmares had begun the night
they left Cheom Pram and continued to come to him ever since.
What could they mean?

The soldier driving the jeep and a black-pajamaed woman
helped him to where the sparse medical supplies were cached.
The woman removed his blood- and pus-soaked bandages, applied sulfa powder and fresh wrappings, and gave him water to
drink and black strips of jerked water buffalo to eat.

He did not see Ly Sokhon approach; she was merely there
when he looked up, standing before him, smiling her ugly serpent's smile. Her face and neck were swollen with insect bites
and some sort of infection, and her upper lip was so deeply
cracked in the center that it seemed split into two halves. It
made him shudder inside to look at her. But it was not just because she was repellent to the eyes; it was because of who she

was, her connections with the inner circle of the Angkar Leu. In spite of himself, he was afraid of her.

"I have news, Mit Chey," she said.

"What news?"

She limped closer to him, favoring her wounded leg. The hilt of the Vietnamese sword at her belt seemed to gleam in the shadowy light; Chey looked away from it. "The Americans will give no more aid to the Lon Nol puppets in Phnom Penh," she said. "It is a certainty that they will soon close their embassy and be gone."

"How do you know this?"

"The American President's speech was broadcast on Radio Phnom Penh this morning and monitored by Angka. The city will be ours in a matter of days; the country will be ours, Chey Han. Think of it! *Chhnea! Chhnea!*"

"Yes," Chey said, "victory at last." He managed a weary smile of his own. "An end to the war."

"An end to it? Perhaps."

"Why do you say perhaps?"

"Our victory must be complete and final."

"It will be complete and final."

"Only when the time of blood is finished," Ly Sokhon said, and her eyes seemed to glow as they had just before she cut off the bonze's head. Again she smiled her serpent's smile, said, "Rest well, Chey Han," and limped away into the shadows cast by the surrounding kapok trees.

Chey felt a vague sense of uneasiness. The time of blood, he thought. What had she meant by that? The war would be over when the victory was won, when the capital belonged to Angka; the time of blood would be past, and there would be the time of peace, Khmers joining hands with Khmers to build a strong People's Kampuchea.

Wasn't that what the Angkar Leu had promised?

The sleep image of the bonze capered again at the edge of his mind, juggling begging bowl and severed head with hands painted in gouts of bright crimson . . .

Foxworth

She was gone.

Foxworth knew it as soon as he swung his Fiat off Avenue Phum Chup into her front yard, saw that the house's front door was standing open and her car was missing from the open area underneath. Not just absent from the house; gone away from it. Gone away from it and gone away from him. Gone.

He slid the Fiat to a stop near the stairs, got out and ran up them. Inside he went into each of the rooms, knocking over partitions in his haste, calling her name in the emptiness the way he had at his own villa last week. In the bedroom he found the lids on two of her painted wooden chests upraised. Neither chest was empty, but both contained nothing now but scattered pieces of Western clothing; all of Kim's Khmer silks were missing. And so was her carved statue of Buddha, the one she always kept amid cut flowers on the bedside table.

Gone. Gone.

She had heard Ford's speech this morning, known what it meant: the White House had written off Cambodia, thrown it to the KC like a splintered and well-chewed bone. And she had also known that he would come rushing to her as soon as he could, with the end as near as it was. So she had packed her things and she had gotten into her car and she had gone away.

Where?

Where would she go at a time like this?

He felt a kind of wild gnawing terror. He should have come here as soon as the speech was over; but in its aftermath everything had been chaotic at the embassy . . . Emergency evacuation committee meeting in the top-floor security "bubble," Dean calling the State Department to request immediate pullout, Dean and Keeley hurrying off to break the news to President Saukham Khoy, preparations, instructions . . . He couldn't get free until just a little while ago and at that he was only supposed to return to his villa and gather vital possessions and await word via the embassy radio net, not go anywhere else because of the curfew and the heavy artillery fire raining down on the city.

Where would *she* go?

Her aunt? he thought. He remembered that she had an aunt, a seamstress named Thirith something, who lived in the Toek Loak sector of the city. But what was the address? Not far from the Bonzes' Hospital and the road to Pochentong; Kim had taken him there once not long after they met. Toek Loak sector —that was northwest, and northwest was where the communists were concentrating their cannon fire because of the airport. Would she go there, knowing that? He didn't know what she might do anymore.

Her aunt's address, damn it. He had seen it listed in Kim's file at the embassy . . . what was it, what *was* it?

Samdach Phuong, that was the street. Two hundred and something Samdach Phuong.

He wheeled out of the bedroom, out of the house and down into his car. Away from there, driving too fast on the near-deserted streets, heading north toward Olympic Stadium. Sweat dripping off his face, matting his shirt and trousers to his skin; not a breath of air stirring anywhere. And the sunset sky streaked and smeared with red, like bloody finger marks on a smoky blue canvas.

What if she isn't there? he thought. What if I can't find her? No, Jesus, he *had* to find her. It was only a matter of hours now; if Ford agreed to the ambassador's request and ordered them out, they'd go first thing in the morning. All of them. Operation Eagle Pull—twenty-four marine CH-53 Sea Stallion helicopters, "Jolly Green Giants," ready to fly in from the carrier *Okinawa* out in the Gulf as soon as matters were settled, 1100 hours at the latest. Plenty of room on those big bastards, even with maybe three hundred embassy officials, Defense Department workers, U.S. journalists, and Third World civilians to take out; even with Long Boret, Sirik Matak, Lon Non, Saukham Khoy, and the other government leaders and their families Dean would extend written invitations to. There'd be room for one more Khmer; he'd *make* room for her, he wasn't going to leave her behind, he was going to get her out safely, because—

Because he loved her.

Admitting it to himself now for the first time, no more uncertainty in his own mind, no more sham. He loved her.

The sunset colors were already fading when he passed Olympic Stadium and swung around to the northwest, into Toek Loak. Night shadows pressed down, stained with the smoke-tinged glow from at least three separate fires. The radio on his belt kept crackling, issuing forth a steady stream of coded numbers and information. He barely heard it; if one of those Control was trying to reach was nine-three, his number, he just didn't give a damn.

Another kilometer disappeared. And one of the fires looked to be dead ahead of him then, a big blaze vomiting globs and streamers of gray-black smoke. Foxworth wasn't close enough yet to see the flames, but he could judge the approximate location: near the Bonzes' Hospital and the road to the airport.

Samdach Phuong?

No, he thought, it's one of the other streets. But he bore down harder on the accelerator, veering around and through what traffic there was, almost sideswiping a cyclo that cut toward him out of a side street. From throat to bowels he felt squeezed up, cramped with tension. More sweat came out of him, flowing and greasy like animal fat, and the smell of it, the smell of his own fear, put the taste of bile on his tongue.

He could see the flames when he neared the southern entrance to Samdach Phuong, a string of them licking up orange and soot-colored for what seemed to be more than a block. There was heavier traffic here, most of it bicycles and scooters, all of it, along with a straggling of pedestrians, heading up Samdach Phuong. Foxworth bulled through, using the Fiat's horn, scattering people and vehicles, and finally made the turn around a jagged shell crater with caved-in sides.

Fire coated the entire northern half of the next block—the two hundred block, the house that belonged to Kim's aunt.

No!

He spun the wheel, braked, and was out and running before

the Fiat rolled to a standstill at the verge. The fire smell was strong in the hot dusk: woodsmoke, gasoline, the pungency of roasting flesh that might have been animal and might have been human. There were seven or eight of the stilt houses ablaze, one of them leaning at a backward angle as if thrown off balance by the exploding force—rocket or mortar shell—that had landed near it. Half a dozen palm trees stood flaming here and there, like giant torches held aloft, and on the unpaved street was the half-consumed corpse of an automobile.

People milled about in a desultory way, staring at the fire but making no effort to do anything about it. There was nothing to do; they had no water to drink, much less to fight fires with, and no one would come from the fire department because they were all too busy protecting the government buildings downtown, the fancy villas on Monivong and Mao Tse-tung Boulevards. Foxworth shoved his way through the crowd, clutching at the women, looking at their faces in the firelight. They stared back at him, some a little surprised to see a Westerner in their midst, most stoic and resigned, none reacting in any way to the frenzy of his movements.

No sign of Kim anywhere; no sign of her aunt. Just a streetful of Asian strangers, the thrumming of the fire, the squeal of pigs and the bawl of a goat, a chicken flapping crazily across his path as he ran—and the smell of meat cooking, flesh cooking, sickening waves of it carried on the hot breath of the fire . . .

He reached the end of the block, dodged across the street into the next one. His breath came in ragged pants; the sound of his pulse was like the sound of her name, "Kim, Kim, Kim," throbbing in his ears. Fewer people here, and a pack of snarling dogs. He turned back, not running so much now as stumbling. Clutched at the women again, some of the same ones as before, some he had missed—

Kim's aunt.

She was standing in one of the yards, half hidden next to an oxcart with one wheel off; he recognized her because she had a goiter on the right side of her neck and had refused to let Kim or anyone else talk her into having it treated. She recognized him, too, when he ran up in front of her and caught her shoulders; but it was just a dull flicker, the clicking of memory circuits in the brain of an automaton. Her face and her eyes were empty—the kind of emptiness that comes at the end of despair, when hope no longer exists.

"Where's Kim?" he said. "Is she here? Where is she?"

The old woman shook her head uncomprehendingly, and through the haze inside his own mind he remembered that she spoke no English, just a little French. He tried again, forcing himself to say the words twice in French, slowly, to make sure she understood.

And she answered, "I don't know."

"She's not here?"

"No."

"She didn't come to be with you today?"

"No, *lok*."

"When did you see her last?"

"Weeks ago," the old woman said. She lifted one of her gnarled hands and pointed across the street. "My house, all that is mine. I have nothing now. Nothing."

He turned away from her and stood trembling with exhaustion, supporting himself against the oxcart. She wasn't here, she hadn't been hurt in the explosion or the fire. But the first rush of relief was gone now. He still didn't know where she was. If she hadn't come to her aunt, then *where?*

Two million people jammed into a dying city, and the city itself sprawled out over several ravaged miles. She could be anywhere, with anyone or with no one at all. Not much time left, maybe only a few hours. She didn't want to be found; how could he find her?

How could he even hope to find her?

Deighan

The sound of shouting voices, of running steps and thumping noises in the hallway outside, woke Deighan and sent him rolling over on his back, wincing at the hangover pain that lashed through both temples.

He opened his eyes to slits. Morning. Early morning: the sky beyond the hotel room window sill had some of the red flush of sunrise. He dragged his left arm up and squinted at the dial of his wristwatch. A little after seven. What the hell day was it? Saturday? Yeah. Saturday, April 12. One day after Ford and the boys officially threw Cambodia to the wolves.

Somebody started banging on the door. Deighan eased his feet off the bed, raised himself slowly into a sitting position. And sat with his head down and his arms folded across his knees, waiting for the dizziness and nausea to pass.

"Deighan? You in there?"

The voice belonged to Michael Irwin, one of the other American journalists who had been at Hotel Le Phnom for the duration. Deighan didn't have anybody he could call a friend among the press corps—or anywhere else, for that matter—but Irwin was one of the few he got along with. At least they shared a taste for liquor and whores, and had a similar outlook on the war and the U.S. involvement in it, Irwin being another graduate of the '60s antiwar movements. They had spent last night together in Irwin's room, smoking pot and drinking vodka and singing "The Star-Spangled Banner" and "Oh, Will There Be a Dreadful Bloodbath When the Khmer Rouge Come to Town?" Celebrating Ford telling the world that it was too late for Cambodia but that the U.S. always honors her commitments and looks out for her friends. Holding their own private wake for Cambodia, even though the corpse was still twitching.

Deighan called, "Yeah, just a minute," and pushed himself off the bed. When his stomach quit kicking up bile he moved over to where his pants and shirt lay in a tangle on the floor. Put the pants on and then opened the door.

"You didn't hear yet, huh?" Irwin said. Behind him, white-uniformed porters were hurrying back and forth, some of them carrying suitcases and other luggage.

"No. What?"

"We're going out this morning," Irwin said. "The embassy just broadcast an assembly message over their radio net."

"How soon?"

"They want everybody at the embassy with bags by eight-thirty. Gates close at nine-thirty; nobody gets in after that. Or out."

"Yeah."

"Better shag ass, Peter."

Deighan shut the door and went back to sit on the bed. So this is it, he thought. Not tomorrow or the next day; right up against it, right now. Was he going to go or was he going to stay? He'd thought about that a lot lately. If he stayed he wouldn't be the only one. The New York *Times* man, Sydney Schanberg, had already indicated that he wouldn't be leaving with the rest of them; some of the free-lance broadcast journalists and photographers had been talking about sticking it out; most of the French and a few of the West German and Swedish correspondents would probably stay too.

But what good would it do him? The others had reasons for wanting to hang on in Phnom Penh as long as they could: a sense of duty and obligation, a personal commitment to the Cambodian people, maybe even the thrill of danger or the chance for a little glory. But none of those reasons applied to him. He didn't give a damn about anything anymore, at least not on a level beyond the abstract; nothing touched him down in the gut, the way some people and some things—Carol, Vietnam, the tenor of the '60s—had in the past. He hadn't written anything in weeks, except a couple of mailed notes and a couple of unmailed and abortive suicide letters to Carol; he had nothing left to say, no comment left to make on the war or anything else. Dead inside, dried up: no more passion, no more poetry, no more Pulitzer Prize nominations. Just Hemingway at the very end—a bitter and disillusioned drunk. And somewhere down the pike, a reenactment of the scene in Hemingway's kitchen in Ketchum, Idaho, all the burned-out brilliance and all the eroded intellect reduced to gore splattered across a wall.

Which was the only valid reason for staying he had been able to come up with: that it might get him killed. If he couldn't do it himself, then by God let the Khmer Rouge do it for him. Except that it would be likely to happen. The communists weren't crazy enough to slaughter a bunch of American journalists; no percentage in that, not when they could avoid an international incident by just rounding up the few that were left and shipping them out to Thailand. Schanberg and the rest knew that; they were willing to risk their necks, sure, but they weren't out to commit suicide. And *he* was. He could provoke the Khmer Rouge into wasting him, of course—refuse to obey orders, attack one of them when the time was right. But working yourself up to that was the same as working yourself up to pulling your own trigger, which in his case, at least for the time being, seemed to be impossible.

No *cojones,* he thought again. No balls at all.

So he would evacuate with the rest of them this morning; there had never been any doubt, really, that he would. And then what? Resettle in Bangkok, maybe. He had nowhere else to go except back to the States, back to California and back to Carol, and you can't go home again. All right, Bangkok—but then what? His money was running out and his magazine editor had already started to refuse him any more advance money without a substantial amount of new copy. Scam some free-lance assignments, latch on with a small wire-service outfit, even do stringer stuff if he had to. Hell, it didn't matter. It was just marking time until he was able to face square up to the old *nada,* put the .45 in his mouth and somehow screw up enough courage to pull the trigger.

On the floor beside the bed was his last bottle, the one he'd carried down from Irwin's room late last night. He reached out and caught it up. Empty—a dead soldier. Hah. Dead soldier in a country of dead soldiers, he thought. Dead soldier among dead soldiers in the Dead Soldier that used to be the Khmer Republic. He threw the bottle into a corner, watched it bounce and roll clattering into a patch of sunlight that filtered in through the window. He'd get another bottle before he left the hotel. No way he was going to face a helicopter airlift ride without some Dutch courage working inside him.

He finished dressing, went into the bathroom to use the toilet. He had quit shaving over a month ago; too damn much trouble. And he had had his hair chopped down to bristle for the same reason. So taking a leak was the only thing he had to do in there. Never mind that he needed a bath and that his mouth both tasted and reeked of stale vodka; he was being evacuated from a war zone, not going to dinner with the ambassador. Which was what he'd done last Sunday, along with most of the other American journalists at Dean's request, because Dean wanted to prepare them for the pull-out. All very civilized and proper, good food and good wine—so civilized and proper that it had made Deighan want to puke. He had gotten drunk and left early to find a whore; that seemed fitting. In the same way that going out this morning stinking of sweat and booze was fitting. It was his last protest, feeble and meaningless but all that he was capable of.

It took him less than ten minutes to pack. The other journalists and photogs had accumulated file material, books, special equipment, art objects, clothing; he hadn't accumulated anything except the black-market .45. All he had was what he had come here with two years ago—the portable typewriter, a few changes of clothes, a toilet kit—and that was all he packed into his Pan Am flight bag. Except, of course, for the .45. That went into the bag too, wrapped in a towel from the bathroom: it was the last thing he would have left behind.

Carrying the typewriter case in one hand and the flight bag in the other, Deighan went out and down the hall. On the stairs one of the porters, looking bewildered by what was happening, offered to help him; but he said no, what he wanted was a bottle of vodka, a quart if they had it, the most expensive in the hotel stock. He gave the porter a handful of riels, followed him the rest of the way down to the darkened lobby.

A dozen or so American newsmen were gathered there, most of whom looked as bleary-eyed as he did. But that was because they'd spent the night chasing down stories or filing dispatches at the cable office, not blowing pot or drinking vodka. With them were several of the Khmers who worked as drivers and translators. Deighan hadn't had a driver or a translator himself since his first couple of months in Phnom Penh; you didn't need any help to guzzle booze or screw B-girls or write abortive suicide letters to your wife. He stood apart from the rest of the journalists, listening to their nervously animated conversations, feeling himself to be at a still, cold distance: not one of them at all.

Irwin came down a couple of minutes later and Deighan bummed a cigarette from him. Not long after that the porter returned with a quart of Smirnoff. Deighan broke the seal and had a drink straight from the bottle; it settled the hangover flutters in his stomach. A couple of the others gave him disapproving looks, so he took a second drink, looking right back at them, before he replaced the cap and tucked the bottle away inside his suitcase. The hell with them, too.

While the last of the journalists hustled down from upstairs, the porters began transferring baggage from the lobby to the cars waiting out front. Stacks of riels changed from American to Khmer hands; the bills were worthless outside the country, worthless outside Phnom Penh now. Worthless everywhere in a few days, Deighan thought, when the Khmer Rouge bulled their way in. He carried his own things out into the early-morning heat.

He stood off a ways and looked up at the crumbling French Colonial façade of the hotel. Home for the past year—another home that he'd never be coming back to. He felt like having another drink, only the first two were mixing with the heat, making him a little fuzzy-headed already, and he didn't want to be drunk for the evacuation. *After* it, damn right, but not during it. Maybe the KC would open up on the helicopters and maybe a rocket or a mortar shell would hit the one he was in; maybe he wouldn't be going out after all. And if that was how it was going to be, he wanted to be alert for it. Death could have him anytime, but it wasn't going to sneak up on him while he was drunk.

Irwin and the rest of them began to file out. There were a lot of handshaking and goodbyes, but not much emotion in any of it—like a convention breaking up. Deighan stayed where he was for a time, watching as the newspeople piled into the cars and the first of the bunch pulled out onto Monivong Boulevard. Then he went over and put his luggage into the last one in line, the one he'd seen Irwin get into. Put himself into the backseat. And pretty soon they were on their way too; and when he turned to look through the rear window the Khmers were still standing there, still watching them with sad eyes and resigned faces.

He rolled the window down to catch a little air and to brood out at the city. It didn't look any different from the way it had on other mornings in the past few months. Not much traffic, aside from bicycles and pedicabs and motor scooters, nor many pedestrians; quiet except for the war sounds in the background. Women in baggy pajamas sweeping the sidewalks with tied-straw brooms. A man selling clothing, probably contraband, out of a cart. A bonze with a parasol and a brass begging bowl. A couple of fortune-tellers. Near the Marché Central, an old lady foraging for food among overflowing garbage boxes—

"Stop the car," Deighan said suddenly.

The Khmer driver jerked his head up and gave him a startled look in the rearview mirror.

"Stop the goddamn car, I said!"

They were all staring at him now, the driver and Irwin and the two others in the backseat. But the driver, either because he was used to taking orders from Americans or because of something he saw in Deighan's eyes, did as he was told; he braked and pulled over to the side. Deighan told him to back up, and when the car was abreast of the old lady at the garbage boxes he said, "That's far enough."

He got out and went up to the woman. She gave him a dull, incurious look . . . until he opened up his wallet and took out all the riels he had left, twenty or thirty thousand total, and pressed the bills into her hands. Then her eyes opened wide with a mixture of amazement and disbelief; she said something in Khmer that Deighan didn't understand. But he was already moving by then, away from her, back to the car.

They were still staring when he got inside and shut the door. Irwin asked him, "Now why'd you go and do that?"

"How the hell do I know?" Deighan said. "I just did it, that's all."

But he was thinking: Because she had her hands in garbage. An old lady with her hands in garbage, trying to find something to eat, on the day the Americans left town.

Foxworth

He had spent most of the night inside the locked and barricaded embassy compound, ever since learning that President Ford had ordered the evacuation for this morning. There was nowhere else for him to go, nowhere else to go looking for Kim; and waiting at his villa, hoping that she would change her mind and come to him there, would have been unbearable. He needed people around him, things to do, other thoughts to occupy his mind. Alone, with nothing to keep a lid on the pain and desperation, he might have lost his self-control and done something irrational.

So he had gathered his belongings, closed up the villa, and come to the embassy. Tom Boyd and most of the others were already there, waiting it out, and because he had to talk to someone, because Boyd was handy and willing to listen, he had poured it all out to him—Kim's disappearance, the fire on Samdach Phuong, his feelings for her, and the changes in her feelings for him.

Boyd was not the most sympathetic of men, but he was at least reasonable—the kind of steadying influence Foxworth had needed just then. "Let's face it, Dave," he'd said, "it's out of your hands. Maybe she'll change her mind; if she does, and if she gets here early enough, there's no problem."

"She won't change her mind, not after Ford's speech."

"All right, then. She won't change her mind and you don't have any way of finding her. The only other thing you could do is stay behind, and that's out of the question."

"Is it?"

"Don't be a fool," Boyd said. "An embassy official? You'd

be the first one the KC would kill when they get here. You know that."

"All right. I know it."

"It's her decision and her country, Dave. That's what you've got to keep telling yourself. Her decision and her country. It's out of your hands."

Fatigue had made him sleep for a while, but he had dreamed of her—a dream so vivid that he believed she was there, that she *had* changed her mind and come to the embassy to be with him. Waking up was like being shattered all over again. And after that, sleep was impossible. Instead he had worked with some of the others at salvaging certain file materials, incinerating others in the furnace out back; at making the rest of the necessary preparations for the evacuation and abandonment of a war-zone embassy.

At 6 A.M. Dean had sent written invitations to all the high-placed Cambodian officials to join the airlift. All had declined politely in return messages, except for one member of Prime Minister Long Boret's cabinet and interim president Saukham Khoy, who was concerned for members of his family and wanted to see them to safety in Thailand. Typical of the letters of rejection was the one from Sirik Matak, which Foxworth had read in Dean's office just after it was delivered.

Dear Excellency and friend,

I thank you very sincerely for your letter and for your offer to transport me towards freedom. I cannot, alas, leave in such a cowardly fashion.

As for you and in particular for your great country, I never believed for a moment that you would have this sentiment of abandoning a people which has chosen liberty. You have refused us your protection and we can do nothing about it. You leave and it is my wish that you and your country will find happiness under the sky.

But mark it well that, if I shall die here on the spot and in my country that I love, it is too bad because we all are born and must die one day. I have only committed this mistake of believing in you, the Americans.

Please accept, Excellency, my dear friend, my faithful and friendly sentiments.

At seven the marine radio operator had broadcast the assembly message to all employees and to the warden at Hotel Le Phnom. Originally, when the evacuation plan was first conceived, there had been six wardens, each one responsible for gathering all Americans within his geographical ward at a central location, where the helicopters would pick them up. But there weren't enough of them left in the country to need more than one evacuation site.

The first evacuees began to show up within a half hour of the broadcast. Foxworth went down to the lobby a couple of times to check on arrivals before they passed through a special door, had brown nametags placed around their necks, and were moved out to flatbed trucks that took them to the landing field. Now, a few minutes before nine o'clock, with not much more than an hour to go before he would leave the embassy for the last time, he felt himself sliding exhaustedly into a pit of indifference. It would not last long, he knew; it was only a remission of the pain which would come again and again. But at least it enabled him to continue to function in these final few minutes.

He was in the lobby, helping to process Saukham Khoy and his party, who had just arrived, when the last carload of journalists came in from Hotel Le Phnom. They brought too much baggage in with them, as most of the others had, because somebody had neglected to tell them they would only be allowed one handbag each. There was some grumbling when the word was passed, but the instructions were inflexible: either they complied or they would be left behind.

A few of the newspeople gathered around Saukham Khoy, who looked haggard and old and who spoke in a hollow voice of going to Bangkok to contact Khmer Rouge leaders for neutral-ground peace talks; but he knew and so did the journalists that his evacuation, like their own, would be permanent. One correspondent who didn't seem interested in what Saukham Khoy had to say was Peter Deighan. Foxworth noticed him standing off by himself, a cigarette in one corner of his mouth; he appeared to be either drunk or hung over, or maybe both.

When Deighan realized he was being looked at he pushed away from the wall and came over to where Foxworth was. "How's it going, Foxie?" he said. "All set for the big run-out?"

"Leave me alone, Deighan."

"Call me Peter. You don't look so good this morning. But then, none of us Americanskis looks so good this morning, do we?"

Foxworth wanted to hit him. Not because he hated the man, although his dislike had always been considerable; he didn't have the capacity to hate anyone this morning. But because there was an impulse in him to lash out, strike something, break something to keep from breaking himself. Only he couldn't do it, of course—not here, not under these circumstances. It would have added tension to a situation that was volatile enough already; it would have been a selfish act, and more than that, an act of disobedience to his country.

Deliberately he put his back to the other man, moved away. The laugh that followed him was mocking, and he felt his cheeks grow warm; he had to force himself to keep walking toward the opposite side of the lobby.

He told himself that Deighan didn't believe in anything, had lost the capacity to believe somewhere, and this cynical, bearded, whiskey-reeking husk was all that was left of the man he had once been. And yet, he thought then, with abrupt insight, the same thing could happen to a different kind of man too. A man like himself, for instance.

Andrea: You're pleasant, you're bright, you're dedicated, you make reasonable arguments for what you think you believe in, but the truth is you've never believed in anything that wasn't handed to you straight out of Grosse Pointe or a college textbook.

Not true, he thought, not true. But wasn't it a fact that he had always followed the advice and the examples set by the role models—his father, his conservative teachers and college

professors, even Richard Nixon—in his early life? Adopted their
political and moral beliefs, rather than established his own?
He'd gone to a good university, gotten a good safe academic
job, avoided all subversive influences, stayed away from dangerous causes. He'd also avoided matrimony because it was
entangling and passionate affairs because they could be emotionally crippling (forcing Andrea to walk out on him because
he was too weak to take the responsibility himself?). He had
waved the flag with patriotic zeal, worked long and hard for the
Republican Party and Nixon's '72 campaign because it was
what was expected of him. Yes, and it was his father who had
talked him out of enlisting in the Army and going to Vietnam,
as he had wanted to do; talked him into joining the State Department, where the only allowable line on the war was the
official line. And it was the State Department and the White
House and the CIA that had told him what to do, how to feel,
how to think, ever since. Where was *he* during all of this,
through all those years? Where was the essence and the intellect
known as David Foxworth?

*You think you're a feeling person, you always talk about
your concerns; those middle-class superstitions and traditions
you call beliefs incite the same passion in you that other beliefs
might in the kids who resist the draft, and you just don't know
the difference. There's a part of you that can't be touched, that
hasn't learned how to give a damn . . .*

But then Cambodia had come into his life, and Kim had
come into it, and now there were things stirring inside him that
he had never known were there. He was a man in flux: the essence beginning to emerge at last, changes beginning to take
shape. Changes that would make him into someone like
Deighan? Or into someone who thought and felt and acted for
himself?

Someone alone . . .

There seemed to be an infinite extension of empty time,
heavy with movement and voices that had no meaning for him.
Then the announcement came that it was time for the rest of
them to leave for the landing zone, everyone out now except
the ambassador, his closest aides, and some marine escorts, be-

cause a final cable had to be sent to Washington officially shutting down the embassy; and it was Dean, too, who would perform the last act of all, the carrying out of the American flag. He was the acting captain, and that meant he had to be the last one off the ship.

Foxworth went out through the special door, clenching his bag, squinting into the sun glare as he took his nametag, still looking for some sign of Kim. Seeing her materialize in his mind and come running toward him, arms outstretched, the two of them like characters in the climactic scene of a John Wayne movie, march music playing in the background and the Stars and Stripes unfurled and fluttering in the breeze overhead . . . and then he was inside the truck, crowded into it with several others, including Tom Boyd, and it occurred to him that only the embassy people wore business suits on this day, that all of them had dressed for the evacuation, sprayed their armpits with deodorant and neatly knotted their ties so they could maintain the illusion, the pretense of dignity throughout . . . and then the truck began to roll across the compound and out through the rear gate.

The landing zone was several hundred yards from the embassy, between it and the Royal Palace near the Bassac River—a dusty soccer field behind a row of apartment buildings. "Landing Zone Hotel," that was the official name for it. Operation Eagle Pull from Landing Zone Hotel. Bureaucratic labels and false dignity. Masks, all of it, he thought. Hiding the truth, and the truth is we're running away.

The truck reached the field and stopped and everybody clambered out. All around the field's perimeters were three or four hundred marines in full combat gear: camouflage uniforms and helmets, flak jackets, M-16 rifles, and grenade launchers. They had come from the *Okinawa* on the first relay of Jolly Green Giants. Over near the apartment buildings, dozens of school-age children, attracted by the noise of the choppers, stood staring at the marines and the weapons they held, not afraid, only excited and curious, some of them smiling and laughing, unaware that they would probably be shot if they tried to come any closer.

There were also small clusters of Khmer adults in the area, watching curiously, as Foxworth and the others queued up; but none of them came to challenge the marine guns. That was something Dean and the rest had worried about all during the night—that they would have a repeat of the Da Nang evacuation, when the Vietnamese realized *they* were being abandoned and started to riot, storming the landing field. Everything peaceful here, though. Everything orderly.

And maybe they don't know or suspect they're being abandoned, Foxworth thought. Maybe they just can't believe we'd do it to them. Sirik Matak didn't believe it; why should anybody in the streets believe it until it's all over? And maybe not even then. Maybe they'll think we're coming back.

God help them, maybe they'll all think we're coming back.

Before long the stillness fragmented in the chattering of heavy rotor blades and the last relay of helicopters swept down out of the sky. The hot wind from their blades, swirling dust, sheared at Foxworth's face and made him squint and shade his eyes. But he wasn't looking at them; he was looking at the Khmers outside the field, looking at all the Cambodians he couldn't see in the city beyond. And there was nothing inside him in that moment, no pain, no indifference, no vision of Kim running toward him while the flag waved, nothing at all . . . he was just a cipher feeling the hot wind and shading his eyes and looking into the distance while the choppers settled and the children laughed and pointed and the whole mad drama went on and on.

Dean arrived from the embassy just then, and something made Foxworth glance at his watch: it was a little after eleven o'clock. When the ambassador stepped out of the car, wearing a dark suit and a striped tie, Foxworth saw that he carried the Stars and Stripes, furled and wrapped in plastic film, under one arm. Furled and wrapped forever, as far as the Cambodians were concerned.

The Jolly Green Giants were down, their doors open. Boyd jostled him, said in a commanding tone, "Come on, Dave, what's the matter with you?" and obediently, still obeying as an automatic response, still not feeling anything, Foxworth ran forward through the dusty prop wash. Over by the apartment houses the children were waving; he was aware of that as he ran. And he heard what they were shouting, in English in their piping voices, before he passed under the spinning rotors and started up the steps.

They were shouting, "Okay, bye-bye. Okay, bye-bye."

He went inside the chopper and found a place to sit and put on his seat belt, all without thinking, still hearing the voices of the children like echoes inside his mind. Somebody came by and handed him a leaflet. He stared at it blankly for several seconds until the printed words registered.

"Welcome Aboard," the words said, "Marine Helicopter, Inc., Flight 454 Non-Stop to the Gulf of Thailand."

Okay, bye-bye.

"The Pilots and Crew of this aircraft are the most professional and highly trained known to man," the leaflet said. "We hope you enjoy your flight."

Okay, bye-bye. Okay, bye-bye.

The doors were closed and secured; the whining roar of the rotors lifted in volume. And a moment later the helicopter lifted too, and they were airborne and banking away over the field where the children were, over the city where Kim was, over the countryside where the Khmer Rouge were, and the numbness went out of him and he felt physically ill with a sudden welling of emotion, surge after surge of it that buffeted him the way the hot wind had buffeted him down on the field.

She was gone, and he loved her. She was gone, and the chances were he would never see her again. She was gone, and what would happen to her when the Khmer Rouge took Phnom Penh?

Okay, bye-bye.

What would happen to her and what would happen to all the rest they were leaving behind?

PART TWO

‹‹‹‹‹‹‹‹‹‹‹‹‹‹‹‹‹‹‹‹‹‹‹‹‹‹‹‹‹‹‹

April 17 to October 1975

Cambodia File: War Calendar

April 13—Declaring a state of emergency, the government bans all celebrations in honor of the traditional Khmer New Year, at which the Year of the Tiger ends and the Year of the Hare begins. All places of business are required to remain open. Many residents of Phnom Penh ignore these orders, however; a number of religious festivities are held privately.

April 14—Shortly after FANK chiefs hold an emergency meeting at their Phnom Penh headquarters, a government army plane drops two bombs on the building. This act, and the announcement that the KC have seized control of the airport road some six miles from the city's gates, puts an end to all New Year's celebrating. Later in the day, hundreds of communist rockets begin to assault the city and floods of refugees pour in from the perimeters; there is rampant panic among civilians, soldiers, and government officials alike.

April 15—Fires rage through fuel reserves, factories, and munitions depots in the outlying districts of Phnom Penh. The Khmer Rouge pushes to within five kilometers in the north, seizes the Monivong Bridge in the south, closes in on the

Bonzes' Hospital in the northwest. Government troops abandon the northern line of defense; there is a mass falling back of men and matériel to the center of the city. A forty-eight-hour curfew is declared, although the huge influx of refugees makes it impossible to enforce.

April 16—General Sak Sutsakhan, head of the newly formed Supreme Council, and Premier Long Boret offer a conditional surrender through the International Red Cross, but Sihanouk rejects it. In a telegram from Peking he says that "if second-rank traitors wish to save their lives, they should immediately lay down their arms, raise the white flag, and rally unconditionally to FUNK. As to the first-rank traitors, forming what they call the 'Supreme Council,' we advise them to flee Cambodia if they can, instead of wasting time digging bunkers." The end is in sight . . .

Kim

Even before the radio announcement came at ten o'clock on the morning of April 17, Kim knew Phnom Penh—and all of Kampuchea—had fallen to the Khmer Rouge. She had felt it in the atmosphere both inside and outside the *wat* on Sokun Boch Thom, near Monivong Boulevard, where she had been for the past six days. The stream of refugees into the sanctuary, heavy and constant all week, had slowed to a trickle at dawn and then ceased altogether; the whine of rockets and mortar shells had also ceased and an eerie, almost breathless stillness had descended on the city. Then Radio Phnom Penh, silent for nearly twenty-four hours, had begun playing military music at 0930 hours.

But it was the official announcement that she and the others waited for, because only then would they have an idea of what to expect from their new conquerors. With the bonzes who lived at the *wat,* with two hundred starving disease-riddled men, women, and children, she sat listening to the music and to the silence outside. Waiting.

The announcement, when it finally came, was made by the patriarch of the Buddhist community, Samdech Sangh Huot That. "The war is over," he proclaimed, "we are among brothers! Stay quietly in your homes!" And not long after that, while excited murmurs still rippled among the refugees, General Mey Si Chan, head of the third bureau of the Republican armed forces' general staff, ordered all FANK officers and soldiers to lay down their arms at once. Peace negotiations, he said, were in progress and further announcements would be made shortly.

The release of tension inside the *wat* was palpable; there were jubilant cries, laughter, weeping, and embracing. Kim, who took no part in the rejoicing, knew that this same reaction to the war's end would be taking place throughout the city. The beginning of the great *fête*—the joining in celebration of all Khmers, victors and losers alike—which Prince Sihanouk had claimed would happen when the Khmer Rouge liberated Phnom Penh? Perhaps. And perhaps not. Unlike the others, she could not be sure for some time yet. But no matter what the intention of the conquerors, it would be a long while before she herself rejoiced again.

Some of the refugees gathered their meager belongings, spilled out of the pagoda into the street; others followed, still shouting, still laughing and embracing. An end to the fighting, their voices said, was an end to the terror, to the rationing of food and medical supplies, to the compulsory military service ordered by the GKR. Now they could return to their villages, their farms, their rice paddies. Now they could begin to live again.

Hail to the victors! their voices said. Hail to our brothers, the Khmer Rouge!

C'est la paix! C'est la paix!

Kim went to the doorway, out onto Sokun Boch Thom. White laundry draped the balconies and fluttered from the windows of the nearby buildings, shining in the hot morning sun:

Phnom Penh in the flower of surrender. In the distance, from the direction of Monivong Boulevard, she could hear a din of honking automobile horns; a military truck, laden with waving civilians, roared past flying its own white flag. People swarmed every which way, heading north, south, west, some on bicycles and motor scooters, most on foot.

And among them, dozens of young Khmers, some no older than twelve with cigarettes dangling from their mouths, dressed in pajamas, T-shirts, flowered shirts, jeans, pieces of khaki uniform, black Mao caps, checkered scarves, rubber Ho Chi Minh sandals; all of them carrying automatic weapons and festooned with grenades, antitank explosives, and bandoliers of ammunition. The ones she could see clearly seemed exhausted, less than joyous, and they did not join in the merrymaking around them. Instead they began to station themselves at the nearest intersections. At the west corner three of them stopped another military truck, ordered the people out of it, and sent them away on foot; the truck remained where it was, blocking the center of the street, impeding traffic.

When the last of the refugees had flowed out past her and away into the turbulence of the city, Kim reentered the *wat*. The stench of waste and corruption, mingled with the perfume of burning joss sticks, was thick on the humid air. As was the coating of flies that glistened in the dull light. Rats scurried among the garbage and cast-off supplies strewn over the colored-tile floor. But she was used to it by now and it did not bother her. No odors, no sights, no manner of pain and suffering bothered her anymore; she was used to it all.

At the altar one of the bonzes knelt before the statue of Buddha; his chanting voice, asking the mystical jewel of the lotus to protect them from evil, was barely audible above the buzzing of the flies, the staticky radio, the noisemaking outside. Another of the bonzes approached Kim as she sat on one of the cots, stood before her with his hands clasped. Neither of them spoke until she raised her head to look up at him.

"They will come here," he said then. "Soon."

"Yes."

"And they will kill us."

"No, brother. We will not be killed."

"They will kill us," the holy man said again. There was no emotion in his voice; he had prepared himself according to the teachings of the great sage. "There is no holiness in the Khmer Rouge. They do not believe in religion, they have no God. The Enlightened One provides the breath of life; the Khmer Rouge provide the breath of death."

"We will survive," Kim said. "All of Kampuchea will survive as one."

"There will be no Kampuchea," the bonze said. "There will only be death and pestilence upon the land."

Kim was silent.

"Prepare yourself, sister," he said, and bowed to her, and moved away to light another joss stick in another urn.

She sat quietly on the cot, with the flies and the stench all around her, looking up at the ceiling fresco of the seven heavens and the seven hells of Buddha. Buddhists cannot kill or actively pursue war, she thought. The Lord Buddha forbids it. She lifted the ivory image on the chain around her neck, placed it inside her mouth. The Lord Buddha forbids any more killing. He forbids it. He forbids it.

For a while she listened to the military music and the occasional pleas for surrender that came over the radio. But there were no new announcements; all that was important had already been said. She stopped listening before long and thought instead of many things and, intermittently, of nothing at all.

She thought of the smug, swaddled face of the new American President until it blended with the faces of David and all the other Americans she had known: they were all the same, they were first protectors and then betrayers, just like children. She thought of how she had been different people all her life—peasant, university graduate, wife, American collaborator, American whore—and how these different Than Kims had existed in perilous balance for three decades, collaborated with one another truly; but she was no more one person than Kampuchea was one country, and perhaps she never would be, as perhaps Kampuchea never would be. She thought of the Khmer Rouge and the stories of atrocities told by the refugees, the wounds and the suffering of the people. She thought of Charoun. She thought of living, and of dying, and she was afraid and she was not afraid.

So many thoughts, so many Than Kims.

And time passed. And outside the noisemaking subsided slowly, by degrees, until all at once she was aware that it had grown quiet, that even the radio was silent. There was nothing to hear now, in the late afternoon, but the praying of the bonzes and the sated, heat-drugged droning of the flies. It was as if a great cloth had once again been cast over the city, as had happened in the dawn hours, muffling its sounds, turning them into inaudible and dying whimpers.

She was still sitting on the cot, with her eyes closed and the ivory Buddha inside her mouth, when the slap of many sandals and the metallic clicks of weaponry came to her from outside the *wat*. Then, when the bonzes ceased their chanting and were quiet, she lifted her head and allowed her lids to open.

A half dozen Khmer Rouge soldiers came inside, assault guns upraised in their hands, wearing B-40s and grenades like necklaces of death, and moved to different parts of the room. Kim looked at their faces in the dim light, saw that they were all boys, none of them older than twenty. And all had eyes that were cold and dead, as if everything that had once been inside them had been scooped out like the seeds of a melon. Boys, she thought. A legion of boys without souls.

One of them stepped forward. "The Americans are planning to bomb the city," he said in a voice as dead as his eyes. "We must all leave the city at once; we must flee into the country-side."

They have no God, the bonze had said; they provide the breath of death. There will be no Kampuchea, the bonze had said. There will only be death and pestilence upon the land.

The Than Kim who was afraid closed her eyes again and bowed her head and prayed.

"Do you understand?" the soldier said to her. He came to the cot, jerked up her head; then he ripped the ivory Buddha from her mouth, tore the chain from around her neck, and flung them away across the tiles. "Stand up, woman, and acknowledge your captors. Do what you're told or you'll be shot as the traitor you are."

Death and pestilence upon the land.

Chey Han

It was the first time he had been in Phnom Penh, and even though he did not want to admit it to himself, he was awed by the aspect of the city. He was only a soldier of the revolution, a peasant from Preah Vihear Province; the city and all its sights had been his only in dreams, after his recruitment into FUNK, and in photographs before that, and always it had frightened him because it was something he did not understand. It no longer frightened him now, for he had come not as a supplicant from the provinces but as one of the conquering army of the People. But there was simply no question that he was awed by it.

In recent days, throughout the last of the fire fights, the anticipation that he would soon walk the streets of the imperial capital had grown and become a sustaining excitement, helping him to forget the pain of the shrapnel wounds he had suffered at Khmounh, the recurring nightmare of the headless bonze. It had even kept him from thinking too deeply about the disturbing orders which had come to him from the Angkar Leu only a few days ago—orders calling for the complete evacuation of the city as soon as it was secure, the forced march into the country-side of every person except any high-ranking FANK officers who attempted to resist and government traitors such as Sirik Matak and Cheng Heng, who were to be rounded up and immediately executed.

Yesterday the excitement had become acute. The day of victory was at hand; everyone knew April 17 would be the day Phnom Penh was liberated, and with it all of Kampuchea. There was only token resistance now from the government forces; once the Americans had left the country, FANK's spirit had also departed and there were wholesale military desertions, an utter crumbling of discipline. The teachings of the Angkar Leu, as always, had been good and true: the oppressor had been driven out and the People had reclaimed their birthright. And that other oppressor, the tiger of fear in the soul, had been vanquished as well.

There had been no premature rejoicing among the soldiers. Much was still to be done after the day of liberation, so that the Angkar Leu could establish a People's government and implement plans for reconstruction. And yet, in his heart Chey had rejoiced and was drunk with his excitement. The city! The victorious march through its streets to the Royal Palace! The end of conflict!

Ah, no, no, he had not been disappointed: the city, the march, was everything he had expected it to be, and more. The railroad station and the Western-style hotels and that symbol of corruption, the French cathedral, along Monivong Boulevard; the apartment buildings and decadent villas lining Norodom Boulevard; and now, looming ahead of him, the pastel pavilions and gilded spires of the palace itself. French and American automobiles littering the streets, headlights gaping like blind eyes before the procession of soldiers on foot and riding, as he was, in military vehicles. White flags and white handkerchiefs flying everywhere, even from the gunboats on the Tonle Sap and Mekong Rivers; people shouting, dancing, embracing. Horns honking, music blaring from radios and loudspeakers. Shop windows displaying machines and gadgets Chey had never seen before and did not know the usage of. These sights and sounds, and a hundred more.

Awesome.

The truck in which he rode slowed as it neared the palace grounds. The advance guard of soldiers under his command had already begun to secure the area: fewer people milled about, fewer symbols of surrender fluttered in the faint hot breeze. The same thing was happening elsewhere in the city—music and automobile horns growing still, replaced now and then by bursts of gunfire. Nearby several of his troops were destroying a line of Western automobiles—slashing their tires, methodically kicking in grillwork and smashing out windows. Another young soldier, who did not know how to operate an automobile, was backing a Citroën down the street at a wild seesawing angle; a moment later it sheared sideways into a tree, crumpled and nearly overturned. The soldier staggered out, cursing, and fired several rounds into the wreckage, as if making sure the machine was dead.

Chey stepped down from the truck, stood looking at the curving snakes that arched outward from the shiny green-and-yellow-tiled roofs of dance pavilions, royal treasure houses, the palace itself. Most of the pavilions were open on three sides, allowing a distant glimpse of murals depicting celestial dancers, temples, birds, people. The colors were dazzling in the bright sunlight; they made his eyes hurt to look at them. And his heart ache to think what all of this had cost the people—not in terms of riels, for money was meaningless to Angka, but in terms of sorrow and corruption. Would the Angkar Leu order the palace destroyed? Or would they—

"Dreaming, Comrade?" a voice at his elbow said.

Chey turned, saw the coldly smiling face of Ly Sokhon. It was flushed, that face, damp with sweat; and in the eyes that stared up at him there was an almost feverish passion. But it was not the same excitement as his own; it was another kind, one that made the nightmare image of the headless bonze leap up in his memory. A kind that was . . . unclean.

As always, he masked his dislike for her and stayed the sharp words that came to his tongue. "Dreams are for dreamers," he said.

"And not for you? Your soldiers are uncontrolled."

"They are controlled."

"The city is to be cleared as quickly as possible," Ly Sokhon said. "This area must be secured before the evacuation can begin."

"I know this as well as you, Mit Ly."

"Then why do you stand gawking at the palace?"

"I am not gawking. I am only looking at what we have fought so long to reach. I am only exulting in our victory."

"Victory? The war is not over."

"But it is. This is the day of liberation."

"True. But the war is not over. It will not be over until all that has gone before is ground to dust and scattered on the wind."

He did not understand what she meant and she seemed to sense his confusion; her smile returned, cold and fevered at the same time, a mixture of fire and ice. Then she was gone, moving away to where a group of other *neary* waited nearby, favoring her leg where she had been shot in the perimeter fighting. Chey stared after her, saw again the image of the bonze juggling begging bowl and severed head with hands painted in bright blood. He looked directly up into the glare of the sun to burn it away.

For the next few hours he issued orders, led several soldiers on a sweep of the palace grounds, and saw to it that a dozen captured army officers in uniform were transported to Lon Nol's Chamcar Mon, on Boulevard Mao Tse-tung, for interrogation. The city grew progressively quieter during that time, until the only sounds to be heard were those of sporadic gunfire. Along Monivong and Norodom Boulevards by now, and in the Chinese sector near the Marché Central, shop windows would have been smashed and the Western goods, the unknown machines and gadgets, carried out to the streets and either liberated, if they could be of use to Angka, or destroyed. Everything American or European—automobiles, villas, signs, tools, books, weapons—must be liberated or destroyed, just as the city itself must be emptied.

Just as its population must eventually be liberated or destroyed?

The thought was unsettling to Chey. Could that be the true hidden reason for the evacuation of Phnom Penh? The Angkar Leu said it was because there was not enough food in the city, and too many people to effectively control, too much opportunity for resistance and insurrection—and the Angkar never lied. And yet, there were speculations among the other officers that once Phnom Penh and Battambang City were securely in the hands of the People, not only high-ranking military and government officials were to be executed but all other FANK officers as well. It was not farfetched to assume that still more executions would follow those, of civil servants and other members of the old regime who might be considered too dangerous, too corrupt for repatriation.

Could this be what Ly Sokhon had meant when she spoke of the time of blood, of grinding all that had gone before to dust scattered on the wind?

Chey told himself he was not a profound man, not a thinker nor a political strategist; he did not know what was best for the People, for Kampuchea. He must not question, he must only obey. And glory in the day of liberation. And bask in his excitement at being in the awesome city.

At midafternoon he stood before the palace and looked at the ragged and growing knots of refugees and city dwellers, some clutching bags of their belongings, a few on bicycles and motor scooters, a few more in automobiles, some pulling or pushing wagons and carts, who were being herded into the area by the soldiers. There were no more flags of surrender now; there were only the black-clad soldiers and the black muzzles of their assault guns.

The face of one frightened teen-age girl jarred his memory and made him think of his half-sister, Than Kim. She had been a teen-ager the last time he saw her, more than a dozen years ago in Rovieng, when she had been on her way to attend classes at the university. Chey had heard nothing about her since. Had she gone to the university, become educated, become as corrupt as the rest of those in the bandit regime of Lon Nol? Was she still alive, still here in Phnom Penh?

But of course the fate of Kim meant nothing in any case. Angka was all; the revolution was all. Family relations mattered little in the great struggle. Hadn't it been more than two years since he had seen his wife Doremy? Even if Kim were alive, even if she should happen to be among the milling throng before him and he should see her and recognize her, there was nothing he could do in her behalf. She would either be repatriated or, if it was the will of Angka, she would be sacrificed for the greater good.

No one could be spared. No one.

Ly Sokhon

At 1600 hours Ly Sokhon led a squad of two dozen soldiers and other *neary* to the Soviet-Khmer Friendship Hospital. The streets surrounding the complex had been secured; there was no sign of resistance. Nor was there any resistance when she and the others moved inside the grounds, made their way through rows of abandoned refugee lean-tos covered in blue polyethylene. She deployed half her troops to the outbuildings, took the other half inside the main building.

Two frightened women in the blood-smeared uniforms of nurses met them, both carrying white handkerchiefs; the lobby was otherwise deserted. One of the nurses came forward hesitantly, saying, "Welcome, brothers and sisters," and attempted an awkward embrace. Ly Sokhon could smell the stink of corruption coming from her, could almost taste it, and shoved the woman away. The nurse cowered against a wall. The fright in her eyes had given way to raw terror.

Ly Sokhon smiled at her. "Where are the others?" she demanded.

"Others?"

"Doctors, other medical personnel."

"Most have gone," the woman said. "There are only a few of us left now."

"There will be none left in an hour. This hospital is to be cleared immediately. The Americans are making preparations to raze the city; everyone must be evacuated into purified zones in the countryside."

"Everyone? But most of our patients are unable to move, they cannot travel—"

"Then they will die." Ly Sokhon looked at the woman with a level, penetrating gaze. The nurse seemed to tremble. "Do you understand? No one resists the revolutionary Angka. If you do not swim in the ocean of history you will drown in it."

There were no more protests. The two nurses were sent outside, and Ly Sokhon and her soldiers then deployed through the building. On each floor beds and folding cots stretched from wall to wall, overflowing into bloodstained hallways. Other patients lay on wooden benches or on grass mats placed on the floor; one of the mats held the uncovered corpse of a newly born infant. In the surgical wards, hundreds of wounded civilian and military personnel lay moaning or unconscious, some with wounds open and festering, untreated, coated with flies like meat hanging in an open market. The stink of pus and blood and excrement created a miasma that was almost palpable—a kind of shimmer on the hot dead air.

Three of the remaining doctors were in the main surgical ward, working feverishly on two and three patients at once. When Ly Sokhon ordered them out, ordered the ward cleared, one of the men attempted to argue with her. She beat him to his knees with the butt of her AK-47 and had him dragged away.

On an empty medical-supply cabinet, near where one of the doctors had been working, was a small plastic transistor radio. It crackled to life just as Ly Sokhon was about to turn out of the ward. She heard a voice say, "This is the United National Front of Kampuchea," and paused to listen.

"We are in the Ministry of Information," the voice went on. "The northern, southern, eastern, and western fronts have shaken hands in Phnom Penh. We have conquered by arms and not by negotiation. Samdech Sangh, venerable patriarch of the Buddhist community, and General Lon Non are standing beside us. We again order all ministers and generals to come to the Ministry of Information at once to organize the country. Long live the courageous and extraordinary People's National Liberation Armed Forces of Kampuchea! Long live the extraordinary revolution of Kampuchea!"

Long live the Angkar Leu! she thought, smiling. Long live the leaders; long live Pol Pot!

While the soldiers began clearing the wards and the hallways she found her way to the staff offices. But they contained nothing worth liberating; most of the offices had been turned into an emergency unit. Hidden in a storage closet, however, she did discover one item of passing interest: a framed color photograph of the former American imperialist President, Richard Nixon.

It was strange to find such a photograph in the Soviet-Khmer Friendship Hospital and the irony was not lost on Ly Sokhon. But she chose rage instead of contempt as her reaction. She stared at the photograph for several seconds, at the dignified posture, the hooded eyes, the smiling mouth, until the rage boiled and seethed over into violence. Then she drew her Vietnamese sword, slashed at the picture, kept slashing at it until the American's face was ribboned and unrecognizable. Her only regret was that it had not been a real face, so that she could have seen the blood pour forth around the flayed strips.

She returned to the entrance lobby to watch the exodus of patients onto the grounds outside. Most of the ambulatory were already out: the blind groping along with the aid of the crippled; the legless propelling themselves with their hands like monkeys; mothers carrying babies in filthy blankets and plastic bags that dripped; fathers with half-dead young children draped over their backs; a soldier with one arm and a gaping wound in his side, walking a few steps, falling, crawling, getting up, falling again, crawling again, chased by a cloud of flies, leaving a smeared trail of redness behind him like the track of a snail. Then there were the ones who could not move by themselves, pushed along in beds by hospital aides or other patients or relatives who had stayed behind to be with them, broken plasma and blood bottles leaking fluid onto the floor, some of them screaming in pain, some of them dying before they reached the sun-beaten streets outside the complex.

Ly Sokhon watched it all with a detachment that bordered on amusement. She was not moved; she had seen worse, much worse, in the jungles and on the battlefields during the long years of revolutionary struggle. Let them die, she thought. They deserve to die. Let the old order perish; let the city be emptied and destroyed so that the reconstruction can begin.

The city. She despised it; it was the festering center of all the forces which had betrayed and dishonored Kampuchea, kept the People from achieving their birthright long ago. If its abandonment resulted in pain and death for the corrupt, then it was a just and fitting punishment. The refugees and the traitors and collaborators of Phnom Penh were a gigantic, poisonous colony of insects, she thought, with the capacity to breed madly amid the sewage. If only a few were left they would multiply yet again and spread their disease throughout the country. In the land lay rice and salvation. In the cities lay death.

The outpouring stream of patients slowed and finally stopped altogether. One of the young male soldiers approached her from the direction of the first-floor ward. "We have reached the end, *mit,*" he said. "The last of them are being removed now."

"Good. But you're wrong that we have reached the end; we have only reached the beginning."

"Yes, Mit Ly."

"There can be no birth without death," Ly Sokhon said. "There can be no joy without pain, no freedom without imprisonment."

"Yes, Mit Ly."

There were noises from the hallway beyond the lobby—the cry of a man, the clatter of something hitting a wall or the floor, the angry voice of one of the soldiers. Ly Sokhon hurried there to find out what had happened. But it was nothing of import: one of the last patients, a middle-aged man with his head swathed in blood-caked bandages, had toppled off a wheeled stretcher and now lay curled on the floor, his hands crossed at his chest and his head pulled down into them like a turtle. The soldier stood above him, shouting *"Krok lên!"* and prodding him with the muzzle of his weapon.

"Baat, tee," the man kept saying, "my head aches, I want to stay here."

Ly Sokhon joined the soldier. "No one can remain here," she said to the casualty. "You will go with the others."

"But I am too weak, I can't walk."

"Then you'll be carried."

"No, *dekkun.* Please—"

"I am not *dekkun.* There is no *dekkun.*"

"Please, sister. Let me stay here."

A hot bright light began to burn behind Ly Sokhon's eyes; she felt her pulse quicken. "You wish to remain here?"

"Yes," the man said.

"Because you are too weak?"

"Yes."

"The weak can never be of use to Angka," she said coldly. "So you shall have your wish. You shall remain here."

She drew the Vietnamese sword, held it above her head just long enough for understanding to register in the traitor's eyes, for fear to replace the blank grimace of pain. Then, as she had with the photograph of the American President, she brought the sword flashing downward. And again. And again.

The blood, she thought then. Ah, the blood!

Kim

The Khmer Rouge soldiers took Kim from the *wat* to Monivong Boulevard, through streets littered with smashed crockery, articles of clothing, appliances, broken furniture, automobiles with slashed tires, and left her there in the company of several thousand other citizens jamming the wide avenue. She was not allowed to take anything with her except what she wore and her handbag. The bonzes were also taken from the pagoda, but to a different and unknown destination. Among the mass of people on Monivong Boulevard she saw only two holy men, both of them elderly, their parasols open and shading them from the rays of the sun.

There was no longer any rejoicing, no jubilant cries or laughter or attempts to embrace the silent young Khmer Rouge who moved here and there, purposefully, in their midst. There was only confusion and an atmosphere of fear that seemed to gain magnitude with each passing minute, mingling with the heat and the city's sweet-sour odors to make the sensitive among the children weep and cling to the hands of their parents.

From time to time one of the soldiers would shout for everyone to move closer together, that the evacuation had already begun south of them on Highway 1, as it had on the other main roads out of the city, and soon it would be their turn. All around her Kim heard the frightened whispered questions of the people. What would happen after they reached the countryside? Were the Americans really going to bomb the city? Would the Khmer Rouge allow everyone to return when it was safe? What would happen? What would happen?

Listening, the Than Kim who was hopeful thought: The Khmer Rouge will not harm us. We are Khmers; they are Khmers; we are all of the same race, the same blood. We have nothing to fear from our own. We must trust them, obey them and trust them—bend with the breeze, as the old saying tells us —and together we will rebuild all of Kampuchea.

And yet, the Than Kim who was afraid thought, these soldiers, these boys, do not seem to be Khmers at all. They speak a strange new revolutionary language that is difficult to understand. Their eyes are dead, their minds are closed, they act not like saviors but like conquerors from another land, perhaps even another world. Are their leaders like this too? It would seem that they must be. The followers are always reflections of the followed.

The Americans are not coming to bomb the city, this Than Kim thought further. They are many things, the Americans, they have dropped bombs and murdered the innocent before; but there is no reason for them to do so now, no advantage for them, no excuse for them to make for such an act. To bomb the countryside in the name of peace, to kill for the preservation of their own ideals . . . yes. But to bomb a city is for them an act of war, and in the eyes of the world they do not wish to be seen as warmongers.

What would happen?

Shortly past 1700 hours, when the street was packed with people and every manner of vehicle, and clouds of smoke from perimeter fires half-obliterated the sky, a KC loudspeaker truck pushed through the crowd and an amplified voice ordered everyone to begin moving. And the procession, the mass exodus from Phnom Penh to the south, was under way.

Progress was slow; the density of human bodies, of vehicles and baggage that some had managed to carry with them, made it impossible to move except in a shuffling painful gait, and then only a few meters or so at a time. Stop and go, stop and go. And all the while the heat sucked moisture from Kim's body until she felt cracked and brittle inside, and babies wailed and a man near her began to cough up blood, and the soldiers shouted and forced stragglers back into the ranks when they tried to break free to rest in the shade of the *koki* trees.

Kim attempted to withdraw into herself, in the manner of a bonze in religious meditation. But she could not. Her thoughts danced here, danced there, flicked into the past, out into the present, ahead into the future. Once, in spite of the promise she had made to herself one week ago, she thought of David. If she had gone with him as he had begged her to do, she would be in Bangkok now—sitting in the lounge of their hotel, perhaps, drinking a cocktail, looking out upon the streets and trying to recapture images of Kampuchea that might already have begun to fade; or lying with him in his room or hers, bodies rising and falling gently in the act of creation. But the thought did not linger, did not bring her sorrow or sadness. It was the image of David Foxworth which had already begun to fade.

The struggling lines turned east and crossed the Monivong Bridge and the Bassac River to Highway 1, the route south to the Vietnam border and Saigon. The afternoon waned toward night; the brutal sun had fallen down the sky and left behind it a blaze of copper overlain with columns of smoke. Some of the people asked if they would be allowed to stop for the night, if they would be given food and water; many of them had not eaten since the previous day, or the day before that.

"Ask Angka for your food and water," the soldiers told them again and again. "Angka will provide."

"But who is Angka?"

"You are Angka; the People are Angka. Angka will provide— provide for yourselves."

Near where Kim was at the outer edge, a pregnant woman, stomach swollen massively, lay comatose inside an oxcart drawn by an emaciated older man. A little girl of no more than six walked alongside and kept trying to climb into the cart to be with her mother. But the emaciated man, the father, would not allow it; he could barely manage the task of pulling as it was. The child started to cry, to complain that her legs pained her and she could no longer walk. The father paid no attention. No one paid any attention until the little girl, crying, half-blinded by tears, stumbled and almost fell beneath the wheels of the cart.

Kim pushed forward, caught the child's arm before she could stumble again. And then, on impulse, drew the little girl close and lifted her. She was light, no more than twenty-five pounds, with stick-thin arms and great shining black eyes. She looked at Kim dully at first, then wrapped her arms around Kim's neck, as if on an impulse of her own, and clung to her; the weeping gentled into dry muffled sobs.

The father did not once look up from his cart.

"Tell me your name," Kim said to the little girl.

"Sang Serey."

"I am Than Kim."

"I'm afraid," the child said. "Where are we going?"

"To a safe place. A place with rice and fruit."

Serey was quiet again. Kim held her with both arms, continued to hold her even when the added weight began to tax her strength. The child was someone for her to cling to as well: the daughter she and Charoun had never had.

Darkness settled over the land, tinged with the glow of firelight, but still the Khmer Rouge prodded them forward. The cries of the children, the pleas for food and water, were ignored. A few people had already collapsed from the heat and the close-packed movement, had been put inside vehicles or carried along by relatives until they revived and were able to continue under their own power.

All along the highway, flanking it on both sides, were the signs of war: shell craters, scorched vegetation and burning buildings, damaged *paillotes* where pigs rooted among the rubble, helmets and uniforms discarded by fleeing FANK troops, abandoned military and civilian vehicles. But it was not until they approached the National Glass Factory that the first corpses appeared. There was enough fire- and moonlight to make the bodies visible—more than a dozen of them scattered beyond the road, all FANK soldiers in green khaki, all steaming, already beginning to decay from the intense heat of the day.

The appearance of the corpses sent ripples through the lines —a freshening of the terror that had grown dull with hunger and thirst and fatigue. No one dared to stare at the bodies in passing, or to look at the Khmer Rouge soldiers moving alongside; no one dared to speak except in whispers. Kim walked with eyes downcast, clutching the tiny form of Sang Serey, willing herself again to withdraw inwardly until her whole being was but a single black dot. Unable to withdraw. Feeling the ripples and listening to the whispers.

What will happen to us?
What will happen?

Foxworth

He was in Bangkok, staying at the Dusit Thani Hotel, trying to put himself back together, when word came that Phnom Penh had fallen to the Khmer communists.

He had been there for five days, since another of the marine helicopters had flown him in, along with several other ex-embassy personnel, from the *Okinawa* in the Gulf of Thailand. Officially he was on R&R for an indeterminate period, awaiting a decision as to whether he would be reassigned immediately or returned to Washington first for briefings and discussions. But there was no R&R for him. For Tom Boyd and some of the others, maybe—Boyd had already left for a week in Tokyo—but not for David Foxworth. He didn't even want to go home. He had requested immediate reassignment to the Bangkok embassy, because it was as close as any American diplomat was likely to get to Cambodia and the only way he could keep his finger on the pulse of what was happening across the border.

But the bureaucrats in the State Department hadn't made up their minds yet. And he was left in a kind of limbo.

Most of the time he haunted the embassy on Wireless Road, monitoring intelligence reports from Phnom Penh. A couple of the post people seemed worried about him. "You're just out of a war zone," one of them said, "you've had a rough experience. Why don't you try to relax, put a little distance between yourself and the Cambodian situation, regain a little perspective."

"Sure," he said, "sure," and came back again, sometimes twice a day, to monitor incoming reports.

The rest of the time he spent aimlessly roaming the city. Sitting alone in his hotel room was intolerable; the one time he'd tried it he had drunk too much gin and made himself sick. For some reason he had lost his tolerance for alcohol, left it behind in Cambodia. Along with a number of other things. Along with Kim.

So he walked along the Chao Phraya River and the much-publicized *klongs* that were supposed to make Bangkok something of an Asian Venice. He visited the Grand Palace and several of the Buddhist monasteries and the Thieves' Market in Chinatown. He wandered the tree-shaded paths of the Dusit Zoo, where parasols bloomed in the sun like the parasols in Le Phnom Park and made his eyes grow wet when he saw them.

And all the while, in the embassy, along the *klongs,* in the wide streets and the narrow *sois,* he thought of Kim.

Where had she gone when she disappeared from her house on Avenue Phum Chup? Was she all right? What would she do when the Khmer Rouge overran the city? If she admitted she had worked for the American embassy, they would kill her. Would she admit it? Would she believe the KC could be reasoned with, dealt with on levels of compassion and trust? These and a dozen, a hundred more questions, repeated over and over, on and on, like an intricate litany whose climax had yet to be written.

The mixture of guilt and yearning had solidified inside him until it became a hard knot of pain that could not be dislodged. And each passing day, each new intelligence report, only made it worse. The situation in Cambodia was utterly hopeless;

Phnom Penh and the rest of the country, like a terminally ill patient, was expected to die any day now. It could happen at any moment; it might only be a matter of hours. He knew this, accepted it, had known and accepted and expected it from the moment that Sea Stallion helicopter lifted off from Landing Zone Hotel at the tag end of Operation Eagle Pull.

And yet when the news came that Cambodia had finally fallen, the patient had finally died, he wasn't prepared for it at all.

He was in the embassy at the time, upstairs in one of the staff offices, reports and media dispatches spread out on the desk before him. A junior AID official came in and told him, almost offhandedly, as if he were reporting a change in the weather. Foxworth sat there stunned. He had difficulty breathing, so much difficulty that the AID official seemed to think he was having some sort of seizure and tried to get him to lie down.

When the shock passed, after a minute or so, it left him feeling empty and battered inside. He left the office, left the embassy building and compound, stood on Wireless Road staring at the placid civilian traffic, the people going about their placid lives. There were no military vehicles here, no men in khaki uniforms armed with automatic weapons. There were no rockets overhead, no dull thudding booms of exploding shells, no smoky fires painting the horizon. There were no dead bodies lying among garbage and rolls of barbed wire, no black-clad soldiers steeped in the art of brutality. Not here, not in this place. But in Phnom Penh, even though the fighting was over, the war was over, the patient was dead, in all of Cambodia . . .

We killed that country, he thought. We killed it with bombs and diplomacy and righteousness. We killed it dead.

Kim, he thought.

Kim!

Deighan

April 17 was a banner day for Deighan: not one but two pieces of lousy news were handed to him within hours of each other.

The first one, the fall of Cambodia, came while he was sitting around the embassy press room with Michael Irwin and some of the other journalists who had been with him in Phnom Penh. It was only his second visit to the chancery since his arrival in Bangkok; the first one had been the day before. He'd spent his first three days in the Thai capital getting gloriously drunk, first in his second-class hotel and then in the modernistic massage parlors and whorehouses in the Patpong district. The only reason he had sobered up was that he'd run out of money and the whores wouldn't let him stick around unless he came up with some more baht for the privilege.

So he had dried out forcibly, and after which sent collect cables to three of the magazines that had used his material in the past, including *Worldview,* the one that had sponsored his stay in Phnom Penh; another cable had gone to a major newspaper syndicate. Each said the same thing, promising immediate dispatches containing "provocative and secret material" about the Cambodian situation, in exchange for return-cabled expense money. One of the magazines hadn't responded at all; a second, and the newspaper syndicate, told him politely to screw off, which meant his newfound reputation for undependability had spread back to the States. *Worldview* came through, but the editor, Ed Saunders, was leery and sent him an advance of only two hundred and fifty dollars.

That put him right up against a decision: two-fifty wasn't going to pay his hotel bill and keep him in vodka and whores very long, and unless he dug up some provocative if not secret material for a dispatch, forced himself to write a couple of thousand words to string Saunders into sending him another and larger advance, the last goose with the last golden eggs would disappear and he'd probably wind up being deported as a vagrant undesirable. There *was* one other alternative, of course. He could take that black-market .45 of his, which he had managed to smuggle through Thai customs, and blow his head off with it. But he didn't have any more *cojones* now than he'd had in Phnom Penh. Instead he steeled himself, cleaned up his appearance just enough so that the marine guards would honor his press credentials and pass him through the front gates, and went to the embassy to look for something to write home about.

There was a poker game going on in the press room when somebody from the Public Information Office came in with a handful of hurriedly prepared media releases. Deighan wasn't playing in the game, just kibitzing, listening to the conversation, trying to pick up an angle. The PIO staffer gave him his angle, all right. Gave all of them just the angle they'd been waiting for. The press room was empty inside of three minutes.

The difference between Deighan and the other correspondents was that they took their releases and hurried off to telephone or cable the news back to their Stateside employers; he took his release and hurried off to get drunk. He had a left-over bottle in his hotel room, so he went straight there from Wireless Road. If he could have spared the money he'd have taken a taxi, or at least a *samlor*; as it was he made pretty good time on foot.

But he made the mistake of stopping at the desk, to see if one of the other magazines had maybe changed its mind and cabled him some money after all, and that was when he got his second piece of lousy news. It came in the form of an airmail letter, addressed to him care of the Hotel Europe, Bangkok, Thailand. There was no return address, but he didn't need one to tell who it was from even before he opened it. He had seen enough of Carol's neat backhand printing to recognize it when he saw it.

He almost didn't open the letter. He hadn't heard from her in weeks, since sometime in February; he hadn't written to her in weeks either, or at least mailed anything to her in weeks. He didn't really want to know what she had to say. That was what he told himself as he carried the letter upstairs, still sealed, and laid it down on the table next to his leftover bottle. But it stared up at him as he poured a glass half full of vodka, the canceled stamp in one corner like a bright square eye smudged with mascara. Carol's eye. And Carol's face in his mind, super-imposed over the faces of six hundred thousand dead Khmers. Or was it a million by now? *Pax vobiscum,* he thought, and drained the glass in one long convulsive swallow.

Then he was ready for the letter. He still didn't want to read it, but there it was, staring up at him with its square eye, Carol's eye, and finally he picked it up and tore it open. One sheet of paper, backhand-printed on one side only: Carol never had been very prolix, even though she was well educated. He held the paper up close to his eyes and read what the printing said.

Dear Peter,

I hope this finds you well, if not solvent. I tracked you down through Ed Saunders at *Worldview.* He said you'd just cabled him for money and he told me where you're staying in Bangkok.

Peter, I've decided to come to Thailand to see you. I'll explain when I arrive. I already have my airline reservation, and I've made arrangements to rent the house here for a while, so you needn't bother writing or cabling or telephoning to change my mind. This isn't a rash decision, believe me. I made up my mind to do it even before I found out where you were, when I heard you'd been evacuated out of Cambodia.

I'll be arriving on April 23rd and will be staying at the Victory Hotel. Please come to see me that evening. If you don't I'll come to you.

It was signed "Yours as ever, Carol" and below that there was a drawing of the peace symbol, something she always included on the bottom of her letters.

Deighan refolded the sheet of paper and laid it down on the table. Then he said, "Jesus Christ" aloud, poured his glass full this time, drank it off the same convulsive way he had the previous one. "Goodbye Cambodia, hello Carol Deighan. Bang, bang, both barrels, just like that."

Just like that. And he didn't even have the guts to give himself the one real barrelful that would put an end to all of it.

Pax vobiscum, all right. And *Kyrie eleison.*

And damn her, what did she want to come here for?

Natalie

It was while she was with her father in his New York City apartment that Natalie learned of the Khmer Rouge takeover.

She was helping him prepare an official request for action from the United Nations High Commissioner for Refugees, the two of them working on it there instead of downtown at the Refugee Relief Fund offices because it was quiet and easier to concentrate. They were sitting in the dark-paneled study, at the table set between the high windows overlooking West End Avenue and 101st Street below—Natalie's favorite room. She had grown up in this apartment, lived in it until she was eighteen and ready to leave for her first year of college, and it was still and always would be home to her. More of a home, certainly, than her own three-room flat in the East Eighties.

Her father had lived there for close to thirty years, ever since his arrival in New York in 1947. He had come close to giving it up when Natalie's mother had been carried away in her final agonies to Lenox Hill Hospital to die of cancer four years ago; he said he could not bear living here alone, stopped sleeping in the master bedroom—he still refused to sleep there—and consulted a real estate agent. But Natalie had talked him out of it. And he had endured, as he had endured after his ordeals in the German concentration camps: he went on with his work, he taught his one weekly class on the sociology of fascism at Columbia University, he took his long daily walks up Broadway to the Columbia campus and back again seven days a week.

When the telephone rang, jarring into the silence, she watched Abraham Rosen get up and move across the room to answer it. He was seventy years old and he walked with a slight stoop and his hair had been gray for as long as she could remember; and it was true, as she had reflected in Cambodia, that he had been burned out inside by his experiences. But he still had a great deal of energy, testified to by the daily walks up Broadway, and his body was remarkably free of disease or age dissipation. He would live a long time, she thought. He had said it to her himself once: he was doomed to a long life.

He spoke into the telephone in soft monosyllables and she made no attempt to listen; she had her own thoughts. She was remembering something else her father had said to her, after her mother's funeral. "I have died twice," he'd said. "I hope that when it happens the third time it will extinguish consciousness."

But how did you extinguish consciousness? Once you knew something, could you refuse to know it?

You could, she thought bitterly, if it has to do with Cambodia. A lot of people knew what was going on there, or at least part of what had been happening there, and most of them refused to admit it. They just didn't care enough to let it touch them, affect their consciences. Here in New York, if there was talk of Southeast Asia, it was of the fall of the Thieu government, the terrible scenes at the American embassy in Saigon. Cambodia barely existed in the eyes of the populace, had all but disappeared from the American consciousness in 1973 with the end of Nixon's three years of terrorist bombing.

Nobody gave a damn. Posters were up all over Manhattan; a huge celebration of the close of the Vietnam War was being held in Central Park, an unofficial reunion for members of the fabled Peace Movement. Intellectuals and entertainers and former student demonstrators would join together for the last time to give speeches, sing songs, hail the triumph of their efforts to bring about peace in Vietnam. But would any of them think of Cambodia and the refugees, the children, who were dying there by the thousands right now? Would any of them remember what had been done to *that* tiny neutral country in the name of bringing about the very peace they had all sought?

Her father replaced the telephone receiver, stood for a moment as if in reflection, and then came back to the table. He was a phlegmatic man in many ways, a controlled man; his face showed no emotion when he said, "That was Sam Richardson in Albany. The communists have taken Phnom Penh."

A chill moved downward along her back, like someone running a finger from neck to buttocks. No words came to her. There was nothing to say; it was an inevitability and she had resigned herself to it some time ago.

"There's not much information so far," Abraham Rosen said. "Only fragmentary reports."

"Does it look like a bloodbath?"

"Evidently it's still too early to tell."

Ever since her return from Southeast Asia, those four brutalizing days she had spent in Phnom Penh kept returning to her in nightmares, in flashes of memory at odd moments while she was awake. One came to her now, bright and vivid and ugly: Preah Ket Melea Hospital, the rows of filthy cots, the faces of the wounded and the sick, flies crawling inside the mouth of a sleeping child. The chill came again; she felt physically ill for a few seconds.

"Papa," she said, "what are we going to do?"

"Do?" He shrugged. "What we have been doing. What we've always done."

"Write formal requests to the High Commissioner of Refugees? Recruit volunteer medical personnel and private funds? Step up the program in Thailand?"

"Yes."

"But that's not enough!" she said. "Papa, that's just not enough. There'll be more refugees pouring into Thailand now; it's bound to happen. They'll need food, medical supplies—and you know how the Thai government feels about housing and feeding refugees."

He studied her, his hands busy with one of his pipes and a leather pouch of tobacco. His expression was shielded, the same kind of expression he wore when he listened to politicians making statements on Vietnam and when he talked about her mother—a closed-in, protective mask. "What do you suggest?" he asked her.

"I don't know. Maybe I'll go to Washington."

"For what purpose?"

"To talk to people, try to get somebody to understand that we need a coordinated aid program, government-sponsored—"

"Which people?" he asked. "Where do you go that we haven't gone before?"

Her thoughts shifted back and forth, casting for a positive direction. Unaccountably, one of the first persons she thought of was David Foxworth. He had been involved with the refugees in Phnom Penh, he had a certain amount of compassion and sympathy. But what could he do, even if he was willing? He was only a middle-echelon foreign service official. Besides, she had no idea where he had been sent after the U.S. evacuation. It could be Washington or Bangkok or any place at all.

"I'll go to Bella Abzug's office," she said impulsively. "I'll see her. And Congressman Koch—he's also sympathetic to our cause . . ."

"Yes, sympathetic." His tone made it plain that sympathetic meant nothing in terms of positive action. "Well, you can try."

"I've *got* to try," Natalie said. "I can't just stay here and write formal requests and organize fund drives and wait for the media to tell me how many people are dying over there. And pretend all the while that none of it is my fault. It *is* my fault, papa; it's all our faults. We're all implicated."

Abraham Rosen lit his pipe and said nothing. But his silence was eloquent. On more than one occasion, particularly since her return to New York, he had said to her that she cared too much, that caring too much was almost as dangerous to the accomplishment of their purposes as caring too little. You had to strike a workable medium between the two. It was plain to her that behind his shield he was thinking the same thing now.

"I'll give them some hard facts," she said, trying to convince herself as well as him. "They'll listen; there are hearings being held right now in Congress—"

142

"Hearings?" Abraham Rosen shook his head. "Discussions, panels, testimony, documents, statements. They had hearings in 1940 in England and this country, too. Oh, yes, they had a great many hearings in those days."

"Papa, that kind of thing can't happen again. There can't be another Holocaust."

He looked at her with his wise burned-out eyes. "Natalie," he said, "dear Natalie—*can't* there?"

Cambodia File: Translation by U.S. Intelligence of Instructions to KC Troop Commanders Broadcast over Khmer Rouge Communications Network, April 18, 1975 (Secret Cable)

Eliminate all high-ranking military officials, government officials. Do this secretly. Also eliminate provincial officers who owe the Communist Party a blood debt.

Chey Han

The convoy of two-and-a-half-ton Czech Skodas and liberated American GMCs crossed the Khmero-Japanese Bridge of Friendship and turned north on a secondary road along the Mekong. Inside the lead truck, sitting hunched forward to ease the pain of the burns across his back, Chey Han stared broodingly at the empty roadway ahead. He imagined he could hear the FANK officers in the trucks behind, talking to each other in the stifling heat, chattering and clucking like chickens. That was how he had convinced himself he must think of them—as chickens. No one concerned himself with the fate of poultry. They were meaningless creatures; and these were poisonous, they could only harm the People if ingested among them, there was no choice but to destroy them. They were chickens.

Did they know they were on their way to die? he wondered.

Perhaps. But when they were loaded into the trucks at Lambert Stadium they had obeyed orders peacefully, almost cheerfully; most of them seemed to have believed the lies they were told—that they had been granted amnesty and were being trucked to a revolutionary camp in order to follow courses of reeducation, so they might be allowed to work with the new regime. They had believed because they wanted to believe. Few of them had ever been interested in the ideological aspects of the war; they had fought because they were trained to fight, and because they had believed the lies told to them by Lon Nol and the Americans.

Lies.

Why does the Angkar Leu instruct *us* to lie? Chey thought. We tell the officers they will be welcomed after a period of retraining, we promise them positions in the forces of the People's army; we give them false hope in the hours before their deaths. We have nothing to fear from them, we have arms and power and they have none. Why then do we lie? What is the sense in this new stream in the river of lies we have struggled against for so long?

It was not that he questioned the necessity of the executions. The FANK officers were traitors, poisonous chickens; once enemy leaders, they might someday again become enemy leaders if they were allowed to survive. The cause was just and sufficient; shouldn't they then be told the truth? Shouldn't they be given the opportunity to prepare themselves for death?

There was something else which disturbed him, added to his brooding. It was said among the cadres that in parts of Phnom Penh, the wives and families of high-ranking FANK officers and government officials were also being readied for execution; that in the north, in Battambang and Siem Reap, some families had already been killed. The women and children were marked for death, it was believed, because they had been polluted through contact with the corrupt and their loyalty to the revolutionary Angka would always be questionable.

The execution of officers and government bandits was one matter; it was another, Chey thought, to slaughter women, children, the elderly. If this truly was the will of the Angkar Leu, then so be it. And yet it did not seem right. What was the sense of it? Could a child of five or a baby of a few months have been polluted beyond redemption?

The truck was beginning to slow. Chey blinked and focused on the road, saw that they had reached the first prearranged stopping point. He did not want to get out of the truck here. He was not the only commander in the convoy; Phlek Puok, with whom he had fought at Kompong Luong, Dang Prak, Khmounh, rode in the truck directly behind. But he could not stay in the cab. He must stand before his soldiers, even though his presence would not be needed yet; it would not be proper if he failed to do so.

He opened the door, went back along the road to where the soldiers were already beginning to unload the FANK officers. Phlek Puok was moving along the line of trucks, shouting unnecessary orders, brandishing his sidearm. He was proud of that sidearm—an American-made .45-caliber military weapon— and drew it whenever he had the opportunity. He also seemed to be enjoying himself as he strutted this way and that, his round face slick with sweat.

Chey watched the FANK officers strip off their clothing, strip down to their underwear. Watched the soldiers use strips of rope to tie their hands behind them. Watched the belief in the lies fade from their faces and knowledge of the truth seep in. They knew now that they were on their way to die, and some began to plead for their lives; but most were silent, stoic, gathering courage and dignity as they were herded back inside the carriers. Not at all like chickens. Except that they were. Poisonous chickens.

Phlek Puok came up beside him. "All goes well, Comrade," he said. "Soon it will be time for the killing."

"Yes," Chey said. "Time for the killing."

Looking at Phlek Puok made him think of Ly Sokhon. They were soldiers of a similar type: their dedication to Angka, to the new social order, went beyond revolutionary zeal into fanaticism. Ly Sokhon even more so. Her fanaticism was perilously close to the insane; the woman was possessed. Yesterday, in the late afternoon, she returned from evacuating a building which had turned out to be a place of prostitution, and in her hand she had carried a plastic bag containing the liver of a whore who she said had insulted her. She had ordered the liver cooked and had eaten it, for an old Khmer belief held that the liver of one slain gave greater courage to the slayer. And earlier today she had brought another liver from the Soviet-Khmer Friendship Hospital, making a point to show it to Chey. This one, she had said, smiling, was that of a child.

At least he would not have to deal with her this afternoon; she had been detailed elsewhere in Phnom Penh, possibly on another series of executions. Of the wives and families of officers and officials? No, he must not think about that. Or about Ly Sokhon. Or about the chickens and the killing that was soon to come.

Inside the truck again, he willed his mind empty of thoughts. The convoy moved along the road for another kilometer, to where a trail curled away into jungle not far from the village of Phum Takeo. The trail, too, was deserted; with the cut-off of gasoline and the seizure of all civilian vehicles, all motorized movement in the Phnom Penh area had come to a halt.

Less than one kilometer into the jungle, they came to the clearing which had been chosen as the killing field. It was more than a hundred meters wide and seventy-five meters long, large enough to accommodate the trucks in the convoy, as well as the additional trucks and the squad of soldiers awaiting them there. Across its far perimeter, close to the forest wall of broadleaf evergreens and tangled creepers and stands of bamboo, were the lines of trenches dug by the soldiers. Shallow, narrow, stretching the entire width of the clearing, the earth from them mounded loosely along their sides.

Chey's driver took his truck to the left-hand side of the clearing, where the waiting troops were deployed; Phlek Puok's driver did the same. The trucks containing the FANK officers backed into position some twenty meters from the trenches. When Chey stepped out he noticed how still it was here, with the engines shut down and the soldiers silent, awaiting orders to commence. No birds sang, no monkeys chattered, no *koprei* or other wild creature made its rustling way through the undergrowth. Stillness. And the dripping heat of late afternoon, wrapping itself around Chey, making his throat burn with thirst.

In a corner of his mind the headless bonze began juggling head and begging bowl, redly—the nightmare image reborn yet again.

Chey shook his head, realized Phlek was looking at him, and stiffened his back and moved toward the nearest of the trucks. Phlek gestured to the execution squad; the soldiers took their places, weapons unslung, some of them still carrying the long-handled hoes they had used to dig the trenches.

At the truck Chey stopped and waited for two of his men to untie the tarpaulin across the rear; the same thing was being done at the other trucks in the line. Then he called, "All FANK officers are ordered to step out immediately, one at a time. Do not stop. Keep moving, walk forward."

There was a stirring inside the truck. Chey moved back and to one side, away from the execution squad, away from Phlek Puok. The first of the condemned men stumbled out, his movements made awkward by his bound hands. Others followed hesitantly, blinking at the sunlight, at the trenches stretched out before them, at the soldiers with their guns nearby.

And it began.

The stillness fragmented in AK-47 and M1 bursts, in shouts and cries and screams of agony. The first bodies rolled into the trenches. More officers spilled out of the trucks, staggering, some of them trying to run, some refusing to walk, some begging for mercy, some cursing the souls of their captors, all of them spinning and falling and dying. Bodies piled up, in and out of the trenches, sprawled over each other, forming layers of torn flesh. Blood filled the air, stained the earth, stained the corpses—blood everywhere, painting the landscape in gouts of bright bonzelike crimson—and still the trucks were not emptied, still more FANK officers emerged and ran and screamed and died under the horizontal rain of bullets.

What are we doing? Chey thought. These are our own people; we are killing our own people. What is the difference between the Angkar Leu and the old regime if the lies and the deaths go on?

Inside his mind the headless bonze laughed.

"Cease firing!" he heard Phlek Puok shout. "Enough! There is no need to waste ammunition on the rest of these traitors. Use your gun butts, your hoe handles instead. *Danh chet! Danh chet!*"

Beat them to death.

And the firing stopped, but the screams went on and the blood went on, I must not be disloyal, Chey Han thought, more men being dragged out, more men dying, I must not think disloyal thoughts, the dull melon-splitting sound of wood driven against flesh and bone, over and over like the faint hollow echoes of the gunshots, Angka is good, the Angkar Leu knows what is best, I must not think disloyal thoughts, *I must obey without question.*

He stood stiffly, obediently, and watched the rest of the chickens being butchered.

Kim

Along with many of the other Highway 1 evacuees, Kim spent the night in a tobacco field near the Stung Meanshey radio station.

It was after 2100 hours before the Khmer Rouge soldiers allowed them to break ranks and forage for food and water. There was a muddy brown stream in the area, a tributary of the nearby Mekong worn down to a trickle by the dry-season heat, and along its banks a line of abandoned *paillotes* and some jungle growth that included wild orange and banana trees. But there was no rush to get there, at least not at first; everyone was terrified of moving too quickly, doing anything which might incur the wrath of the soldiers. Rumors were rampant that in the lines behind them several long-haired students who had attempted to defy Khmer Rouge orders had been bound, led away into a stand of trees, and executed; that another man, a merchant who had dared argue with a KC officer, had been decapitated at the roadside. Kim had seen nothing like this, but she *had* seen people roughly treated, and the bodies lying strewn and steaming near the National Glass Factory, and the KC platoons methodically searching for FANK troops, and she *had* heard sporadic gunfire. She did not doubt the rumors.

When it became clear that the soldiers would not shoot them for foraging—"You must forage," they were told; "no one will feed you if you don't"—the people spread out more quickly to the stream, the stilt houses, the shadowed forest. Kim still carried the child, Serey, as she followed the others. Serey's father had made no effort to reclaim her; her pregnant mother was ill, delirious from pain and sunstroke, and demanded all the father's attention. The child herself was too drowsy with fatigue, too drugged with heat, to offer complaint.

The water in the stream tasted of pollution; Kim spat out the mouthful she had taken and would not let Serey drink. Most of the others drank from it regardless. Death from dehydration seemed a much more immediate threat than a potential death from cholera or some other disease.

At the perimeter of the jungle, where Kim went with the child, the rotting corpse of a water buffalo filled the air with carrion stench and waves of insects. She made a wide detour around it. And detoured away, too, from the men and women she saw here and there, squatting to empty their bowels and swollen bladders.

A wild orange tree yielded several small bitter fruit—moisture for their parched throats, nourishment for their enervated bodies. Kim also found edible plantain leaves and green bananas, placed them inside her clothing for a meal to be eaten tomorrow. There was no way of knowing when the Khmer Rouge would allow them to forage again.

In one corner of the tobacco field Kim turned dry grass and a discarded mat into a bed for Serey and herself. She lay looking up at the velvet-dark sky, the child asleep beside her, one tiny hand touching her breast. She had grown attached to the little girl—too attached, perhaps. But someone had to watch out for her, at least until the time when her mother gave birth. That time was not far off, Kim thought; another day or two of travel like the one which had just passed would surely put her into labor.

For a while there were sounds—low murmurs of conversation, more rumors passing back and forth, children crying, the coughing and retching of the sick, all of it like desultory breezes blowing across the sweltering night. Then the sounds faded as those who made them were overcome by exhaustion, by a need to escape the fear and the uncertainty for a few hours in sleep. It was the same for Kim. Her mind worked briefly, weakly, like that of an old woman; then it closed down, took away the ache in her body and in her heart, set her adrift in blackness.

The hollow crack of gunfire awoke her and the others at dawn. It was only their captors firing into the air to rouse everyone, but the fear roused with them nonetheless. Several of the children were weeping, Serey among them; she begged for her mother and Kim could not comfort her.

The soldiers began moving among them, confiscating motorbikes, Western-style bicycles, and all jewelry, watches, radios, gold damleungs, and other personal belongings of any value, including ballpoint pens which seemed to fascinate the younger troops. Some of the women managed to hide valuables on their person, in body orifices or clothing, but Kim surrendered the hammered silver bracelet from her half-brother Chey Han and an emerald ring which David had given her. The bracelet was too large to conceal and she saw nothing to be gained in hiding the ring. If it had been a gift from Charoun, she might have done it. But jewelry had not been among the gifts her dead husband had chosen for her.

The reason the soldiers gave for confiscating valuables was that Angka needed them; everything would be returned later, they said. But they did not say why Angka, whatever Angka truly was, should need such objects as rings and wristwatches, and no lists of items or names of owners were made. The one personal belonging they did not confiscate was paper money. Kim saw one soldier crumple several thousand-riel notes, spit on them, and grind them into the earth beneath his sandal. The revolutionary Angkar had no use for riels, he told them. The revolutionary Angkar had abolished money as a tool of capitalism and made everyone equal in a system of barter.

A short time later a Land-Rover outfitted with a loud-speaker came along the highway from Phnom Penh. An amplified voice from within issued instructions for all FANK officers from the rank of second lieutenant upward to present themselves at the radio station, where they would be registered and returned to Phnom Penh. All students, schoolteachers, professional people, and civil servants were also required to present themselves for registering. Everyone except FANK officers would soon be allowed to return to the villages where they had been born.

These announcements lessened the tension somewhat, created an overall attitude of cautious relief. But not in Kim. It was understandable that the Khmer Rouge would want to have the names of all former FANK officers, but what would they want with students, schoolteachers, civil servants? Unless it was not integration and repatriation which the Khmer Rouge intended, but eventual reprisal against the educated and the military for their ties to the Lon Nol regime—a seeking out of potential revolutionaries against the revolution. If that was the case, those who had collaborated with the Americans would be the most hated, the most feared, and therefore the ones to suffer the worst reprisals. Imprisoned? Or taken away and shot

—slaughtered like the militant students yesterday or the soldiers near the National Glass Factory?

She must not present herself at the radio station, she thought; she must not declare herself. Of that she felt certain.

The choice was not hers to make, however. The mass of people, stirred into activity by the loudspeaker announcements, had begun to break up along the highway; some families set off immediately toward Neak Luong, perhaps with the idea of escaping into Vietnam, while others turned back toward Phnom Penh. But not everyone was allowed to leave. Unchallenged were those who were obvious peasants, plus a scattering of youths, bonzes, fortune-tellers, and old people; but most of those in Western dress and long or Western-styled hair, who looked as though they might be educated, were detained. And Kim, although she was dressed in Khmer clothing, bore the unmistakable features of intelligence.

It was a soldier of not more than seventeen years, with a face pitted by smallpox scars, who stopped her. Serey was still crying, still begging for her mother; Kim had picked the child up and was carrying her toward the road, where her father was struggling to help the mother's bloated form into their cart. The soldier told her she could not leave the area yet, she must first go to the radio station to be interviewed. If she did not lie, if she gave her true biography, the soldier said, she would be allowed to proceed to her native village.

Kim did not argue. There was no arguing with the Khmer Rouge; of this, too, she was certain. It pained her to give Serey up to the father, while the pockmarked soldier looked on stoically, because now she might never see the child again. But she had learned that it was best not to become too attached to anyone in wartime—not husband, not lover, not a child who might be a surrogate for the one which had never sprung from her own loins. They were only torn away by death and circumstance, or you yourself were, in this country of dead Khmers.

She was taken to the radio station along with several dozen others, some of them willingly, most, like herself, unwillingly but without protest. Once there, she was made to wait two hours in the dry climbing heat of early morning, in line with the others, until her turn came to enter and face one of a dozen black-pajamaed interrogators behind a long row of tables.

"You look like a teacher," the KC officer said immediately. He was a lieutenant, no more than twenty-two years old, with the same empty eyes of the others, the same blank mask for a face. Kampuchea has been conquered by children, she thought. Children who have grown old and monstrous while they are still young. "Are you a teacher?"

"No," she said.

"You must tell the truth," the lieutenant said. "If you tell the truth you will be permitted to leave. But if you lie I will know it and you will be punished by Angka."

"I will tell the truth," she lied, because the one thing she must not do from this point forward was to reveal the truth about herself and her past.

"What is your name?"

"Mey Yat," she said.

He wrote this down on a sheet of paper. It occurred to Kim as she watched him that perhaps the reason why he had been made an officer, a leader, was that he was able to read and write. "The date and place of your birth?"

"May 16, 1947. The village of Kus in Takeo Province."

"Name of father?"

"Mey Somnang."

"Name of mother?"

"Hang Samoeun."

"Brothers?"

"None. Nor sisters."

"Tell me what you did in Kus."

"I worked in the rice paddies."

"You did not teach school?"

"No," Kim said. She stood with her hands clasped behind her back. The lieutenant must not examine her hands, she thought. This was obviously a routine interrogation and at this time she would not be pressed; but if she were not careful her hands would betray her. They were not the hands of one who worked in the rice paddies. They were soft delicate hands, hands of collaboration, hands that had held documents and writing tools, hands that had touched jasmine flowers and caressed the naked flesh of an American . . .

"When did you come to Phnom Penh?" the lieutenant asked.

"Several months ago."

"For what purpose?"

"Kus was overrun by soldiers and we were frightened," she said. Other interrogations were going on around them but her perspective seemed to have narrowed to this one, as if she and the KC man-child were alone together in a pocket of space. "We fled to Phnom Penh because there was nowhere else to go."

"You say 'we.' Your husband fled with you?"

"I have no husband. My husband was killed three years ago."

"In the fighting?"

"No. In the paddies, by American bombs."

"Your children, then?"

"I have no children."

"Then who fled with you from Kus?"

"Other peasants such as myself."

"Your father and mother?"

"No. Both are deceased."

"Where did you live in the city?"

"With a cousin, Long Sambath, and his family."

"Where is this family now?"

"I don't know. I was separated from them yesterday."

"Do you speak French?" he asked abruptly.

"No," she said.

"Do you speak any other language?"

"No."

"Will you serve the revolutionary Angka?"

She inclined her head. "Yes," she said. "The revolution will return us to our land. I wish only to go home."

This seemed to satisfy him. He made a final note on the sheet of paper, looked up at her for several seconds, and then said, "You are permitted to proceed to Kus."

"Thank you, brother."

He waved her away with a gesture of contempt.

Outside, she stood blinking in the sun glare. Highway 1 was still jammed with people, some in carts and wagons, most on foot, carrying their belongings in bundles balanced on their heads. The motorbikes and bicycles belonging to the evacuees had disappeared, and the tires on the few private automobiles had been slashed. The main flow of people was still to the south, proceeding at a more rapid pace, though still closely packed and still watched over by soldiers with unslung weapons. Fewer citizens were making their way back toward the Monivong Bridge—and among them, as she watched, the third truckload of FANK soldiers under heavy guard she had seen since yesterday.

There was no question as to what she herself must do. To return to the city, occupied as it was by the army of liberation, would be suicidal; even if she had somewhere to go within it, which she did not, the risk of discovery was much greater than it would be in the countryside. No, she must continue south, perhaps to Kus, perhaps to another village near the Vietnam frontier. And if her suspicions about the Khmer Rouge proved correct, she must find a way to cross the border to Saigon. She must do what she had told David she would not do: abandon her country to a new set of conquering oppressors.

And in the meantime she must not show defiance in any way, she must remember that her name was Mey Yat and she came from the village of Kus in Takeo Province. I am a peasant, she thought. I am of the land, a refugee farmer. I know nothing and I want nothing except to return home.

Bend with the breeze, she thought. Even though the breeze carries the odor of death.

Foxworth

Foxworth's orders came through on April 19: the people at State had finally made up their minds to reassign him to the Bangkok chancery, as he'd requested, effective May 1, but meanwhile they wanted him back in Washington for talks and briefing sessions. He didn't want to leave Thailand even for two weeks, especially not now with all of Cambodia in the hands of the communists and the fragmentary intelligence information hinting at mass executions in the Phnom Penh area; he wanted to move right into an office in the embassy so he could keep on monitoring reports, so he'd be on hand if any Phnom Penh refugees made it across the border and were brought in for debriefing. But what he wanted didn't matter to the State Department. He was on a TWA commercial flight out of Don Muang Airport that same night.

He slept most of the way around the world. Part of the reason was that he was worn out, haggard mentally as well as physically; he had never driven himself harder than he had this past week of R&R. And part of the reason was that it kept him from thinking about Kim. It didn't prevent him from dreaming about her, of course, but the dreams were vague and as fragmentary as the reports filtering out of Cambodia. He couldn't remember any of them when he woke up.

Washington, when he got there, was basking in balmy spring sunshine. The cherry trees were in full puffy bloom along the Tidal Basin and there was a kind of festive carefree attitude among the populace, the way there always was when they had shed the mantle of winter. It all depressed him instantly. He was used to the choking dry season heat of Southeast Asia, the brown Asian faces, the alien landscapes. Being here made it all —Thailand, Cambodia, Phnom Penh, Kim—seem remote and indistinct, and that was the last thing he cared to have happen. It should have been the first thing, according to the embassy people in Bangkok and the great minds at State, but it wasn't. He couldn't make himself be insensitive, not anymore, not even for his own self-protection.

He had been booked into a suite at the Mayflower. By the time he checked in it was midafternoon—the worst time of day because he didn't know what to do with himself. It was Sunday and everything would be shut down at State; he couldn't even go over there and scrounge for the latest Cambodian developments. Or telephone Ralph Chadwick, the senior official on the

Southeast Asia desk he was scheduled to see in the morning; he didn't have a home number for Chadwick, and there was no listing in the Washington, Maryland, or Virginia directories.

Foxworth went out for a walk and spent two hours chasing himself up and down Connecticut Avenue from Du Pont Circle to Farragut Square. Then he went back to the hotel and had a drink in the lounge that he wanted badly but only finished half of. Then he went up to his suite and put in a long-distance call to his parents' home in Grosse Pointe, Michigan.

He had spoken to his father briefly from Bangkok the day he'd been flown in from the *Okinawa*. The connection was bad, as connections always seemed to be between Southeast Asia and the United States, and he had been too wrought up to do more than offer monosyllabic reassurances that he was all right and they shouldn't worry about him. Now he felt like talking. Not necessarily to his father, or to his mother—to someone, anyone.

His father answered the phone. It surprised Foxworth that he was home, considering it was four-thirty in Grosse Pointe and cocktail hour at the country club. That was where Benjamin Foxworth spent most of his Sundays, at the country club playing golf and indulging in the cocktail-hour festivities, as befitted an executive of American Motors.

They talked for a while, all of the talk nonspecific, all of it tolerable. His mother, who had got on the extension, began to natter away at him in her motherly fashion and that was tolerable too. But then his father had to get into specifics, as he should have known would happen, and the kind of specifics his father got into weren't tolerable at all.

"We should have used full armaments on the Khmer Rouge," Benjamin Foxworth said. "Our policy there has been wishy-washy ever since the damned Congress forced Nixon to halt the bombing runs. There are no half measures in war."

"Look, Dad—"

"The country wouldn't be in the hands of the Reds now if we'd handled it right," Benjamin Foxworth said. "We'd have wiped the bastards out long ago."

I don't want to listen to this, he thought. Then, surprising himself, he said, "We'd have wiped out more than just the Reds; we'd have wiped out all the Cambodians. As it is we almost did."

There was a small silence. "What kind of talk is that?" his father said.

"I don't know. Straight talk, maybe."

"Are you sure you're all right, David?"

"I'm not sure about anything anymore," he said.

"You're still worrying about that girl," his mother said. "That's it, isn't it. That Cambodian girl."

"She's not a girl. She's a woman."

"Forget about her, son," Benjamin Foxworth said. "You're operating under enough pressure as it is."

You don't know what pressure is, he thought with a kind of dull anger. You drive seventy miles a day in an air-conditioned limousine and read *Barron's Weekly* and applaud Goldwater speeches and complain at your lunch clubs about the niggers. What the hell do you know about pressure?

"How am I supposed to forget her?" he said. "I was in love with her; I still am. Do you understand?"

Another small silence. "David," his mother said, "you need rest. Why don't you come home for a few days? You can arrange that, can't you? Do you realize it's been more than two years since we've seen you?"

"You'd like that, all right," he said. "That way you could introduce me to a nice Grosse Pointe girl, somebody like Andrea Vernon. Take my mind off the Cambodian."

"David . . ."

He said he had things to do, he would call again before he left Washington for Bangkok, and hung up on them.

He ate a light supper he didn't want, went to bed early, slept deep and hard and dreamed of Kim and the night on Avenue Phum Chup when they had almost been killed, and woke up sweating and still tired, still strung out. He reported to Ralph Chadwick's office at State promptly at ten o'clock. Chadwick, however, didn't arrive until ten-twenty. Which was one of the perks, Foxworth thought sardonically, of being a senior State Department official in Washington.

Chadwick was in his late thirties, mostly bald, mostly stone-faced, and the owner of a degree in political science from Georgetown University; his framed diploma hung on the wall above his desk. He was also a professional fence-straddler: he expressed no opinion, took no stand, on Cambodia or any other issue. That was how he'd gotten to where he was and it was how he was going to maintain his position in the pecking order.

The briefing session lasted two hours and consisted mainly of a general review of his duties in Phnom Penh and a general statement of what his new duties would be in Bangkok. Refugees, of course. Not that a refugee problem was expected; Chadwick would be the last to admit there would be or ever had been a refugee problem. Political liaison efforts. Debriefing and intelligence work for the CIA, who wanted to see him later in the week to discuss specifics. The usual procedures, Chadwick said. He should have no trouble fitting right in.

The usual procedures. No trouble fitting right in. And meanwhile, in Phnom Penh, Khmers were dying, Khmers were being executed, and he had no idea if the woman he loved was one of them.

Chadwick had nothing to tell him about that. Intelligence reports were still sketchy: intercepted communications broadcasts, on-scene media dispatches, a lot of speculation and unconfirmed rumor. There were still a few hundred Westerners in Phnom Penh, including the handful of American newspeople who had refused evacuation on the twelfth, and more would be known about the situation when they came out. If they came out.

Foxworth had the afternoon free. Chadwick wanted him back for another conference but not until tomorrow morning; and the rest of his meetings, such as the one with his CIA contact, were scheduled for later in the week. So he went around to Red Cross Headquarters on Seventeenth Street and found out that their communications to Cambodia had broken down even before the fall, on the sixteenth, when the crumbling GKR government set up a Red Cross shelter zone in Hotel Le Phnom. What had happened to the shelter zone, no one knew yet. And of course there had been no comment from anyone in the newly constituted Royal Government of the National Union of Kampuchea.

He left there feeling grim and wandered by the Cambodian embassy on Sixteenth Street, along Embassy Row. The rectangular blue-white-red flag of the Khmer Republic no longer flew above it; that made him feel even more grim. He debated going inside—people were being permitted to enter if they had official business—but what was the point? They wouldn't tell him anything; and he was in no frame of mind to listen to polite "no comments" from the Khmer staff.

Well then? he thought. What do you do next? Go back to the hotel and brood out the window at the Washington skyline and wait for tomorrow? Take another walk up and down Connecticut Avenue? Go to a movie, go to a singles bar, go get laid? That would be his father's solution—getting laid. Help relieve the pressure, son, help get your mind off the Cambodian girl. Nothing wrong with a one-night stand. Even American Motors executives from Grosse Pointe knocked off a little extramarital piece now and then, just so long as they were discreet.

Try another relief agency? There were several in Washington —all privately maintained, all small, all looking for government assistance and trying to do their best without it, but not doing half of what they could if they were organized. He knew that as well as anybody; he'd had to deal with some of them in Phnom Penh—

Natalie Rosen, he thought.

The name popped into his head, and along with it an image of a tall dark-haired attractive woman. Natalie Rosen. The one who had baited him so vehemently the night he'd almost had the fight with Peter Deighan, the night of the nightmare on MV Phum Chup. The one who had spoken out so strongly to him at the embassy of the need for government recognition of the refugee problem, government sponsorship of a major relief program. The liberal, the bitchy New Yorker, the woman who had had tears in her eyes when she talked of what she'd seen in the hospitals in Phnom Penh. The woman who cared.

Odd that he should think of her now; he hadn't thought of her at all since she'd walked out of the embassy and out of his life seven weeks ago. Or maybe not so odd, after all. She worked for a refugee relief organization, and she cared about the Cambodian people, and she had known Kim, however briefly. She was someone to talk to, even if she couldn't tell him anything about the situation in Cambodia, even on the telephone.

He went back to his suite at the Mayflower, called New York City Information, and then dialed the number the operator gave him for the Refugee Relief Fund. As he waited for a connection it occurred to him vaguely that he was being impulsive, maybe even a little irrational. But he didn't care. It was something to do; it was better than doing nothing. Did it make any less sense to call Natalie Rosen, talk to her, than it had to call and talk to his parents?

A woman's voice answered with the words "Refugee Relief Fund, good afternoon." Foxworth explained who he was and asked to speak to Miss Rosen. And the woman said she was sorry, that wasn't possible; *Ms.* Rosen was out of town.

Ms. Rosen was in Washington.

Staying at the Mayflower Hotel.

In other circumstances Foxworth might have added laughter to his surprise; it was the kind of coincidence that fiction writers steered clear of, and that Hollywood loved, and that happened more often in real life than most people imagined. His mother might have approved of it, because it meant that now he could talk to the nice American girl face to face. On the other hand, though, his mother might not have approved of the fact that the nice American girl was Jewish. But what the hell, she couldn't have it both ways, now could she?

Foxworth picked up the phone again and asked the desk to connect him with Natalie Rosen's room.

Cambodia File: Postwar Calendar

April 19—A clandestine radio station calling itself the "Voice of the Future Nation" and claiming to represent the Khmer Rouge, says that several GKR leaders, including former Premier Long Boret and former General Lon Non, have been beheaded. The official Khmer Rouge Radio, however, has been silent since the fall of Phnom Penh, when it claimed that FUNK had seized nine provincial capitals, among them Battambang City and the deepwater port of Kompong Som.

April 20—The news blackout from Phnom Penh continues, with the Khmer Rouge Radio broadcasting only heroic descriptions of the city's capture and revolutionary songs. One song, titled "Red Flag of the Revolution Is Flying over Liberated Phnom Penh," makes reference to "killing the abject Phnom Penh traitorous clique," but it is not certain whether or not this refers to actual executions.

April 21—Exiled President Lon Nol, who is currently staying with his family and an entourage of twenty in special quarters at Hawaii's Hickam Air Force Base, is said to be buying a home in Honolulu valued at $103,000. The home is located in the Mariner's Cove section of the exclusive Hawaii Kai subdivision, near an inland waterway which many residents use to shuttle their yachts to the Pacific Ocean.

Kim

Early on the afternoon of the twenty-first, Kim and a ragged pack of several hundred others reached the Mekong ferry town of Neak Luong.

The trek south along Highway 1 had been slow and torturous—even more difficult than the mass evacuation of Phnom Penh on the eighteenth. The people were exhausted, weak from hunger and malaise, and still fearful of what lay in store for them. Despite what the Khmer Rouge soldiers had told them at Stung Meanshey, most of the evacuees had not been allowed to splinter off for their native villages. Their villages were already too crowded, the shepherding guards told them now. They must go where they were needed by Angka. And where was that? The Angkar Leu would inform them when it was time for them to know.

A few of the more courageous had slipped away in the night; but it was whispered that they had all been hunted down by KC patrols and executed for disobedience, and though no one knew this for certain, the majority were too frightened to take the risk. One fact they did know for certain was that here and there along the route, particularly in the area around the abandoned village of Chroi Dang, there were more corpses—some decayed but others still fresh and steaming. The Khmer Rouge guards said that the bodies were those of government loyalists who had refused to surrender, who had offered last desperate pockets of resistance. But at least some of them, Kim could tell, had died not in combat but with their hands tied behind their backs.

There was no food and no water except for what they could forage from the land. Kim developed huge blisters on the soles of her feet and her ankles swelled painfully; the green fruit and impure water she had been forced to ingest gave her, as they did many of the others, an attack of diarrhea. She had foraged a pair of peasant pajamas and a straw hat, and as soon as she had been able after leaving the Stung Meanshey radio station she had set to work cutting and roughening her hands with stones. But she had not been questioned again thus far.

The hardship might have been worse for her if she had not been strong-willed and determined to survive. And, too, if she had not been reunited with the child, Sang Serey, the evening of the second day.

The cart belonging to Serey's father had suffered a broken axle and it had taken him hours to find material with which to repair it. The guards refused to help him or to allow anyone else to help him; Kim learned this later, when she reached the place where the cart was drawn off the road. The pregnant mother had not yet given birth—still had not two days hence—and remained delirious with fever and heat sickness. The father had been too frantic, too busy with the cart to forage more than enough for his wife; Serey had been neglected, given nothing to eat or drink all day.

Kim's spirits had risen at sight of the child. And Serey, though dazed with fatigue, had seemed glad to see her; had responded to her in the same trusting way as before. Together they had found food, water, and then helped to make the mother comfortable for the night while the father finished work on their cart. In the darkness that came soon afterward, Serey had lain with her by the roadside and talked herself to sleep, saying that she and her family had come from the village of Tonle Bet near Kompong Cham, that the soldiers and the big guns had made them flee to Phnom Penh and they had stayed for weeks with her mother's sister in a house with one room, twelve people in one room, and had always been hungry in this new place and her mother had cried often and was sick because of the little one that lived in her stomach. The father wasn't her real father, she said, her real father had stopped being a blacksmith and become a soldier and then been killed in a battle, and her mother had married the new father; but the new father didn't like the old father's children very much and her brother had gone away in Phnom Penh and never come back and now they were going away too and she was very frightened. Where were they going? Would it be much longer before they got there? When would they have enough to eat, and a place to sleep at night, so they wouldn't have to be afraid anymore?

"Soon," Kim said to her, and the word was bitter on her tongue.

All the following day and part of this one she had walked beside the cart, sometimes helping the father pull it, more often carrying Serey in spite of her own weakened muscles and swollen ankles. It was midday of the twenty-first when they crossed the Mekong and reached the place just south of Neak Luong where Highway 15 intersected with Highway 1. Here, the Khmer Rouge made what seemed to be an arbitrary division in their number: more than two thirds, Kim and Serey and her family among them, were diverted back to the northeast along Highway 15, while the rest were pressed on toward Svay Rieng on the Vietnamese border. No explanation was given for this action; all the guards would say was that they must go where Angka needed them, do what the Angkar told them to do, and then they would be rewarded with food and shelter and a prosperous new existence under the revolutionary flag. Perhaps even tonight, some of the soldiers said. Perhaps there would be rice for all of them this very night.

But they had lied about everything else and Kim knew that this, too, was a lie; there would be no rice tonight, no prosperous new existence. The Khmer Rouge were prepared to starve them to death if necessary. Or march them to death. Or do whatever else to them their Angkar instructed them to.

Not everyone accepted the division docilely. One Vietnamese peasant lost control of himself; he began to shout angry protests at the soldiers, demanding to be allowed to go south, saying that his native village was there and he had been promised safe passage. When the soldiers ordered him to be silent he attacked one of them with his hands, beat on the soldier pitifully, weeping, and was himself beaten to the ground and kicked unconscious. Then he was carried away by two other soldiers, into a stand of broadleaf trees nearby. The soldiers were alone when they returned, and one of them had blood on his hand.

Kim felt a strange emotion possess her: she wanted to kill those soldiers, as they had surely killed the Vietnamese. Something had happened to these troops in all the months and years of fighting; something had carved the souls out of them, made them less than human. They had the appearance of men but they were machinery. To plead with them was to plead with the mindless ticking of a bomb. She repressed the primitive feeling, forced herself to look away from the soldiers, to stroke Serey's matted hair and press her face against the child's. One of the purposes of this forced march might be to make them all welcome death, but Kim would not allow herself to die in such a way. She would not lose control. She would not capitulate.

An almost unrelieved silence, heavy with hopelessness, hung over them on the trek to Neak Luong. On the previous day, even this morning, there had been conversation, a sense of animation; they had been a group of people carried on a common plank of anguish, but with hope alive in most of them, hope that they would not be harmed, hope that they would be allowed to work the land again, hope that they might escape to Vietnam. Now the fragile strands that held them together seemed to have snapped. They might have been cattle herded slowly along the river. They were no longer people but animals —or, still worse, a kind of inanimate cargo that retained only the ability to propel itself. And that, too, Kim thought, might be one of the purposes of the great Angkar: the less community and humanity, the less the possibility of resistance.

There was very little left of Neak Luong. The last time Kim had been there, more than two years ago, it had been a busy river town full of barges, fishing boats, paddle-wheel ferries, goods and produce awaiting transshipment up or down the Mekong. Now, after its more than three months as a key target of the communist offensive, it was a shell, a place of the dead. Everywhere there were burned and bombed-out buildings, piles of rubble, the shattered skeletons of river craft littering the Mekong's muddy banks. Some effort had been made to clean up the debris and what must have been hundreds, perhaps thousands, of corpses. A series of shallow graves seemed to have been dug in the vicinity, but so haphazardly that some had been torn open by dogs or wild animals. It was just as well that none of these was close to the highway, where their contents could be seen and perhaps smelled by the evacuees as they shuffled by.

They were allowed to camp for the night on the northern outskirts of the town, where dry brown paddies, separated by grassy dikes and lines of palm trees, stretched away from the Mekong and from the highway. Kim took Serey with her and began the night's foraging. At first she went back to the nearest group of buildings, but when she saw a pair of putrefying bodies, crawling with insects and maggots, she reversed herself and went out into the paddies. There was a strip of jungle at the far edge, fronted by a stand of bamboo. At this time of year, before the monsoons came, there were no tender young bamboo shoots; Kim pushed deeper into the tangled vegetation. It yielded no edible fruit, but she found several of the black beetles that were abundant in the dry season, killed them, and gathered their crushed bodies together in her straw hat. She also found some edible bark, and, as her father had taught her when she was a child in Rovieng, located several buried locusts by their airholes. The bark and the insects would do little to appease their hunger, and nothing to appease their thirst; still, they were better than no nourishment at all.

It was dark by this time, too dark to continue. If she stayed out, there was the chance she would be seen by a KC patrol and accused of attempting to escape. Perhaps someone else had found a better variety of food and would be willing to barter away some of it. Kim had little with which to barter—she wished now that she had not given up David's emerald ring to the Khmer Rouge at Stung Meanshey—but Serey's parents possessed a few items of small value. The father had not been willing to part with them thus far, but he would if he grew hungry enough. Just as she herself would trade the use of her body in exchange for food, if she grew hungry enough.

With Serey draped across one shoulder, Kim made her way back across the paddies. Fires had been built off to one side by the KC soldiers; she could see several of them squatting there, cooking rice and boiling tea for themselves, as she approached.

The lust for their death came to her again; to dispel it she looked away and said a Buddhist prayer inside her mind.

But the urge and the prayer both disappeared when she and Serey reached the cart: the child's mother was in agony, having finally gone into labor.

Several other women were grouped around where she lay beside the cart, one of them acting as midwife. The father was in a frenzy; each of his wife's screams made him clutch his head and stare about himself with wild eyes. Serey struggled in Kim's arms, drawn by the cries, wanting to go to her mother, not understanding what was happening. Kim held her away. Whispered to her, tried to soothe her. Nearby two of the soldiers looked on incuriously; one drank now and then from a field canteen. But when the midwife turned to him and begged for water he said, "Let the woman suffer as we have suffered," and walked away from her.

The mother's shrieks ceased not long after that, so abruptly that Kim turned Serey's head against her breast and kept it pressed there as she stepped closer. There was blood and a twisted little shape on the midwife's hands—a shape that did not move. The baby had been stillborn. And the mother was unconscious, still bleeding, hemorrhaging internally.

Moaning, muttering disjointed invocations to the Enlightened One, the father tried to lie on the ground beside her, take hold of her hand. The midwife and the other women pushed him away. They did what they could for the woman, but there was no light except that of the moon and removed fires, no water, no medicine or tools. There was nothing, there was no hope.

Serey's mother died forty minutes later.

And the father, crazed with grief, first tried to throw himself on the body and then, after he was restrained, ran away into the darkness. No one was able to stop him or to search for him because the Khmer Rouge would not allow it. He did not come back in the night and he was not there in the morning when the soldiers prodded them up and put them back on the road, started them north toward Prey Veng. Kim never saw him again.

The child, Serey, belonged to her.

168

Natalie

David Foxworth had changed.

That was Natalie's first thought when he walked into the Mayflower's lounge five minutes after the time—six o'clock—they had agreed to meet. It had been less than two months since she'd last seen him, that day at the embassy in Phnom Penh, but it might have been two years, or even two decades. The bright young foreign service officer was gone, replaced by someone she had never met before. He had aged, that was the main thing. His face was still unlined and his hair was still the same dark brown, but his eyes seemed to have receded into their sockets, to have taken on a dull, haunted sheen, as if ghosts rustled and whispered behind them; and he walked with the stoop of middle age, projected a kind of superannuated ponderousness. There was nothing comical about any of this. It was just the opposite, in fact—the appearance of someone in the midst of a great tragedy.

Could the American evacuation, the fall of Cambodia, have done all this to him? No, she thought, it had to be more than that. And much more personal than that, to have affected him in such a profound way. But what?

She felt intensely curious about him. His telephone call earlier had amazed her—not just because of the coincidence, both of them in Washington and both staying at the same hotel at the same time, but because he had sought her out in the first place. It seemed uncharacteristic of a product of the Nixon administration. Why her, of all people? He had said that he wanted to discuss the refugee situation, but there were other relief organizations right here in Washington, including the headquarters of the International Red Cross. And they hadn't exactly had the best possible rapport in Phnom Penh . . . although she remembered the poignant exchange of dialogue between them just before she left the embassy, and how it had caused a shift in her feelings toward him. Maybe he remembered it too; maybe it had helped shift his own feelings toward her.

You really care, don't you, Miss Rosen?

Yes, I really care. Don't you?

I always believed I did.

But now you're not so sure?

Now maybe I'm starting to learn how.

It was the tag end of the cocktail hour and the lounge was crowded and noisy. Foxworth didn't say anything to her at first, possibly because he didn't want to raise his voice to be heard; just nodded and sat down across the table from her. Their eyes met and held for a span of seconds; then his gaze flicked away, as if he didn't want to let her see the depths of the pain that glistened there. But she did see it, and felt moved by it. Pain had always had that effect on her, ever since the first time her father showed her his scrapbook of photographs from Auschwitz, Dachau, Buchenwald.

"Thank you for seeing me, Miss Rosen," he said at length. He still didn't raise his voice; she had to lean forward to hear him.

"Not at all. You can call me Natalie, if you like."

"All right."

"And you're David."

"Yes. David."

A waitress came and took their orders for drinks and went away again. David cleared his throat, looked at her, and cleared his throat again, as though he didn't quite know how to begin. Then he said tentatively, "Have you been in Washington long?"

"Two days."

"On business for the Relief Fund?"

"After a fashion," she said. "Trying to raise support for a government-sponsored relief program."

"Any luck?"

"No," she said, and made no effort to keep the bitterness from creeping into her voice. "None at all."

"Who have you seen?"

She told him who she'd seen. Or rather, who she had not seen. The first place she had gone was to the Sam Rayburn

Building and Bella Abzug's office, as she had told her father she would; but Bella Abzug had been unavailable. So had Representative Richard L. Ottinger, Congressman Peter Peyser, Congressman Edward I. Koch. One of Koch's aides was pleased to tell her that Congress had passed a bill authorizing a hundred and fifty million dollars in Indochinese aid; surely this was a step in the right direction, didn't she think so? She reminded him that both Cambodia and Vietnam had already fallen to the communists; what good was all that aid going to do the *people* of those countries now? The aide hadn't had an answer for that.

Then she had gone to the office of Senator Brooke of Massachusetts, she told David, because Brooke had spoken recently in opposition to any Indochinese relief, saying it would "become another temptation for extensive graft and corruption." But she had convinced herself that if she were able to talk to him at length she could make him understand the desperateness of the refugee situation, and get him to publicly recant his position; a positive statement from Brooke at this time might have had some real impact. But Senator Brooke, his polite assistant had told her, was in New York and the time of his return to Washington had not been determined. Perhaps she could make an appointment at some later date, he'd said, stressing the word *appointment*.

Then she had gone to the State Department and managed to get an entry pass on her credentials. And walked its Byzantine corridors past the Auditorium and the International Conference Room where Kissinger met the press—there had been no sign, of course, of either Kissinger or the press—and eventually found her way to the office of the Assistant Secretary of State for East Asian and Pacific Affairs, one Philip C. Habib. But Philip C. Habib, like everyone else in Washington, seemed to be unavailable. (She didn't tell this to David, but on the way out of the building she had had a sudden fantasy: Washington was so insulated, so careful, so bureaucratically maintained that if it ever fell, as Phnom Penh had fallen, its collapse would be invisible. Any invader coming into the State Department would have to apply for a pass and then would become lost in its sterile corridors, looking for a way out. Just like all the politicians, just like the Cambodian refugees, just like she herself—looking for a way out.)

"So that's my tale of woe," she said to David. Which wasn't quite true. She also hadn't told him about the reporter, Wade Collins, she had met in Habib's outer office. Nor was she going to; that particular episode had nothing to do with the futility of her ride on the Washington merry-go-round. Or maybe it did, but she wasn't about to get into that with herself, much less with David Foxworth. "Nobody's available, nobody wants to listen."

"I want to listen," he said.

"Do you?"

"Of course I do."

"But are you in a position to do anything about it? You're not a politician, David. A bureaucrat but not a politician. It's the politicians we have to convince, or nothing will ever get done."

"I know."

"Politicians on both sides of the fence."

"Yes," he said. "You're not trying to maneuver me into a polemical debate, are you? I don't want to argue liberal versus conservative tonight; I don't want to discuss political ideology."

"Neither do I. And no, I wasn't going after controversy."

"Good."

Their drinks came. David looked at his without touching it. Natalie sipped hers—a brandy-and-water—and then put it down again and said, "You do see the refugee situation as a major problem, don't you? One that can only get worse as time goes on."

"I see it that way, yes."

"And that we've got to have a coordinated aid program."

"Yes."

"That isn't quite the way you saw it two months ago," she said. "I don't mean that critically; I'm only making an observation. What changed your mind?"

"A lot of things have changed in the past two months. My mind is only one of them."

"Doesn't answer my question."

He shook his head. It didn't mean no; it meant he didn't want to deal with her question. Natalie thought again, as she had in Phnom Penh, that he might fascinate her if she got to know him. There was so much pain in him that she could almost feel it, like waves of heat radiating across the table. It touched places inside her, evoked responses—one of which, even though she wasn't eager to admit it, was sexual. She had found him attractive enough in Phnom Penh, but there had been something missing. Character, maybe; that nebulous stamp of maturity and individuality. The pain, ironically enough, had given him character and made him almost magnetic.

She shifted position on her chair, sipped again from the brandy-and-water. "Do you think there's anything you *can* do?" she asked. "I mean, if you don't mind my being frank, do you have much influence in high places? Can you help pull some strings?"

A wry smile quirked one corner of his mouth. "I know a few people," he said. "I could probably get some strings pulled, all right. The only trouble is, they're all the wrong strings. Or the right strings pulled in the wrong way."

"I'm not quite sure I know what you mean."

"Never mind. I was thinking about my father." He looked at his drink again but still didn't taste it. "The truth is, Miss Rosen—"

"Natalie."

"Yes. Natalie. The truth is, Natalie, I doubt if there's very much I can accomplish in my position."

"But you do intend to try?"

"I'll do what I can. Here and in Bangkok both."

"Bangkok?"

"I've been reassigned to the embassy there," he said. "Effective May first."

"Oh, I see," Natalie said, and felt just the slightest bit disappointed. "The same duties you had in Phnom Penh?"

It seemed to her that he hesitated before saying, "Yes. That's why I'm in Washington. Meetings, briefing sessions—putting things together before I fly back to Thailand."

"Don't you get a vacation first?"

"You mean R&R after Cambodia? I had a week in Bangkok. That was enough."

"Only a week."

"I want to get back to work," he said.

"Well, at least your friend's here with you, isn't she?"

"Friend?"

"Your Khmer friend. Than Kim."

There was a rippling movement along one side of his face, as of a wince half controlled; then his facial muscles were still and she was looking at a blank, a matrix with features molded onto it. But the sunken eyes still had ghosts rustling and whispering behind them, and the pain that radiated out of him now was so acute it made her quiver inside.

Another four or five seconds passed before he said, "No, she's not here with me," in a voice that he tried and failed to make as emotionless as his expression.

"Waiting in Bangkok?"

"No. She . . . didn't leave Cambodia."

"My God," Natalie said. And knew, sensed intuitively, that this was the primary source of his pain. This was what had changed him, aged him, put the character into his face, put the stoop in his shoulders. Than Kim. Gentle, compassionate, beautiful. Khmer. "Why? Why did she stay?"

He shook his head again, the same way he had earlier: it was a question he didn't want to deal with.

Natalie said, "But you tried to bring her out?"

"I tried," he said, but there was something in his tone that told her he believed he hadn't tried hard enough. "It was her decision; I couldn't force her to leave against her will."

"You . . . haven't had any word?"

"No. No word."

Silence, then, for what must have been a minute or more. Unspoken between them, like something ugly that had been dropped onto the table, was the knowledge—or half knowledge —that Khmers were dying all over Cambodia, being executed, suffering God knew what other reprisals at the hands of the communists, and that those who had had dealings with Americans, had worked with the Americans, were likely to be the primary targets. It was no wonder he was being torn up inside, she thought. The war had stopped being an abstract for him; now it was personal. And when it became personal it had opened him up like a surgeon's knife and let all the other anguish, all the other horror, come spilling in. It had made him a kind of empath, just as those photographs in her father's scrapbook had made her one. Only he couldn't handle it, hadn't learned how to function with that kind of sensitivity. He was ODing on it, that was what was happening. And if he didn't reach a point of remission pretty soon, it was going to break him down one way or another and keep him from functioning at all.

But she couldn't tell him any of this. How could you tell a person, a man you barely knew, that he was ODing on pain? What good would it do? Maybe he already knew it or suspected it; and if he didn't, talking about it wouldn't solve anything. Words, other people's or your own, didn't teach you how to deal with pain or the fact that you had become empathic. The coming to terms, the remission, had to happen inside yourself, if it was going to happen at all. It had to come from inside David Foxworth, not across the table from him in a crowded lounge in the Mayflower Hotel.

So she just sat there, feeling his pain, trying to think of something that she *could* say to him. Hollow reassurances were out; she hated hollow reassurances, people telling her everything would be all right, you had to have faith, look on the bright side. Change the subject, then? And talk about what? The weather? The brand-new baseball season? Washington in cherry-blossom time? "Did you know, David, that the cherry trees were a gift from the Japanese government in 1912?" For God's sake—

He cleared his throat. It was a small sound, almost lost among the voices and laughter and clinking glasses around them, but it made her blink and look at him more intently. Then he said, "I think I'd better go," and started to push his chair back.

"No, wait," she said. She didn't want to lose him, not now, not like this. "Why don't we have dinner together? You're not doing anything for dinner, are you?"

Hesitation. "No, but—"

"L'Orangerie is close by," she said, "if you like French food. They do a really nice poached oyster dish." I'm talking too fast, she thought. What's the matter with me? "All right? Will you join me?"

She watched him think about it and she wished she knew what was going on in his mind. Finally he said, "I guess I don't really want to eat alone. We could talk over ideas for a refugee program; and I'd like to know more about how your organization operates."

"Fine," she said, feeling relieved. "Shall we go?"

They went to L'Orangerie and ate *les huîtres Normandie* and drank a half bottle of French Chardonnay. And they talked about a coordinated aid program, and possibilities for an airlift of supplies into Thailand, and she told him about her father and the inner workings of the Fund. There was a certain intimacy in it—table for two, candlelight, French wine, soft music —and yet there was a distance, a chasm that she couldn't seem to cross. The chasm was Than Kim, of course. She knew it and she accepted it, but she kept trying to reach him just the same. It was almost a compulsion now, probably transitory but nonetheless intense, fed by her sensitivity to his emotional upheaval.

It was after nine when they came back into the Mayflower's plush lobby. "Did you know, David, that Gene Autry once rode his horse through here as a publicity stunt?" She shook herself mentally, got her thoughts straightened out as they crossed to the elevators. There was an open car waiting there, empty, and they stepped inside.

"I'm on twelve," she said. Then, as the doors closed, she said, "We can have brandy in my room, if you like."

It was a clear sexual invitation and he knew it; he'd have had to be a dolt not to know it. But he let it hang in the air for three or four seconds, while the car whirred upward, and she could tell by his face that he was going to turn it down, reject it, even before he said the words.

"I don't think so," he said. "No."

"Are you sure?"

"I'm sure. I've got an early appointment in the morning, I'd better get to sleep right away."

The car stopped at the twelfth floor and the doors whispered open. Natalie said, "Then I guess we won't see each other again. I have an early-afternoon flight back to New York."

"We should keep in touch," he said. "Maybe we can work together on some of those ideas we talked about."

"Yes, I'd like that."

She stepped out, turned to look back at him. And he said, "I'm sorry, Natalie," just before the doors slid closed again, like a wall between them.

She went down the hallway to her room, let herself in, and plopped herself down in one of the chairs. The first thought that came to her then, not irrelevantly, was of Wade Collins, the reporter she had met at the State Department yesterday. Well, no, not a reporter exactly—a free-lance writer who was putting together what he called a "Washington Diary" and hoped to sell it to one of the national magazines. As soon as he'd found out who she was and that she'd spent some time in Cambodia, he had said he wanted to interview her, make her the subject of a "primary entry," and he wouldn't take no for an answer. He had been nice enough, sort of like a polite, cleaned-up, noncynical Peter Deighan, and he had had enough published credits to make him credible, and any chance for free publicity for the Fund had to be jumped at, particularly now. So she'd let him take her to a dark restaurant on J Street, where she had answered a lot of questions and then listened to him talk with great sincerity on whether or not the Indochina experience would enable America to confront its soul. The war in Southeast Asia, he said, had been an American happening; the Cambodians and Vietnamese had merely been metaphors for the sickness of the post-technological 1970s. That was why nobody was responding to the plight of the refugees. People just didn't care anymore, not after all that had gone down in the past decade.

Then casually, over their third drink, he'd asked her to stop in at his apartment so they could get better acquainted.

She had looked at her watch, said that she had to leave, thanked him for the drinks, got up, and left the restaurant—all with such grace and speed that he hadn't had time to say another word. A fast, sure rejection; the best kind if you wanted to avoid an uncomfortable situation. But no faster and no surer than David Foxworth's rejection of her just now.

Not that she blamed David, of course. She understood why he had done it. Just as she understood why she had done it: been prepared to let him spend the night with her. She may have been liberated and all that but she wasn't promiscuous; she didn't go around propositioning men because of their animal magnetism or her own need for physical gratification. It was his pain, the depth and intensity of it. There had been no pain in Wade Collins, nothing except false sincerity and a kind of guile; he had never wanted to make her the subject of a primary entry in his "Washington Diary," he had only wanted to make her. David wanted nothing from her—and yet he needed something she could give him.

Sitting there alone, she wished fervently that he hadn't said no. But it wasn't for herself, her own sake, that she wished it; it was for his.

Because she could have made some of his hurt go away, if only for a little while.

Deighan

I'm playing this game under protest, Deighan thought.

It was five o'clock on the afternoon of April 23 and he was on his way to the Victory Hotel, off Charoen Krung Road in downtown Bangkok, to see his wife for the first time in more than a year. He was also moderately drunk and in better spirits than he had any right to be. The way he wanted to feel was depressed, angry, dripping with cynicism; but here he was, walking along Charoen Krung Road, very steady on his feet, very steady inside his head, not looking forward to facing Carol but not dreading it anymore either.

He had even cleaned himself up for the occasion. Shaved for the first time in weeks, combed his hair, gotten his suit pressed and the worst of the stains taken out. The suit didn't fit him very well anymore because he'd lost more weight since the evacuation—he was down to a hundred and sixty pounds now—but what the hell. He was an expatriate American journalist and expatriate American journalists were supposed to look a little seedy, a little underfed; it was like a badge of honor, anyone caught looking prosperous and well stuffed gets his membership in the Overseas Press Club revoked.

He wondered how she would look.

Well, she would probably look the same; Carol had one of those lean, willowy figures that stayed the same from fifteen to fifty, and she had never fiddled much with her hair, kept the same long natural style, the natural chestnut color. No, she wouldn't have changed much. Not like him. Not like the old Pulitzer Prize nominee, fresh from another exotic assignment, fresh from the only war we had, fresh from unsuccessfully trying to knock himself off for the hundredth time in the past few months. Or was it the two hundredth?

What he couldn't figure out was why she'd made up her mind to come to Bangkok. She'd never liked to travel and she'd always been just a little bit of a xenophobe, even though she would never admit it; the Vietnamese and the other Asian races were fine, dandy, but they ought to be left to their own culture and their own devices; the thought of killing them upset her but the thought of screwing one of them would probably make her throw up. He made a note to tell her how many little brown women he'd screwed himself, just to watch her reaction. Like the one last night, the Thai whore who had reminded him vaguely of Carol and whose contempt for him had been so open and savage that it had acted as a kind of perverse aphrodisiac and excited the hell out of him. He ought to tell Carol about *that,* all right; how the whore had spread him out like Prufrock's London, a patient etherized upon a table—

etherized with vodka, of course—and done a Luftwaffe blitz on his private parts. Carol would love it. Especially the resemblance angle.

So why was she coming to Bangkok? Why did she want to see him? It couldn't be that she was pining away for him; it had been more than a year since they'd laid eyes on each other, add another three months since they'd laid each other, he hadn't written in weeks, she hadn't written in weeks, they hadn't had anything to *say* to each other in months, the damn marriage was over. It was over. She knew it too; there hadn't been any pretense in any of her letters to him while he was in Phnom Penh. Maybe that was why she was here, eh? Deliver the old Dear John in person? No, not Carol. That wasn't her style. She didn't have a lot of *cojones* herself, figuratively speaking. If she decided to divorce him she'd just go out and do it, desertion or similar grounds, and maybe send him a letter about it and maybe not, maybe just let the lawyer ship the papers himself, along with a businesslike covering letter. He'd half expected to get an envelope like that in Phnom Penh; if he had, it might have given him just enough impetus to squeeze the trigger on that .45 of his. But then, Carol wasn't very decisive either, at least not where major decisions were concerned.

Except that coming to Bangkok, eight thousand miles from home, to be reunited with her drunken husband, was a pretty major decision and had required a certain decisiveness. The question was still *why?*

Well, he'd find out pretty soon now. Pretty soon. No use worrying about it now, right? Now he ought to be thinking about what kind of bar they had at the Victory Hotel and whether or not they opened it up on time. They were *supposed* to open at five; all the bars in Bangkok were. If there was one thing he had firmly fixed in his mind, it was the local schedule for public consumption of alcohol. Sunday through Thursday, eleven in the morning to two in the afternoon, then 5 P.M. to midnight. Friday and Saturday, the same hours during the day and until 1 A.M. It was a pretty thoughtful schedule, when you thought about it—the weekend extensions and also the drying-out period during the afternoon. The Thai government was damn paternal in its corrupt little way.

The plan, then, was to head straight into the bar, assuming it was open, and space out four or five more drinks until Carol's arrival. Not enough for him to release his hold on the chinning bar of lucidity (look at that, boys: I can write rings around that old son of a bitch Hemingway even when I'm drunk and walking down a stifling-hot street in Bangkok, Thailand; I'm good, I am). No, just enough to keep a fine edge on and his spirits high, so he could face her and so she'd know that all the rumors floating around about his degeneration were true to the last bloody word.

Be that as it may, he thought, and winked at himself in a storefront window as he passed; be that as it may, I'm *still* playing this damn game under protest. Heigh-ho! Under protest, by God.

A *samlor*, one of those three-wheeled motorized-bike contraptions that choked the streets of Bangkok, almost ran him down halfway across an intersection. Deighan raised the middle finger of his right hand at the startled driver, got a blank stare in return. Nobody else paid any attention to him. Damn city. It didn't seem to have been touched by the wars across its border in Cambodia and Laos and Vietnam. But it would be someday; it would be touched, all right. The good old U.S. would see to that. Fix these poor bastards the way we fixed the Vietnamese and the Cambodians, damn right.

He was almost to the Victory Hotel now. He thought about the plan again and stopped and leaned against the wall of a building to check the number of baht in his wallet. Enough. Not a hell of a lot, but enough for tonight and tomorrow and another couple of weeks. By then he ought to be getting another advance from Ed Saunders at *Worldview*. He'd done the bugger three thousand words and mailed it off two days ago. In spite of Carol, in spite of Cambodia, in spite of the vodka and the whores . . . three thousand damn words. It might be another four months until he wrote anything again and it might be never, but they couldn't take those three thousand away from him. Some of it was crap, but some of it had the old touch, the old Pulitzer Prize-nomination flair. "Reflections on the Day of the Fall," that was what he'd called it. The old flair. Saunders would come through with another two-fifty as soon as he read it; Deighan was sure of that. Maybe even five hundred this time. He wouldn't have to think about the typewriter again for at least a couple of months.

The hotel loomed up in front of him and he went inside. The blast of the air conditioning chilled him, iced the sweat on his body. Reminded him of how thirsty he was. He could see the bar sign ahead of him, winking in nice soft colors; the lounge had opened up right on time. He started over there to put his plan straightaway into action.

Carol was standing at the desk.

When he saw her he came to a sharp standstill, blinked, stared. It was her, no doubt about that: wearing a white tropical dress, chestnut hair falling long out from under a wide-brimmed white hat. She was facing away from him, but enough in profile so that he could recognize the lines of her face. He hadn't thought he would react when he saw her, but then he'd expected to be pretty well insulated by that time; there was a jolt of emotion and his pulse quickened and the sweat drying on him seemed to grow colder. He felt himself start to tremble. He couldn't face her yet, not without another couple of drinks, not cold this way, unprepared, uninsulated. The bar sign beckoned him again; he took another step toward it.

Too late. She turned from the desk and saw him.

"Peter," she said.

He stopped again, looked at her, looked at the entrance; he felt trapped. I don't want to see you, he thought. Damn it, I don't want to see you. But he didn't move as she came toward him. Just stood looking at her, trying to stop the jangling inside him, trying to hold himself together.

"Peter," she said again when she reached him, and touched the back of one of his hands. That was all: no kiss, no embrace. Just the touch—and eye contact. She had always been very good at eye contact; her eyes were enormous, brown with little amber lights in them, and she could make them say things more plainly than words, she could make love with those eyes better than some women could make love with their bodies. But the eyes weren't saying anything to him now, nothing at all. There was a shield down behind them, as impenetrable as lead. Same Carol: same features, same figure, same hairstyle. But her eyes weren't talking to him anymore; her eyes, too, had run out of things to say.

It's over, Carol, he thought, you know it's over. Why are you here? The cheerful feeling was gone; he felt confused, almost desperate. And sick. His stomach was jumping and he could taste bile pumping into the back of his throat.

"You're early," he said, because they were the only words that came into his head.

"The plane landed early. I just got here in a taxi five minutes ago. You didn't know that—about the plane landing early?"

"No."

"Then why are you here now?"

"I was going to get a drink."

"Oh. I see."

"I've been drinking," he said.

"Yes, I know. You haven't exactly kept it a secret."

"I mean I've been drinking today."

"That isn't a secret either. You reek of liquor."

He couldn't think of anything to say. No sharp retort, no cynical wit. Nothing. His mind was a well of muddy thoughts.

"Peter, you look terrible. Why are you doing this to yourself?"

"Why do you think?"

"Not because of me—of us?"

"No. Hell no. You don't look so bad, though; not so bad."

"I . . . well, I've found a little peace."

"You have, huh?"

"Yes."

"Chemically?"

"You mean drugs? No, nothing like that."

"Est, then? Religion?"

"No."

"What, then?"

"Just an inner peace, that's all."

"Is that why you came all the way over here?" he said. "To tell me you've found inner peace? Christ, Carol—"

"I came to see you," she said.

"Why? What for? It's finished between us, you know that."

"I don't know it. That's why I'm here."

He looked at her without speaking.

"I know we don't have much of a marriage left," Carol said. "I hardly know you anymore and you hardly know me. But I did love you once and maybe I still do; and maybe the same is true for you. I have to find out, Peter. That's part of my peace, too: finding out the truth, dealing with it."

Deighan still didn't say anything, just kept staring at her. And the more he stared, the more serene, almost radiant, she seemed. Was this really Carol? Full of peace, undergoing some kind of spiritual rebirth, wanting to find out if there was anything left of what they'd once had together? Then why the shield behind her eyes? Why weren't her eyes talking to him too?

He couldn't cope with it. It was too unexpected, too foreign, and he was too damn drunk. But not drunk enough, by God. "I need a drink," he said to her. "We'll talk about this in the bar—"

"No," she said.

"What?"

"I won't talk in the bar. I won't talk with you at all anymore when you're like this."

"Like what?"

"Drunk. Reeking of liquor. You can either come with me into the restaurant and have enough coffee to sober you up, or you can leave and come back tomorrow or whenever you've dried out. I mean it, Peter."

"I don't have to sober up for you," Deighan said. "I don't have to sober up for anybody." He was suddenly angry, but it was the pouting anger of a small boy. He knew that and it made him even more angry, even more confused. None of this was turning out the way he'd expected it to when he left his hotel; it was off key, off center, a kind of deadly farce that he simply could not cope with because he didn't understand what was going on. What the hell was going on here?

"You do if you want to find out what's left for us," Carol said. "It's been over a year, Peter; I don't know you any longer and I don't want to know you this way. Now will you come with me and have some coffee? Will you sober up so we can talk?"

I don't want to sober up, he thought.

Then he thought: I'm playing *this* damn game under protest too. And let her take his arm and lead him across the lobby to the hotel restaurant.

Kim

The ordeal for her and Serey came to an end on the sixth day, the twenty-third of April, at an abandoned rubber plantation a few kilometers northeast of Phum Veal.

Then the new ordeal began.

There had been another division of ranks at Phum Svai Antor, above Prey Veng. Half of the people had been driven on along Highway 15 to an unknown destination; the other half, including Kim and the child—more than a thousand of them altogether—had been diverted to Phum Veal and then through a section of arid rice paddies to the edge of the plantation. The sky was already boiling with clouds by then: white clouds, haloed by gray and purple; clouds with darkening colors, a deep bluish-purple that created an eerie afternoon light. The air was thick and wet with humidity. It would not be long, Kim knew, before the rains of the northeast monsoon began.

Immediately after they arrived a group meeting was held, presided over by a Khmer Rouge civilian official. "You are prisoners of war," he told them. "You are *opakar*." Instruments. Not people, not even animals—instruments. "You must work for the People to prove that you are no longer enemies of the revolution; you must help to rebuild what you have helped to tear down. This land once belonged to an imperialist Chinese rubber planter and is no longer productive; it has been assigned to you for reclamation. The People must have rice, maize, cassava, yams. We must all unite to provide food for the new and liberated Kampuchea."

The official went on to say that they would be split into *krom* of from ten to fifteen families, with a chief appointed by Angka as the head of each. Each unit would be allotted a section of land, approximately three hectares per family, as their responsibility. First they would clear this land as rapidly as possible and build cabins of wood, grass, and bamboo in which one or two families, depending on their size, would live. Then they would plow the land, plant rice, plant crops, construct dams and dikes and irrigation canals in preparation for the heavy rains which would come in July and August. Until they were able to grow enough food to feed themselves, the Angkar Leu in its benevolence would furnish them with rice, water jars, kettles, and rice pots. They were to keep in mind, however, that these rations would be distributed in proportion to the amount of work and effort shown by the prisoners.

That night there were milk tins of thin rice gruel mixed with green bananas. As Kim fed herself and Serey—the child had been listless, withdrawn, since the death of her mother and the disappearance of her stepfather—she felt a faint hope for the first time in a week. Perhaps life under the direction of the Angkar Leu, the Organization on High, would not be so terrible after all. It was possible the cruelty and indifference with which they had been treated was no more than an overzealous postwar reaction, one which would not last, by troops against those who had been their enemy. She would not mind working with them then, even under such conditions as these, even as an *opaka* in a labor commune. For it would be for the benefit of all Kampuchea.

But in the days that followed the hope guttered like a candle flame and died and was not relighted. Kim and the others in her *krom,* in all the *krom,* were roused from sleep by gongs at 0500 hours every day and put to work until 2000 or 2100 hours, with short rest periods for meager midday and evening meals. The soldiers treated them no more humanely than they had on the march; they drove everyone as if they were truly *opakar,* using threats and occasional beatings to take them to the limits of physical endurance—and beyond. No one was spared, regardless of age or sex. The women suffered alongside the men, the children alongside the women, the elderly and the sick and the crippled alongside the children.

Most of the people were city-bred and unused to long hours of manual labor. Muscles stiffened, backs and limbs ached, hands bled; women and children collapsed in the heat, old men were stricken with heart failure. There were widespread dysentery and diarrhea, scattered cases of cholera; the waves of mosquitoes brought malarial infection. Not a day passed but that someone died and was dragged away immediately for burial in a shallow unmarked grave.

One of the men in the commune, in a neighboring *krom* to Kim's, had been a doctor in Phnom Penh, and there were others who had worked as pharmacists; but the Khmer Rouge would not allow them to help the sick because they were "more urgently needed by Angka to prepare the land for its rebirth." Except for native remedies—herb teas for intestinal ailments, coconut milk, a medicinal syrup distilled from tree bark—there were no medical supplies of any kind. Whenever anyone complained about this or any of the other hardships, the soldiers said, "We were forced to suffer for five years; now it's your turn." And if the complaints continued, or if anyone refused to work, or if anyone failed to achieve his daily quota of work on more than two occasions, the person was accused of malingering and "sent to the Angkar." No one sent to the Angkar was ever seen or heard from again.

The acreage to which Kim was assigned was secondary jungle along the perimeter of an unproductive rubber kaboon. With those in her unit and in two others she felled trees, cut sawgrass and bamboo, stripped the land to bare earth and used the cleared vegetation to build a series of primitive cabins—not traditional Khmer *paillotes* but ground-level structures in the Sino-Vietnamese style; all identical, all covered with straw and palm leaves, all just large enough to accommodate six to eight persons. Because the war had depleted the number of oxen and water buffalo, there were no draft animals to help them; everything had to be done by hand, with a slim assortment of tools: saws, axes, hoes, sharpened bamboo canes. The monsoon rains made the task even more arduous. As did unexploded bombs and mortar shells lying hidden in the tall grasses; a woman in Kim's own *krom*, a shopkeeper who had lost two of her sons in the war, was blown apart when she accidentally struck one of the shells with her hoe.

Through all of this, by day on the land, by night inside the barren cabin—there were no furnishings; no mosquito netting to keep off insects or beetles, no blankets, nothing except the barest essentials—she guarded Serey with a protectiveness more fierce than that of any mother. The child's belly was swollen, her skin had become scaly and ulcerous, and she developed a small constant cough. Kim fed her some of her ration of rice, made certain she had simple duties to perform which would not tax her, and was so obsequious to the Khmer Rouge, worked so hard herself, that they neither warned her about the child nor bothered Serey directly. Nevertheless Serey was so terrified of the soldiers that she would begin to tremble and weep uncontrollably when any of them came near her. And she remained listless, uncommunicative, saying almost nothing during the work hours. It was only at night, when Kim held her, soothed her, whispered and sang to her in the darkness, that she responded in any way at all.

On one of those nights, with the heat pressing down on them as they lay curled together on a grass mat, Serey said to her, "Will I go to see my mother soon?"

"Your mother is with God."

"Will I see God soon?"

A chill brushed Kim's neck. "No," she said. "Not for a long while."

"I hate this place," Serey said. "I hate the soldiers. It would be better with my mother and with God. Wouldn't it be better there?"

"Perhaps. But that isn't a decision for us to make. We must try to live in this life before we embrace the next."

"But why?"

"For each other," Kim said. "For Serey and for Kim."

It has truly come to that, she thought later, when she had rocked the child to sleep. We must survive for each other, not for Kampuchea, not for the extraordinary and benevolent Angkar Leu. I must live for Serey and for myself. Serey must live for me and for herself. There is no one else any longer. There is nothing else.

But this she could not deny: Serey, in her child's wisdom, had been right.

It would be infinitely better with her mother and with God.

Cambodia File: Postwar Calendar

May 3—After a grueling four-day trip by truck convoy, the six hundred foreigners who have been in the French embassy in Phnom Penh since the city's fall arrive in Aranyaprathet, Thailand. Many of the refugees, which include five hundred Frenchmen and a handful of U.S. citizens, are weak and ill from their ordeal. Newsmen and French officials among them confirm reports that Phnom Penh was emptied immediately after the communist takeover and is now a ghost city. They are unable to confirm, however, reports of mass executions in the Phnom Penh area and in the countryside.

May 3—because of his experience in foreign affairs, Richard Nixon has stated he believes he could offer some useful suggestions on foreign policy. He has reminded visitors to San Clemente that he and Secretary of State Henry Kissinger "made a good team." He is dismayed over the collapse of the anti-communist governments in Cambodia and South Vietnam, and suggests that the failure of Congress to back up the Saigon regime with military aid precipitated the crisis.

May 12—The S.S. *Mayaguez,* an American container ship enroute from Saigon to Sattahip, Thailand, carrying a cargo of U.S. government supplies, is accosted and boarded by the crew of a Cambodian gunboat. At a hurriedly convened National Security Council, Henry Kissinger insists that the United States must use force to free the captured ship. A twenty-four-hour ultimatum on the release of the ship and its crew is delivered by President Ford to the Khmer Rouge, via the Chinese government.

May 13—The crew of the *Mayaguez* is transferred by fishing boat to the island of Koh Tang. A contingent of American marines in Thailand prepares for an assault on the island.

May 14—Another fishing boat leaves the island carrying the *Mayaguez* crew, bound for the mainland port of Kompong Som. U.S. planes strafe and gas the boat but fail to halt it. When it reaches the mainland, the U.S. planes are ordered to sink all boats around Koh Tang and seven are destroyed. Kissinger insists that more force is necessary and demands a renewal of air strikes against Cambodia, even though this is in direct violation of the August 1973 ban on the bombing of Indochina. The Joint Chiefs of Staff, operating under instructions from the White House, order all Cambodian small craft sunk in the target areas of Koh Tang, Poulo Wai, Kompong Som, and Ream, and B-52 strikes against the Kompong Som and Ream airfield. Nine additional Cambodian vessels are sunk and many buildings are destroyed at the Ream naval base.

May 15—At dawn, in spite of the 1973 War Powers Act which requires the President to consult with Congress before committing U.S. troops to combat, American marines land on Koh Tang. Because the island is more strongly defended than intelligence reports indicated, the marines are subjected to heavy fire and suffer casualties: forty-one men killed, forty-nine wounded. A short while later Radio Phnom Penh promises to release the ship and its crew. Ford and Kissinger, however, order Kompong Som to be bombed, which places the men of the *Mayaguez* in danger. At 10:08 A.M. the *Mayaguez* crew is returned to their ship via Thai fishing boat and are picked up by the U. S. Navy. As soon as this news is received by the White House, a fresh bombing assault is ordered on the Cambodian mainland.

May 16—President Ford and Secretary of State Kissinger receive praise from political leaders in the United States and elsewhere for their actions in "protecting American lives in a piracy attack." In an interview Senator Barry Goldwater says, "It was wonderful. It shows we've still got balls in this country."

May 19—Despite consistent denials by the revolutionary government of Kampuchea, and the lack of confirmation by the six hundred foreigners evacuated from the French embassy, fragmentary intelligence reports continue to support the theory that a bloodbath is taking place in Cambodia. Intercepted radio transmissions claim that close to a hundred Cambodian military officers and their wives have been executed; dozens of former GKR and provincial officials are also believed to have been killed; and countless hundreds of civilians are thought to have died during the forced evacuation of Phnom Penh. The intelligence reports describe terrible suffering and warn that huge numbers of deaths from starvation, disease, and communist reprisal may still follow.

Foxworth

"Why don't you slow down a little, Dave?" Tom Boyd said to him. "You've knocked yourself out the whole month we've been here. Keep it up, you'll have a nervous breakdown one of these days. Or buy yourself a cardiac arrest."

They were on their way down to the cafeteria on the main floor of the Bangkok embassy. Foxworth hadn't wanted any lunch and still didn't; but Boyd had come into his twelve-by-twelve office on the second floor—wood-paneled, nice furnishings, nice view of Wireless Road, not as large as the office in Phnom Penh but nicer, very nice, nice—and started lecturing him about the need for a proper diet. So he had let Boyd talk him into lunch in the cafeteria, which was a clear mistake. The damned lecture was still going on.

"Look, Tom," he said, "it's my life, all right? I'm working hard because I want to work hard."

"The hell you are," Boyd said mildly.

"No? What's your theory, then?"

"It's not a theory. You're busting your hump because of Kim and we both know it. Why don't you admit it?"

Foxworth clenched his teeth and was silent as they went out through the glassed-in security enclosure, past the stone-faced marine guards and the Thai receptionist, and into the cafeteria. It was about half full with other officials, Thais attached to the embassy, and journalists freeloading under the guise of conducting interviews. There was both Thai and American food; Foxworth got a tray and put some of the food on a plate, not paying any attention to what it was, and put the plate on the tray. As soon as he sat down, even before Boyd was settled at the table, he began to eat. Steady, mechanical eating, barely tasting the food. The sooner he finished, the sooner he could get away from Boyd and back to the stack of refugee and intelligence reports on his desk.

Not that the reports would do anything other than add to his frustration. As had the debriefing sessions he'd conducted, on behalf of the CIA, of one French and two American journalists who had come out in the evacuation of all remaining foreigners on May 3. As had every other piece of information connected with Cambodia so far.

He'd spent a good deal of time, for instance, in interviewing refugees. There were a number of them in and around the embassy—filling out forms, waiting in the halls for interviews or for visas which would allow them to leave Thailand to live with relatives or sponsors in the States; and he'd also visited Aranyaprathet and a couple of the other border camps. But none of the refugees had been in Phnom Penh when the country fell; none had taken part in the death marches. Only a few, in fact, had been anywhere in Cambodia after April 17, and of those, all were from Battambang and Oddar Mean Chey Provinces, close to Thailand. To date the seals which the Khmer Rouge had placed along the Cambodian borders were more or less leakproof.

And yet it seemed probable that sooner or later refugees would start coming out, in trickles if not in streams; there were always ways for people to escape a country, to bypass minefields and barbed wire fences and military patrols, if they wanted out badly enough. That was his opinion and it was shared by most of his coworkers; already there was talk of opening a private house on Sukhumvit Road, where he and Boyd and most of the other staff were living, to accommodate the interrogation and processing of refugees when they came. And when they finally did come there would be answers, more information to help form a clearer picture of conditions inside Cambodia. Until then, there was nothing to do except to wait and monitor incoming information and talk to available refugees and file routine reports to the CIA and establish liaisons with local politicians and generally keep busy-busy in his nice air-conditioned wood-paneled office and his nice air-conditioned stucco house on Sukhumvit Road.

The days weren't so bad; it was the nights, the long nights, when he had no embassy function to attend or social gathering to host, no more paperwork to shuffle through, that were some-times intolerable. Mostly he was able to keep Kim's face out of his mind, but on those nights it would loom suddenly and drive him out of the house and into the streets where there were peo-ple and lights and noise. Walking made him tired enough to sleep; he walked for hours sometimes, not only at night but on Sundays too, and got to know the *klongs* and alleyways of Bangkok better in one month than others at the embassy had in years.

He never thought about Kim if he could occupy his mind with other things: like a man with a terminal disease, he tried to bury that knowledge just below the level of consciousness so that he'd be able to go on. He did think about Andrea once in a while, because of the things she'd said to him that last night and because there was truth in them after all, as he'd admitted to himself just prior to Operation Eagle Pull. And he thought about Natalie Rosen too: the evening they had spent together in Washington, her involvement with the plight of the refugees. And because she was the kind of woman he could have cared for once, a long time ago, in a different world. Maybe Natalie would show up in Bangkok one of these days; she had indicated she might in one of the two letters he had received from her. If she did he would see her, to discuss the refugees, but if she didn't he was sure he would think of her less and less as time went on.

The truth was, he had lost the capacity to care about any-thing anymore except Kim and what was happening to the Cambodian people. He had undergone a metamorphosis, all right; his values had shifted, what had once been peripheral and abstract had become central and intensely personal. And vice versa. The real David Foxworth was still emerging, but until the emergence was complete he felt as if he were in a kind of limbo. In a sense he had lost control of his circumstance—lost it on the twelfth of April, as he sat in that big green Sea Stallion helicopter watching Cambodia dwindle away beneath him for the last time—as wholly as the United States had lost control of the situation in Southeast Asia. The primary difference was that he was willing to admit this loss of control, to maybe benefit from it, and the people in the White House and the Pentagon and the State Department refused to admit anything. An old American tradition . . .

Boyd was saying something to him. He looked up from his plate, looked up from his thoughts. "What was that?" he said.

"Lost in another one of your fogs, Dave?"

"Just thinking, that's all. Did you ask me something?"

"I asked you if you were going to admit it."

Foxworth blinked at him, confused for a moment because he thought Boyd had somehow read his mind and was talking about admitting to a loss of control. Then he realized it was Kim the man was referring to, the uncertainty of her fate being the reason for his descent into overwork: Boyd still playing his role of lecturer and big brother.

"All right," he said, "I admit it. Does that satisfy you?"

"No. Now you've got to do something about it."

"Like what?"

"Like stop working so damn hard."

Boyd didn't look as though *he* was working so damn hard. He wasn't haggard, he wasn't tense, he wasn't emotionally torn up by the events in Cambodia. He looked fine, in fact, almost as fine as he'd looked after his three weeks of R&R in Tokyo. Along with the other reassignees from Phnom Penh, he had settled into the Thai environment like an eager tourist determined not to act like one—which, Foxworth had learned, was the key to success in the foreign service. Boyd had even found himself a Thai mistress already. His Khmer mistress, Samthan, hadn't come out with him; like Kim, she had chosen to stay behind, in the hope of working with the Khmer Rouge regime. But that didn't seem to matter a great deal to Boyd. He obviously wasn't losing any sleep over Samthan's fate.

Foxworth said, "What would you suggest, Tom? Find myself another woman, get my mind off Kim that way?"

"Well, it might not be such a bad idea, you know."

He could feel the jangling start up inside him. "Don't you ever think about Samthan? Don't you care what might have happened to her? Or still could happen to her?"

"Of course I care," Boyd said. "But there's nothing I can do, is there? Nothing any of us can do. Hell, man, she made her choice, just the way Kim made hers."

"Did she?"

"Now what's that supposed to mean?"

"Did any of those Khmers have a choice to make?" Foxworth asked him. "Or did we make their only real choices for them along about 1970?"

Boyd had been sipping from a glass of milk; he put the glass down carefully and leaned forward. For the first time—he hadn't even had it while he was lecturing—his expression had taken on a certain intensity. "Listen," he said, "I can understand you being upset about Kim, but that's as far as it goes with me. Cambodia itself, the whole business . . . Dave, we just have to put that behind us. And the sooner you realize it and accept it, the better off you'll be."

"Put it behind us? You mean sweep it under the rug."

"I mean put it behind us. We tried, we failed; we did everything for them we could. They didn't want our help."

"No, you're right about that. All they wanted was to be left alone. And all we did was to kill a few hundred thousand of them—"

"That's enough," Boyd said. His voice was still quiet, even, but there was an undercurrent in it like wires of steel.

"It's *not* enough. What would you have us do, Tom? Make believe those reports coming over the border aren't valid?"

"Relief isn't our affair," Boyd said. "Ours is administrative, goddamn it. Let the agencies worry about the refugees."

You tight-assed son of a bitch, Foxworth thought. "And we just keep right on treating it all like a bad dream, right?" he said, making an effort to control the rise of anger. "Nobody died over there in the past five years; nobody's dying over there right now; nobody's going to die over there tomorrow."

"I told you," Boyd said, "that's enough." The steel in his voice had expanded from wires into thick bands. He glanced around, as if to make sure no one else had heard Foxworth's comments. "I don't like that kind of talk and I don't think the people upstairs would like it either."

"Is that a threat? Are you going to put me on report?"

"Not unless you force me to."

Foxworth felt reckless, dangerously so. He wanted to force the issue, all right, see just how much it would take to make Boyd into a snitch. Tell him he was acting like a minor-league Kissinger: pissing in a swamp, then buttoning his pants and walking away. Tell him that maybe they were all too insulated, too rich, too spoiled, and the fact that no living American had ever undergone the ravages of war in his own country had made it impossible for them to understand what war really is; made the Southeast Asia fiasco possible in the first place.

But then, as he stared at Boyd across the table, their eyes locked, reason got hold of him again and chased away the rashness. What good would it do to antagonize Boyd, get himself put on report? The way things were now in the State Department, everybody on edge and oversensitive to criticism, it might even get him transferred out to some post on the opposite side of the world, the Azores or one of those places they sent recalcitrants, screw-ups, and not very promising newcomers. He wouldn't be able to bear that. Here, even with the frustration, he was close to Cambodia, close to Kim, he had access to the intelligence reports and the incoming refugees. Besides, Boyd wasn't his enemy; nobody here was his enemy. Boyd was just a functionary, a product of the system, just as he himself had been and effectively still was. What could you expect from a Nixon-administration foreign service officer except the good old party line? It was *his* line too, wasn't it? Even after Vietnam and Cambodia and the *Mayaguez* incident just two weeks ago, which Boyd thought was a terrific show of force and which he himself, in the privacy of his own head, considered ruthless and unnecessary, even after all of that it *was* still his line too, wasn't it?

He let out a heavy breath. "Okay, Tom, you win—" he said, but that was as far as he got. Somebody had come up and stopped alongside the table, laying his shadow over them. When Foxworth looked up he saw that it was Peter Deighan.

"Mind if I join you?" Deighan asked them.

Boyd glared up at him and said glacially, "As a matter of fact, I do." He got to his feet. "You coming, Dave?"

Foxworth hesitated. Then, because he had had enough of Tom Boyd for the moment, and because he couldn't resist one last little barb, he said, "No, not just yet. I'll see you later."

"Sure." Boyd's expression was accusing now, as if he suspected Foxworth of having cultivated left-wing relationships. "Sure," he said again, and went away into the lobby.

Deighan sat down. He was smiling his crooked cynical way, but it was a different smile than it had been in Phnom Penh: there was no longer any real malice in it. Something had happened to Deighan since the airlift out of Cambodia; he no longer baited embassy employees, or showed up drunk at places or functions they frequented; he had been almost polite in the few glancing dealings Foxworth had had with him; he had even begun to pay attention to his grooming. Maybe it was some sort of aftershock to the whole Cambodian experience. More probably, it was the attractive dark-haired woman— Deighan's wife, he had heard—who had shown up in Bangkok a month or so ago. Whatever, it was a definite improvement over the Peter Deighan he had nearly come to blows with in Le Royal Restaurant.

"Boyd doesn't like me much, does he?" Deighan said as he lighted a cigarette.

"Not very much, no."

"How about you, Foxie?"

"I like you better now than I did in Phnom Penh."

Deighan made a barking sound through his nose. "I like myself better than I did in Phnom Penh. Not much, you understand, but a little."

There was one of those brief, transitionary silences. It occurred to Foxworth, looking across at the other man, that in some ways the Phnom Penh environment had been reconstructed here in Bangkok. The embassy, the villa with its tropical garden, a lot of the same Western faces: Boyd, the other reassignees, Deighan, dozens of other journalists, even a few of the war profiteers and other knaves who had hung around Hotel Le Phnom until the end. The brown Asian faces were Thais instead of Khmers, but they were still brown Asian faces.

Only the sights and the sounds of war were missing. And Kim. And Kim.

"I'll be frank with you," Deighan said. "I'm looking for material, something to base an article on for *Worldview.*"

"You won't get it from me. *Worldview* is a far-left publication; nothing I could tell you would interest their readers."

"Oh come on, Foxie, loosen up a little. *Worldview* is no more left-wing than Teddy Kennedy. Besides, I'm not after polemic this time."

"No? I thought polemic was your stock-in-trade."

"It used to be," Deighan said. "Maybe it still is. But this time I want human interest stuff. People, not politics."

"I still can't help you."

"Sure you can. If you're willing."

"I don't see how."

"I want to do a piece on the relations between Americans and Khmers in Phnom Penh," Deighan said. "Not public relations, all that diplomacy and East-meets-West crap; personal relationships, one-on-one, man-and-woman. Specifically, you and Than Kim."

Foxworth went tight inside; he could feel himself closing off all at once, retreating from what Deighan had just said to him. He said, "No."

"Why not? Look, I know she didn't come out with you and I know you were close and I know you're knocking yourself out trying to get some word on what's happened to her over there."

"No," Foxworth said.

"I won't play up the political angle; I promise you that. Only the human angle. It's the kind of story that should be told, even you've got to admit that. Maybe it'll help make the boys and girls back home understand that it's *people* getting hurt in Southeast Asia, people just like them, on both sides."

"No," Foxworth said.

"I won't even use your name or hers, if you're worried about possible reprisals. Just the basic facts, as much as you're willing to release for publication—"

"No," Foxworth said, "I told you, no," and stood up and went away from Deighan, out of the cafeteria, across the lobby, through the security enclosure, up the stairs to the second floor, into his office. And sat down at his desk and began to shuffle through the reports and copies of cables and prescreening refugee bios, busy-busy, keep his mind occupied, keep his mind off Kim because it hurt too much to think about her and their relationship, he couldn't talk about it to Deighan, he couldn't stand to see it laid down in cold print; it was *his,* it was all he had left. And his superiors at State wouldn't like it, that was another thing. Even if his name wasn't used they'd know it was him—Boyd and too many others from Phnom Penh would keep it from remaining a secret very long. Then he'd be transferred out to the Azores or someplace, just the thing he was afraid of, just the thing that would break the last threads linking him to Kim and Cambodia . . .

Rationalizations.

Good and valid reasons, but rationalizations nonetheless.

Because Deighan was right about the boys and girls back home; right about the people over here being hurt, people on both sides, the human angle. Deighan, the cynical drunk, the belligerent agitator, the flaming liberal who stood for everything Foxworth had stood against his entire adult life—Deighan was one hundred percent right.

Chey Han

On the first of June, Chey Han received orders to immediately transfer part of his battalion from Phnom Penh to Sisophon, in Battambang Province.

No explanation was given for this decision, but Chey sought none. The news gladdened him. In the first place he would be leaving the city, which no longer awed or fascinated but only depressed him, and leaving Ly Sokhon and Phlek Puok and all the chickens as well. He had seen enough of desolate war-torn streets, empty except for his own soldiers searching for barricaded townspeople among the rubble. He had seen enough of chickens herded into trucks with weapons and lies, chickens clucking and squawking and bleeding and dying—not just roosters now but hens, oh many hens, and even some chicks, baby chicks peeping and peeping and lying broken on earth made muddy by rain and blood, oh many chicks. He had seen enough death; now he wished to see life again.

And in the second place, Battambang was a northern province and Sisophon was not all that distant from his home village of Rovieng, in Preah Vihear. He had not had any message contact with Doremy in close to a year, or seen her in close to two, and his yearning for her had become acute in the past month. He had wanted to send word to her ever since the glorious seventeenth of April, tell her he was alive and well, ask her to be patient a while longer—but his duties, the chickens, had kept him from it until just two days ago. Now he would surprise her; instead of sending another message to Rovieng from the capital, he would wait until his arrival in Sisophon, until he could ask permission of Angka to bring Doremy to live with him. Then once more he would hear her call him her Great Ox, feel the warmth of her body and the touch of her hand, see the serenity of her features after they were finished making love. Then he would taste life again, and all the death would be behind him, and together he and Doremy would join in the building of the new Kampuchea.

Chey was in good spirits the following day, June 2, when he and some two hundred of his soldiers left Phnom Penh by truck along Highway 5. But it was not long before his mood changed to match the sky: dark, brooding, swollen with clouds. All along the two-hundred-kilometer route northwest to Sisophon, there were razed villages, the black bones of buildings and trees burned by napalm, sewing machines and electric fans and other Western goods rusting in piles; lines of abandoned howitzers and sometimes overturned automobiles, doors hanging open, tires stripped away to make Ho Chi Minh sandals; ragged bunches of peasants with oxcarts full of meager belongings, being transferred, just as he and his troops were, to another place—all these, and thousands of New and Old people working in the fields, building dikes, cultivating yams, planting the light quick rice called *srauv sral*. Few of them were smiling, happy at their work; this was one thing Chey noticed. And another was their weariness and the pall of fear that seemed to hang over them, that made them look away from the soldiers who watched over them, from the convoy as it passed them by.

There was a sameness to all of them, Chey thought—not just the peasants but the soldiers too. An absence of ambition and desire, of the feelings and simple pursuits which made life good. Was this to be the true outcome of the revolution? Was *this* the future of Kampuchea—all of them trapped together in a joyless reconstruction, sentenced to control and to be controlled, still prisoners in a system no less severe than that of Lon Nol and the Americans?

Disloyal thoughts; dangerous thoughts. Chey tried again to suppress them, as he had tried to suppress his distaste for the slaughter of the chickens. He was not disloyal. He could not have spent five years in the jungles, fighting for Angka, suffering terrible hardships, without loyalty and conviction. The oppressor had to be overthrown or else there would be no peace, no future at all; this he had believed, still believed. But the thoughts came nevertheless. They would not be suppressed, only pushed aside into a corner which seemed to become more and more crowded as the days passed.

Did the fault lie with him or with the Angkar Leu? None of the others appeared to feel as he did. Some, such as Ly Sokhon and Phlek Puok, relished the killing of chickens and the new militaristic order. But that was not so much a result of loyalty as of aberration. Perhaps they could not function at all in a peaceful society; perhaps they needed militarism and butchery and dreams of revolution to sustain them. It would explain Ly Sokhon's dissatisfaction with Angka's reward for her services: a minor position in the Ministry of Commerce, joining her husband, Im Chung, with whom she had been reunited. She had not wanted such a post; she had wished to remain as leader of the *neary*. There could be little doubt that she wished it so she might find further uses for her AK-47 and her Vietnamese sword.

But the rest of the troops went about their work methodically, neither liking it nor disliking it, and spoke in glowing terms of Angka, and believed the revolutionary slogans they heard over Radio Phnom Penh and spoke among themselves. Were they all blind? Had they all been deluded, betrayed by lies, robbed of joy forever by the voices of deceit?

He had no answers; it was too soon for absolute knowledge. He had had his fill of ideology, just as he had had his fill of death. He must take each day as it came, and not allow himself to be robbed of joy. In Sisophon, in his new duties there, he would take life in both his hands again; and with Doremy, there would be happiness such as he had not known before in all his thirty-two years.

When they arrived in Sisophon the following morning he learned the nature of his new duties: military reconnaissance and supervision, and execution of dissidents in Battambang's northwest sector.

Two days after that he learned that Doremy had been dead since late November, when FANK napalm was dropped on the field where she was working outside Rovieng.

Deighan

They had an early dinner, as they often had in the past five weeks, at Chitr Pojana on Sukhumvit Road. Carol liked the atmosphere and the way you had to sit on large pillows on the floor, without your shoes, like in country-style Japanese restaurants back in the States. She had also developed a taste for Thai food, particularly *khao pat,* a fried rice dish flavored with bits of crab, chicken, pork, and saffron, and a shellfish curry that she sprinkled with *nampla* sauce.

That was what they had on this night, sitting cross-legged on the pillows, eating off a low teak table in one of the air-conditioned rooms; not saying much to each other, at least not with words. Her eyes were talking to him again. The shield was still down behind them, he couldn't penetrate that shield, he couldn't see through to the source of that mystifying inner peace of hers, but at least the eyes were no longer silent. It was similar to the way it had been in the early days of their relationship, before they were married, when there was a kind of exciting mixture of strangeness and intimacy between them— knowing each other and yet not knowing each other at all.

Once, while they were eating, she said to him, "You look so different, Peter."

"Different?"

"Than when I came here in April."

"Maybe I am different. A little, anyway."

"Are you happy?"

"Yes," Deighan said, and although it was a lie there was still a budding truth in it. "For the first time in years and I hate myself for it."

"Why?"

"Because of where I've been and what I know and what's happened to what I left behind."

"You couldn't have made any difference," Carol said. "You did all you were able to do."

"I did nothing."

"But you did. You wrote the truth."

"Not enough of the truth."

"Then you'll write it all now," she said. "You're back to work again and as good as you ever were; that last piece you did for *Worldview* was really first-rate. All you needed was some distance and perspective."

"Distance and perspective." He shook his head. "I sat over there and watched Cambodia being systematically sacked and now I'm sitting over here watching the same thing."

"*You* aren't the one who sacked it in either case," Carol said. "You can't take everything personally, Peter."

"I take you personally," he said.

"Good. I'm glad."

He sipped some of his tea, watching her. They never drank anything except tea or coffee, at dinner or at any other time when they were together. Carol wouldn't allow it; she seemed to have developed a phobia against alcohol, or maybe just the smell of it and its effects on him. At first he'd had a difficult time drying out, and the only way he could get through an evening was to think about the drink waiting for him back in his hotel room. But then, gradually, the evenings had grown less uncomfortable, and he hadn't needed several shots or even one to put him to sleep at night. The desire to humiliate himself in front of her went away; the pain of being with her went away. The need to be drunk in order to face her and their marriage went away.

He had even cut down on his drinking on those days when he wasn't seeing Carol, two or three days a week now, where it had been three or four up until mid-May. It hadn't been his idea to space out their dates; he would have seen her more often, every day if she'd allowed it. But she thought it would be good for their new relationship if they didn't saturate themselves with each other.

Not saturating themselves included not sleeping together, and that was the hardest thing of all he'd had to contend with—much harder than not drinking. He had wanted her with a kind of self-contemptuous lust at first, the way he'd wanted the whores in Phnom Penh and here in Bangkok: sack her and them and himself the way Cambodia had been sacked. Then he had wanted *her*, Carol, his wife, with a desire that went beyond lust. Now his need had shifted again to a sort of wistful desperation; just looking at her, feeling her eyes on him, remembering how it had been for them in the past, made him ache inside.

But she kept saying no. She had moved out of the Victory Hotel because it was too expensive, and rented a little bungalow off Issraphard Road, on the west side of the Chao Phraya River; she seemed to have a little money (although she always let him pay when they went out) and wouldn't discuss where she'd got it. From renting the house in California, maybe; it didn't matter. What mattered was that after every date she kissed him once, more chastely than anything else, and said good night to him at the door. He hadn't even seen the inside of that bungalow yet. "It's too soon," she kept saying. "Peter, don't you think I want you too? But it's too soon, we aren't ready to take that step yet."

This wasn't the Carol he knew. The Carol he knew had balled him twenty-four hours after they first met, and always approached sex with the same clinical intensity with which Henry frigging Kissinger approached the idea of military force. But the Carol he knew didn't have a shield behind her eyes, or a glow of serenity, or would have come chasing halfway around the world just so she could go out on dates three times a week like a college frosh. This Carol was a stranger in the old Carol's body. This Carol made him feel angry, frustrated, inept, silly, strong, weak, tender. This Carol kept him from drinking, kept him away from the whores in spite of her refusal to sleep with him, kept him from thinking about suicide, and even gave him a certain impetus to work again on a regular schedule. He didn't know why he was willing to go on playing this game of hers, but he was. And not under so much protest anymore, either.

When they were done with dinner she spent several minutes chattering and laughing with their Thai waiters. They liked her, you could see that, and she liked them. Genuinely. There was no trace of the xenophobia he had always intuited in her; if the Carol he knew had ever had it, this new Carol had shed it somewhere in the past year. The waiters were so delighted with her, in fact, that with smiles and gestures they pushed back two of the baht Deighan laid out for them because they said he'd overpaid. Which was unprecedented in Bangkok, but then, just about everything that had happened since Carol's arrival had been unprecedented.

They went out and walked along the river for a time. It had been raining when they entered Chitr Pojana, but the sky had cleared now, at sunset, and the heat-heavy air had an almost dazzling clarity. In the distance the crenellated white walls of the Grand Palace seemed to have an ice-cream pink glow, and the yellow tiles and bits of colored glass imbedded in its roofs and towers glittered like precious stones. Deighan looked at the palace, and at the rest of the city's mosaic spread out on both sides of the river, and let the sounds wash over him—automobile horns, boat horns, bicycle bells, temple bells, Asian and Western music, the ribald voices of actors in a nearby *likay* theater, the singsong voices of Thai monks begging alms and food. And he thought that if Vietnam and Cambodia were places of enclosure, places of fire and death and the slow sealing off of self, then Bangkok had become an opening, a place in which he might be able to recover the man he had once been. That man had been a true believer; he'd thought he could help to change the shape of the world. In the last few years his conviction had been leeched away, along with most of his desire, by too much exposure to the ravages of war, but here with Carol he could hear the faint soulsong of purpose again. It was far off, almost an echo, but still he could hear it. It was Carol, of course, who had made it happen—the new Carol, the one who believed there was something to be salvaged between them. Believing and making him believe too, on a night like this, strolling along the river with the musical-comedy sights and colors and sounds all around them.

They walked without touching, and later, after they had haggled out an agreeable fare with the driver, they sat without touching in the taxi that took them across the river to Issraphard Road. Deighan told the driver to wait while he saw Carol up to the door of her bungalow, as he always did. The porch was shaded by an acacia tree and very dark, and there was the scent of frangipani in the muggy air, and he felt the ache well up inside him again when he kissed her. Well up and then spill over into words that came out of him unbidden once they stepped apart from each other.

"I love you, Carol," he said.

She was silent. In the darkness he couldn't see her face; but he felt her eyes on him, the flutter of her breath against his cheek. Then she reached up and traced the curve of his mouth, gently, with the tips of her fingers.

"Tell the taxi driver he can go, Peter," she said. "You can stay with me tonight; I want you to stay."

When he went into the bungalow with her he kissed her again in the dark, once more after she put the lights on, and she smiled and talked to him with her eyes, and it was then he understood why she hadn't let him sleep with her before, why she was going to let him stay tonight and all the nights from now on.

She had been waiting for him to tell her he loved her.

Cambodia File: Column by Jack Anderson, June 4, 1975

Washington—What has happened to more than three million Cambodians who were driven out of their city homes into the hinterland by the conquering communists?

This is the great mystery of Southeast Asia.

The United States, with all its intelligence resources, has been unable to find out. The communists have hermetically sealed Cambodia so that almost no information leaks out.

Aerial photographs have established only that the cities have been emptied. The marketplaces, which used to be teeming, are now virtually deserted.

The communists have shut down almost all their broadcasts, so the Central Intelligence Agency has intercepted few messages that shed any light on the displaced population. There are also no travelers coming out of Cambodia for the CIA to debrief.

In CIA jargon, the agency has "no assets" left in Cambodia. The analysts can merely make agonizing guesses as to what has happened to the three million men, women and children.

For many, the sudden exodus must have been a death march. The aged and the ailing probably didn't survive the trek. Patients were even cleared out of the hospitals and herded into the hinterland with the rest.

So far as is known, there also aren't enough food stocks in the backwoods to feed the masses from the cities. Analysts believe that hundreds of thousands will die of starvation. One shocking estimate is that at least a million people will perish.

It appears that the Khmer Rouge, as the Cambodian communists call themselves, may be guilty of genocide against their own people. Certainly, the ruthless uprooting of three million people is an act out of the dark ages.

Yet no one—not the United Nations, not the Red Cross, not an individual nation—has called upon the Cambodian authorities for an accounting . . .

Natalie

She read the Anderson column on the Fifth Avenue bus, on the way from her apartment to the Refugee Relief Fund offices on West Twenty-ninth Street. It enraged her, particularly the paragraph which accused no one, not the United Nations nor the Red Cross nor a single individual nation, of demanding an accounting from the Cambodian authorities. Why were all those bloody fools so complacent, so blind? They knew what was going on over there, just as she knew it and Jack Anderson knew it. Why did they keep on ignoring the truth? How *could* they keep on ignoring it?

The rage was something new for her. She had always been angry, but it had been a low-key anger, a small flame burning beneath passion and purpose, even beneath frustration. But ever since early May it had flared up into a genuine all-encompassing fury. She was furious all the time now, and with each day that passed without anything being done about Cambodia, about the refugees who were already in Thailand, the flame burned hotter and brighter and began to consume everything in its path.

It had been a pair of news stories in the New York *Times* that first kindled the rage. The first dealt with a charter flight from the Utapao camp in Thailand to El Topo, California, arranged by the International Committee for European Migration and carrying the last of the 850 Cambodian refugees brought to Utapao by American evacuation ships and planes. The second story had to do with Lon Nol, the deposed head of the Khmer Republic, who had been given red-carpet treatment by the State Department on his arrival in Hawaii and who was being put up in plush quarters at Hickam Field by the U. S. Air Force, while a special team worked to find him a new home in Oahu's Diamond Head area.

How many refugees, she'd thought, could have been resettled in the United States using just the money which was being spent to resettle Lon Nol? A hell of a lot more than eight hundred and fifty, that was for sure. And if you took all the money Lon Nol was supposed to have been paid as a buy-off by the CIA—a million dollars, one political acquaintance of her father's had estimated—and all the money Lon Nol himself had allegedly smuggled out of Cambodia . . . how many refugees could you resettle with that? Eight thousand and fifty? Eighty thousand and fifty?

But no, not a penny had been allotted by the government for refugee relief. Since the beginning of the year the United States had directed thought to the plight of the Khmer people on only three futile occasions: January 27, when the Study Mission for the Refugee Subcommittee of the Senate Judiciary Committee met to discuss the humanitarian problems in South Vietnam and Cambodia—two years after the cease-fire in Vietnam and a year and a half after the halt of bombing in Cambodia; February 24, when the Supplemental Assistance to Cambodia hearings were held before a subcommittee of the Senate Foreign Relations Committee; March 13, with the Military and Economic Situation in Cambodia Staff Survey Report for the House Committee on Foreign Affairs. And nothing substantive since. Committees, subcommittees, survey reports, study missions. Zero accomplished, and all the while people were dying and being displaced in wholesale lots.

She had grown to maturity under a certain set of assumptions: you accepted the policies of your government, you assumed that the government of the United States was at least trying to perform in a benign fashion. But now she was having second thoughts; a whole new set of assumptions had opened up to her. That the government as it was being run and had been run from the Johnson administration to the present one was no longer benign; that put to a hard choice, these administrations had always seemed to have chosen the worst possible course of action; that the government of today was as much an enemy of the American people as any foreign power. And this didn't make her a communist or a traitor to the flag, either, as the Nixon boys might have accused. She loved this country as much as anyone, in some ways maybe more. No, it only made her an American who was enraged at all the injustice being perpetrated and condoned by the politicians she and the rest of the nation, God help them, had put into office as their elected representatives.

Natalie brooded the rest of the way downtown on the bus, on the short walk west on Twenty-ninth Street to the Fund offices. By the time she entered the small office in the large building, the fury was like something lodged just under her Adam's apple, so that she could barely answer when one of the volunteer workers, Mrs. Edmonds, said hello to her. There were three other volunteers on duty, and the phones were moderately busy, and Mrs. Edmonds said that they had just received a five-thousand-dollar pledge from a wealthy matron in Larchmont; but none of this did much for Natalie's mood, or for the knot of rage in her throat. Spitting into a fire, that's all the Fund and the other independent relief organizations were doing. Just spitting into a damned *holocaust*.

Her father was in his cubicle at the rear; she could see him in there, talking on the phone, through an open doorway. She went in and sat down in the old wooden armchair across his desk, to wait for him to finish.

He was talking to someone in Washington about the refusal of the new communist regime in Cambodia to accept outside assistance of any kind. Their leaders said it would be an interference in their domestic affairs and might have an adverse effect on Cambodia's independence and sovereignty. They had even turned down an offer from UNICEF to help the Khmer children, saying that "Our Angka has everything it needs." Monsters, Natalie thought as she listened. We're culpable and foolish and uncaring, there's no excuse for us—but the Khmer

Rouge are evil. What kind of government refuses to accept food and medical supplies for its children? What kind of ideology condones genocide against its own people?

When he replaced the telephone receiver Abraham Rosen wore his characteristic nonexpression. "You look grim, Natalie," he said.

"That's because I feel grim."

He sighed. "It's an old, old story," he said. "It's the oldest story in the world. Men think and men lie and men make war; and it's the children who suffer."

"There's no hope for a massive airlift into Cambodia, is there."

"I'm afraid not."

"Or for the UN to take any action."

"It doesn't look that way."

"Or for Congress to pass a relief bill."

"Natalie . . ."

"Or for the Thai government and ours to get together on a coordinated aid program."

Her father picked up one of his pipes and tapped the bit against his front teeth. "You're leading up to something, Natalie. What is it?"

"I want to go back to Thailand," she said.

Silence for a moment. Then he asked, "Why?"

"Because I can't stand to stay around here any longer, doing nothing and watching nothing being done. I'm not needed here; but I am needed over there."

"In the camps, you mean?"

"Yes. And maybe I can do some good in Bangkok, too—see some of the people I met in February, try to get something accomplished on the Thai end."

"Are you certain this is what you want?"

"I'm certain."

"When do you propose to leave?"

"As soon as possible. As soon as it can be arranged."

Another silence while her father lighted his pipe. Natalie thought that he was going to try to talk her out of it; that he would deliver another of his warnings that caring too much was almost as dangerous to their purpose as caring too little. But he said only, "I don't suppose any objections I might have would change your mind."

"No, Papa, not this time."

"Then if you feel it's what you must do, you have my blessings."

She stood and went around behind the desk and kissed him on the forehead. And as she did so she thought that David Foxworth was in Bangkok and that he was certainly one of the people she would see when she got there. Not that that had anything whatsoever to do with her decision to return to Thailand. David Foxworth was incidental, if not irrelevent. Of course he was.

Wasn't he?

Kim

One day in the commune is like any other day, like all days in what has become her life: it passes with a terrible, enervating, monotonous slowness, and blends into tomorrow, and the to-tomorrows blend into weeks, and the weeks blend into months . . .

0500 hours. The gong awakens them and they rise in the hot damp darkness of the cabin, file out under the watchful eyes of the Khmer Rouge. No one speaks; everyone is afraid to speak, even in the cabins. There are fewer soldiers now—many have been transferred elsewhere, or shed their weapons and uniforms and mounted tractors to cultivate the rice paddies, the fields of fast-growing yams and sweet potatoes—but the commune is full of *chhlop,* those who spy for the Angkar in return for favored treatment, and even the most innocent comment can be overheard and become distorted in the retelling. Many of the *chhlop* are children; the KC indoctrinates them to spy on their parents and other elders, and succeed often because of hunger and privation. Some people have been warned for voicing complaints, for expressing anti-Khmer Rouge sentiments. Others, whose complaints and sentiments were deemed subversive, have been "sent to the Angkar Leu."

Serey stays close to her, as she always does in the morning and evening hours. During the day, now, they are separated by the rules of the commune. While Kim and the other women work at planting rice and yams and building dikes, and the men cut trees and form teams to pull the oxless plows, the children toil together under constant supervision, at a steady stream of small chores and handicraft projects. The child is pathetically thin, even though her belly remains distended, and her cough has not gone away; the skin on her arms and legs is flecked with scabs, there are abcesses on her neck, a patch of her hair has fallen out. She says almost nothing anymore, to Kim or to anyone else. She has retreated inside herself, into a child's fantasy world, perhaps, or the world she once knew in her native village. And her eyes are as empty as those of the Khmer Rouge soldiers.

Kim, too, has grown thin and suffers from back spasms, cramps, and aching joints. Vitamin deficiency. Protein deficiency. Calcium deficiency. They were not permitted any of the first crop of yams and sweet potatoes; these were trucked away to an unknown destination. They have never been given meat or fish or *prahoc* to eat. They are allowed two meals per day, and each consists of a blackish soup which the Khmer Rouge taught them how to make: rice, green bananas, white maize, the water plant *tracuon,* and banana stems cut into thin strips. At first the KC laughed and said, "You are pigs; you must be pigs because you eat the food of swine." Now they no longer laugh. No one laughs in the commune anymore; Kim has not heard the sound of laughter for many weeks.

But there is more than enough meat and fish for the Khmer Rouge, who consume these items with open taunting relish. Some of the people were able to barter with the communists in the early days, trading gold damleungs and other valuables which they had managed to conceal for extra rice, fish paste, and other rations; now, however, no one has anything left to barter with. The choice is either to become a *kang chhlop,* which is not so easy or safe because the Khmer Rouge mistrust the motives of everyone and have sent *chhlop* as well as non-collaborators to the Angkar Leu, or merely sufferers like Kim and Serey.

0530 hours. Together with the other women, Kim trudges out into the paddies a half kilometer from the commune to plant rice seedlings in the first muddy light of dawn. She has no thoughts as she walks; she has been transformed into a creature virtually without thought by day, without the will for anything other than obedience and a kind of numb survival. It is only at night that she allows herself to think and to pray to the Lord Buddha, and then in small careful rations, as the Khmer Rouge ration their food.

A few of the other women have bags slung over their shoulders, and their eyes are cast downward as they shuffle along the mud levees between the seedbeds. Ever since the rains came and the rivers and streams overflowed their banks, flooding the paddies, it has become possible to find frogs, freshwater snails, fat beetles, paddy crabs. Kim has no bag, but if she sees a frog or snail or beetle, and if none of the KC supervisors is too near, she will make the effort to capture it for Serey. But she will not pick up a paddy crab. Their flesh has no blood and she knows that if the child eats it, it will give her boils instead of nourishment.

0800 hours. The rice shoots in the seedbeds are bright green and glisten luminously in the early sunshine, as if glowing with an inner light. She takes no notice of the color, the luminosity; she only carries the seedlings from the beds to the flooded paddies where she will transplant them later in the day. Like the other women, she moves slowly and is learning how to steal moments of rest, little lapses into unconsciousness between strides. She has not quite learned the whole secret of it yet but she will. She will.

0940 hours. The sound of shots comes from beyond a patch of forest which has been left standing between the paddies and the commune. Kim does not look up, does not stop working. Neither does anyone else.

1100 hours. The two-hour midday break begins. The sky has

turned the color of molten lead and the heat is intense, dripping with moisture; but there is no shade, no cool place to rest. In the early days she and the others went into the forest to forage for bark, leaves, fruit, gecko lizards, and to escape the lambent rays of the sun. Now they are too exhausted, too listless, to make the effort.

One of the soldiers stations himself near her and watches as she eats her milk tin of rice gruel, prepared the night before. He does this every day and has for some time. He is short and muscular, with a round bulbous head and large crooked teeth which protrude when he opens his mouth. He reminds Kim of a rabbit—but a hungry rabbit, a predator. At first she thought he suspected her of some transgression and sought to catch her at it. Then she came to understand that he finds her attractive and stations himself as he does so he can admire her. When he comes close enough she can see the sexual desire squatting naked in his eyes.

But he has never spoken to her except as a soldier to a prisoner of war. It is forbidden for the Khmer Rouge to have sexual relations with the *opakar* under their charge; they are only allowed to marry other Khmer Rouge, or to bring wives and brides from Old Villages—those long liberated by the KC—to live with them. Among the people themselves, no one is allowed to show affection or to talk of love. Sex is forbidden except between married couples, and then only by special permission; if a woman, married or not, becomes pregnant without permission, it is grounds for her and her husband or lover to be sent to the Angkar Leu.

1300 hours. The dark-purple clouds churn across the sky, creating the eerie light of early afternoon, forming intricate shapes. As a child Kim would play the game of studying monsoon clouds, identifying their shapes as those of birds and animals. Now they all look the same to her, like a herd of a single creature: they all look like dragons.

She is standing knee-deep in one of the flooded paddies, planting the rice shoots, when the rains begin. But neither the paddy water nor the rain offers any respite from the heat; both are warm and flow and beat against her skin with a sameness which is as monotonous and enervating as the days themselves. She leans forward, pushes one of the shoots into the mud, pinches it firmly in place. Takes a step, leans forward, pushes one of the shoots into the mud, pinches it firmly in place. The agony in her back is acute, but she does not vary the rhythm of her movements. Again she practices stealing moments of unconsciousness between strides.

1530 hours. A middle-aged Chinese comes running along the dike path from the direction of the yam fields. He has an armload of yams and he is screaming what might be obscenities in his native tongue; it is obvious to Kim that he has gone mad and stolen the yams. Behind him two guards emerge, neither of them armed, and shout for assistance from the ones supervising the paddies.

Kim straightens and stands watching. The other women do the same. They have nothing to fear at the moment; the eyes of Angka are all on the Chinese.

As he runs screaming through the rain, at an angle to where she is, Kim recognizes him: he is the one who complained about the lack of food after their arrival and has been made to work with excrement as his punishment. Sanitary conditions are poor at the commune; everyone uses open trenches for the elimination of body waste. Each day the Chinese digs new trenches, and when he is finished digging he transfers feces into the fields to be used as fertilizer. He is given no tools for this except a hoe and a pair of buckets; he lives part of every day with his hands in feces, with feces all around him, with the smell of feces clinging to him like a thin layer of cloth. Kim is not surprised that he has finally gone mad. Others have gone mad just working in the fields; the Chinese has had a great deal of strength to last this long before releasing his hold on sanity.

The Khmer Rouge guards catch him and begin beating him with their hands and with hoe handles. Kim looks away. She knows the Chinese is dead now; even if the guards do not beat him to death, he is dead. She leans forward, pushes one of the shoots into the mud, pinches it firmly in place while the rain hammers down in thin gray sheets against the agonized curve of her back.

1700 hours. Kim and the other women leave the field and trudge back through the forest to the commune. The soldier who looks like a rabbit watches her with his hungry eyes as she passes, but still says nothing to her. He is one of the guards who beat the Chinese, one of those who used a hoe handle.

1800 hours. The rain has stopped for the day, but the air continues to drip moisture; Kim can hear it on the thatched roof of the cabin as she and Serey and the other family that shares it weave baskets and make rope. There is no free time in the commune, no time for anyone except Angka. When they are not working in the fields they must "keep our hands busy in order to rebuild our history."

1900 hours. Kim washes herself and Serey with water from their waist-high jar, then prepares the evening meal on the cookstove—stones arranged on a bed of ashes, a gap in the eaves above acting as an outlet for the smoke. This is one of those rare days when the KC has permitted them a small amount of salt with which to flavor their rice; Kim mixes it in carefully. She has no snails or beetles or frogs for Serey, but the child does not ask for anything more than what she is given. The pupils of her eyes are as black as night, as hollow as hope. She coughs repeatedly now and Kim is fearful of tuberculosis. One of the Khmer Rouge wives gives the child a small cup of herb tea mixed with Pepsi-Cola, offers an incantation of protective magic as Serey drinks. This, she says, will cure the child's ailment. She is quite serious about this; she believes what she says.

1930 hours. They return to their weaving and rope-making. On nights when the moon is full they are sent out into the fields and paddies again to work until 2300; on this night there is only a slivered crescent moon, and faint starlight broken up by clouds, so it is too dark to plant rice shoots or harvest yams or build new dikes. Later, the guards have told them, there will be lanterns and field lights so that they may work well past midnight, perhaps all night long. Kim does not know if this is a lie to taunt them or the truth. She prays it is like all else with the servants of Angka: a lie.

2100 hours. The nightly propaganda and indoctrination

218

meeting. The head of the commune, the Khmer Rouge administrator, has a radio which he plays for them over loudspeakers when they are all assembled. The program broadcast each night over Radio Phnom Penh seldom varies: revolutionary music and slogans, interspersed with detailed reports of projects under way in different regions.

The slogans are always the same. "We must rely on our own strength, take our own destiny in our hands, to achieve independence-sovereignty." And "We used to rely on the sun or on nature alone to grow rice, but now we must control the water throughout the year, in dry and rainy seasons alike; we cannot become masters of our fate unless our struggle against nature is victorious." And "We must hasten to build dikes and canals, and clear the forest to increase the amount of land for rice-growing. The land must not be allowed to remain unproductive."

The detailed reports are always the same. Numbers of dams, canals, reservoirs, ponds, wells being built; their lengths and widths, depths and heights; how many cubic meters of earth have been displaced, or hectares irrigated or cleared of forest. Nothing is ever said of what is happening in Phnom Penh or in the world outside Kampuchea. There is no world outside Kampuchea. There are only slogans and music and statistics and exhortations, and fatigue-numbed minds to be assaulted with them, and the ghosts of children and of a madman beaten to death because he could not bear to work all day with his hands in feces.

After the radio is switched off at 2200 the KC administrator delivers his lecture on communism as the only alternative to the dacadent oppression of the West. It is the same lecture every night, almost word for word; Kim thinks that the administrator has had it engraved upon his brain cells, as if they were the grooves of a phonograph record. Communism is good, imperialism is corrupt. Communism is the savior of the people, the capitalists are their destroyer. There are CIA spies still operating within the country, he tells them, but they will soon be uncovered and sent to the Angkar Leu. Anyone who thinks subversive thoughts, anyone who complains too much about his lot, anyone who disobeys the rules, he says, is either a pro-Western spy or a potential recruit and sooner or later will feel the wrath of Angka. Then, over and over, he repeats the word *samuhaphiep*—unite. And over and over they must repeat it with him.

Unite. Unite. Unite.

In death, Kim thinks each night. Unite in death.

2315 hours. She lies in the darkness of the cabin, the odor of sweat and earth thick in her nostrils, Serey's warmth against her hip. These are the only minutes of the day, the ones before sleep, which belong to her. They are the only minutes in which she allows herself prayer and open thought, and the true spirit of Than Kim to emerge battered but still whole from the inner cell where it is caged.

The first thing she does is pray to the Lord Buddha for salvation. The first thing she thinks of is escape. The Vietnamese border can be no more than forty kilometers from the commune, and it would be simple enough for her to slip away in the night. But she will not leave Serey; she cannot. And the child is not strong enough to travel such a distance, nor is Kim strong enough to carry her. Besides, how would they eat? How would they avoid the Khmer Rouge patrols? How would they cross the border when they came to it? The soldiers have told them that all of the frontier is mined and heavily guarded and that anyone attempting to cross it will be killed. It is possible that this, too, is a lie, but Kim does not think so. Sealing the borders seems certain to have been an early priority of the Angkar Leu.

So she cannot escape, at least not now, not on this night. Therefore she must survive another twenty-four hours. Therefore she must think of life, take out the small good memories and examine them one by one—the laughter of children at play, the music made by the xylophone called *roneat-ek,* the outer galleries of the temple of Angkor Wat and their vast bas-reliefs displaying the entire ancient history of Kampuchea, the shape of the monsoon clouds when they were all bears and elephants and cats instead of dragons, the smile on Charoun's face when she told him she would become his wife, the first touch of his

220

hand and the first touch of his lips on her breast. These, and more, many more until the spirit, revitalized, returns to its cage and she begins to drift away on the darkness.

Midnight. And sleep . . . so that she can be torn from it by the gong in five short hours and it can all begin again.

One day in the commune is like any other day, like all days in what has become her life: it passes with a terrible, enervating, monotonous slowness, and blends into tomorrow, and the tomorrows blend into weeks, and the weeks blend into months . . .

Ly Sokhon

The long-awaited day of her reunion with Pol Pot did not arrive until late August.

He had been in Phnom Penh since some time after the glorious seventeenth of April, just as she had, but he had been busy with Khieu Samphan, Ieng Sary, and the others in the hierarchy of the Angkar Leu—too busy establishing the new proletarian government to meet with a minor official in the Ministry of Commerce who wished to see him. Not that she was bitter about this. She was not bitter. She understood the more pressing demands on his time; he was, after all, the Premier of Democratic Kampuchea. And yet she was anxious, disappointed at the refusals which met each of her requests for an audience. Could he not find a few minutes for her, in honor of all they had shared at 17 Rue la Cepede, Place Mouffetard, when his name was Saloth Sar and the liberation of Kampuchea only his dream?

She had seen him once, in July, after a meeting at the Ministry of Information. Just a glimpse, but it had been enough to set up tremors of excitement within her. He had not changed a great deal since Paris; he was heavier, his face rounder and lined with the long years of revolutionary struggle, but the way his hair seemed to jut from his head like spikes was the same, and the fire in his eyes was the same, and she thought shame-lessly that the fire in his loins would be the same as well. If there had still been a fire in her own loins, or if it was possible for one to be rekindled, she would have matched the flames of Pol Pot's passion with flames of her own, as she had during the long pulsing nights at 17 Rue la Cepede.

But there was none of the loin fire left from her youth. She had been reunited with her husband, Im Chung, in early May—Im Chung but not Saloth Sar—and on the night of the first day he had sought to possess her body. She had been repelled, and had repelled him. He was a stranger to her, a dried-up fish of a man, with hands cold and damp and eyes that bulged and sel-dom blinked. She did not know him after three years, nor did she want to know him. She could not even imagine why she had married him. Pol Pot was better known to her, more cherished, after twenty-five years than Im Chung after three. They lived together, but they did not sleep together and spent no time in each other's company except for their duties at the Ministry of Commerce and Party meetings.

When she was not working for Angka she prowled Phnom Penh alone and took pleasure in its emptiness, in the way it had been picked clean like the bones of a slaughtered calf. Not only had all the people been eliminated from its streets and buildings, so had all the symbols of decadent imperialism: money, religion, books, formal education, telephone service, postal system. And yet she felt vaguely dissatisfied. The cities still stood, still existed—monuments of the filth and corruption she had spent her years in the jungle fighting to destroy. They were breeding grounds for the poisonous insects of subversion; they gave off waves of fetor which would, she was convinced, pollute anyone if he exposed himself to it long enough. If she had had her way she would leave Phnom Penh at once and order it razed to the ground, so that the earth hidden now be-neath buildings and asphalt and concrete could be reclaimed and made productive for the good of the People. No one should live in the cities, least of all the leaders of Angka. Least of all Pol Pot. What if the corruption of Phnom Penh should pollute *him* one day?

The possibility was unthinkable; she thought it no more. But with each new day her hatred for the city grew and made her restless with the need to get away from it, relocate herself in the countryside, join the People in mastering and purifying the land. There were still spies among the New population, still American collaborators and sympathizers, still FANK and GKR personnel masquerading as peasants; she could help to unmask and destroy them, if she were not shackled to a task she did not want in a place that repelled her as much as Im Chung's cold damp fishlike hands. She would enjoy executing more of the enemy. She would enjoy using her Vietnamese sword—she had kept it honed and polished and had hung it on the wall near her bed, where she could look on it often—and watching the blood of more traitors flow in rivers as long as the Mekong, as wide as the Tonle Sap. This was the task she was suited for. This was the task she longed for.

Her hatred and her restlessness had become acute by late August, when the latest of her requests for an audience with Pol Pot was granted. When her initial excitement ebbed she thought that she must tell him how she felt about the cities, ask him to let her leave Phnom Penh. "I do not belong here," she would say to him. "Perhaps none of us belongs here. The cities are corrupt and if we do not destroy them we ourselves might be corrupted. We must not become what we despise. Remember how this was our fear in Paris in the days of our youth? Remember our discussions of how the revolutionary must never reenact the ways of the barbaric oppressor but must create anew?"

He would understand the force of her argument. Dialectically she was inferior to no one except him and perhaps Khieu Samphan and Ieng Sary. His eyes would gleam with understanding and insight, as they had at 17 Rue la Cepede, and he would give her permission to go into the countryside to search for the hidden enemy. Perhaps he would even come himself, relocate the government structure on the land where it belonged. Perhaps he would order Phnom Penh razed immediately and she would be allowed to watch its demolition. There would be passion in her loins then. Passion would sear her at the sight of Phnom Penh reduced to rubble.

She slept little the night before she was to see him. And arrived thirty minutes early at an office in the Foreign Ministry where the meeting would take place. Neither Pol Pot nor any of the other leaders had a fixed headquarters, and most of the administrative buildings of the bandit Lon Nol regime were empty; it was a precaution against assassination attempts by the spies and lackeys of the American CIA and the deposed GKR. Her credentials were checked by an assistant and she was made to wait in a guarded anteroom until the appointed hour. Then, without ceremony, she was ushered into the presence of the Premier.

He sat behind a desk flanked by the national flag and by the red Party flag with its hammer and yellow reaping hook in the middle. He was gazing straight ahead, his hands folded together, and as soon as she saw him it was as though a quarter of a century had fallen away. Even up close he looked little different than he had in Paris: still quiet, introspective, his eyes full of fire. The only difference was that some of the intensity of expression had been smoothed over and in its place was the calm assurance of the victor—the look of one who has become that version of himself which he had always dreamed of being. He wore traditional black pajamas, as she did, to demonstrate his alliance with the People, but anyone who looked on him could tell that he was not a peasant. No, a brilliant revolutionary, a great leader, the head of Democratic Kampuchea and the vanquisher of the running dogs and parasites of the enemy.

Ly Sokhon felt herself trembling inside. There was a stirring in her loins as well, the first such stirring in many years; in that moment she thought fleetingly of Pol Pot's wife, Khieu Ponnary, and the bitterness of hatred spiced her pleasure at seeing him again.

She raised her arms and said in a voice hoarse with feeling, "Saloth Sar."

His eyes fixed on her; his face remained impassive. "I am Pol Pot," he said.

"Yes. But in Paris, in the days of our youth, you were Saloth Sar."

A silence. "What do you know of Paris, Comrade?"

"What do I know of it? You cannot mean that."

"I do mean it. Who are you?"

"I am Ly Sokhon, of course."

"Do you expect me to know you, Mit Ly?"

The sensual stirrings and all her excitement vanished. Confusion gripped her. What manner of reunion was this? What sort of strange dialogue?

"Have I changed so much?" she asked him. "Look beneath the wrinkles of my skin; the woman who lived with you at 17 Rue la Cepede, the woman who shared your dreams and your passions, is still visible."

He seemed to stiffen. "I know of no such woman," he said. "Why have you requested this meeting? What is it you want?"

"To see you again, to talk with you of Paris—"

"I will say once more and for the final time that I do not know you. Now state your business. Have you come on a matter concerning the Ministry of Commerce?"

The confusion had shifted to something else, something with impact: she felt stunned. Her head wobbled from side to side, answering *No* to his question.

"Then you must leave," Pol Pot said. "There is much to be done. I have no time for foolish reminiscences, no taste for the past. The present and the future are all that matter to the revolutionary Angkar."

Her mind would not coordinate itself. She wanted to blurt out to him that she did not belong in Phnom Penh, none of them did, the city was evil, it was a nest for poisonous insects, it must be razed to the ground and she must be returned to the land to search out the hidden enemies and make their blood flow in rivers as long as the Mekong, as wide as the Tonle Sap. Instead she found herself backing away from him, turning, fleeing the office. Fleeing into the empty hateful contaminated streets of the city.

And through the daze inside her mind thoughts thudded and bounced like hurled rocks. Why had he done this to her? Why had he lied about not remembering her and the nights in Paris? It was only a quarter of a century ago, he could not have forgotten her or her name, he could not have forgotten the heights to which the flames of their passion had soared. That he no longer had a taste for the past was hardly an excuse for his refusal to acknowledge her. Why had he lied? Why?

The answer came to her later that day, after she returned to her post at the Ministry of Commerce. It came to her in the form of a question, but she sensed with rising horror that it must be true—the unthinkable must be true.

What if the city's corruption *had already* polluted Pol Pot, Saloth Sar, the leader of Democratic Kampuchea, and made him that which he had always despised?

Cambodia File: U.S. Intelligence Report, September 10, 1975 (Top Secret)

Phnom Penh gave Prince Sihanouk and his party a festive welcome when they arrived in the Cambodian capital yesterday.

The Prince was accompanied by Deputy Prime Minister Khieu Samphan. Deputy Prime Minister for National Defense Son Sen delivered the welcoming address.

The Khmer communists apparently have been trying for some time to entice Sihanouk to return. The invitation, tendered to the Prince when he was in Pyongyang in mid-July, evidently was not the first one offered him. Although Sihanouk has dutifully served as a mouthpiece for the communists since their takeover in mid-April, the Cambodian leadership is well aware of his record of unpredictable behavior and probably wants to have more control over his actions. They may also have been concerned about the Prince's earlier reported threats to renounce his title and go into permanent exile abroad, from where he could snipe at regime politics.

The Prince's current visit to Phnom Penh will be short. He will return to China to attend the National Day celebrations on October 1, then travel to New York to address the UN General Assembly. From New York, he will go to Pyongyang for the anniversary of the Korean Workers' Party on October 10, and finally return to Peking to commemorate his birthday on October 31. Following this round of travel, Sihanouk may be resigned to spending most of his time in Phnom Penh.

The communists appear to have assuaged the Prince's earlier fears for his personal safety. According to a recent clandestine report, a member of Sihanouk's staff has stated that the communists assured the Prince he would be able to leave Cambodia if he chose. He was also told that he could live in the Royal Palace compound and be provided with a staff. Nevertheless, he knows that, once back in Phnom Penh, his future role and lifestyle will be determined by the communist leadership. When the Prince reportedly said recently that he would spend a "good deal" of time in Peking and Pyongyang in the future, Khieu Samphan replied that the place for the Cambodian head of state was in Cambodia.

Sihanouk's decision to return to the inhospitable political climate in Phnom Penh was a difficult one, but he apparently decided that the trappings of high office, at least for a while, are better than obscure retirement abroad. He has, in fact, little leverage in dealing with the Khmer communists.

Foxworth

On the tenth of September Foxworth left Bangkok for an extended tour of the refugee camps in southern and western Thailand—Trat, at the southernmost tip, across the border from Boi Russey in Cambodia's Cardamom mountain range; Aranyaprathet, opposite Poipet in Battambang Province; and Prasat and Surin, above the frontier of Oddar Mean Chey Province. These camps had been established for some time, since before the Khmer Rouge takeover, but were now beginning to expand with the small but steady stream of refugees flowing out of Cambodia. He had visited each of them before, briefly, in late May and again in July—and had come to Aranyaprathet in early May when the last six hundred Westerners crossed the rickety, barbed-wire-barricaded wooden bridge from Poipet; but both of those tours had been more orientation and sociopolitical maneuvering than anything else. This time he intended to participate in the debriefing of incoming refugees, to talk to as many as possible while their experiences were still fresh in their minds. Not that the interpreters and embassy field officers hadn't done a credible job. But still, most of the information supplied by the refugees was coming to him secondhand, in the form of more reports to wade through. Some refugees have been brought to Bangkok, of course, to the new facility on Sukhumvit Road, and he'd had a chance to talk to them there; only by then too much time had elapsed. They had already forgotten places, dates, faces.

And one of those forgotten faces might have been Kim's.

It was a slim chance, he admitted that to himself. Cambodia was a fairly large country, there were still several million people left alive within its boundaries, and Kim could have been evacuated out of Phnom Penh in any direction, to any destination. She could be anywhere at this time. She could even have slipped across the border into Vietnam or Laos, along with hundreds of others; neither of those countries was a picnic but at least it would mean she was free of the KC. She could be dead, too, but he refused to even consider that possibility. With the passage of time some of the edge had dulled off his pain and he had settled into a kind of gray existence, no highs, no lows either, just gray all the time, an emotional limbo in which he floated, waiting and hoping, while he went about the business of filling up his days. At the least, touring the camps was movement, activity, a sense of direct involvement—much better than sitting around the embassy in Bangkok, spinning his wheels, reading intelligence reports of widespread cholera epidemics and starvation, speculations that Cambodia's forthcoming rice harvest would yield two hundred thousand tons below minimum domestic needs.

As far as the State Department and the CIA were concerned, the central reason he was touring the camps was to ferret out intelligence on and from the resistance movements that had formed and were being formed along the Cambodia-Thailand border. The Khmer Rouge had been having some problems consolidating their control in the northwestern provinces— several hundred Cambodian families had managed to escape from Pailin, midway between Trat and Aranyaprathet—and there were several reports of border skirmishes between KC troops and guerrilla fighters. The groups were all small and disorganized but seemed to be gaining strength, mainly through recruiting efforts in the camps. Support in terms of money and weapons was allegedly coming from Cambodian businessmen in Bangkok, as well as some right-wing Thais. The largest of these groups, according to a recent clandestine report, was the Khmer Serei Liberation Front, with eight hundred former FANK army troops under its command; it had plans to launch commando raids into Cambodia, for the twin purposes of harassing the communists and obtaining information, and considered its ultimate objective to be the capture of Sisophon. Most of the other groups were comprised of anywhere from twenty to two hundred ex-soldiers, civilians, and mercenaries, and operated, for security reasons, in strict secrecy from jungle base camps on both sides of the border, under the blanket code name of Cobra.

The Thai government, as usual, was fence-straddling on the issue. Foreign Minister Chatchai had said recently that Thailand would not interfere in Cambodian "internal affairs," but would also not stop giving aid to political refugees. If you could call what they were doing "giving aid." Conditions in the camps were miserable, because the Thai had no desire to make things better for homeless Khmers than they were for their own peasants.

As for the Khmer Rouge, they had adopted a variety of measures to cope with the situation: increased border security, with troop patrols, the laying of unmarked minefields and the planting of *punji* stakes; arrest, interrogation, and execution of "spies," "enemy elements," and persons caught trying to escape; strict restrictions on travel by villagers; and political indoctrination of villagers, particularly of family members of those who had escaped, and relocation away from the border. Not that any of these measures was likely to staunch the flow of refugees or decrease the number of border fire fights between KC troops and the resistance teams. There was simply no way the communists could seal the entire length of their frontier with Thailand.

So Foxworth's job was to gather as much new data as possible, principally by interviewing alleged guerrilla leaders based in the camps and anyone else who might be able to provide pertinent information. No one in the embassy, including Foxworth himself, held out much hope that the Khmer Liberation Front or any other group could do much more than bedevil the KC for a while; but that didn't stop the CIA from wanting extensive documentation. You never knew when something might develop that you could turn to a political if not military advantage; that was the motto of the boys in McLean. The more you knew about resistance and KC deployment and strategy, why, the better equipped you were to help punch holes in the enemy's defenses, force in new sticks of democracy, light the fuses, and blow everybody to hell again.

That was the trouble with the CIA's brand of militaristic thinking: it ignored the refugees, it ignored the human element. Instead of trying to find ways of improving their lot, giving them food, medicine, entry permits to the United States, or help in relocating to France or elsewhere, the CIA and the State Department and the Pentagon and the White House wanted to go right on playing war games. Well, they had played war games in Cambodia and Vietnam and look what it had gotten them there; look what it had gotten several hundred thousand bystanders. The lesson loomed as plain as death, but nobody seemed to want to read it. *He* read it, all right, but that didn't keep him from doing what the CIA told him to. David Foxworth, minor embassy official, minor human being, first-rank hypocrite.

There's nothing else I can do, he kept telling himself. I'm only one man, I can't tell the CIA to go to hell, I have to work within the system. What can I do?

Nothing. Not a damned thing.

But he was beginning to build up a nice little resentment for the CIA. He could feel it growing inside him, like a tiny tumor. Along with other tiny tumors. Kissinger, for instance. Nixon. His father. Men he'd always respected. And the biggest tumor of all, the biggest cancer growing in the world: war.

I'm turning into a pacifist, he thought. One of those long-haired hippie freaks with their make-love-not-war T-shirts and their peace marches and their communal draft-card burnings. Where's your protest placard, Foxworth? Where are your marching shoes?

Except that maybe they weren't freaks after all.

Except that maybe the real freaks were the boys in McLean and the boys in the White House . . .

There were several others on the tour with him—two junior embassy officials attached to POLMIL, three journalists, the usual contingent of marine bodyguards—and the first camp they went to was the closest to Bangkok, Aranyaprathet. It had grown since July, but only in size; it still looked the same, felt the same, smelled the same. A ramshackle collection of thatch huts and row houses with bamboo partitions—little rooms three or four meters square that housed up to six people—and wood-and-tin roofs. Watchtowers and surrounding fences that gave it all the aspect of a prison compound. Water tanks and lines of buckets. Rattan stalls set up on the camp's boundary, attended by Thais selling or trading local handicrafts and other goods to the refugees. A camp liaison shed, storage facilities, a dispensary and infirmary. Disembodied voices calling names over a loudspeaker. And the refugees themselves: raggedly dressed, showing signs of illness and malnutrition; the elderly sitting in front of the huts, staring at nothing, young women moving in the painful shuffle steps of the very old, groups of men standing or sitting together and talking in low earnest voices. Only the children showed signs of life—playing games, shouting, even laughing, because there were no exploding rockets here, no threat of execution, and the squalid surroundings were still better than what they had had in their homeland.

Ten minutes after the group's arrival, one of the children said to Foxworth, giggling, "Okay, bye-bye," and it made him think instantly of Operation Eagle Pull, the crowd of children at the edge of the helicopter landing zone. *Okay, bye-bye.* Where were those children now? he wondered. How many of them were still alive?

On impulse he embraced the child, a boy of nine or ten, and then gave him ten baht. But as he watched the boy run off, squealing with delight, he wished he hadn't done it. Buy them off with money, he thought. Buy off our own guilt with money. Isn't that what's become the American way?

He spent an hour in private with the Thai officer in charge of the camp and an interpreter. The officer professed no knowledge of resistance efforts in the area, no knowledge of anything controversial. See no evil, hear no evil, speak no evil. Enough food for the refugees? Oh yes, there was plenty of food: four kilograms and eight hundred grams per family per week, plus fish or chicken once every fortnight. Sometimes pork too. Enough medical supplies? Oh yes, the International Rescue Committee and the other relief groups saw that they had sufficient medical supplies. Of course, some refugees died every week from malnutrition and other ailments, but this was through no fault of anyone at the camp.

"One expects refugees to die," the officer said, and shrugged.

After that interview ended, Foxworth asked to see a man named Chuon Van, one of the camp leaders, who was reputed to be involved with the guerrilla movement. Chuon was in his mid-thirties, quiet, well educated, and spoke excellent English: he had been a high school teacher in Battambang, before becoming a soldier in the Republican army. He had escaped to Thailand just after the Khmer Rouge takeover in April; his wife, two sons, and a daughter had not escaped with him and he feared that they might be dead. He was very matter-of-fact about this, either because he had been drained of emotion or because he was a philosophical man by nature; Foxworth couldn't tell which. Chuon didn't seem to blame the Americans for what had happened to his country and offered cooperative answers to questions about the camp and conditions in Battambang. The resistance movement, however, was another matter.

"I know of no resistance groups in this sector," he said in a guarded voice.

"Are you sure?"

"Quite sure."

"You don't belong to one yourself?"

"No."

"If there was such a group here, would you join it?"

"Perhaps."

"Would others in the camp join it?"

"Perhaps."

"Have you heard of the Khmer Serei Liberation Front?"

"I don't believe so."

"What about the code name 'Cobra'?"

"That is also not familiar," Chuon said.

All of which told Foxworth that there *was* a guerrilla team operating at or near Aranyaprathet, and that it was probably fairly substantial, as these groups went, and either active at the moment or soon to be active. If Chuon Van refused to discuss it, it was unlikely that anyone else would: he didn't figure to get anything in the way of details no matter how many refugees he interviewed. All right, so he would make a token effort, note his suspicions in his report to the CIA, and let it go at that. The hell with the CIA. The rest of his time at Aranyaprathet he could devote to the problems of the refugees themselves.

With Chuon as their guide, Foxworth and the others made their way through the camp, inspecting facilities, talking to the people. Every time Foxworth passed a young Khmer woman he found himself peering at her face: looking for Kim, of course. Ridiculous, of course. He knew she wasn't here; if she had been here he would have heard about it. And yet he kept expecting, with a kind of stupid surreal faith, to see her at any second, have her come running toward him from one of the huts or row houses, through the mud and the garbage, her arms spread wide; to see her and hear the sound of her voice—

"Hello, David."

It jarred him. At first the voice was Kim's, echoing inside his head; then he knew it was a real voice, coming from somewhere behind him; then, even before he turned, he knew it wasn't Kim's voice at all. It belonged to Natalie Rosen.

She was standing with three other people, all of them Thais, and she was wearing a white bush jacket and white slacks and a native sun hat even though the sky was overcast and threatening rain. There was a small tentative smile on her mouth when she came over to him.

He said stupidly, "What are you doing here?"

"The same thing you're doing here."

I doubt that, he thought. Jesus, I doubt that. "How long have you been in the camp? You weren't here when we arrived, were you?"

"No. We just got in from Bangkok. You don't seem very pleased to see me."

"I'm just surprised, that's all."

"So was I, when I found out about your tour," Natalie said. "In fact, if I'd known about it sooner we'd have made arrangements to join you. We may still, unless you have objections."

"Why?"

"Why not? It's always easier to travel with other Americans, particularly you embassy people." She gave him a quizzical look; her eyes, he noticed, were very dark and sad and pained, like mirrors of the suffering that was going on around them. "I'm not exactly a stranger to the camps, you know."

Well, he did know. She had been to Aranyaprathet and the even more squalid camp at Trat in February, before coming to Phnom Penh; she'd told him that at the dinner they had shared in Washington. And she'd visited them again on at least one other occasion since her return to Thailand in mid-June. She had gotten in touch with him soon after her arrival, and they'd had lunch and discussed the refugees, only the refugees, nothing personal because he still couldn't respond to her on that level, and then she had gone off to work in the camps. There had been another meeting in July, just a drink that time at Nick's and twenty minutes of conversation, and a third and final meeting in August, no lunch, no drinks, five minutes of conversation in the embassy lobby sandwiched between other appointments.

He also knew, or sensed, that she wouldn't object if a personal relationship were to develop between them. Her invitation to him to spend the night with her at the Mayflower Hotel hadn't been capricious, or the automatic gesture of what his father would have called a roundheel; she felt something for him. Which was surprising, because what she had seemed to feel for him in Phnom Penh, he remembered, was contempt. What was it that had changed her outlook? Maybe it was just that he had come around to her way of thinking on the refugee question, shared her outrage at what was happening, or not happening, to them. Or maybe it was something else that he didn't understand. Christ knew, there was a lot he didn't understand—about women, among any number of other things.

But it was all moot anyway. He couldn't respond to her, even if he'd wanted to. And in other circumstances he might have wanted to: Natalie Rosen was the kind of woman who had always attracted him—gentle, compassionate, intelligent—and there was a kind of nascent chemistry between them each time they met. All moot. All pointless. His love for Kim made an affair untenable; Cambodia made it untenable.

Sorry, Natalie, he thought. Sorry, Kim.

Okay, bye-bye.

"Why are you staring at me that way?"

He blinked. "Was I staring at you?"

"Yes," Natalie said, "you were."

"Sorry." Sorry. Sorry, sorry.

"You *don't* have any objections, do you?"

"Objections? To what?"

"To my group joining yours."

It occurred to him that she might have contrived to come to Aranyaprathet at this time, join the official camp tour, because of him. No, that was being unfair, that was chauvinism; she was here because she cared about the refugees. What's the matter with you, Foxworth? Put your filthy ego away and take another look at what you're standing in the middle of.

"I don't have any objections," he said.

"Good. Maybe we'll be able to help each other along the way. You know, as we discussed in Washington."

"Yes," he said. "Maybe we will."

Natalie and the three Thais accompanied them as they continued their rounds of the camp. And each time Foxworth talked to someone newly arrived from Cambodia, he had an irrational impulse to take hold of the person and say, "Do you know what happened to a woman named Than Kim? She's thirty years old, slender, beautiful, she has a strawberry birthmark on her left shoulder, she used to work at the American embassy in Phnom Penh. Where is she? Can you tell me where she is?" The desperation was back inside him, and the edge of his pain had sharpened again, and he didn't know why it should be that way all of a sudden. He had to exercise a strong effort of will to hold himself in check, maintain his outward composure.

Finally he gave up the questioning himself and let the junior officers handle it. And watched Natalie talk to the refugees, watched how she was able to establish an instant rapport with them, and the gentleness and compassion with which she treated them. Watched how they responded to her. Everyone seemed to respond to her, including the two junior officers, both of whom hovered around her like drones. But not him, not Dave Foxworth. He couldn't, he mustn't respond to Natalie Rosen—to the way she moved, to the way she used her hands, to the sadness in her eyes, to the emotion that flowed balmlike out of her and over those ravaged brown faces. Not him. All moot. Not him.

Damn it, not *him* . . .

Kim

It was a night toward the end of September, during the fortnight when the Festival of the Dead had once been celebrated, when the soldier who looked like a rabbit raped her.

She had suspected it would happen hours ahead of the act itself, from the time of the midday rest period. The soldier had stationed himself near her in the rice paddies, as he usually did, and watched her eat her ration of rice gruel. But then he had come forward, his Ho Chi Minh sandals making sucking sounds in the paddy mud, and spoke with a furtiveness which might have been pathetic if all pathos had not been purged by the revolutionary Angkar. And if the lust had not lain bright and glistening, tumescent, in his eyes.

"Tonight there will be a full moon," he said. "Unless there are clouds, we will work late in the fields."

"Yes," she said.

"But if this happens, you will not leave with the others. You will wait in your cabin until everyone else has gone, before taking the path through the wood. Do you understand?"

"Yes," she said.

"If you don't obey, you'll be sent to the Angkar Leu."

"I will obey."

He wet his lips and went away from her. Kim looked up at the heavy monsoon clouds overhead. I am an ox, she thought, I am a water buffalo; I am not a woman. Draft animals do not care if they are mounted by other draft animals. Draft animals do not understand rape, they do not worry about rape, they only endure it. Then she stopped thinking altogether and slept standing up, with her eyes open, because she had finally mastered the trick of it.

The afternoon passed, the rains passed, the evening meal passed. There were clouds, but they moved swiftly across the sky and the moon was not obscured for more than a few seconds at a time. The indoctrination and propaganda meeting was held early, immediately after they ate. "We must transform the quality of the soil," the voice of Radio Phnom Penh said. "This can be accomplished by using natural fertilizers, such as the manure of buffalo, oxen, and pigs; or by using human excrement, which is also rich in the minerals necessary for the growth of fertile crops." And a short while later the Khmer Rouge administrator said, "Unite. Unite. Unite."

In rape, Kim thought. Unite in rape and death.

The announcement came that they were to return to the

fields tonight, to work until 2300 hours. There were no mutterings of protest; draft animals do not mutter or protest. Kim held Serey's hand for a few seconds, while the others began to trudge out of the commune, and the child looked up with her enormous eyes, as if sensing that something was about to happen; but she did not speak, and Kim did not speak either. The soldier who looked like a rabbit was watching from nearby, his face shining blackly in the moonlight; she released Serey's hand as soon as she saw him, made her way across to her cabin, and entered it.

Five minutes passed. No one else came in, although someone would have if she were to stay very long; the guards, she knew, always checked the cabins after the work periods began, looking for malingerers. She did not think while she waited. Her mind was an emptiness, a cavity—the mind of an ox, the mind of a water buffalo.

When she stepped outside again there was no one visible in the commune except several of the children and the two Khmer Rouge wives who watched over them, and a pair of soldiers talking some distance away. Kim slipped into the shadows alongside the cabin, went around behind it and through the patchy moonlight to the path leading through the section of forest.

It was much darker in there; only random shafts of moonshine penetrated the vault of leaves and branches overhead. And damp in there too, from the afternoon rain. All the leaves dripped water, like a thousand leaking faucets, and the magnified sound drowned out all other noises. Nothing lived in this patch of jungle, not anymore, but she sensed an animal presence nearby: a rabbit, a giant brown rabbit.

He came at her out of the darkness, as she had expected he would—suddenly, with the stealth of a predator—and caught hold of her and clapped a hand over her mouth and dragged her back off the path. She did not struggle. There was no purpose in struggle; there was only obedience. The place where he stopped dragging her was a tiny clearing, and along the near edge of it, she realized dimly, was a strip of damp steaming leaves and palm fronds. He had made a bed for them here. He had built her an altar for the ceremony of rape.

"You know what's about to happen, don't you," he said. He was very excited. His voice was broken by ragged pants and she could feel his tumescence against her hip.

"Yes," she said.

"If you fight me I'll have you sent to the Angkar Leu."

"I will not fight you."

"If you tell anyone I'll kill you myself."

"I will not tell anyone."

He turned her toward him and then let go of her, tentatively, as if testing the truth of her words. She stood still, looking at him but not seeing him, her arms flat against her sides. He caught hold of her again, put his mouth over hers—and pulled her down onto the palm fronds, fumbled at her clothing, fumbled at his own, I am an ox, she thought, his breath clawing at her face, his fingers clawing at her thighs, I am a water buffalo, she thought, and felt him plunge into her, make an incision into her body, begin to grunt as he moved above her, his hands urgent on her breasts, the grunts becoming little squealing sounds against her mouth, I am an ox, I am an ox, and he was a rabbit in every way because then it was over, after only a few seconds, in a soft muffled cry as he emptied himself inside her.

She lay without moving, without touching any part of him with her hands. But he withdrew from her almost immediately, reared back in a way that told her he was frightened now that his passion had been sated, afraid of being discovered and punished by the other Khmer Rouge. He fumbled at his clothing again, and when he said to her, "Dress yourself, hurry," she obeyed without hesitation. Then he pulled her to her feet, took a rough grip on her shoulders and laid his face close to hers.

"Tell no one of this, do you hear? No one."

"I will tell no one."

"If I want you to come here again you'll come. You'll come as often as I tell you to."

"Yes," she said.

Something seemed to shift inside him, a brief flicker of humanity within the machine. His grip on her arms eased; the tension left his features and only the fear remained, like that of a boy with his hands full of forbidden sweets. "I'll give you extra rice," he said, more softly than before. "*Prahoc* and *tuk-trey* too. You want more to eat, don't you?"

"Yes," she said. Thinking of Serey, not herself; of how malnourished the child was.

"Go, then," he said. "Join the others in the paddies. Say nothing, do as I command you, and you'll be rewarded."

When he released her she turned and made her way through the damp foliage to the path. Her pajamas were damp too, where she had lain on the bed of palm fronds, but the night air would dry them so that her sweat could make them wet again. There was an itching sensation between her legs, but she thought that this might be her imagination. It did not matter. Even if it was not her imagination, even if he carried disease, it did not matter.

Without looking behind her, she followed the path out to the paddies, where the other women worked like black crows in the moonlight. She felt huge among them: an ox, a water buffalo, among crows. *Do as I command you and you'll be rewarded.* The words of a machine to a draft animal. There were no longer any human beings in the commune, perhaps not in all of Kampuchea. There were only machines and animals and crows, trampling and plowing under the bodies of dead Khmers.

She stood knee-deep in one of the flooded paddies, harvesting the first meager crop of *srauv sral* with a reaping knife, and thought of the Festival of the Dead. Once there had been great respect for the dead in Kampuchea. Once *ben,* rice balls cooked in coconut milk, had been placed on large silver dishes each night for two weeks, and there were huge banquets on the final night of the festival, during which the head of each family symbolically invited the souls of the ancestors and those of their closest friends to share the banquet, and on the morning following, solemn religious rites were held on behalf of the souls of the dead. Now there were no solemn religious rites because there was no religion. Now there was no respect for the dead because there was no respect for the living.

Kampuchea had been raped, just as she had tonight—plundered, filled with alien seed, robbed of will and spirit. And like her, it would continue to be used without compunction, without shame, a receptacle for the power lusts of men in far-off places and those behind the revolutionary Angkar. And in the end it would die, just as she would die, because no matter how strong you were and how much you wanted to survive, you could only withstand physical and spiritual rape for so long. And when it did die, who would mourn? Who would give banquets in respect for her and all the others? Who would hold solemn rites for the soul of Kampuchea?

No one. No one anywhere.

In all the world there would be no Festival of the Dead.

PART THREE

*December 1975
to April Fool's Day, 1976*

Cambodia File: Postwar Calendar

September 25—Task force representatives at Camp Pendleton, California, report that Khmer refugees anxious to return to Cambodia remain confident the Phnom Penh regime will welcome them back. Their optimism is based on continued contacts between the refugees and the Khmer delegation in New York, which has assured them that Phnom Penh has already formally approved their return, and on the fact that Prince Sihanouk has already been welcomed back from his own forced exile in Red China.

October 6—According to intelligence reports, a large number of Khmer refugees who opted for repatriation and returned to Cambodia have been summarily executed. Eighty-seven military men were effusively greeted at the Thai border, taken down the road out of sight, and then told they were no longer Cambodians but imperialists and killed on the spot. Another 247 officers and noncommissioned officers were reported executed on an abandoned farm, and other military and nonmilitary returnees are said to have met the same fate.

October 9—Tension continues between Cambodia and Vietnam, both in the offshore island area and along their mainland border. Both sides appear to be increasing their coastal defenses, reportedly as a result of Vietnamese forces shelling the Cambodian-held island of Koh Thmei in early September, and there is no evidence that either side is willing to compromise on who owns the disputed islands and surrounding undersea resources. Also, despite the fact that the Cambodian Party Central Committee stressed recently that border questions should be settled by "political means," the Cambodians are planning to form a new army division in the eastern region bordering Vietnam.

November 3—"Secret Spoke" intelligence documents speculate that one reason why the Khmer Communist Party (KCP) has never made a direct public acknowledgment of its existence is that they are still encountering some of the factionalism which characterized the insurgent movement during the war. They are being forced to cope with active resistance as well as, in all probability, passive but widespread popular dissatisfaction. To help counteract this, and to strengthen and expand the party organization, a twenty-day cadre-training class was reportedly due to open in Phnom Penh in October. Both civilian and military officials were to attend—regional and sector standing committee members, district committee chiefs, military commissars down to battalion level, and at least some provincial officers.

November 4—Cambodian Deputy Prime Minister Ieng Sary and his Thai hosts in Bangkok have apparently established a favorable atmosphere for future contacts between the two countries. Thai agreement to the pledge that both parties would not allow their territory to be used for hostile purposes against the other, it is speculated, was intended to allay Cambodian fears of Thai government support for resistance groups operating in the border area against Cambodia. No reference is made in the joint communiqué issued by the two nations to the refugee issue, although Ieng Sary tells reporters that both Thailand and Cambodia share a "common desire" that the refugees return to their homeland.

Deighan

In the little bungalow off Issraphard Road, in the corner of the living room they had partitioned into an office for him with teak screens, Deighan rolled another completed page out of his battered Underwood and laid it on the growing stack of pages alongside. Then he sat back, set fire to another cigarette, and looked out into the rear garden, where purple bougainvillea and several other tropical flowers and shrubs grew lushly, including one, something-or-other ixora, which was the color of fresh blood.

But he didn't want to think about blood right now; he had been thinking about blood all morning, two thousand words of blood and about blood, and it was time to take a break and think about something pleasant. So he thought about Carol, and how they had made love out there once, not long after he'd moved in with her, thrashing around on a blanket spread out over the patio tiles. That was in their abandoned period, when the heat of passion burned at a high constant flame and they were at each other all the time—in bed, on the furniture, on the floor, anyplace and any way the mood happened to strike them. Carol had always had a fondness for sex, even beyond his own fondness for it, but this new Carol brought dimensions to the act of love that surprised him: a kind of consuming intensity that demanded everything from him, physical and spiritual, and gave him everything in return, as if she were trying to fuse the two of them in ways beyond the sensual.

So they'd been having a go out there in the garden, with the high wall around it keeping out the voyeurs, and just after the climactic moment Carol had burst into delighted laughter. When he asked her why she said it was because he'd bayed like a sheep when he came. Sheep don't bay, he said, and she said Maybe they don't but you certainly did, Peter, and imitated a noise that he couldn't remember making, a really funny noise, and they'd laughed about it for the rest of the day. And maybe she had a point, too: maybe sheep did bay. Embittered and drunken war correspondents didn't all of a sudden quit drinking and rediscover purpose and love, but that was what had happened to him these past few months. The baying sheep was becoming an animal of a different sort—the sober, pointed wolf emerging from the liquor-soaked wool. His thoughts didn't exactly mesh sometimes; his mind was full of mixed syntax like that. But hell, that was what love was supposed to do to you, wasn't it?

The mixed syntax didn't carry over to his writing, though. His writing was as good as it had ever been, better in some ways, closer to the center of his talent and his vision of the world—sharp, clearheaded, savage prose that might just kick a little ass back on the home front, might just make the Pulitzer Prize folks sit up and take notice again, not that he gave much of a damn about the Pulitzer Prize. But the remarkable thing was that he was writing with a sense of commitment again. The year in Cambodia had been a sodden nightmare of bottles, bars, whores, emotions in many colors but mostly gray and black, and wadded-up sheets of paper: abortive dispatches, abortive letters and suicide notes to Carol, lying letters to his editors, and discarded cables from them in reply. He hadn't written five thousand words of any value whatsoever in that year. But now, in just two months, October and November, he had turned out fifty thousand, and all of them pretty damn valuable, at least to him.

Fifty thousand words, a short book's worth, only not a book yet, just the opening third of what he intended to be the last word on the life and death of Phnom Penh. He had sent the opening sections off to the agent he'd used on *The Only War We Had,* and she'd made approving noises over the trans-Pacific telephone wire: she would try to lay those sections off to one of the bigger-pay slicks, while at the same time going after Scribner's—Hemingway's publisher, that was where everybody

went first when they had a manuscript by a war correspondent—
to sign up the book rights. She wanted big money, she'd said; if
Scribner's wouldn't play, then she'd run an auction among some
of the other houses. Deighan listened to all of this and then for-
got it as soon as they hung up on each other. It had no reality
to him; the only reality was Carol. She was where the book was
coming from, and she was where he was coming from, and
along with the poor poor bastards in Cambodia she was all he
gave a damn for.

He poured himself a cup of the strong Thai tea Carol had
made for him before she left to go shopping. That was all he
drank these days; he hadn't had a shot of vodka, a taste of anything stronger than tea, in thirty-three days. Amazing. Incredible. He alternated sips from the cup with drags on his cigarette,
and thought how quiet the bungalow was when he wasn't using
his typewriter and Carol was away. Like an island set apart
from everything. Which was what he'd been himself without
her. No man is an island, according to old John Donne, but
John Donne hadn't spent two war years in Vietnam and one
war year in Phnom Penh. You got to be an island in places like
that, all right. You got to be one of those atolls in the Pacific
where they used to test atom bombs: blackened and torn apart
right down to bedrock.

Where Carol had gone was to James Thompson's Thai
House and its little village of Thai silk weavers. She went there
often, to watch the craftspeople and to bring back this or that
example of their art. He'd told her to go ahead and furnish the
house with Thai silk and handicrafts if she wanted to, but she'd
said no, the bungalow was only rented, it wasn't a permanent
home. Which had prompted him to ask if she wanted to move
back to California, an idea which appealed to him not at all—
you can't go home again, he still believed that—but which he
was willing to follow through on if it was what she needed. But
it wasn't, she said. She liked Bangkok just fine. He sensed again
that she was keeping something from him, because that damned
shield had come back down behind her eyes. Most of the time
now it was gone and her eyes told him everything he wanted to
know, but the shield was an occasional reminder that she was

harboring some sort of secret. She spoke freely enough of the fourteen months they had been apart: the things she'd done, the people she'd met, her job as a research assistant at UC Berkeley, even a brief affair she'd had (which pained him more than it should have, considering his own adventures with the whores of Indochina). It was none of that. Nor was it some sort of religious conversion; she said it wasn't, and her serenity wasn't exactly spiritual. He just didn't know what it was. In time maybe he could get it out of her. But not just yet, not until she was ready to let go of it.

Bangkok was a place he liked himself, as much as he could like any place in Southeast Asia, but more and more lately he'd found himself thinking of Paris. It wasn't the Hemingway *shtick* this time; he'd pretty much exorcised that particular demon. It was that he'd spent some time in Paris after Vietnam, and it was an ideal location for a working journalist because you could keep your finger on the pulse of what was happening anywhere in the world, especially in Cambodia because of the French connection. It was also a city for lovers, corny but true —walks along the Champs-Elysées, visits to the Louvre and the Eiffel Tower, picnics along the Seine, the ghost of Maurice Chevalier singing "Louise" on every street corner and in front of every sidewalk café. An all-around good city, Paris. A place for Carol and him to complete their new start together.

Except that she didn't want to go there either.

He'd suggested it just the other day, a visit over Christmas and New Year's first—it was already December, where did the time go?—so she could get to know the city because she'd never been. No, she said. She didn't want to live in Paris and she didn't want to visit Paris. Christmas in Bangkok seemed fine to her, she said; they had each other and they had the bungalow, what did they need to travel all the way to Europe for, fighting other holiday travelers every step of the way? And the shield banged down again behind her eyes.

Deighan shook his head. He'd have to talk to her again when she got home from the Thai House. Maybe it would be a minor hassle getting to France, but ten days or so there would do them both a lot of good; he could use a vacation from the book, because it was painfully visceral stuff and taking a lot out of him, and she could use one from the oppressive heat that always lay over Southeast Asia at the beginning of the dry season. She'd been looking a little wilted lately, and had been less enthusiastic in bed; the Paris landscape was bound to perk her up. And they could afford the trip: his agent was so hyped up on *The Rape of Cambodia,* his working title for the book, and so convinced there was big money in it, that she'd sent him a two-thousand-dollar advance out of her own pocket. Plus, in the last letter he'd had from her, four days ago, she'd promised "important news" by the end of the year, which had to mean either a substantial slick sale on the portions or a book contract, with a sizable chunk of additional money to follow.

He thought about writing her a letter, asking status, but decided against it. Prodding agents was likely to make them unhappy and therefore uncommunicative; there was enough lack of communication between writers and agents, not to mention between writers and editors, without complicating things. Instead he rolled a clean sheet of paper into the portable, lighted his fifteenth cigarette of the day, and set out to finish the chapter he'd started two thousand words ago.

> We watched the choppers come down. Across the field, behind a row of apartment houses, a group of kids were watching them too. Their eyes were not filled with mockery or recrimination or astonishment or loss: they were filled with nothing at all. They bore witness, just as the country itself had borne witness. The children, the land, all the dead Khmers humping the riverbanks had no more meaning and no less meaning than the Nixon Doctrine, than the Kissinger Twitch.
>
> History is plunder, I thought, that's the truism. I was very drunk on the vodka from Hotel Le Phnom. History is plunder and property is theft. But here, now, with the choppers coming down, all of us going out, all aphorisms were lies, all metaphors unfunny jokes. History is history, I thought, that's the answer

now; theft is theft, death is death. Everything is exactly what it is. And we were all exactly what we were: nothing at all.

This is what I thought as I waited. And this is what I saw refracted in the eyes of the kids as they watched the choppers come down.

The rest of the chapter went about the same way. Good enough, the old power, but so central and so painful that he had to crawl down inside himself to drag it out. Which meant that when he reached the last page he had to surface again in stages, like a diver coming up through deep water. The final sentence brought him all the way out, and he pulled the page from the typewriter, laid it aside, stood up to work the kinks out of his muscles. And only then did he realize, looking past the teak partitions, that Carol had come home and was perched on the rattan settee in the other part of the living room.

He went in there and bent to kiss her. "How long have you been home?" he said.

"A few minutes."

"I didn't hear you come in."

"I know. You were engrossed in your work."

"Why didn't you say something?"

"I didn't want to disturb you," she said. "I thought I'd just sit down and rest until you were finished."

She looked tired, in that same wilted way of the past couple of weeks. Damned heat. It was tolerable in the bungalow or one of the restaurants, because of the air conditioning, but outside it was like being steamed in a giant open-air wok. He sat down beside her, put his arm around her shoulders, meaning to comfort her, but she misinterpreted the gesture and seemed to stiffen and withdraw under his touch.

"Not now, Peter," she said. "It's too hot."

"I wasn't going to do anything."

"It isn't a matter of *doing* anything. It's . . ."

"What? Carol, what's wrong?"

"Nothing," she said, and the shield snapped into place again.

He felt her closing off, drifting away from him; the sensation was frightening.

"Hey, look," he said, "I know you. Something's wrong."

"Do you?"

"Do I what?"

"Know me."

"I think so. Better than I ever did before."

"That's true," she said. Her voice was wistful now, almost melancholy. "Better than you ever did before."

"Carol—"

"I'm just tired, that's all. The heat . . . I probably shouldn't go out in the afternoons. But I don't want to disturb you."

"You don't disturb me."

"Well, I feel as if I do."

"You need a change of scenery; we both do. I still think Paris over the holidays is a good idea. You will too, once you get there."

"I don't want to go to Paris, Peter."

"Why not?"

"We don't have time to go to Paris."

"Why don't we?"

"Because . . . you have to finish your book."

"I can finish it after we come back."

"Why are you so eager to go to Paris? It's not that Hemingway business again, is it?"

"No, it hasn't got anything to do with Hemingway."

"Because he's been dead for fifteen years," Carol said. "And Scott Fitzgerald and Gertrude Stein have been dead longer than that. Paris hasn't been a literary mecca for half a century."

He felt a flicker of his old annoyance at the way she had of patronizing him sometimes. "I want Paris for us," he said, "not because of any literary ghost."

"But I don't want it at all. Peter, please, I don't want to talk about it anymore, all right?"

"Will you at least give it some thought?"

"Yes, I'll give it some thought. Right now I'm going to go and lie down for a while, take a nap. You can join me later, if you want. Then we can make love."

He watched her get up and walk slowly down the hall to the bedroom, and he thought: Something's wrong, there's something very wrong here. Then he thought: No there isn't, nothing's wrong, what could be wrong? He got up himself, went past the teak screens again. He read what he'd written, making ink changes here and there. David Foxworth's name appeared a couple of times . . . he'd have to get in touch with Foxworth again, try to change his mind about discussing his relationship with the Khmer woman, Than Kim. Deighan still wanted to do something on that, a chapter for the book now, although he could still sell it as a separate article if he made it self-contained enough. He wrote out a note to himself. He put fire to his eighteenth or nineteenth coffin nail of the day. He stared out at the garden and followed the flight of a small blue-and-green parrot.

So she has a few secrets, he thought, so what? Everybody has a few secrets, including me. That doesn't mean there's anything wrong, does it?

Something's *wrong,* he thought.

Natalie

She finally talked David into going out with her on December 7, the anniversary of the Japanese bombing of Pearl Harbor. Not that there was anything significant in the date; there wasn't. It just happened to be the day she got through to him, the day that he let his defenses down for the first time and admitted her into his personal life.

Up until then, ever since the two-week tour of the refugee camps in September, he had pretty much avoided her. And pretty much avoided her during the tour too, although there were times when she caught him looking at her, studying her, maybe thinking about her. She would have given anything to know what those thoughts were. But then, maybe she was better off not knowing. The emanations of pain from him were enough as it was—much less severe than on the evening in Washington in late April, but still palpable, still the same deep subjective anguish. He hadn't reconciled himself to the loss of Kim yet and it was possible he never would; but she preferred to think he was making inroads in that direction, whether he knew it consciously or not.

Her own feelings for him were less clearly defined. Or maybe they *were* clearly defined and she just wasn't ready to admit it to herself yet. She thought about that as she rode in one of the three-wheeled *samlors* from the house near Lumpini Park, where she was staying with a Thai family active in refugee relief, to Prakanong Bridge to meet David. Just how did she feel? Well, there was his pain and her own responsiveness to suffering in others. But it had become more than just a matter of empathy. He had been on her mind a good deal since her return to Bangkok, she had even dreamed about him twice, and she kept wanting to know him, to get close enough to look past that pained and walled-off exterior at the man who dwelt within. If that man, the real David Foxworth, was the good and sensitive human being she suspected he was, then maybe she could let herself love him. Assuming, of course, that she didn't already love him. Assuming, of course, that she didn't already want him, no matter who he was, in a way that she'd never wanted any other man.

Assuming, of course, that she wasn't a damned fool, groping around for love in the midst of all the agony in Southeast Asia —searching for flowers on a dung heap, as her father might say.

Because loving David Foxworth would very probably mean hurting herself. How could she compete with a memory kept alive and burning bright by guilt? How could she hope to dislodge his love for Kim so she could insert herself in Kim's place?

Natalie had an impulse to call her father in New York later and ask his advice. But that was childish, and besides, she knew what he would tell her. "You care too much about everything, Natalie," he would tell her. "You haven't learned how to temper your emotions with either perspective or common sense.

You walk around naked all the time; you don't cover any part of yourself, you don't protect your vitals."

Yes, Papa, she thought, but how? Tell me *how*.

David was waiting when the driver of the *samlor* deposited her at Prakanong Bridge. He stood apart from the crowd queued up for the three-hour *klong* trip, looking out over the congested brown waterway beyond. He struck her as a forlorn figure, alone, like a piece of flotsam adrift in the city. Illusion. Fantasy. It was how she wanted to see him because it allowed her to feel closer to him, gave rise to her maternal instincts.

"Hello, David," she said when she reached him. "Did I keep you waiting long?"

He had a smile for her, pale but still a smile. "No, I've only been here a couple of minutes."

"It's almost nine. Shall we join the queue?"

"I guess we should."

He was looking at the noisy crowd of tourists on the quay and she sensed a mild distaste in him. She said, "If you'd rather not take the boat trip, we can do something else."

"No, the boat trip's fine."

"It'll be more peaceful once we get under way."

"Sure," he said. "More peaceful."

There was a ten-minute wait before they were able to board the *hang yao,* a long-tailed, shallow-draft boat with square sails and an awning to protect passengers, that waited at the quay. David seemed fidgety, uncomfortable, and she thought: He doesn't want to be here with me, he thinks he's betraying Kim in some way. She could feel his pain again and she wanted to reach out, touch him, soothe him, heal him. More maternity: Mama make the hurt go away. Except that she couldn't. She didn't have the power to heal him or anyone else. No one did. No one could make his kind of hurt or her kind of hurt go away.

The *hang yao* took them through several large canals into a network of smaller *klongs,* maneuvering past and through rice barges, sampans, fishing boats, produce boats laden with vegetables and fruits, log rafts, and a variety of other craft. The *klongs* were lined with houses built out over the water, lush gardens, a school, a sawmill. And *wats* decorated with gold leaf, enamel, glass and pottery mosaic, glazed-tile snake roofs glistening with color in the morning sunlight. From the eaves of the pagodas tiny silver bells made gentle tinkling sounds, in counterpoint to the discordancy of shouting voices and motors and horns.

Natalie looked at the sights, listened to the bells and to the voice of a guide pointing out landmarks, and the feeling of rage began to rise inside her again—directed at herself this time, as much as at anyone or anything else. The contrast between all of this, what they were doing and seeing and hearing, as against the stark horror of the refugee camps was glaring; in a just world there was no way in which she and David would be allowed to do this while the refugees suffered in places like Trat and Aranyaprathet. It was a reenactment of Phnom Penh. It was unfair. In its own way it was monstrous . . .

You see? she imagined her father saying to her, extending the overseas telephone conversation they would not have. *You're caring too much again. Of course there's injustice in the world; there has been injustice in the world for more than two millennia. Do you have to live in filth and ugliness to want to abolish filth and ugliness? And why do you always search for that in every situation which makes you sad or angry or unhappy? You feed on pain, Natalie, the pain of others; but it's your own pain you have to be careful of, or else you'll end up feeding on yourself.*

Yes, Papa, she thought, you're right, Papa—and looked at David to see if he felt the same sort of reaction to their surroundings. But there was nothing in his face to indicate what he was feeling or thinking. In fact, he seemed less uncomfortable now that they were under way, as if he were slowly and cautiously allowing himself to unwind. He sensed her looking at him, met her eyes, and gave her another small smile. Allowing more of his defenses to lower, too? She smiled back at him, and made an effort to douse the flare of rage. It wouldn't do her any good, or him any good, or their relationship any good. Her father always did know what he was talking about, in person or in her imagination.

They were out of Bangkok proper now, into the countryside: rice paddies, farmers in wide straw hats, floating produce markets, motorized pirogues and narrow paddle boats, boys and girls on bicycles waving from the road that followed the *klong*. The voice of the guide said in several languages that they would stop at a typical Thai farmhouse near Hua-Pa and then make the return trip on a converted rice barge. Several of the tourists kept snapping photographs of the landscape and of each other. One of them, a fat American, threw a paper bag full of sandwich leavings into the canal.

Thousands dying of starvation and disease in Cambodia, hundreds dying of starvation and disease in the refugee camps—she wanted to stand up and scream it into the American's fat bovine face, into all the fat bovine complacent faces . . .

Stop it, she warned herself. That's enough.

"This could be Cambodia," David said beside her.

She heard him but at first she didn't understand what he meant. "Cambodia?"

"The countryside, the way it looks. Except that there aren't any war scars here."

"Did you go into the countryside very much?"

"Not very much, no. Kim and I—" He stopped and then, after two beats, like an engine that had faltered briefly, he went on. "Kim and I once took a paddle-wheel boat to Kompong Cham, before the communists closed in. About the only difference is that all along the Mekong you'd see women washing clothes at the water's edge."

His pain flowed into her again, made her wince. "Maybe this wasn't such a good idea," she said. "I mean, maybe we should have stayed in Bangkok . . ."

"No, it's all right. I'm glad we're doing this."

"Are you? Why?"

"Because I needed it," he said. "I needed to get away for a few hours, into surroundings like these." He paused. "I guess I needed someone to talk to, too. I don't talk to people anymore, except at the embassy or an embassy function. Sometimes I think I've forgotten how."

"You haven't forgotten how," Natalie said, and understood

that he was opening up to her for the first time. Not much, and very tentatively, but opening up just the same. "You're doing fine, David."

"No I'm not. I'm not doing fine at all."

"Someday you will."

"Will I? I don't think so."

"But I do."

The conversation had shifted subtly, become something different than what it had started out to be. David knew it too but it didn't make him withdraw again; he said, not quite looking at her, "You're a good person, Natalie. I wish I'd known you a long time ago."

"You know me now. Isn't that enough?"

"I'm afraid not."

"It could be, David."

"Not the way things are."

"They could change. Time passes and things change." She hated the sound of her voice, the words that kept coming out of her. It was the voice and the words of every social worker she had ever known: platitudinous, pedantic, emptily comforting. "David, look—"

"You know what I do at night sometimes?" he asked her. "I try to imagine what it's like for Kim in Cambodia, under the Khmer Rouge. And I can't. I can't imagine it because it's out of my experience, it's nothing that ever happened to me or could happen to me. That's almost as bad as not being able to do something to help her. But I keep trying. I have to keep thinking about her because if I stop, then I'll be admitting she's dead or as good as dead. I'll be abandoning her again. Does that make sense to you?"

More of his anguish funneled into her and was absorbed. "Yes," she said.

"And the rest of the time I pore over reports, I talk to others with a pipeline to McLean, I ask refugees if they know of her. I even went around looking at faces in the camps, hoping one of them would be hers. That's the way it is, Natalie, and it's not going to change, not unless I find out one way or the other. And I expect not even then."

The *hang yao* slid into another canal, this one flanked by stilt houses with corrugated iron roofs. Natalie was silent. Something he'd just said, probably without realizing it, had triggered a thought—an obvious thought, considering who he was and what he did, and considering some of the things Peter Deighan had said to him that night at the Le Royal in Phnom Penh, and yet one that she hadn't considered before. Or hadn't let herself consider before.

He said, "Why are you looking at me that way?"

"David, do you work for the CIA?"

She hadn't meant to put the thought into words, at least not as abruptly as that; and what the words did, as she might have known, was to close him off from her again. His face went blank and she could feel him withdrawing, even though he still sat close to her on the bench. Damn, damn, just when he'd begun to place those bleeding parts of himself in her hands! Her first impulse was to apologize, let it drop, but the thought and all its implications held her back. That, and the way his gaze flicked past her, probing the faces of the other sightseers— a concern that was groundless because she had spoken in an undertone, and the guide was talking loudly about the life-style of the Thai peasants, and no one was or had been paying any attention to them.

"David?"

"What kind of question is that?" he said.

"A reasonable question."

"What made you ask it?"

"You said you talk to others with a pipeline to McLean. That implies you have a pipeline to McLean yourself. Do you?"

"You know I can't answer that."

"Because it's true?"

"Because I can't answer it, true or not."

"I want to know," she said.

"Why? Is it that important to you?"

"It might be. I hate the CIA; if they hadn't engineered the coup against Sihanouk in 1970, things might be different today. A lot different."

"The CIA didn't have anything to do with the '70 coup."

"Oh didn't they?"

"All right then, believe what you want. The point is, if you found out I was CIA-connected, you wouldn't want anything more to do with me. Right?"

"I didn't say that."

"You didn't have to."

She looked out over the muddy brown water, at the farmers harvesting rice in the paddies, stacking the cut stalks in bunches to dry in the sun. I don't know, she thought, I don't know what I feel. All your pain, David, that's genuine; but what about the rest of you? Still loyal to the Nixon-Kissinger machine? Still the basic hawk—and a basic CIA spook too? And if you are, what then? *Does* it make that much of a difference in how I feel about you?

Yes, she thought, it does.

And her father's voice, still whispering in her imagination, said, *You walk around naked all the time; you don't cover any part of yourself, you don't protect your vitals. You feed on pain, Natalie. Watch out you don't end up feeding on yourself . . .*

Kim

As she had been torn from sleep on all the other mornings, she was torn from sleep on the second morning after the last of the rice was harvested—but this time it was by the roar of many truck engines, not by a ringing gong. The trucks were maneuvering into the commune along the access road which the Khmer Rouge had ordered built some months ago, before the first crop of yams; patterns of light danced through the darkness inside the cabin, creating a nightmarish shadow play. Then doors slammed and voices began shouting for the *opakar* to rise and assemble immediately.

The married couple with whom Kim and Serey shared the

cabin spoke together in low frightened voices. But she did not listen. She bent to where Serey lay stirring and lifted the child into her arms. Serey's face was warm and damp, but the heat of her fever seemed to have lessened. This was a good sign. Kim had been afraid it might be virulent malaria, because the fever had lingered for several days at high heat; the mosquitoes had been thick during the monsoon rains, and several people had been stricken and a few of the weaker had died. Serey whimpered softly, asked about the light and noise. Instead of answering, Kim stroked the little girl's head, pressed her close, and then carried her out of the cabin.

There were at least a dozen trucks, all of them with headlights burning, all of them six-wheeled canvas-covered Molotovas with Chinese characters visible on their sides. Twenty or thirty armed soldiers, some in black pajamas and some in khaki uniforms, swarmed about the trucks, opening the canvas flaps at the rear, supervising the assemblage of the people, shouting for everyone to begin entering the trucks. We are being displaced again, Kim thought without emotion. Transported to another commune? Taken to slaughterhouses and butchered? Only Angka knows. Not even God, because the Angkar Leu has abolished God and shackled His holy men and put them to work in the fields. There is no God in Kampuchea.

Some of the people, when they realized what was happening, reversed their movements and tried to return to the cabins, to gather what was left of their belongings. The soldiers would not permit it; the only items which could be taken, they said, were kettles, rice pots, and small amounts of rice. Kim made no effort to reenter her cabin. Nor did she feel any of the fear that rippled through the others in the predawn darkness. She had nothing worth taking with her except Serey's life and her own, and it made no difference to her where they were being taken. Here there was death; wherever they were being transported would have more death. She simply stood motionless, holding Serey, waiting for it to be their turn to enter one of the trucks.

The KC administrator stood on the hood of a nearby truck and spoke to them all through a bullhorn. "You are being returned to Phnom Penh," he said. "You have worked well for the revolutionary Angka, and proven your worthiness, and now you are ready to join with the Old People in the independence-sovereignty of Democratic Kampuchea."

Lies, Kim thought. But the words seemed to allay the fear all around her, to calm the *opakar* and make them docile again. As they had no doubt been intended to.

"There is no need for you to take anything with you," the administrator said. "Everything you need awaits you in Phnom Penh. You will each have a house of your own, and in each house there will be food, utensils, clothing, sleeping mats, mosquito netting."

Lies. All lies.

The soldier who looked like a rabbit passed near her, paused to look into her face. In the glare of the truck headlights, his own face contained traces of sadness and disappointment—perhaps because she was being moved elsewhere while he would remain here, perhaps because she was being taken away to be executed, in either case because she would no longer be available to him. He had raped her six times since the first rape in September, each time on the altar he had built for her in the patch of jungle; and not once had he kept his promise—one more in the string of KC lies—to provide her with extra rations of food. She had had no difficulty enduring the act itself: she was so adept now at snatching moments of unconsciousness while she labored in the fields that she had been able to do the same thing while he plundered her body. The one thing she had not been able to endure was the prospect that he would make her pregnant. If that had happened, she knew she would have killed herself before the Khmer Rouge could do it; the thought of his seed growing within her, forming another child of the revolution with its dead and soulless eyes, was repugnant beyond tolerance. But the rabbit had not given her a child. Her menstrual blood had flowed each month, and had flowed again one week ago, two weeks after his last assault.

The soldiers kept telling everyone to hurry, shouting *"Di! Di!"* over and over. The knot of people ahead of Kim unwound into one of the covered trucks. She moved forward, ox away from rabbit, obliterating him from her consciousness; if she was to die soon, it would not be with thoughts of a rapist penetrating her mind as he had penetrated her body.

When she reached the truck she shifted Serey's weight across her shoulder, climbed up past another of the armed soldiers. In the darkness, as she groped toward one of the slat benches that lined both inner sides, she jostled someone and was jostled twice in return. The truck had been built to hold no more than thirty, but at least half as many as that had already been wedged inside: the benches were full and so was part of the floor space in between. She forced herself between two people near the opening, upsetting one of them onto hands and knees, not feeling regret when she realized it was an old woman—*this is what they have made of us, this is what we are reduced to*—because it was suffocating in the narrow confines and Serey, weak with fever and coughing again, would need air. Then she braced herself and the child against the wooden side supports, closed her eyes, and waited for the trucks to begin moving.

It did not take long. Inside of five minutes the engines roared, gears ground, and the convoy began to jounce out of the commune. When Kim opened her eyes again she saw that two of the soldiers rode standing outside on the tailgate, hanging on military fashion with their automatic weapons slung over their backs. From time to time, in the bobbing lights from the truck behind, she could see them glance inside. Perhaps they were there to keep anyone from attempting to jump off and escape. Or perhaps they were there merely to listen; the ears of Angka the Omnipotent were always open. But if that was so, there was nothing for them to hear. No one spoke aloud, for they had all been trained well, and the only sounds were the cries of a baby and the whimpering of a boy-child.

Once they were clear of the access road, the convoy gathered speed. The soldiers in the cabs drove recklessly, so that the trucks bucked, swayed, vibrated every time one of the wheels struck a pothole in the road and sent them spilling against each other, sent the unwary toppling to the floorboards. The constant violent motion, the exhaust fumes mingling with the stench of sweat and body waste to foul the hot dry air, made Kim short of breath and nauseated. The effect on Serey was the same; she vomited a thin stream of fluid at Kim's feet, and her sticklike body was wracked with spasms of coughing. The fever had taken hold again and made her face feel hot and slick. Kim shifted the child's position, tilting her head toward the rear opening where the breeze of their passage could fan it. At least she could do that much for Serey. Deeper within, where the breeze did not reach, others were not so fortunate; the sporadic sounds of moaning and retching grew as the kilometers fled away beneath them.

It was difficult to tell, even after the coming of dawn, in what direction they were moving. From glimpses of the landscape, past the guards and the other trucks, Kim thought they might be retracing the route that had brought them to the rubber plantation in April: west through Phum Veal to Highway 15, then south toward Neak Luong. This was confirmed when the familiar landmark of the airstrip at Prey Veng appeared to her some time later. She half expected them to stop at any time, at any place along the road, and for her and the others to be herded out into the fields that lined it and then shot. After which their corpses would be buried in the soft earth so that their flesh and their bones might fertilize it and bring Angka fine new crops in the coming year. But this did not happen. The trucks neither stopped nor slowed their pace anywhere along Highway 15.

When they reached Neak Luong Kim saw that there were barges on the Mekong again, all of them heavily laden with rice and other goods and all of them drifting south toward Vietnam. Was this what happened to the crops they had harvested at the commune? Were they being exported to Saigon and other places outside Kampuchea, instead of distributed to the starving population? It was possible; she knew nothing of what had become of the country under the rule of the Khmer Rouge, nothing of their policies or their dealings with the outside world. Except for coverage of Prince Sihanouk's return from exile in September, Radio Phnom Penh spoke only of dikes and soil yields, unity and sovereignty. Factual news reports, like truth, were as much an enemy of the new order as imperialism and democracy.

Much of the forest in the vicinity of Neak Luong had been cleared away to make paddies and yam and cassava fields. Little had been done to the ferry town itself; few of the burned-out buildings had been torn down and replaced and few people seemed to be living there. There was no automobile traffic on the road except for an occasional military vehicle which passed them going in the opposite direction, and only scattered bicycles, carts, and draft animals. But the fields were full, just as they had been at her commune, with women harvesting rice and planting new crops, with men digging canals and building dike roads and plowing newly cleared acreage. This was communism at work—and it was a lie, like everything else, because the people were not working for themselves but for the Angkar Leu. Not freedom; oppression. Not life; death.

The caravan crossed the Mekong and turned northwest on Highway 1. Near Chroi Dang the trucks slowed, drew off to the side of the road; the two soldiers hanging on at the rear looked in and said there would be a ten-minute stop for the emptying of bowels and bladders. A few of the people begged for time to cook a little rice; they were ill from lack of food, the children needed nourishment, would Angka give them just a few more minutes? Angka would not. "If you complain too much," one of the soldiers said, "we'll let you complain to Angka yourself. How would you like that? How would you like to be sent to the Angkar Leu with your complaints?"

Kim took Serey into the shadows of a palm tree and held her while she urinated. The child's face was flushed, her eyes lusterless. She said, "I'm thirsty. I'm so thirsty."

"There's no water, little one. I'm sorry."

"Where are we going this time?"

"To Phnom Penh, the soldiers said."

"Do you believe the soldiers?"

"If we stop in Phnom Penh I'll believe them."

"I don't want to stop in Phnom Penh," Serey said. "I want to go far away from Phnom Penh."

"To your home village?"

"To where my mother is. To look at the face of God."

Kim hugged her and said nothing, thought nothing. There

were no words to speak and she must not think; she must only be strong until they came to whatever their destination, because weakness would not help her or the child.

They returned to the truck, crowded inside. But their place had been taken by a man and his wife, who would not give it up; they snarled at Kim when she tried to argue and forced her and Serey toward the center of the truck. She fought rearward again, managed to displace another woman weaker than herself, on the opposite bench near the opening. The still-strong preying on the weak; the law of the jungle. Animals turning on themselves, betraying themselves as they had been betrayed. Animals.

The convoy set out again along the highway. It was past noon when they crossed the Monivong Bridge and reentered Phnom Penh, and there was a tentative air of excitement in the truck, whispers echoing the promises of food and shelter made by the KC administrator. But the excitement waned as the caravan skirted the Tuol Tompoung and Toek Loak sectors, avoiding the city center, and then passed straight through Tuol Kauk to the north. And it waned, too, because the city was lifeless: there were no people on the streets, no sign that any of the houses or buildings were inhabited. In some places weeds and other vegetation had begun to encroach on what had been built by the hands of civilization. In other places there was just emptiness and the unhealed scabs of war.

The excitement vanished altogether and was replaced by a combination of apathy and fear when the trucks turned north along Highway 5. Kim felt neither; she had prepared room inside herself for no emotion other than concern for Serey. If you did not believe in lies, you would not be disappointed when you discovered the truth. If you did not have hope, you would not be crushed when you found nothing but despair.

Highway 5 had been impassable prior to the Khmer Rouge takeover, when the war still raged beyond the city's perimeters. Now it had been repaired and held more traffic than either Highway 15 or Highway 1. But it was the same type of traffic: military vehicles, soldiers on bicycles, unsmiling people with carts and draft animals. The landscape was the same too:

fields, men and women working listlessly, remnants of the war—abandoned cars, napalmed trees and buildings—being slowly erased not because they were ugly, not because they were reminders of a bitter struggle, but because they were unproductive.

All afternoon they traveled without stopping, except to refuel with gasoline from military tins, through Phsar Oudong and Kompong Chhnang toward the Tonle Sap. The sun fell down the sky and disappeared in a trail of fire; darkness blotted out the terrain; the headlights on the trucks behind created the same dancing glare of predawn. The children and the one baby in the truck screamed continually for food, for water. The mingled odors of gasoline fumes and close-packed bodies worsened. And so did Serey's fever and cough; the child vomited again, complained of a headache and pains in her abdomen. Kim tried to rock her to sleep, but the violent motion of the truck made that impossible.

Sometime after 1930 hours the trucks slowed again and drifted over to the verge. When they stopped, one of the guards looked in and said that a camp would be made at this location; anyone with rice would be allowed to cook it for an evening meal. Then he and the other soldier jumped down, stood with weapons held at port arms as Kim and the others stirred and began to file out.

In the darkness a woman's voice cried out—a thin shriek like that of a parrot—and then broke into shrill words: "He's dead, he's dead!" Kim, thinking only of food for Serey, did not hesitate or look behind her; nor did any of the others. When everyone else was out of the truck the soldiers swung inside. And reemerged a few seconds later carrying the limp body of a middle-aged man by wrists and ankles. The man's wife, the woman who had shrieked, came out behind them, moaning deep in her throat, plucking at the corpse as if trying to coax it back to life. The soldier holding the dead man's feet let go of them, so that the heels bounced and kicked up a thin puff of dust, and shoved the woman roughly to one side.

"Why do you mourn, old woman?" he said to her. "Your husband is better off dead. Everyone who is not strong enough to support the revolution is better off dead. There is no place in Angka for the weak."

The woman sat down in the dirt behind the truck and rocked herself, weeping silently, as the two guards carried her husband's corpse into the night. But once they were gone she got up again, fumbled inside a pouch at her waist, produced a small amount of rice, and went zombielike to join the others. Kim moved after her, because she had no rice for herself and the child. She helped the woman gather wood for a fire, fetch water from a stream near the highway, cook her few kernels of rice. The woman said nothing to her the entire time, and made no protest when Kim claimed some of the sticky cooked rice in payment.

Serey did not want to eat at first. She drank a great deal of water, vomited part of it, and gagged when Kim attempted to feed her some of the rice. "I want to sleep," she said, "can't I sleep?" But Kim said, "No, you must eat first—then you can sleep," and finally managed to get the child to swallow a few grams. Serey's face was still hot and damp, but the cough had gentled and become sporadic. Her eyes, heavy with fatigue, seemed clearer than they had in the truck. A night's rest, here where the air was clean and water flowed close by, might help break the fever again. Kim sat down with her back against a fruitless mango tree, pillowed Serey's head on her thigh, waited until the little girl was asleep, and then sought sleep for herself.

It was not to be. Less than three hours had passed since the convoy halted, and she had only just slid into a fitful doze, when the soldiers set up a shout. Dully Kim sat up. "Return to the trucks, take your places inside the trucks!" they were shouting. "We will leave here in five minutes!"

So there was to be no overnight camp after all. More lies, Kim thought. She leaned over Serey, saw that the child was breathing congestedly and had not yet awakened, and lifted both of them from the turf. Walked on pain-stiff legs to the line of trucks. Found a place inside one of them, on the edge of the bench near the opening.

Ten minutes later, not five—that, too, a lie—the engines

roared, the headlights flared, and the convoy set out once more through the darkness toward its unknown destination.

Foxworth

Three weeks before Christmas he made another trip to the refugee camp at Aranyaprathet.

There were several reasons for him going this time. One was that the CIA wanted more information on resistance activities in that area, because things were heating up along the border between Cambodia and Thailand: an increasing flow of refugees, despite stepped-up preventive measures by the communists; skirmishes between KC patrols and guerrillas that threatened the fragile relationship between the Bangkok and Phnom Penh governments. Relations between the Thais and the United States were also what Boyd, in his best British colonel manner, called "sticky." The fact was, the Thais were in a difficult position. For years now, despite the wars raging in Cambodia and Laos and Vietnam, they had managed to preserve their neutrality—but they had also accommodated American troops and matériel, permitted GKR training instruction and exercises within their borders, and were giving sanctuary not only to thousands of Cambodian refugees but, unwittingly, to burgeoning resistance groups. On the one hand they wanted to establish both trade and friendship agreements with the Phnom Penh regime, because of their geographic proximity and because they were afraid of attracting the serious attention of Red China and the Viet Cong, and they were determined to prevent ex-Cambodian military personnel from launching full-scale rollback operations from within Thailand. They were also determined to rid themselves of all the Cambodian and Laotian refugees as soon as possible, by any means short of forcing them back across the borders. On the other hand they needed American aid, and American aid was more or less contingent on doing what they were asked by the White House: accommodate the refugees, make no real effort to break up resistance efforts, maintain a certain aloofness in dealing with the communists. It was a delicate balancing act any way you looked at it, with all sides jockeying for some kind of leverage. Which was why the CIA wanted to know more about resistance efforts in the Aranyaprathet and other areas. And which was where Foxworth, like it or not, came in.

Then there were the refugees themselves. The inevitable corruption in the Thai bureaucracy had eroded even the bare-minimum living standards in the camps: less than fifteen of the forty cents allotted daily to each refugee was believed to be reaching them, with the rest being cut up among various officials. There were also reports of harassment and brutality, of young refugee women being kidnapped and sold into prostitution and slavery. Thai Premier Kukrit Pramoj had denied all of this, of course. He had also formally ruled out local settlement of the refugees and recommended voluntary repatriation or admission to third countries such as France; and at the same time he made noises about issuing seven-day entrance visas to all incoming refugees, at the end of which time the visas would not be renewed and the refugees would be returned. So much for Kukrit Pramoj. Foxworth's section head at the embassy wanted more information on the matter of corruption and brutality; so did Foxworth.

His third reason for going to Aranyaprathet was less well defined. It had to do with Kim, but it wasn't just the same mindless groping for news of her among the people in the camp. It was something else, a kind of act of desperation that he didn't want to admit to himself ahead of time. He had pushed himself physically and emotionally these past months until he was near the borderline; he couldn't go on this way, something had to give one way or another pretty soon. The presence in his life of Natalie Rosen wasn't helping matters, either. She had touched something inside him, opened him up. He kept fighting it and fighting her, but he was weakening. He sensed that all he had to do to drive her off was to tell her that he worked for the CIA; yet he couldn't bring himself to do that. He didn't *want* to drive her off. Except that he did. Except that he didn't. He kept having confused dreams about her and Kim and Andrea Vernon, one in particular where he was walking with the three of them in Le Phnom Park, and they each kept twirling a parasol high over their heads because the sky was raining blood, and then Andrea faded away and there was only Kim and Natalie, and then Kim began to fade, he could see her becoming transparent and falling away under the blood-rain, and at this point he would wake up drenched in cold sweat and trembling violently. You didn't need to be a Freudian psychoanalyst to interpret what all of that meant.

It was midafternoon when he and his marine driver arrived at the Aranyaprathet camp. There was a middle-aged American relief worker in the administrative shed, talking to the Thai officer in charge. The American seemed to recognize him, although Foxworth had no recollection of ever having met the man, and looked vaguely embarrassed, as if he and the Thai officer had been talking about embassy officials in general and Foxworth in particular. Which was ridiculous. Guilt, depression, paranoia . . . what was the next stage in his deteriorating mental state?

"I'll be going," the relief worker said perfunctorily, and nodded at Foxworth, and went out. Going where? Foxworth thought. Where were any of them going, refugees and relief workers and embassy officials alike?

He spent some time talking to the Thai officer, but he could feel himself growing restless. And so he foreshortened the discussion and asked to see Chuon Van, the camp leader he had spoken to on his previous visit. The Thai officer sent someone out into the compound. Ten minutes later Foxworth was sitting in a small side office with Chuon, watching the former schoolteacher chain-smoke unfiltered Thai cigarettes.

"I'd like to talk to you about the resistance movement," he said.

Chuon's expression was placid, but there was a flickering in his black eyes. "I know very little about it, as I have told you before."

"I think you know a great deal, Chuon."

"Such matters are forbidden by our Thai hosts."

"But you can't deny that there *are* guerrilla teams operating from Thailand, forbidden or not."

Chuon said cautiously, "I have heard this said, yes."

"Raids across the border, sabotage, things like that."

"Yes."

"And helping other Khmers to escape," Foxworth said. "That's another thing the resistance groups are involved in."

"Perhaps."

"At random—whoever they happen to encounter who wants to escape? Or could they find somebody if they had enough information, break that person loose from the KC and get her back across the border?"

Chuon squinted at him through the smoke from his cigarette. "Her? Why do you use the female pronoun?"

And there it was, out in the open now, all his cards on the table. He'd bluffed himself long enough. "*Would* something like that be possible, with enough information?"

"Why do you wish to know?"

"Please, Chuon—answer my question."

There was a thickness in his voice; he heard it and felt himself swallowing, as if to swallow the thickness. Chuon seemed to sense the emotion in him. He lit another cigarette, and his eyes were both probing and compassionate as they studied Foxworth. The situation was all wrong, turned upside down, like a scene in a play by Ionesco: it was the Cambodian who felt compassion for the American, the Cambodian who was calm and reasonable and the American who seemed to be coming apart under the strain.

"Yes," Chuon said at length. "It may be possible, if the location of the person is known and if it is within a reasonable distance from the border."

"What if the person's whereabouts aren't known?"

"Then I would say the chances are slim."

"Would there be any hope in trying?"

Chuon shrugged. "There is always hope. We live here on little else—hope that one day we will reclaim our homeland, hope that we may be allowed to live in a free country, hope for enough food to feed ourselves and our children."

"Suppose I gave you a complete dossier," Foxworth said. "Physical description, past history, everything. Would your people try to find her for me and bring her out?"

"You forget that I don't belong to the resistance."

"All right, then. Would you help me put the information in the right hands? I'll do whatever I can for you in return—money, an American visa, anything you want."

"You are most generous," Chuon said. If there was irony in the words, it was carefully concealed. "But you realize that such an undertaking would be dangerous to the person you seek. The resistance might never find her, and even under the greatest secrecy, word that she is being sought might reach the Khmer Rouge. If that happens, there is little doubt she would be executed."

"My God." Foxworth slumped back in his chair, ran a hand through his hair. He should have thought of that himself. He couldn't take a risk like that; he couldn't play God with Kim's life. Too many Americans had played God with too many Cambodian lives already.

"Perhaps you would like more time to consider the matter," Chuon said gently.

"Yes. More time. Thank you, Chuon."

"I did nothing. I will be here if you want me again."

When Chuon had gone Foxworth sat with his elbows on the table, chin resting on clenched hands. He felt like a fool. And driven, being pushed toward some profound, maybe devastating, crossroads decision in his life. He had felt the same sort of way in Phnom Penh, just before Operation Eagle Pull—a shifting and rearranging of values, feelings, attitudes, toward what this time he didn't know. All he knew for certain was that he had backed himself up just about as far as he could go; if he tried to maintain the pattern of existence he had followed since April, he would crack up just as Tom Boyd had predicted. The pressure was too intense, it was already leading him into irrational and desperate acts like this conversation with Chuon Van. The next thing he was liable to do was agree to spill everything to Peter Deighan, out of some insane belief that it would help Kim or purge his own demons. Either that, or he'd load up with an M-16 and a bandolier of ammunition, and join one of the guerrilla outfits so he could go looking for her himself.

No, he couldn't let anything like that happen, he couldn't let himself crack up. Which only left him with one alternative.

Somehow, in some way, he had to go sane.

Kim

Sunrise. The railroad yard at Pursat, west of the Tonle Sap on Highway 5. The banging of couplers, the hiss of steam and air brakes, the thunder of steel on steel as a train comprised of several passenger cars curled in from the north through an early-morning mist.

Kim stood watching it with Serey drowsy and fevered in her arms. There were at least a thousand others watching it too, on both sides of the repaired meter-gauge track. Some of them had been here when Kim's truck-convoy reached Pursat two hours past midnight; intermingled, they had all spent the time of darkness sleeping on the open ground inside the yard and along the tracks. Others had been trucked in just before dawn. From what desultory conversation had passed among them, Kim understood that they had been brought from all over the country: Takeo, Kompong Thom, Kompong Cham, Angkor Wat. None knew what their new destination might be, although Battambang Province seemed likely because this line, the oldest of the two in the country, stretched north to Battambang City and Sisophon. And all were images of those from Kim's commune, of Kim herself: skeletal, hollow-eyed, hopeless—a legion of dead souls standing motionless in the mist and heat of another day, awaiting transport to a different corner of hell.

The soldiers had stirred everyone awake just past dawn and begun a systematic search of each person, confiscating any goods which might have been overlooked or concealed, leaving them with nothing except sleeping mats, kettles, and rice pots.

Then portions of rice, enough for three days, and a minuscule amount of salt had been distributed. And now the train, like a demon with one eye and a breath of fire, was coming to swallow them all.

The clattering noise and a single whistle blast woke Serey, and she moved her head around to squint at the oncoming locomotive. Her lips were cracked, bleeding in two places; the skin of her face was spotted with flame-colored blotches and pinpoints of sweat. She said something so softly that Kim could not hear. The child repeated it against her ear, in a voice as cracked and dry as her lips.

"Are we going on the train?"

"Yes, little one."

"To a good place this time?"

"Yes," Kim lied. "To a good place."

The train drew closer. When it was within a hundred meters of where Kim stood with Serey, passing the first lines of people, a man in tattered clothing broke free from the others and ran screaming at the string of cars. Without hesitation he threw himself under the wheels of one of them. There was no audible sound; there was only a redness, and then something disgorged into the air, spat out by the demon, that landed a dozen meters away. Kim did not look at what it was.

Two other people, a man and a woman, attempted to take their lives in the same way as the train's speed slackened to a crawl; the soldiers stopped them, dragged them away. But on the opposite side of the tracks there were more screams, like faint echoes of the train whistle, and more redness appeared and disappeared beneath the cars.

The locomotive chuffed to a halt amid a grinding and hissing of brakes, seemed to stand panting under the red-and-gold sky. It was an old steam locomotive, run on coal and wood, and it belched steam and cinders that fell in a faint dark rain on those nearest the tracks. The cars were old too, thick with grime, the windows streaked to opaqueness. There were a dozen of them, all identical, all empty except for a contingent of soldiers.

Immediately, with no time wasted, the loading began. Soldiers clambered off the cars to open doors or to help the ground troops herd everyone close to the tracks; still other soldiers climbed up on top and stood with automatic weapons at port arms. People filed up the metal steps in a steady stream, hurried by shouts and weapon nudges.

Kim and Serey were among the first dozen into one of the cars midway along. The interior had been hollowed out, stripped of most of its seats, to create a giant oblong room—a giant oblong garbage bin, because the floor was littered with filth and the heat-choked air was alive with flies. The stench of vomit and excrement formed a palpable miasma, but it was overridden by the stench of death. Many people had died in this room, this garbage bin, this charnel place.

Bile lifted into the back of Kim's throat. She fought down the need to gag and went to one of the windows, tried to tug it open; it had been nailed shut. She turned away from it and grasped the handle on the connecting door to the next car. Bolted. More people kept coming in, and more, and more. Serey made whimpering sounds, other children cried, babies squalled. Kim fought toward the entrance, thinking the air might be fresher there, but she could not get past the center of the car: the density of bodies was too great. And yet still more people were forced inside by the soldiers—at least a hundred now, packed together like so many draft animals.

Draft animals. Oxen. Cattle. In her studies at the university, that other Kim in that other Kampuchea had read of the Second World War and of Jews being packed into cattle cars and sent to Nazi concentration and extermination camps. The book had said that such atrocities could not happen again, that the nations of the world would not let it happen a second time. But what was this? Was there any difference between the hand of Hitler and the hand of the Angkar Leu?

She was driven back against one of the windows, into a space just large enough for her to stand with Serey, or to sit with knees drawn up and the child braced against them. Still more bodies wedged inside. They were not people now, not even draft animals; they were a black swollen mass, a single grotesque creature with arms and legs like tentacles, with a hundred mouths gasping for breath and for mercy that would never come. Then, finally, over the panting and the wailing of children, Kim heard the entrance door slam shut and an outside bolt being thrown. The locomotive's whistle sounded. And after a long dreaming instant, the train began to slide around out of the yard and back onto the northbound track toward Battambang.

It was a little better after they were under way, because most of the people managed to find room to sit or kneel on the filth-caked floor and this relieved the milling crush of bodies. But the heat and the stench made breathing difficult, then painful, then torturous. Serey's fever raged; her body leaked fluid, drenching Kim's pajamas, and the whites of her eyes had a curdled look. She was coughing continually, and between coughs making words that bordered on delirium—calls for her mother, a fragment of a song she had once been taught, something about the face of God.

Kim closed her eyes and prayed to the Lord Buddha. Then, as the bonzes had done when there were still bonzes in Kampuchea, she made an effort to block out her surroundings and meditate herself to another plane of existence. She could not do it, but in the attempt she was able to endure the passage of the morning. The sun beating in through the opaque windows made an oven of the car. Flies crawled on her face, buzzed in her ears, fed on the salt of her sweat. A woman at the other end of the car died; Kim knew this because there was a small outcry from her husband. A young man stood and began to beat his head against the metal wall between two of the windows. No one tried to stop him. He kept beating it until blood flowed from several wounds, harder and harder, moaning, and then fell down and was either unconscious or dead.

Serey jerked awake and put her face close to Kim's, looked at her with bright fevered eyes. "Kim," she said.

"Shh. It's all right."

"I love you," Serey said. She closed her eyes again and put her head against Kim's breast.

More time passed. The rhythm of the train wheels, fast and steady on the straight stretches, slow and uneven on the curves, singing low notes when they crossed a rickety trestle bridge, began to deaden Kim's mind more effectively than her effort at meditation. She drifted within herself, afloat on the rhythm and the heat and the waves of pain throughout her body. Drifting, floating—

Something cold went through her, something thin and icelike and terrible. And this was strange because there was nothing cold in the place where she was drifting, nothing cold in the savage heat which surrounded her. She struggled back into awareness, opened her eyes. Her arms were around Serey; she withdrew them and lifted the child's head in her hands.

Then she knew what the cold thing was. Then she let out a soft mewling sound, a single helpless cry of anguish.

Serey was no longer breathing.

Serey had gone to look at the face of God.

Chey Han

Chey and a number of his soldiers were waiting at the railroad station in Sisophon when the latest trainload of redeportees arrived from Pursat. There had been several such trains since September, when Angka first ordered the relocation of the Phnom Penh prisoners of war for the rice harvest, and Chey had been on hand to meet all of them. This had been made part of his new duties in Battambang Province—to meet the trains, to have his soldiers ready with stretchers to remove the dead and the dying from the cars, to help supervise the exodus from Sisophon into the surrounding countryside by truck, tractor-drawn trailers, oxcart. How many dead chickens had come off the trains so far? he wondered as he waited on the platform this fine December afternoon. Oh, thousands. Thousands. And how many had he seen on the roads to Mongkol Borei, Phnom Srok, Phum Thmel and Svay Chek? Oh, tens of thousands. And how many had he executed so far, by command of the extraordinary Angkar Leu, for such heinous crimes as lovemaking and stealing a bit of rice to fill a shrunken belly? Oh, too many to count. Many too many to count.

And there would be many too many more to come, because a new round of purges was to begin soon. All those who had served the Lon Nol government as enlisted soldiers, as civil servants, as doctors and lawyers and teachers, were to be weeded out by collecting, checking, and rechecking written biographies. Only then, Angka said, would the old order be destroyed so that the new order could flourish. Only then would the People be safe from spies and traitors and imperialist corruption. Only then . . . when half the population had been reduced to bones in the killing fields.

"But after all," the headless bonze said to him, "they're only chickens. What can chickens matter?" And the bonze juggled his crimson head and prayed to Buddha and laughed and laughed.

The bonze had begun to speak to Chey inside his head not long after his arrival in Sisophon, at about the time he learned his wife had been killed in the war. At first he had not been able to understand what the bonze was saying and he was very frightened. The laughter frightened him too, even though he had heard it before; it rang like temple bells in his mind, sometimes throughout the night so that he was unable to sleep. But then the words of the bonze had become clear, and Chey realized there was nothing to fear. The bonze did not hate him because Ly Sokhon had chopped off his head with her Vietnamese sword. The bonze was his friend. The bonze was a wise man and counseled him well. He could not talk to any of his soldiers, he could not talk to any other commanders or military chiefs, he could not talk to civilian district committee or village chiefs. He could only talk to the bonze. Inside his head, intimately, where no one else could overhear.

They shared a great secret, Chey and the bonze. It was the headless one who had first whispered it to him, and now he knew, beyond any doubt, that it was true. The Angkar Leu was not extraordinary and not benevolent and not a salvation; Pol Pot and the other leaders had simply assumed the role of Lon Nol and the imperialist Americans. Chey and the bonze

discussed this truth at great length, but only between themselves. They dared not take anyone else into their confidence. It
would mean certain death for Chey, his own head severed and
juggled in someone else's bloody hands, inside someone else's
mind.

On some occasions they spoke of escape to Thailand; on
other occasions they spoke of revolt, of joining a clandestine
group of disgruntled officials which, he had learned in strictest
confidence, was being formed in Damban 106, the provinces of
Oddar Mean Chey, Siem Reap, and Kompong Thom, and
which wanted to bring back some of the old ways of living. But
the bonze did not care for either of those alternatives. The
bonze counseled caution, a longer period of waiting to see if
another choice presented itself, and Chey agreed that this was
the wisest course to follow. So he continued to perform his
duties as instructed, without question; he read communiqués,
filed reports, led patrols, carried out executions, waited at the
train station to supervise the removal of the dead and the dying
by stretcher, by trailer, truck, oxcart. And he ate his rice and
fish and meat, chewed his betel leaves with tobacco and cloves,
dreamed his dreams of Doremy and the joy he would never
have. And he spoke to no one of the Angkar Leu and to no one
of the bonze.

The train from Pursat glided in across the flat terrain from
the southeast, through the shimmers of afternoon heat haze.
Chey shouted orders, positioning his men and the lines of
trucks which would take this particular load of poultry south
along the Mongkol Borei River to the new commune in the
paddies near Lovea. Time was of the essence. The chickens
must be on their way by 1500 hours, so that they would reach
the commune before nightfall and be rested and available for
harvest work in the morning.

When the train stopped Chey saw to it that the doors were
unbolted immediately, that the outspill of poultry began with
no wasted minutes. Some of the chickens looked stunned as
they emerged; some could not walk by themselves and had to
be carried or supported; a few were laughing, chattering, and
squawking like hens in a farmyard, their eyes shining madly in

the sunlight. Chey moved among them, up and down the platform, impervious because he had seen them all before: one
chicken was like another, alive or dead, whether or not it had
lost its senses.

The flow from within the cars became a trickle and finally
stopped altogether. As soon as this happened Chey sent the
stretcher bearers inside, the third car from the locomotive first
because it contained at least a dozen bodies stacked in one
corner like cordwood. He went down to the rear car, where two
of his soldiers had gotten into an argument, and shouted at
them to resume their duties. Then he started back toward the
locomotive again.

"Look there," the bonze said suddenly. Blood spurted from
one of his eyes; he juggled it away. "That hen—isn't she familiar? Don't you know her, Chey Han?"

He stopped, staring ahead, shading his eyes from the sun
glare. The female chicken had just come out of one of the cars
and was walking alongside a stretcher carrying the body of a
young chick. Chey saw her only in profile, at some distance, but
the bonze was right, she did seem familiar. He moved forward
several steps, at an angle to the hen so that he might better see
her face. When he did see it clearly it appeared to him as ravaged, streaked with grime and sweat, no face he had ever
known. And yet, perhaps he *did* know it . . .

"Than Kim," the bonze said.

"No," he said, "no."

"It's your half-sister Than Kim."

Two of the soldiers had taken hold of her, were pulling her
away from the stretcher, dragging her into the crowd of other
chickens. Chey lost sight of her, and as soon as he did he
stopped moving and wiped sweat from his face with his uniform
sleeve. Then he reached into his shirt pocket, took out the tin
he kept there, pinched up a few grains of salt from inside, and
put them on his tongue. While he was doing that the gaggle of
poultry moved out of his line of vision, toward the trucks waiting outside the station.

"It couldn't have been Than Kim," he said to the bonze.

"Are you sure?"

"Yes. Than Kim is dead."

"Are you sure?"

"I have no one, bonze, no family left in all of Kampuchea. I have only you."

But she had resembled Kim in some ways, and in truth he did not know what had happened to his half-sister in the years since she had left Preah Vihear Province for Phnom Penh and the university. Was it possible that it *had* been her? That her unimaginable journey, his own years of fighting in the jungles, all that had happened since the seventeenth of April, had brought them together again here, in this place and time, at a train filled with death? Than Kim, he thought, remembering. Younger than him by two years, playing together as children, taunting each other because they were only half-sister and half-brother . . .

"Chickens," the bonze whispered, and laughed and laughed and laughed.

Cambodia File: Letter from (Name Withheld), Aranyaprathet Refugee Camp, to Ethnic Affairs Officer, Refugee Section, U.S. Embassy, Bangkok

On Tuesday you came to Aranyaprathet camp. Then I wanted to talk to you, but I didn't because you were very busy and I didn't want to disturb you.

I was very excited when I saw you coming the other day—I thought that I would have a chance to go to the U.S.A.

I want to get married. I asked for the hand of an unmarried

woman. I am engaged. My fiancee's name: (withheld). She is a Christian.

I want to know whether I can take my future wife with me to the U.S.A. I'm afraid that if I want to take a wife with me I will not be accepted.

Is it possible for me to take her with me to the U.S.A.?

If it is impossible, would you please cross her out.

In the U.S.A. I heard that it is hard to find a Khmer wife. That's why I want to get married. On the other hand, I'm a Christian. I want to marry a Christian woman.

Do my plans fit with the American criteria?

Would you please tell me the truth so that I can make up my mind about marrying or not.

I would be very grateful for a reply. Finally I wish you a long life.

God bless and keep you and your family always.

Natalie

New Year's Eve.

In Cambodia, as the refugees and the Bangkok *Post* reported, people were dying from starvation, disease, and genocidal brutality. In Aranyaprathet and the other camps, there was not enough food or medical supplies, despite the efforts of the Refugee Relief Fund and a dozen other foreign and local relief organizations, and more than a hundred and fifty refugees had died since May. In Washington, State Department officials were saying that at most ten thousand Laotians and Cambodians could expect to receive entry permits in 1976—this contrary to the fact that France was expected to admit at least triple that number, and 139,000 Vietnamese had been admitted to the U.S. after the collapse of the Saigon regime. And in the American embassy in Bangkok, while all this was happening on the last day of 1975, there was going to be—predictably enough—a nice festive New Year's Eve party complete with band, champagne, hors d'oeuvres, and no doubt funny hats and noise-makers.

Hooray for our side, Natalie thought sourly. *Vive les Americains.*

She did not want to go to the damn party. But David had invited her, which was a little surprising, saying that he didn't want to go either but that it was mandatory for him and why didn't they suffer through it together. So it was either attend or do what she had done on Christmas: sit in the house near Lumpini Park, talk to her father on overseas telephone long enough to exchange more Hanukkah greetings, talk to her Thai hosts for a while, go to bed early, and feel sorry for herself and the world at large the whole time. She just didn't feel capable of that on a New Year's Eve in Bangkok, halfway around the world from home.

So here she was, all prettied up in an appropriate gown, riding in a taxi along the paved asphalt driveway toward the grayish concrete embassy building. She was an American, after all, and this was what Americans did on holidays. Dressed up, went to parties. Danced, laughed, ate too much, drank too much, kissed each other at midnight, sang "Auld Lang Syne," maybe did a little drunken groping, and woke up hung over in the morning telling each other what a great time they'd had. A tradition, that was what it was. A great American tradition.

Vive la tradition.

The drive curled past a grassy area and a pond with geese floating in it, and made a loop around an oval with a fountain poking up from the middle. The fountain was turned on and floodlit, and there were American and Thai couples moving between it and the embassy entrance and the parking lot straight ahead. The lot was already half full, even though it was only a quarter of eight.

The taxi turned in past the fountain, drew up at the entrance. A uniformed marine opened the door for her, handed her out, checked her invitation, and allowed her to proceed up the steps.

Two things smacked into her as she stepped into the lobby. One was the rarefied air conditioning, in sharp contrast to the pressure of the heat outside. The other was Peter Deighan. He was with another man, one of the minor embassy officials whose name Natalie had forgotten, talking to him earnestly as they walked toward the doors; he didn't see Natalie and she didn't recognize him until they collided.

"Sorry," he said, and then saw who she was and gave her a crooked smile. "Well, hello there."

"How are you, Mr. Deighan?"

"Call me Peter." He gave her an appraising look, but there was none of the drunken arrogance or machismo in it that there had been in Phnom Penh. There was something different about him, and not just in his more presentable appearance; she'd noticed that on the other two occasions she had bumped into him, not quite so literally, since her arrival in Bangkok. Like David, and like herself in some ways, Deighan was not the same man he had been back in February. "On your way to the ball, are you?"

"Yes. Under protest."

"I wouldn't go even under protest," he said. He was wearing a rumpled tropical suit, no tie; the embassy official wore a business suit and, naturally, a tie. "We just got back from the refugee camp at Surin."

"Oh?"

"I'm doing a book on Cambodia, and I wanted to talk to some of the refugees. George here helped arrange it." George here looked a little uncomfortable, as if arranging a trip to Surin for Peter Deighan was not something he had done happily. "Conditions there are miserable."

"Yes, they are."

"Were you at Surin recently?"

"Last month."

"Worse now," Deighan said. "More people coming in every day." He gave her another appraising look. "How would you feel about an interview?"

"What sort of interview? Like the one in Phnom Penh?"

"No," he said seriously. "I'm off booze these days, and my wife's here in Bangkok; in fact, I'm on my way home right now. I mean a legitimate interview on your relief work. You were in Phnom Penh, you saw what things were like there firsthand.

That's the kind of slant I'm after in the book—personal experience."

"Well—" She hesitated. "Would you let me read anything you write before publication? And make changes if I object to something?"

"Sure. Fair enough."

"Then I suppose it'll be all right." She gave him the telephone number of the Thai Relief Organization offices on Vorachak Road, which was where the Fund had its Bangkok office. "Call me and we'll set up a time."

"Right. I've got to go; enjoy the party."

"I'd rather enjoy the new year, Mr. Deighan. But I doubt if I'll like either one."

"You never know," he said. "And will you please, for Christ's sake, call me Peter?" He went to the doors with George-here, who still looked uncomfortable, and the two of them disappeared into the night.

Natalie found her way to the main reception area. She had half expected to see crepe-paper streamers draped from the ceiling and walls, but they had more dignity than that, at least. And no noisemakers and party favors in evidence either. Just a bar, a buffet table, the usual embassy furniture strategically arranged, and a dais on which a Thai band played a combination of Western and Asian music, none of it very well but all of it softly, thank God. The crowd numbered about fifty so far, an equal mixture of Americans and a few other Westerners in tuxedos and ballroom gowns and glittering jewelry, and Thais and a few other Asians in tuxedos and patterned silk, star sapphires, and princess rings. Several white-jacketed Thai waiters circulated among them, bringing drinks and passing out hors d'oeuvres.

She looked for David but didn't see him. He was probably still at dinner with the Thai politicians, which was the reason why he hadn't called for her, as gentlemen were supposed to do on social occasions such as this; he had apologized for it too, not that it mattered one bit to her. She did see several other people she knew, a couple of whom began to make their way toward her. In self-defense she got to a passing waiter before the acquaintances got to her and plucked a glass of champagne off the tray he was carrying. A little insulation, that was what she needed, because this whole atmosphere was giving her a vague crawly feeling already. Peter Deighan had started her brooding again, with his talk of the conditions at Surin and his request for an interview, and she found herself contrasting the expensive gaiety here with the squalor in which the refugees were forced to live. It was going to be a long night.

She spent the next hour talking to people, answering questions, smiling, dancing with the deputy chief of mission, the head of the Economic Commercial Section, the Thai vice-premier, and in fending off Tom Boyd, whom she had met in Phnom Penh and who was there with an attractive Thai woman and who seemed intent, in a suave and unctuous fashion, on seducing a nice Jewish girl from New York City. She got through it all with the help of three more glasses of champagne, very good champagne too, private French stock, nothing but the best for the ringing out of the old and the ringing in of the new. She knew she was getting tipsy and didn't care. She had a right to get tipsy, didn't she? Faced with starving refugees, and Thai bureaucracy, and American indifference, and emotional involvement with a man who might just work for the goddamn CIA, faced with all of that and a New Year's Eve party at the American embassy, complete with a jerk who was trying to smooth-talk his way into her pants, she had *every* right to get tipsy, didn't she?

David arrived at nine o'clock, with a contingent of three Thai politicians and their wives. When she saw him she was talking to the ambassador himself, William Kintner, and trying not to slur her words, and she felt more relieved than she ought to have that he was finally there. Shining knight come to rescue the damsel in distress, before she succumbed to boredom, rage, drunkenness, or the lustful intentions of a jerk. Hah. Some shining knight. Shining *spook* might be a better term for him. Hmm?

Still, she felt the relief, and when he came over her way, displacing the ambassador in the space next to her, she enjoyed the lingering touch of his hand. Got a little thrill from it, even.

My God, she thought, maybe I'm horny. Champagne has been known to have that effect on people. Yes it has.

"I wanted to be here sooner," David said, "but we got a late start for dinner. I'm sorry."

"Don't apologize. I'm having a gay old time."

"Are you?"

"No," she said. She held up her empty glass. "But this helps me fool myself a little."

"I wish I could fool myself." The tone of his voice made her look more closely at him. His face was strained, smudged around the eyes; the smile he wore looked painted on. She could feel his pain again, and responded to it as always, absorbing it.

"Try my remedy," she said, and held up the glass again.

"I don't have much tolerance for liquor anymore."

"Champagne isn't liquor. It's medicine." Not to mention an aphrodisiac, she thought.

"Maybe I'll try a glass or two."

"I'll try them with you," she said. "You can tell me all about your dinner with the Thais, and how they've changed their minds and plan to open their hearts and their purse strings to the poor refugees."

They drank a glass of bubbly together, and talked, and danced once because Tom Boyd asked her to waltz and the only way she could think of to refuse him was to say she had promised the dance to David. It was rather nice, dancing with him, holding him and being held by him; in fact, it was very nice. More little thrills, and a warmth down low in her body—part of it the champagne, part of it her empathy, part of it something else that she didn't want to think about. Horny, all right. For all the good it was likely to do her.

It got to be ten o'clock, and then eleven. Most of the time passed in a kind of fuzzy party whirl, even though she only spent part of it with David: he had to circulate, talk to the Thais, dance with Thai wives, play his part in the political game. The problem of Tom Boyd ceased to be a problem when she told him, in a polite whisper, that he might as well go screw himself because *she* wasn't interested. Or words to that effect.

288

He managed to avoid her and pay more attention to his Thai date after that.

The only other problem was that she had to quit partaking of the champagne. Little warning bells began to go off inside her head, telling her she had reached her limit; if she drank any more right now she would throw up, or fall down, or otherwise disgrace herself and the Refugee Relief Fund both. But not drinking any more meant that the effects of all she had drunk began to gradually wear off, and as soon as she started to feel sober again, she also started to think about Surin and Trat and Aranyaprathet, and Washington, and Phnom Penh, and before long it was rage instead of champagne that was bubbling inside her.

A decade ago Southeast Asia had been, in the words of Hubert Humphrey, "a great adventure" for the United States; so the flower of American youth had been dedicated to the reaffirmation of democratic principle. But in those ten years two Presidents had been thrown out of office, fifty thousand Americans had died in Vietnam, ten times as many as that had had their lives destroyed or seriously altered, and Southeast Asia had been bombed, invaded, abandoned, and taken over by the communists. So much for the reaffirmation of democratic principle. But the music still played, the political games still went on, the same attitudes still prevailed. And the people still suffered; the people still died. She wanted to walk up onto the dais and scream it at them: "The people are still dying! Why don't you care about the people!" But of course she wouldn't do any such thing. She didn't have the courage. Any more than Johnson had had the courage to confront the implications of his actions in 1965; any more than Kissinger had the courage to face the truth of a single dead Cambodian.

Bastards, she thought. Bastards, all of them, and her not much better. Not *any* better, because here she was, right in the midst of them, drinking champagne with them, dancing with them, being the same kind of hypocrite they were—

"Natalie?"

She blinked, realized that David had come up and was staring at her intently.

"You look grim," he said. "Are you all right?"

"No, I'm not all right. I hate myself for being here. And I think it's about time I left."

"There's another fifty minutes until midnight."

"I don't care about midnight," she said. "I don't want to be here at midnight; I don't want to sing 'Auld Lang Syne' and pretend the world is going to be a happy place in 1976."

"Neither do I," David said. "I'll leave with you."

The offer surprised her. "Do you mean that, or are you just being impulsive?"

"I mean it. There's no reason why I have to stay until the clock strikes twelve. Just give me time to tell a couple of people I'm going."

He went away and Natalie edged toward the outer archway, refusing another dignitary's dance request on the way. The air conditioning was making her shiver now. Or maybe it was just the let-down from her champagne high. But the chill disappeared once David returned and they were out of the embassy; the thick dry-season heat saw to that. She was sweating—not perspiring, as nice girls were supposed to do even in the tropics; really sweating—by the time they reached David's car, an embassy-maintained Ford, in the parking lot.

When they turned out of the compound on Wireless Road he asked her, "Do you want to go straight home? Or could you stand another drink somewhere?"

"I could stand another drink," she said; "I'm going to have a hangover tomorrow anyway, so it might as well be a good one. But I couldn't take another party or any more cheerful people."

He was silent for a moment. Then he said, "I've got liquor and mix at my villa, if you want to stop there. It's not very far and it's guaranteed quiet."

"Guaranteed quiet is just what I need right now."

He drove around to Sukhumvit Road. His villa—actually a small stucco house, but David was one of those Americans who had fallen into the habit of labeling "villa" anything in this part of the world larger than a tent—was set back from the street and had a screened veranda and a lot of purple bougainvillea growing over it. The interior wasn't such a much: plain stucco walls, tasteless imitation Western furniture no doubt supplied by David's Thai landlord, and almost no personal touches. A place where he lived, but not a place he had tried to make his own. A lonely place.

He switched on the air conditioner, mixed them a brace of gin-and-quinine, light on the gin, and then led her out onto the veranda. She happened to glance at her watch as they went. The time was four minutes to 1976.

It was quiet here, as he had said it would be; the only sounds were those made by insects, plus indistinct party noises from one of the other houses nearby. The air was heavy with the perfume of night-blooming jasmine. She took deep breaths of it, and sipped at her drink, and looked out over the fanciful shadow shapes and glow of lights that was Bangkok, and felt his nearness, his need, and his anguish, and the warmth flared up again low in her body. Neither of them said anything. It was a good soft moment, the kind that didn't want words because words would only have spoiled it.

But then there was a faint burst of cheering from the nearby house, American voices that faded into off-key singing. David said, "It's midnight."

"Yes. Let's go inside, David."

They went back through the veranda doors, stopped again after a few paces as if by tacit agreement. "Happy New Year, Natalie," he said, and his face was close to hers, shadowed in the light from a single small lamp, and she said, "I hope so, for all of us," and felt the warmth rise and make her feel aggressive as well as sensual, and she thought: I don't care if you work for the CIA, I don't care—and kissed him, put her glass down and her arms around him and kissed him, a long kiss that made the warmth spread hotter, made his hands tighten on her shoulders. He broke it finally, saying "Oh God, Natalie—" in a voice heavy with emotion, but she said, "Don't say anything, don't talk," and kissed him again, kept kissing him until he began to match her aggression with aggression of his own, until the kiss turned hungry and for the first time what flowed out of him and into her was not pain but desire, a warmth as hot as hers, hotter, burning, so that when the need to quench it became overpowering there was nothing for him to do except take her into the bedroom, take her to bed, take her.

And a little while after that, she knew beyond any doubt that she loved him.

Deighan

On the way home to Carol, riding with George Spencer in Spencer's embassy Impala, Deighan kept sliding up and down the scale of his emotions—high to low, low to high, happy, eager, worried, angry, bitter, afraid.

Happy: He had spent two productive days in Surin, gathering material for the last half of *The Rape of Cambodia*—detailed refugee accounts that he had taped and would set down verbatim. And tonight, in the chance meeting with Natalie Rosen, she of the nice *tsitskas,* he had lined up yet another strong chapter. The book was going well too, sixty-five thousand words so far, a little less than half finished; if he maintained his present pace, he'd have it done by April. His agent had already sold one of the early sections, to *Pacific Monthly* for two thousand dollars, payable on acceptance, money wired and received on December 15, and she claimed to be "very close to a major deal" with Scribner's on the book rights.

Angry, bitter: Seeing the refugees, the hellhole they were forced to live in—particularly seeing it with George Spencer, who thought Kissinger was a great man and Ford a brilliant political intellect—had transported him back in time to Phnom Penh, made him confront the whole ugly chain of events all over again. And confront not just the weakness of his country but his own weakness too, the liquor, the whores, the lust for war and death. He had come out of Surin feeling even more dedicated to telling the truth in *The Rape of Cambodia,* to rubbing the noses of the White House lads in the kind of dung they had left behind.

Eager: He had not seen Carol in three days, and it was New

Year's Eve, and he had a bottle of French perfume for her that Spencer had finagled in Surin. Spencer was a twit but Spencer was also greedy, malleable, and susceptible to exotic local vices; there was one like him in every embassy, regardless of country or administration, and once you found him you had yourself a neat little arrangement: you told him things, like the location of gambling dens and the names of whores with Asian specialties, and he told you things, like nonclassified information and embassy scuttlebutt; you did things for him, like hand over a few dollars in "expense money" now and then, and he did things for you, like finagle a bottle of French perfume on New Year's Eve in a small Thai town. Deighan would rather have had a bottle of French champagne for the occasion, but he was drinking almost nothing these days and besides, Carol wouldn't want anything to do with liquor, or with him if he celebrated alone.

Worried: The feeling of wrongness in Carol's behavior had persisted all month, nothing more tangible than her refusal to talk about what was on her mind, or about Paris or any other future plans—a feeling that she was slipping away from him. It seemed at odd moments that he could almost see her withdrawing, retracting into herself, swaddling in that inner peace, whatever the hell it was, that sustained her. She had kept refusing to go to Paris for the holidays, until it got to be too late to make any arrangements. She had consented to a week-long tour of upcountry Thailand before Christmas, the now-famous Bridge on the River Kwai, the teak forests in Khao Yai National Park, the Pimai ruins, elephant races, all that tourist crap, but after three days on the road she'd claimed to be tired of the travel and asked to be taken back to Bangkok. She seldom left the bungalow after that, not even to visit the silk weavers at Jim Thompson's Thai House, and spent a lot of her time reading in bed, avoiding his conversation. She was as cooperative sexually as ever, but the eagerness was gone, the sense of involvement had slipped away too, giving him the feeling that she was dutifully going through the motions just to get it out of the way so she could return to that insulated place inside herself, away from him and the pressures of lovemaking.

Afraid: That what all of it meant, added together, was that she intended to leave him. Just as he had left her to go to Vietnam, left her again to go to Cambodia. That the whole purpose of her coming to Bangkok was an elaborate plot, maybe not even a conscious one, to get even with him—reestablish their relationship, pretend to love him again, build him up, and then walk away from him and let him come crashing down from these new heights. If it was true she would succeed well enough because he couldn't bear either the betrayal or the loss of her. If it was true and all of these past months had been a lie, he knew he would dive right back into the bottle and the whores and the suicidal depression, the whole cycle all over again, only much worse. The irony would be intolerable. It was restlessness, a search for meaning—not rebellion, not insensitivity, not a lack of desire for her—which had driven him away to the war zones of Saigon and Phnom Penh. Yet all his search had brought him was shame and a slow erosion of everything he had ever believed in. He had recaptured himself, found a real sense of meaning, only because of her. Without Carol, he was and always had been nothing.

But all of this was a tower of sand, a fiction manufactured by his literary imagination. Sure it was. She wasn't going to leave him. She hadn't set him up to betray him; she was incapable of that sort of malice. It wasn't that at all.

All right, but then what *was* it?

His mind backed off from the question. And he went skidding back up the emotional scale until he was locked in on eager and happy, telling himself that it was New Year's Eve, for God's sake, this was no time to brood, this was a time for celebration, this was homecoming after three days of hell and George Spencer. Carol would greet him with a kiss, they'd talk a little, he'd give her the French perfume, they'd talk some more, they'd have some tea, they'd go to bed and make love and time it so that they'd set off their own fireworks display at the hour of midnight.

He had himself convinced that that was how it would be until Spencer eased the Impala off Issraphard Road and to a stop in front of the bungalow. Then he felt himself backsliding again, down to worried, almost down to afraid.

There were no lights on in the bungalow.

There should have been lights, she should be here. She knew he was coming home tonight; he'd given her his schedule before he left for Surin. She might be in bed, maybe that was it . . . except that it wasn't even nine o'clock yet, why would she be in bed, sleeping, before nine o'clock on New Year's Eve?

He made short work of the amenities with Spencer, swung his bag out of the rear seat, and hurried up past the acacia tree to the front door. When he turned his key in the lock and pushed inside, thick coils of heat clogged around him in the pristine black: the air conditioner was off. The feeling of wrongness seemed to lunge at him again. He fumbled for the light switch, clicked it on. The living room looked the same, nothing different, nothing removed, the teak screens still in place to form his office.

"Carol?"

Silence. He dropped his bag, started for the doors to the garden, stopped, reversed himself, and moved into the hallway that led to the bedroom.

"Carol?"

"Yes, Peter. In here."

The words startled him, even though they were soft-spoken, barely audible. They came out of the darkness inside the bedroom, and there was something in them, a strangeness, that combined with the disembodied quality to put a faint coldness across his shoulder blades. *Wrong, something's wrong.* He ran his tongue over dry lips, went to the bedroom door, pushed it open, and stepped inside. Just enough moonlight filtered in through the chinks in the rattan window blinds to let him see the shapes of furniture, the shape of Carol sitting propped up in bed. In the dark. Propped up in bed in the dark.

"Don't turn on the lights," she said.

"Why not? Carol, what's the matter?"

"I have to talk to you and I'd rather do it this way."

"Why are you here in the dark like this, with the air conditioner shut off?"

"I was cold."

"Cold? It must be ninety in here. Are you sick?"

"Peter, come sit on the bed so we can talk."

"Not until I put the lights on," he said, and before she could protest he touched the wall switch, blinked as the overhead fixture chased away the darkness.

Carol was wearing her nightgown, the blue one, sitting with her hands folded in her lap. Her expression was . . . God, so serene she looked unreal, like a life-size image of a saint. But there was melancholy in her eyes, and a kind of gauntness to her face, a look of both strain and weariness that hadn't been there three days ago. Or maybe it had been there and he'd just refused to see it.

There was something else the lights showed him, over on the carpet near the teak dresser. Carol's suitcases, both of them, sitting side by side and bulging in a way that told him they were packed full.

He felt a wrenching inside, at the center of himself. "What's going on here?" he said. He went to the bed, stood looking down at her. "Why are your bags packed?"

Her throat worked several times before she answered. "This isn't going to be easy, Peter."

"I don't care about that. Why are your bags packed?"

"I was going to leave yesterday, while you were away."

"Leave? To go where?"

"Home. Back to California."

"For God's sake, *why?*"

"Because I didn't want to face you," she said. Wetness glistened in her eyes, but there were no tears. "I was going to write you a letter and put it on the table for you to find. But I couldn't bring myself to do it that way. It would have been cruel and ugly and unfair, and I just couldn't. I guess I knew back in April that I wouldn't be able to when the time came."

"Back in April," he said bitterly. "So there it is. You bitch, you planned all of this. You *planned* it."

"Don't call me names, Peter, please."

"A fraud all along, a calculated lie. You never gave a damn about me—"

"Oh, Peter, that's not true. That's the furthest thing from the truth. I came here because I wanted to find out if I still loved you and you still loved me, and I do and you do. I needed you desperately then. I still need you."

"Then why did you want to leave?"

"I felt I had to. For your sake and my own. But now I know I've been selfish; I can't hurt you like that, I can't make it any worse for either of us than it's going to be already. We need each other more than ever; to see it through together."

His mind was chaotic. He couldn't seem to sort through her words to get at the sense of them. "What are you talking about? I don't understand what you're saying."

"I thought about telling you the truth a hundred times," Carol said, "but I couldn't do that either. I couldn't shatter you just when you were beginning to find yourself again. I can bear the burden alone, or I could until now; I've found the strength to put me at peace. And you're strong again too, and I don't want to be alone when it happens. I don't think I could bear that."

And all at once the chaos settled into clarity, he saw the sense of it all, and there was another wrenching, a terrible inner agony as of hands tearing at his entrails, and he knew what she was talking about even before she said the words, he knew why she had come to Bangkok, he knew why she had wanted to leave without him, he knew the reason she looked strained and tired and spent so much time in bed lately, he knew the cause of her near-religious serenity, he knew he knew he knew—

"I'm dying, Peter," she said. "I have a blood disease. I have terminal cancer."

Kim

In the paddies, as she had every morning since the death trip to Battambang, Kim stood hunched forward and used an ancient rice knife to harvest the ripe stalks. The knife had a small prong which sliced through the stalks on the forward swing, a large wooden curve to gather a new bunch for cutting on the back swing. Slash, retreat. Slash, retreat. The first smudges of dawn were beginning to show on the horizon, but it was still dark: she and the other women worked by lantern light from 0500 hours until daylight. In the afternoon, after the midday break for feeding—half her daily ration of one hundred grams of rice—she would cut the sun-dried heads off the stacked bunches, toss whole rice grains in large bamboo trays to winnow the kernels from the husks. In the evening, she would eat the other half of her rice and listen to the Radio Phnom Penh broadcast sent by loudspeaker trucks over the paddies; then, because she was a member of a *kemlang,* a mobile group of single persons between the ages of fifteen and forty-four, and as such spent all her time in the paddies, day and night until the harvest ended, she would lie on her mat under one of the few trees and live in darkness and nightmare until the cycle began again at 0500 hours.

Slash, retreat.

There was an old saying that Khmers had been put on earth to serve the will of the weather; that it was an overbearing taskmaster and made them slaves to the monsoon and the drought, slaves to the land. Radio Phnom Penh spoke of this often, in its new and altered revolutionary language, urging each person and each "production cooperative," the new official name for the communes, to greater struggle so that the weather, the land, the future could be mastered. But it was all another lie in the spider's web of lies which stretched across Kampuchea. The weather was not the enemy, nor was the land; the future would never be mastered by those who toiled and died in the communes. The enemy was the Khmer Rouge—the soldiers, the civilian guards and chiefs, the *chhlop,* the power structure in Phnom Penh. What they had already done to the old Khmer country of the Moka Nokar was monstrous, far more terrible than anything the Thai, the Annamese, the Vietnamese, the French, the Americans, had done to them over centuries because this was their country too, they were Khmers. No matter how mutated and evil, they were Khmers.

Slash, retreat.

Slash, retreat.

She imagined that each of the stalks was a Khmer communist, and with each forward stroke of the rice knife she was separating heads from shoulders, limbs from torsos. It was a sense-
less game; she knew this, and knew also that it would have
been better if she merely blanked her mind, used her newfound
gift for slipping into unconsciousness while she worked. Still,
she played the game every morning—and played a variation of
it in the afternoons as well. More than once in the night, when
she allowed herself reflection, she had wondered if perhaps she
was insane. If Serey's death and her own ordeal had broken her
fragile hold on sanity. It had happened to others on the train, at
the commune of identical straw-covered huts near Lovea, here
in the fields, and no doubt it had happened and was happening
on all the other trains and communes and fields in Kampuchea.
It was not impossible that it had happened to her.

Except that it had not. Nor would it. What had happened to
her was not insanity, it was hatred.

At first, that lifetime ago in April, she had had hope for
Kampuchea and a will to survive; then she had had hopelessness for all but herself and Serey; then there had been
nothing at all, a numbness, a living just to span the time until
death came; then Serey had died and the hatred had been born,
there in the filthy railroad car, while she held the child's lifeless
body in her arms—hatred that rekindled her will to survive, that
burned as hot and bright as the sun above her now. Because of
it, she had not mourned Serey beyond that first day, when they
arrived in Sisophon and the soldiers dragged her away from the
stretcher bearing those pathetic remains. Serey was only another victim, Serey was better off in death, Serey had gone to
live with God. She would not have been able to keep the child
with her anyway, because at the new commune children and
adults had been separated and the children taken elsewhere for
"reeducation." No mourning, only hate. Hate fed her, hate sustained her, hate gave her the strength to go on.

Hate, and the thought of escape.

Slash, retreat.

Slash, escape.

The Thai border was fifty or sixty kilometers from Lovea, beyond the northern reaches of the Cardamom Mountains; in that respect the Khmer Rouge had done her a favor by relocating her here. Now, if she were able to get away from them, it would be Thailand, not Vietnam, into which she could flee. A free country, not another communist state.

Thailand . . . where David was?

She had not thought of David in a very long time. He was a part of her life which no longer existed; a part of her which no longer existed. His face, now that she sought to conjure up an image of it, was indistinct, a face like all American faces. She could not recall his body, or the touch of his hands, or the words he whispered to her in the darkness. What she did remember was that he had begged her to come live with him in Bangkok, and now, nine months later, the entire focus of her existence was centered on escaping to Thailand. She had come full circle, through incredible misery, to the very decision she had faced in April in Phnom Penh. Which perhaps made her a fool, but that did not matter. Her foolishness was not important. David was not important. Only hatred and escape and survival were important, because if she could reach Thailand she could bear witness to all that was happening in Kampuchea under the yoke of the Angkar Leu, and she could live to fight them and see them destroyed.

Slash, retreat.

She longed to leave now, at this moment. The flat black-and-green earth, the irrigation canals and paddies glistening like mirrors that seemed to stretch endlessly from the Mongkol Borei River toward Phum Siem, made her feel exposed, trapped within their vastness. If she did not flee soon, she felt she would suffocate. Or the Khmer Rouge would learn the truth about her past, what she had done for the Americans and the Lon Nol regime in Phnom Penh, and suffocate her even more quickly.

She had been forced to write out a complete biography after arrival at the commune, and she had been questioned twice since. The KC were looking for former FANK enlisted men, as well as anyone who had been educated beyond village-school level—teachers, students, doctors, civil servants, high-level monks, wealthy farmers. They said it was because these people's skills were needed to assist in reeducation of the population, but of course this was another lie. The truth was that all of these individuals were marked for death, and the reason, Kim suspected, was that the Khmer Rouge now sought to reshape Kampuchean society by eliminating the cultural, social, and political past: the uneducated and the uninformed posed little threat of rebellion. She herself was marked for death for this same reason; it was only a matter of time before Angka discovered that she was not the simple peasant she claimed to be.

Nevertheless, she must be careful. If she made her escape attempt at the wrong time, under the wrong set of circumstances, and she were caught, she would be executed immediately. She must not let them kill her, she must not die by their hand. There would only be one opportunity, and therefore she must choose it well—be patient, continue to work until the harvest was ended and she was returned to the cooperative, where more opportunities presented themselves; say nothing, lie as they lied, and survive until the time came.

Slash, retreat.

Survive to escape; escape to survive.

Slash. Slash. Slash . . .

Cambodia File: U.S. Intelligence Report, February 1976 (Secret)

Prince Sihanouk has made a firm decision to stay on as Cambodia's titular head of state despite his delicate and uncertain position with the Khmer communists.

Sihanouk had considered going into permanent exile several times in recent months. He decided not to do so because he thought there was still a remote chance of his resuming a significant role in Cambodian affairs. The Prince is aware that he is regarded as an anachronism by Cambodia's communist rulers, but he may hope to bend slightly their radical policies.

The Prince's future probably is still a contentious issue among the Khmer communists. Sihanouk says Deputy Prime Minister Ieng Sary is intensely hostile but that others want him to remain head of state.

Although those with long-standing grudges against the Prince would like to get rid of him, the Khmer communists probably will not act hastily to depose him.

Sihanouk is said to fear the possibility of assassination, but believes that the presence of several communist embassies in Phnom Penh will afford him some protection.

Ly Sokhon

"It is the women of the second force," the voice of Radio Phnom Penh said, "the *Kemlang Ti Pir,* upon whom the continued success of the revolution must rest. Whatever the men can do, the women can do equally well. Therefore, you must strive harder; you are not the assistants of men but their collaborators. Just as the Angkar Leu has come out from behind the mask of the guerrilla fighter to take its rightful leadership role in the independence-sovereignty of Democratic Kampuchea, so must the women come out from behind the men to stand and serve beside them."

Ly Sokhon listened to the words from her cubicle at the radio station and felt fury swirling through her. The Angkar Leu! A name, a secret formless body! The Angkar had come out from behind the mask of the guerrilla fighter, yes, but the leaders refused to come out from behind the mask of Angkar. Now there was little threat of reprisals; now there was no purpose in maintaining secrecy, in not making a direct public announcement of their existence and that of the Khmer Communist Party. Unless they were ashamed of being communists. Or unless the motives of Khieu Samphan, Ieng Sary, Pol Pot, were far deadlier than that.

Pol Pot.

She thought of him now with hatred, not devotion. She had been transferred here to the radio station from the Ministry of Commerce in October—a demotion because her duties were limited, unimportant, those of a menial. And her constant requests to be sent out of Phnom Penh, out of the festering city and back to join the body of the People and the search for the cancerous cells within it, had been denied. It was because of her meeting with Pol Pot in August, a form of punishment for what had transpired between them, that she was being kept here in the city, here in this cubicle; she was certain of it.

She was also certain that there was but one explanation for the actions of the Angkar Leu and Pol Pot: corruption. They were turning into a nest of poisonous insects just as lethal as the traitors of Lon Nol and the capitalist lackeys of the United States.

Why else had they treated that dog of a Prince Sihanouk in such heroic fashion on his return from China, allowed him to pronounce the new constitution "excellent" and then granted him living quarters in the Royal Palace? Sihanouk did not fit into the Party's vision, Saloth Sar's vision in Paris, of a new Kampuchea with no connections to its debased past. To reinstall him as head of state, even a powerless head of state, was to acknowledge a tie to Chou En-lai and the Chinese. He should have been permitted to return, yes, but then executed immediately upon his arrival at Pochentong Airport.

Why else would "normalization" of diplomatic and trade relations with Thailand, with China, with the Soviet-backed and hateful Vietnamese become an important priority? It could only be to curry favor, to reenter the political arena of the world outside Kampuchea; it had nothing to do with the ideology of the revolution or the People themselves. Kampuchea must stand by itself on all counts, with total self-sufficiency. This, too, was what Saloth Sar had believed a quarter of a century ago at 17 Rue la Cepede.

Why else would all power, all of it, be maintained in the hands of those few in the hierarchy of the Angkar Leu? There was no question that this was the case. At the Third National Party Congress in December, where plans had been formalized for national elections in March, it had become obvious that an elitist clique had formed under the guise of Angkar. Pol Pot was Prime Minister, Ieng Sary was in charge of foreign affairs, Son Sen was Minister of National Defense. The post of Minister of Education was in the hands of Yun Yat, Son Sen's wife; Ieng Sary's wife, Khieu Thirith, was Minister of Social Action; Pol Pot's wife, Khieu Ponnary, who was Khieu Thirith's sister, was head of the Association of Democratic Women of Kampuchea. The national elections would be a fraud. Pol Pot and his clique would rule in the same fashion as Sihanouk and his noisome monarchy, as Lon Nol and his military bourgeoisie.

No question, no question at all: he *had* become that which he had always despised. His goals were the same as the others'— comfort, wealth, power. He did not care about the goals of the revolution, nor any longer dreamed of remaking Kampuchea into a communist utopia. No wonder he had treated her so coldly in August; she was his conscience, she had brought the old days and the old ways back to him, and to confront them was to understand what he had become. Of course he would not talk to her, of course he had sought to banish her to this place in this city she hated. It was she who embodied the true spirit of revolution, the great and glorious revolution of the People which had crested him to power.

"Did not five thousand *neary* fight alongside the male cadres during our first five years of struggle?" the voice of the broadcaster said. "Did not the women fight even more fiercely, even more proudly? Stand up, women of Democratic Kampuchea! Come forth! The struggle must continue!"

Yes, Ly Sokhon thought, yes. Stand up, come forth, the struggle must continue. The future of Kampuchea was in the hands of women such as her, and men too, all those who still embodied the revolutionary spirit. There had been some of these at the Third National Party Congress, expressing cautious disillusionment over the direction of the Angkar Leu, over the presence in their midst of the dog Sihanouk. One, surprisingly, had been her husband Im Chung; perhaps he would know of still others. She would have to talk to him. He was a fool in many ways, but he would listen to her if she approached him properly, he would help her if she allowed him to exercise his lust upon her body.

Together, all of them could create a new revolution, form a guerrilla force that would take to the jungles—yes, back to the jungles—and dedicate themselves to destroying the Angkar Leu and all that it had already corrupted, destroying Phnom Penh and the other cities, razing them to the ground, purifying the land through fire and blood, purging it for all time, washing away every last trace of corruption on the new tide of bright red blood which would flow in rivers as long as the Mekong, as wide as the Tonle Sap. It could be. It could be.

It *must* be.

And I will lead them, she thought with sudden enlightenment. *I* will make the dreams of Paris come true at last. It is *my* destiny. It is my destiny!

There was great excitement inside her now; she could barely contain it as she sat listening to the broadcaster's voice, busying her hands with the lighting of a cigarette. Her thoughts settled in clear focus on the Vietnamese sword on the wall above her bed. Ah, the sword! Tonight she would take it down. Tonight she would hold it again in her hands. Tonight she would begin to make her plans.

For she understood now what she must do before she could leave the deceitful city for the last time, lead the other true believers back into the jungles and commence the new revolution in all its glory.

She must cut off the poisonous heads of the old monarchy and the new Angkar Leu.

She must assassinate both Sihanouk and Pol Pot.

Deighan

Carol died on the fourth of March, three days before Deighan's thirty-second birthday.

He was with her when the end came, in the bungalow off Issraphard Road. She had refused all along to go to a hospital, saying that she wanted to die in the only place where they had known genuine happiness; it was another reason why she'd chosen to stay with him in Bangkok, instead of going home to die in California. The time was four o'clock in the afternoon and she had been heavily sedated with morphine for the previous twenty-eight hours. She had a rare blood disease, a form of cancer, the kind that wasted you in slow stages and left you functioning in a more or less normal fashion until the last few weeks, and she had been in progressively greater pain since late January, in and out of delirium since the twenty-fourth of February.

The last coherent words she had said to him were "Peter? Tell me you love me, Peter."

The Thai doctor wasn't in the room when she died; neither was the nurse who had been caring for her since mid-January, when Deighan's agent wired him that she'd sold *The Rape of Cambodia* to Scribner's for twenty-five thousand dollars, two thirds payable up front because more than half the book had already been submitted. They were alone, him sitting in the chair beside her bed, half somnolent in the heat, holding her hand in one of his. Then there was a sudden brief pressure of her fingers, a spasm followed by limpness, and when he came up out of the chair and leaned over her in the shuttered half light he knew, even before he felt for a pulse, that she was gone.

He stood there, he never did know how long, still holding her hand, looking down at her. Then he bent and kissed her on the mouth, the last kiss, aware that it was the last, and turned and went out and said, "It's over" to the doctor and the nurse. He walked into the garden, sat on another chair and listened to the sounds of Bangkok, the sounds of life going on, until the doctor came out after a space of time to talk to him.

He was a good man, the doctor, who had been educated and received his medical training in London; Carol had been going to him secretly for months, ever since her arrival in Bangkok, on some of those afternoons when she claimed to be visiting Jim Thompson's Thai House. A good man, a good doctor, but right now Deighan hated him. He wanted to smash the little brown man's face, break him up the way he himself was broken inside, screaming You're a quack, you're all quacks with your chemotherapy treatments and your bloody scalpels, why couldn't you do something for her, why couldn't you save her? But the irrational moment didn't last. As soon as he looked away the hatred fled in stages, dribbled out of him the way the life had dribbled out of Carol, and left him feeling . . . nothing. Nothing.

The doctor said things to him, and he said things to the doctor, and there was a blankness like the passage of time in a dream, and then an ambulance came and they put Carol on a stretcher and took her away, like they took the dead away in the war zones, hurrying a little because corpses decayed fast in heat like this, you had to get them on ice pretty quick or they'd start to stink up the place, they'd—

His mind rebelled from the thought and seemed to shut off altogether. When it came back on again the doctor was asking him if he would be all right, if he wanted a sedative to help him rest. No, he said, no sedative, I just want to be alone, and a little while after that he was alone, sitting out in the garden again, watching streaks of color fade out of the sky as night settled down in velvet shadows.

He wanted a drink desperately, but Carol had made him promise that he wouldn't start drinking again after she was gone. "Swear it on my memory, Peter," she had said to him. "Swear it on your love for me."

"I swear it," he said.

"Because you've got to go on after I'm gone. Finish your book, write other books, go to Paris, find another woman—"

"There'll never be another woman."

"But I want there to be. You have to go on living, Peter."

You have to go on living, Peter.

More time passed. He got up and went back inside, went into the bedroom. The nurse, somebody, had made the bed; it looked neat, unused. Empty. He entered the bathroom and looked at Carol's things arranged neatly on top of the commode, smelled the faint lingering scent of her perfume. He walked back along the hallway again and past the teak partitions and sat down in front of his typewriter; tried to read the top sheet of paper on the manuscript stack beside it, the last page he had written on the book. The words seemed to blur together, meaningless, a jumble of mystical black symbols on a white background.

"Promise me you'll finish the book, Peter."

"I promise."

And she had insisted that he go on with his daily work, even while she was dying in another room, and so he had come in here every day and typed things like "Now is the time for all good men to come to the aid of their country" over and over for two-hour stretches, just so she would hear the sound of the typewriter and think he was writing. But he wasn't writing; he hadn't written a line on *The Rape of Cambodia* since Carol told him she had terminal cancer. He was as creatively impotent as he had been sexually impotent these last two months, even though lovemaking was something else she had wanted him to go on with. The knowledge of her suffering, the impending loss of her, had unmanned him in every way.

You have to go on living, Peter.

Alone?

Promise me you'll finish the book, Peter.

Alone?

Swear that you won't let yourself become what you were in Cambodia.

Alone?

He laid his forehead against the cool metal of the typewriter,

308

clasped his hands across his neck. He wanted to break down into great racking sobs, to expunge some of the pain and grief, but no tears came. His eyes were dry. And his creativity was dry. And his soul was dry.

You have to go on living, Peter.

Alone!

Foxworth

When the doorbell rang at his villa a few minutes past 9 P.M. he thought it was Natalie.

He wasn't expecting her, but she had dropped in on him unannounced one other time since the start of their affair, and he couldn't think of anyone else who would come calling at this hour. Except Tom Boyd, maybe, but he and Boyd weren't exactly close these days; they seemed to have nothing in common anymore, if they ever had, and Boyd also seemed to resent Natalie for some reason and steered clear of her whenever she was around.

He didn't want to see Natalie or Boyd or anyone else tonight, that was the thing. He had been careful to keep this evening free—no social gatherings with Thai political figures, no assignations, nothing—because he needed some time alone to think things through, sort out his options and sort through his jumbled feelings. He was on the brink of his crossroads decision, or one crossroads decision anyway; he had felt himself coming up against it for the past few weeks. Natalie was part of it, and so was Kim, and so was Cambodia, and so were a lot of other factors, all combining to open his eyes and open his mind, not to mention open his old wounds. He thought he knew what that decision had to be, was pretty sure it was the right one, but he still needed to talk himself into it. It was going to take guts, and courage had never been his long suit. On the contrary. Playing it safe, as Andrea had pointed out that night in East Lansing, was what he had always excelled in—in his opinions, in his career, in his relationships, in all aspects of his existence. Always the easy way out, always the party line. Other people had made his decisions for him all his life, his major decisions anyhow, and it was long past time that he potty-trained himself. If his life was going to keep on being screwed up, then at least *he* would be the one to do the screwing.

He went to the door and squinted through the spyhole that had been installed in it. You never knew when somebody might want to knock off an ugly American these days, even an inconsequential ugly American like himself. This might be particularly true right now, in early March, because Thai communist activity had begun to heat up in recent weeks, with efforts to expand their influence in the Khmer-populated provinces along the Cambodian border. In some of the sixteen districts in six provinces where trouble brewed heaviest, the communists had overrun isolated government outposts and killed several people. It was always possible that terrorist attacks could spread to Americans in Bangkok.

But it wasn't a terrorist standing outside; it was Peter Deighan.

Frowning, Foxworth unlocked and opened the door. Deighan said, "Hello, Foxie," in a quiet hat-in-hand kind of voice. "Sorry to come around so late but I need to talk to you."

Foxworth hesitated. He had no desire to talk to Deighan, of all people, and yet he'd heard that the man's wife had died of cancer less than ten days ago; looking at him now, he felt something more than just sympathy—a kind of kinship, a hard bond of pain between them. *The woman I love may be dead too. Of a different kind of cancer.*

"You *are* alone?" Deighan asked.

No, he thought, I'm not alone. There are lots of others here, including guilt. Especially guilt. But he said, "Yes. All right, come on in."

They went into the living room. Foxworth said, "I'm . . . . sorry about your wife."

"So am I."

A small awkward silence.

"Can I get you something? A drink?"

"No, thanks," Deighan said. "I'm off the sauce these days."

They sat down on facing chairs. Foxworth watched the other man light a cigarette and thought that he was holding up pretty well. There was grief in his eyes, in the lines around his mouth, but otherwise no outward signs of anguish. The fact that he had been a drunk in Phnom Penh, and was sober at a time like this, spoke for itself.

He said, "Is it about your book? Why you're here, I mean."

"Yes. I've sold it, you know."

"No, I didn't know."

"Scribner's. Hemingway's publisher."

Foxworth cleared his throat. "Look, if it's about my relationship with Kim, I haven't changed my mind. I just can't talk about her, that's all."

"I can understand that," Deighan said.

And of course he could: he probably found it impossible to talk to anyone about his wife, now that she was gone. It would give him more pain, flay him inside. The only difference was, Deighan didn't have the guilt that made him deserve to be flayed inside and David Foxworth did. The feeling of betrayal that had crawled in on him after that first night in bed with Natalie had been manifest. Kim was trapped in Cambodia, or already dead, and certainly already betrayed, and here he was, humping a nice American lady in a nice warm bed on New Year's Eve with his belly full of champagne and expensive food. Guilt had stalked him ever since, but guilt at least was a companion: it kept him from feeling empty. But it hadn't kept him from going back to Natalie on at least a dozen occasions since—Natalie's arms, Natalie's body, Natalie's passion, and maybe even Natalie's love. He hadn't wanted to, he'd hated himself before and after each time, and yet that hadn't stopped him from going; he didn't care for Natalie and yet of course he did. It wasn't just sex, he knew there was more to it than that, but admitting it opened up possibilities for an even further, and perhaps final, betrayal of Kim. He hadn't been able to face it. He still wasn't able to face it. The crossroads decision, yes. But not the implications of his affair with Natalie Rosen.

Deighan said, "I didn't come to ask you about Kim. You've told me your position and I respect it."

"Then what do you want to talk about?"

"Another chapter I'm going to do. On the resistance movements operating out of Thailand."

"Yes?"

"I need to interview some of the Khmers involved," Deighan said. "Specifically, one of the leaders. I thought maybe you could give me a name."

"Why would you think that?"

"Why not? None of my other sources at the embassy works with refugees, has had contact with Cambodians in and out of the camps, and is probably CIA-connected."

"Now wait a minute . . ."

"Don't get your back up," Deighan said, "I don't give a damn anymore whether you are or aren't connected. The point is, I need a name and I figure you're the one to provide it."

Foxworth took a half dozen slow breaths before he said, "I'd like to help you but I can't. It would be against regulations."

"Sure it would. And the hell with regulations. Listen, we've had our disagreements in the past; we almost came to blows in Phnom Penh. But this hasn't got anything to do with politics, it has to do with humanity. You may be a lot of things, Foxie, and I may be a lot of things, but the two of us are human beings. No?"

Foxworth didn't say anything.

"Human beings," Deighan said again. "What separates the two of us is nothing compared to what separates us from a whole legion of others—the liars, the thieves, the protected, the deluded, the power-mad who run wars from inside their electric bunkers and never give a single thought to the millions they condemn to die. I know it, and you know it too. All I'm asking you is a small favor, not from a diplomat to a journalist—from one human being to another."

The smoke from Deighan's cigarette, caught in a draft from the air-conditioning unit, swirled up in front of his face for a second and seemed to erase the distinctiveness of his features, seemed for that instant to make him look like an image of

Everyman. Handy illusion: it was what Foxworth *wanted* to see, of course. Because he needed to believe that what Deighan had said was the truth—that he *was* separate from all the Tom Boyds and Henry Kissingers and Lon Nols and Pol Pots, he *was* a human being whose main concern was other human beings, not politics or anything else.

"Chuon Van," he said. "One of the camp leaders at Aranya-prathet."

Deighan repeated the name.

"But he wouldn't admit it outright," Foxworth said. "I doubt if he'll talk to you."

"Oh, he'll talk to me, all right."

"What makes you so sure?"

"I can be pretty persuasive when I set my mind to it." Deighan made a note on a small pad from inside his jacket, leaned over to stab out his cigarette in the coffee-table ashtray. Then he said, "But I wasn't doing a number on you; I meant what I said. Thanks. You're a good man."

"Sure."

Deighan got to his feet, and Foxworth did the same and went with him to the door. Before he opened it they stood looking at each other for a span of seconds. There was a feeling between them that might have been the seed of friendship, or at least of mutual understanding. When Deighan put out his hand Foxworth took it immediately and said, "Good luck, Peter," and it wasn't until the words were out that he realized it was the first time, even with all the "Call me Peter" exhortations, that he had addressed the man by his given name.

A faint smile, empty of humor, moved Deighan's mouth. "You too, David," he said.

"I hope you find what you're looking for at Aranyaprathet."

"So do I," and the smile seemed to shift, to become some-thing else, something with darkness in it. "Hang in there," he said, and he was gone.

Foxworth went back inside, made himself a small gin-and-quinine, sat down with it to resume his interior monologue. But he found, with a sense of enormous relief, that there was not much need for it where his decision was concerned. Peter Deighan, with his remarks about human beings, had already talked him into it. There was no longer any question of what he was going to do. The only question left was when he was going to do it.

Cambodia File: Excerpts from Airgram Report by Refugee Officer, American Embassy at Bangkok, March 1976

Virtually everyone in Cambodia is theoretically a member of a "production cooperative," which the KC theoreticians are counting upon to be the agents for genuine economic and social development. Radio Phnom Penh has given considerable attention to cooperatives of late: "Our production cooperatives reflect the character of the revolutionary power of the state. Since the beginning of 1976 our cooperatives have developed considerably." (February 17) Also, "Since the beginning of 1976 our cooperatives have gradually gained the character of a village." (February 3) From what these and other broadcasts report, the idea would seem to be to make the Cambodian cooperative similar in nature to the Chinese people's communes, as relatively self-contained, self-reliant institutions.

Cambodians fleeing into Thailand are particularly cynical about the nature of their participation in a "cooperative." To most, it is a word without meaning. The well-educated know that their involuntary servitude is antithetical to the sense of a cooperative. All recent refugees agree that they observed absolutely no change in the way their cooperative worked last year and this year . . .

Some refugees tell us that all the military in their particular area are the same, whereas others—often the more observant ones—report that the military seem generally to divide into two groups. There are (1) local militia types who do little more than guard the people, and (2) more active soldiers who seem to be responsive to higher levels, carry out executions, and have usually greater responsibility. Their dress may sometimes be different. Most still wear just black pajamas. The number of ballpoint pens in one's shirt pocket served previously as a rule of thumb for determining the rank of KC officers; now, it may be the number of folds in his sleeve.

Many of the KC soldiers are described as young (fifteen years old) and barely educated, if at all. Often the KC began working with them and training them as soldiers when they were quite young. Since the war ended, some of the younger KC have allegedly requested to return home. Some have received permission, but others—particularly those whose families are known to have been killed—are refused, receiving a promotion or some other type of reward instead.

Cambodian refugees often claim that a number of KC, militia types or older soldiers in particular, are disillusioned and would turn against their masters were there to be a general uprising. We have heard stories from Oddar Mean Chey for months that KC are often poorly disciplined and would rather fish than guard the people. Refugees from there reported recently that they have seen some soldiers looking at magazine pictures and commenting that Cambodia looked better before liberation. There have also been cases reported where soldiers became almost friendly with local people. One refugee from Battambang Province told a journalist in January that the KC in his village were transferred to another place every fifteen days, so that they would avoid becoming attached to the people.

Chey Han

Inside Chey's mind, the bonze who had no head said to him through the head that had no bonze, "The woman you saw at the Sisophon railroad station is Than Kim. There is no question that she is your half-sister Than Kim."

"Kim is dead," he said.

"She is not dead. She is at the cooperative near Lovea."

"Then why haven't I been able to find her name among the biographies from that cooperative?"

"Because she is using a false name."

"Why would she use a false name?"

"Oh Chey Han," the bonze said reproachfully. "Because she came from Phnom Penh, of course. Because she was doubtless a member of the corrupt regime of Lon Nol and she fears for her life."

"If that was true, she would have been discovered by now."

"Not necessarily. There are many traitors who remain in hiding among the People. You know this."

"I know it. But the hen was not Than Kim."

"No? Go to the cooperative and see for yourself."

"I don't want to go to the cooperative."

"Why not? Are you afraid the hen *is* Than Kim?"

"Yes."

"And then you'll have to butcher her?"

"Yes."

"But she is only another chicken."

"She is not another chicken."

"Why isn't she?"

"Because if she's a chicken, then so am I."

"You are, Chey Han. We are all chickens."

"I could not execute my half-sister."

"But you must. It is your duty to Angka to unmask and execute all traitors and malingerers. If you don't, and the Angkar finds out you harbored a traitor, *you* will be executed. Then there will be no doubt that you are a chicken."

"I am harboring no one," Chey said.

"Your knowledge harbors Than Kim."

"I have no knowledge. The hen is not Kim."

"She is Kim. You know she is."

"I know nothing. I am nothing."

"Except a chicken."

They had had this dialogue many times, Chey and the headless bonze. In Sisophon, in Phnom Srok, in the jungle along the Thai border where they were sent on patrol, in Battambang City where they were sent for indoctrination lectures, in Siem Reap where they were sent during the national elections. Even on execution details. Many times, in many places. It had begun as an even contest, between opponents of equal strength, but as time passed the bonze began to win. He was very clever and devious, the bonze; he laughed and spurted blood while Chey was talking to him, and juggled his head and laughed and sometimes performed the ancient *lamtong* with head held high above his crimson neck. This made it very difficult for Chey to concentrate on his argument.

The day came, as he had been afraid it would, when the bonze forced him to admit defeat. It was the last day of March and they were in Sisophon, where they had been since returning from Siem Reap. There were no more trainloads of chickens from Pursat, because the rice harvest was long finished and it was the height of the dry season drought; but groups of chickens were still being transferred from this cooperative to that one, along with groups of soldiers as well, for no reason which Chey or the bonze could understand. One of these poultry groups was being moved on April 1 from the cooperative near Lovea to Mongkol Borei, and Chey and some of his soldiers had been assigned to supervise the transferral.

The bonze was delighted when he and Chey learned of this. "Now you have no choice," he said. "Now you must go to Lovea and confront your half-sister."

"My half-sister is not at Lovea. She is dead."

"She will be dead after you arrive at Lovea."

"I won't go, then. I'll ask to be relieved of the duty."

"On what grounds?"

"I don't know. I'll think of something."

"You'll think of nothing that will not be questioned," the bonze said. "The Angkar will become suspicious. They'll know you're concealing something, they'll question you, they'll have you watched, they'll find out about me and about Than Kim. Then they'll butcher you like all the other chickens."

"I won't be butchered."

"Then go to Lovea and confront your half-sister."

"I won't butcher Kim."

"You have no choice, Chey Han. You have no choice." Laughter. Capering and juggling and dancing. "You have no choice. You have no choice. You have no choice."

This was when he admitted defeat. The bonze was right, he had no choice. He must go to the cooperative, he must search out the hen he had seen at the railroad station in December, and he must confront her. And if she was Than Kim, though he still refused to believe it, he would have to expose her as he would expose any other chicken. She was not a chicken, but oh yes, she was. He was not a chicken, but oh yes, he could be. Angka could make anyone a chicken. Angka the omnipotent, Angka the extraordinary, could make anyone in Kampuchea a dead rooster, a bloody hen, a broken chick. He must not let it happen to him and the bonze. Even if it meant executing his half-sister, even if it meant such a thing as that, he must not become one of Angka's chickens.

He slept little that night. The bonze kept him awake with laughter and singing and flashes of blood as bright as exploding rockets; and the song he sang was a song of quest. Chey awakened from a fitful doze an hour before dawn, left his quarters a brief time later, and was riding in a jeep alongside one of his sergeants, out through the gates of the Sisophon military installation, before the eastern horizon had begun to lighten. The other soldiers would not be leaving for half an hour yet; this was how much time he had allowed himself, or allowed the relentless bonze, to find the hen who might or might not be Than Kim.

318

The drive to Lovea along the Mongkol Borei River was a
short one, but the bonze made it seem long by chattering at him
the whole way, imitating chicken squawks and laughing in-
sanely. Chey chose to remain silent and ignore the headless
one. The bonze was already dead and had no worries about his
own fate or the fate of a half-sister; let the bonze carry on like
a fool. But if the hen was not Kim, it would be Chey's turn to
laugh, Chey's turn to dance and imitate the bonze's prayers and
perhaps make taunting gestures with an imaginary statue of the
great parasite Buddha.

On the way to the cooperative, along a newly built levee
road two kilometers beyond Lovea, Chey saw two hundred
roosters and hens already out building new irrigation canals
and a new dike. He ordered his driver to stop the jeep, got out,
and walked among them for a short while, looking at the faces
of the hens. None was familiar. And none dared to look at him
in return; they all knew who he was and were afraid he would
take them away to be slaughtered. This gave the bonze pleasure
and he laughed and pointed to those who carried bamboo
poles, to which were affixed a pair of woven baskets, across
their shoulders. When the baskets were full of rocks, stones,
and other debris, the weight bent the carriers double as they
took them away to a dumping site.

"Look, Chey Han," the bonze said. "What do they resemble?
Gaunt and yoked oxen? No! Chickens! Chickens with broken
wings!"

Chey was not amused. "Be still," he told the headless one as
he returned to the jeep. "I'll deal with you later."

The bonze roared with laughter.

The *sahakoo toic* itself was like many others Chey had seen
in Battambang, Oddar Mean Chey, and Siem Reap Provinces.
It contained the desired number of one thousand persons and
consisted of a series of identical thatched huts set ten meters
apart from one another; a group of communal dining halls—
communal feeding of all chickens had become mandatory in
January; a blacksmith's forge; storage sheds and separate quarters for the chief and the other KC military and civilian residents. It also contained the heavy dry-season smells of dust,

heat, and manure. What it did not contain was trees, recreation facilities, or chicks above the age of four. All those from ages five to twelve would live in a neighboring commune, where they would work on small handicraft projects, carry night soil to adults working in the fields, and receive Party indoctrination; all those above the age of twelve would have been taken away to work camps in other parts of the country.

Most of the compound was deserted now, in this hour past dawn, except for several old ones making fish traps or bamboo poles, and a group of eighty or ninety roosters and hens near a small livestock pen. These, no doubt, were the chickens being transferred this morning to Mongkol Borei. As Chey's driver brought the jeep to a stop on the dusty central clearing, a middle-aged man wearing a red scarf detached himself from the group and hurried up. The red scarf said that he was a man, not a rooster, because in some KC quarters it was a symbol of power and identified him as a Party member, probably the local *srok*. Just as Chey's green-khaki uniform and sidearm identified him as a military officer. Without acknowledging the chief, he swung out and stood looking at the gaggle of poultry. None of these haggard, empty hen faces seemed familiar either, although he could not be certain at a distance.

The *srok,* who was doubtless an ex-military officer himself, judging from his posture as he stood before Chey, offered a greeting and then his name, which was Dy Phon. "You are early, Mit Chey," he said. "Where are your soldiers?"

"They will be here shortly."

"Is there a reason for your early arrival?"

"He's going to confront his half-sister Than Kim," the bonze said slyly. "She is one of your hens."

"Shut up," Chey told him. To Dy Phon he said, "There is a woman, one of those in your charge. I am here early because of her."

"The woman's name, Comrade?"

"I don't know her name. At least, I don't know the name she is using here."

"Ah," Dy Phon said.

"Ah," the bonze whispered. "Ah! Ah! Ah ah ah!"

"Be quiet, you fool!"

"Did you speak, Comrade?" Dy Phon asked him.

"No." *Did* I speak aloud? Chey thought. I must be careful of that. I must not let anyone know about the foolish bonze.

"What does the woman look like?"

Chey described her—not Kim as he had known her in Rovieng, the hen at the railroad station in Sisophon. "Perhaps she was once quite beautiful," he said, finishing.

"Ah," the chief said again.

"You know her?"

"I believe so. As Mey Yat, a peasant from Takeo Province. She is not a peasant, then?"

"No," the bonze said, "she is his half-sister Than Kim," and threw his head high in the air and then caught it again in one hand, spraying blood and laughter.

Chey was silent.

"One of Lon Nol's hidden traitors?" Dy Phon prompted him.

"Her background is unimportant. Have her brought to me."

"Brought to you?"

"Is that such a strange request, Dy Phon? Have her brought to me from wherever she is in the fields. Immediately."

The *srok* looked perplexed; one of his hands lifted to touch the end of his red scarf. "But I thought you'd already found her, Mit Chey. I thought that was the reason you came to ask about her."

"What are you talking about?" Chey said. He stayed an impulse to take the chief by the throat and shake him. "I don't understand you."

"I do," the bonze whispered. "I do, I do. Ah! Ah ah ah!"

"The woman Mey Yat is no longer here," Dy Phon said. "She escaped from her *krom* two nights ago."

Natalie

It was 10 A.M. Bangkok time, the thirty-first of March, when Abraham Rosen telephoned her at the Thai Relief Organization offices on Vorachak Road. That was where she worked when she wasn't at one of the camps or out soliciting funds and/or political support from indifferent Thai bureaucrats, and her father had called her there several times. They spoke at least once a month, in addition to keeping in touch through weekly letters; it had been a full three weeks since their last conversation, so it wasn't surprising that he would call today. Or so she thought at first.

But the connection was bad—full of staticky noises, like a badly tuned radio. She could only understand about one out of every three words he said to her. The overseas operator came on before long, no doubt at the behest of her father, and asked Natalie to please hang up, there would be a ring-back when a clearer connection was made.

She replaced the receiver. And while she waited, instead of returning her attention to the paperwork on her desk, she found herself thinking about David again. As she had a great deal of the time since the simultaneous beginning of the new year and their affair. He had become central to her in some of the same ways her father was central to her; the only difference seemed to be that with David it was sexual as well as spiritual. Their relationship, despite the fact that it seemed like a graceless *pas de deux,* choreographed as one step forward and two steps backward, was the most profound she had ever known.

And yet for him it was founded upon falsity: it wouldn't exist if Than Kim had come out of Cambodia with him, or come out at any time in the past year. He knew it and she knew it and each knew that the other knew it, and sometimes the image of Kim, the truth of who and where she was, sat between them in restaurants and walked between them on the streets and lay between them in bed like a physical presence cutting off any deep connection. It was almost as if her soft Khmer voice, the cries of her suffering, could be heard like echoes in the darkness.

But still, still, there were moments when Kim seemed not to be there at all, no one between them, just her and David and a feeling not of pain but of love, or at least the first bittersweet tremors of love. It was those moments that gave her hope for someday.

She tried not to let herself speculate on what would happen if Kim did escape her Cambodian prison, what this would do to the lives of David Foxworth and Natalie Rosen. Nor did she want to speculate on what her feelings really were on that possibility. She wanted Kim to be alive, to live, to somehow find her way over the border into Thailand or Vietnam or Laos, sincerely wanted this because it would put an end to David's pain and guilt . . . and yet the near-certainty that Kim was trapped or had already perished inside Cambodia was the one fragile thread that bound David to her and gave her hope. Down at the bottom of her soul, did she truly want that thread cut? And if not, then what did that make her? She had dedicated her life to the alleviation of human misery, yet in a very real and terrible sense her own happiness seemed based on the continued brutalization or death of another human being who had never hurt her, who had shown her only kindness.

The telephone rang again. Which was fortunate, because her thoughts had taken a turn into the intolerable again, as they sometimes did in spite of herself. You could make yourself crazy with that kind of thinking because there was no answer, no solution; it was a paradox, and the only way to deal with it was to not deal with it on any level.

She said hello into the receiver, and her father's voice said, "Natalie?" much more clearly this time. He still sounded as if he were far away, which of course he was, and talking to her through some sort of hollow tube. The telephone service in and out of Thailand was not the most sophisticated.

"Hello, Papa," she said.

"Can you hear me?"

"Yes. Can you hear me?"

"Yes. How are you? Are you all right?"

"Fine. You shouldn't worry about me, Papa."

"I'm not worried. Just interested."

"How about you? You're not working too hard?"

"No. Listen, Natalie, why didn't you call me?"

"Well, it's only been three weeks since we talked."

"I don't mean that."

"What, then?"

"The news, of course."

"What news? Don't tell me Congress finally drafted a relief bill?"

A pause punctuated by crackling noises.

"I guess not," she said. "Did Ford and Kissinger declare war on Cambodia?"

"Natalie, are you trying to be funny?"

"No, Papa. I'm sorry. Why should I have called you? About what?"

"About David Foxworth, what else?"

She felt herself frowning. She had written her father about her relationship with David—because she had never held back from him anything important in her life, not because she wanted guidance. None of the details, naturally, they were too personal, but enough to let him know she was emotionally involved. He had been supportive, as she'd known he would be, and that was as far as it went; he hadn't tried to act the role of a parent. It didn't matter to him that she was involved with a gentile. The only racial matters Abraham Rosen concerned himself with were those dealing with persecution, whether of Jews, Khmers, or any other ethnic minority. If she wanted to fall in love with a gentile, that was her business. Just as long as she was sure of her choice.

So what was this? Why did he think she should have called him to discuss David at overseas telephone rates?

"What about him?" she said.

"I'm curious what he's going to do."

"Do about what? Papa, what are you talking about?"

Another crackling pause.

"Papa?"

"You don't know," he said.

"Don't know what?"

"I thought he'd have told you himself."

She began to get belated intimations that something was amiss, something of considerable significance; the draft from the air-conditioning unit was chilly on her neck. "I haven't seen David in almost a week," she said. "I haven't talked to him, he hasn't told me anything. Will you please tell me what this is all about?"

"Sam Richardson called me from Albany a little while ago," her father said. If there was inflection in his voice, she couldn't tell what it was because of the interference. "He heard about it from one of his friends in the State Department."

"Papa . . ."

"Foxworth resigned his post at the Bangkok embassy five days ago," Abraham Rosen said. "He's leaving government service, Natalie. Effective tomorrow, April first."

Unreasonably, she felt tears welling. Stupid. There was no reason to cry. What good would crying do her? The refugees, the dead in Cambodia—they were worth tears, not her own dreary emotional complications.

"But it doesn't have to mean he's leaving Bangkok," her father said. "Or leaving you, either."

"Then why didn't he tell me?"

More crackling silence.

Why didn't he tell me?

Deighan

Deighan went back to Cambodia on April Fool's Day.

The irony of the date wasn't lost on him. If he'd told anyone in Bangkok—David Foxworth, for instance—that he was planning to become the first American, the first Westerner, the first journalist, to set foot inside the country since the Khmer Rouge takeover, he'd have been called a prize fool, not to mention a horse's ass. But he hadn't told anyone. It was no one's business but his own, and that of Chuon Van and the rest of his small band of resistance fighters.

It had taken him ten days and ten thousand dollars to convince Chuon to first admit he was a member of the resistance and then agree to let Deighan join a raid across the frontier. Without the money—almost all he had left from the book advance and magazine rights on *The Rape of Cambodia,* after paying off the Thai medical people and arranging for shipment of Carol's remains to California for burial—Chuon and his men never would have agreed to the proposal. But the one thing they needed most was ready cash, and especially ready American dollars, to buy weapons and supplies in order to outfit more guerrillas. And ten grand would bring plenty of automatic weapons, ammunition, grenades, and other firepower from the Thai black market.

Even so, he had had to submit to half a dozen interrogations by Chuon and the others, plus a mock patrol in the Thai jungle south of Aranyaprathet to see how well he followed orders. He was not to speak unless spoken to, and was to obey every directive without question. If he did anything, at any time, to jeopardize either the mission or any of its members, he could expect to be killed on the spot. Chuon said this to him a dozen times, to make absolutely sure he understood that it was not an idle warning, but from Deighan's point of view the warning itself wasn't necessary. He understood the rules of war, all right. If there was one thing left on earth he understood, it was war. He'd accepted the rules, and agreed tacitly to play by them, from the moment he'd made his decision to go back into Cambodia.

Just when he had made that decision, he wasn't sure. Sometime during the vague stuporlike week following Carol's death, when random moments of lucidity would strike him and he'd find himself on a street somewhere—or, once, teetering on the upper platform of the 260-foot-high Wat Sraket—and not remember how he'd gotten there or why. It was exactly like being on a week-long bender, except that he hadn't had a single drink then or since. Keeping his promise to Carol, because that was all he had left of her to hang on to.

But another of his promises was that he would finish *The Rape of Cambodia,* and he knew he couldn't do it as he had intended to before: just hole up in the bungalow and grind out enough words to fulfill the contract length of 125,000. He couldn't do it because the words would be hollow, little more than detached backseat observations, the kind of words any correspondent, or any clever hack back in the States, could string together with enough research material. He had *lived* the first 65,000 words, that was the thing. And those 65,000 words were good *because* he'd lived them, because all the facts and events, all the observations and speculations, were personal. Where was the personal involvement in interviewing people like Foxworth on his relationship with Than Kim, or Natalie Rosen on the refugee situation? Hell, he'd be telling their personal stories, not his own. Which was all right in limited quantities, as sidebar stuff to keep everything in perspective; but it just wasn't enough to hang the balance of *his* book on.

All of this was in his mind one morning when he woke up, and that put an end to the lost week and got him functioning again in a more or less normal fashion. He must have thought about it before, during that week, because it was all clear and sharp and logical, but he couldn't remember having done so. Maybe his subconscious had worked it out for him. In any case, there it was.

And now, three weeks later, here he was—on his way back into the lair of the Khmer Rouge.

They made the frontier crossing near a village called Ban Ra Lom Tim, northwest of Aranyaprathet. There was a rubber plantation there, on the Thai side, and evidently the owner sympathized with the resistance efforts; according to Chuon, he and his men had made a number of crossings from this starting point. They took a pair of jeeps out of the village an hour before midnight on March 31—an even dozen men, including Deighan. The night was heavy with clouds, with heat so humid and intense that you could taste its wetness each time you took a breath.

They followed a laterite road to an overgrown rubber kaboon on the estate's eastern perimeter, a kilometer or so from the border. The kaboon hadn't been worked for some time: the trees were old, leafless in places, their trunks scarred and black-scabbed with spiral tapping cuts, and there was a tangle of underbrush and creepers and liana vines growing among them. All of which made good concealment for the jeeps, and gave the men plenty of cover under which to unload weaponry and to dress in jungle-camouflage fatigues and heavy boots. Then they waited in the thick heat, Deighan restlessly because nobody told him why they were waiting, the others with the stoicism of trained soldiers. As most of them were: former FANK noncoms and enlisted men who had escaped the purges in Battambang and Siem Reap. One of these, Thang Phim, gave most of the orders and had also protested the loudest against the idea of Deighan's presence. But the real leader was Chuon Van, not Thang Phim, and Chuon had prevailed.

It was a full hour before they lined up and began to move through the undergrowth, following a path that was barely visible in the darkness. Deighan's place was in the middle of the pack, by prearrangement—not for his protection, for that of the others. Which was also the reason why they hadn't offered him one of the M-16s they were carrying. Not that he would have taken it if they had. He'd never fired an automatic weapon in his life, even in Nam, and it would have been dangerous in his hands. He was carrying a sidearm, though, in a holster Chuon had given him: the military .45 he had bought on the black market in Phnom Penh, the gun he had tried so often and so abortively to knock himself off with. Irony in that too, but he hadn't dwelled on it. He wasn't thinking about knocking himself off these days, any more than he had during the ten months with Carol.

There had been no conversation while they waited near the jeeps, and there was none now. Nor would there be any, Deighan guessed, until after they were well beyond the border, and then only if imperative. But the jungle was alive with sounds, particularly so once they were clear of the rubber kaboon and into what the French called *fôret clairière,* or medium-dense jungle: monkeys, nightbirds, insects, something slithering through the underbrush, something that was probably a fruit bat making leathery flutterings overhead. The noises made him feel uneasy. So did the thought of snakes hidden in the grasses and among the sinuous roots of white-boled fromager trees. The Asian jungle wasn't exactly alien territory for him; he'd spent some time in one in Nam. But not at night and not on a mission like this, a guerrilla raid on an unknown objective —unknown because Chuon had refused to confide in him, saying that it was best for all of them if he didn't know until afterward where they were going or why.

Deighan turned his attention inward. But Carol was in there, and grief and pain and emptiness were in there, and he came right back out again. The only way he had been able to get through these past weeks, the only way he would be able to get through this adventure and all the rest of his tomorrows, was to deal with things on an external basis, with only superficial subjective involvement. That would have to change when he went back to work on *The Rape of Cambodia,* because you couldn't write a book as personal as his without crawling down inside yourself and drowning in your emotions; but that wasn't now, that was in the future. He'd worry about it when the time came.

He occupied his mind by making little memory notes— impressions, feelings, sensory perceptions—that he could transcribe after they got back. He had developed a knack for doing that in Nam, a mnemonic retentiveness that had given *The Only War We Had* part of its power because it carried with it a sense of immediacy. Most of the reviews had said that the reader felt he was living the experiences of Deighan and the combat soldiers, not just reading about them. The Pulitzer Prize Committee had said the same thing. Then why hadn't the bastards given him the prize? It didn't matter, he had never cared about Pulitzers, but there was principle involved. Something else that didn't matter, some book about something meaningless, had received the award. The damn committee should have given it to him.

It seemed they had been walking a long time, at a good pace for night travel in the jungle, when the signal to stop came back through the line from Thang Phim. The signal was one of several that Deighan had been taught and it probably meant they were close to the border. The terrain hadn't changed much, except for the fact that the jungle growth was no longer quite so dense; there were fewer trees, fewer lianas and trellises of betel vines, and the ground covering was mostly elephant grass and clumps of fern. But there were still plenty of leeches around; when he raised his arm to rub sweat from his forehead he found one of the filthy things clamped between two fingers. He couldn't make out anything in the darkness that even resembled a landmark, but of course there had to be one for the Khmers.

This was as far as they were going to go while it was dark; another signal came back through the line and told him that. They moved away from the trail, serpentining in the same single file through a fernbrake and into a concealed clearing that looked manmade by flattening down ferns and grass. In there they spread out to cover all approaches, hunkered down to wait for the first light. The time, according to Deighan's watch, was a little past 4 A.M., April 1.

Nobody said anything to anybody else, not even in a whisper. Deighan lay on his back after a while and listened to the jungle sounds and watched the movement of the clouds across the sky. He was too keyed up to even close his eyes. He just lay there, marinating in his own sweat, trying not to think about anything. Just trying to get through this static period until dawn came and it was time to move out again, time to cross the frontier. Time to face the tiger in his own den.

As soon as the sky's velvet black modulated into gray, Chuon and Thang had them up and back on the move. Spaced out at wider intervals than before, moving much more slowly than they had during the night. Deighan walked in the tracks of the man in front of him, as everybody else was doing behind Thang at the front; and he kept his eyes cast downward, the way they did, sweeping his gaze from side to side, because the frontier was spotted with pressure-activated mines and pitfalls full of *punji* stakes. The last time the guerrillas had been over this trail was six weeks ago, and that was plenty of time for KC patrols to have found it and laid down traps.

The jungle petered out into a long flattish section strewn with rocks and patches of elephant grass. On the far side the ground rose sharply into escarpments made rugged by water erosion, their slopes coated with more jungle. Nothing moved anywhere around them except birds and something off to Deighan's left that may have been a snake; he had a glimpse of a fat brown body glistening in the early-morning light.

All of his joints felt sore, wired with tension. Sweat kept spilling out of him, melding clothing to skin, making him as sodden as if he'd been submerged in water. He laid his right hand on the butt of his holstered .45—a gesture which struck him belatedly as ridiculous. What the hell good would a .45 do you if you stepped on a mine or plunged down onto a cluster of *punjis*? He took his hand away again and wiped it across his shirtfront, let it hang loose at his side.

The crossing seemed to take a long time, hours, because of the retarded pace. But it was not even sunrise when they reached the slopes and began to climb up into the jungle again, and Thang signaled back for them to close ranks. There had been nothing along the way to indicate at what point they'd crossed the border of a neutral country into one that was communist-held, but Thang's signal meant they had. Now that part of it was finished; now it was official.

Peter Deighan was the first American back inside Cambodia.

It didn't make him feel much, one way or another. He made a mental note about that, the absence of any reaction, his only feeling being one of hyperalertness. Maybe later, when they got to where they were going, or when they were on their way back, he would have some sort of emotional response. Or maybe it wouldn't come until after he was back in Thailand, back in Bangkok. Or maybe it wouldn't come at all.

They climbed steadily through the jungle, for what Deighan's watch told him was better than two hours. Then, when the terrain began to level off again beyond the rim of the escarpment, they turned right off the trail at a place that looked like impenetrable jungle growth but wasn't: another trail, even less well defined than the one from Thailand, was hidden in there. They followed that trail for half an hour, winding back and forth across ground that sloped downward in an irregular descent. Deighan had brought a compass with him; he took it out near the bottom of the decline and made a reading. South by southeast. He tried to visualize the topographical maps he had studied during his stay in the town of Aranyaprathet. What was south by southeast from Ban Ra Lom Tim, over on the Cambodian side? A village called Phum Preav seemed to be the nearest habitation. The nearest place of any size was Sisophon, but that was a good forty kilometers from the border. Chuon and his men wouldn't be—

The soldier ahead of him stopped all of a sudden and Deighan nearly ran into him. He jerked his head up, backing off. The soldier behind him caught his arm and held him motionless. Where they were now, he saw, was in a clearing where the terrain flattened out again, with a fernbrake on the near side and a cluster of silk-cotton trees with flanged roots like flying buttresses on the far side; up ahead, twenty meters or so away, was a kind of crossroads where a larger and just-discernible path intersected the one they were on. At the front of the line, Thang and Chuon stood together, frozen in position, guns up, heads up like animals keening the air.

Deighan didn't understand what the matter was. Nothing moved at the crossroads, there weren't any strange sounds in the surrounding jungle. What was the matter?

Thang made a frantic hand signal. Immediately, all of the guerrillas broke away either left or right, from in front of Deighan and from behind him, like a long thin pod cracking open and leaving him there alone.

Ripples of fear went through him. No strange sounds in the jungle . . . *no sounds at all, no monkeys, no birds.* On reflex he drew the .45, took three running steps toward where some of the others were plunging into the fernbrake.

Then all hell broke loose.

They came out of the jungle on both sides of the crossroads— at least two dozen Khmer Rouge soldiers in black pajamas and khaki uniforms, all of them armed with automatic weapons. All the guns seemed to start chattering and spitting at once, raking across the clearing, bullets whining and buzzing and creating an undersound of pok, pok, pok when they hit solid objects nearby. Two of the guerrillas went down. Deighan, running, his ears and his head full of the guns, saw them go down and saw that one of them was Thang and saw the ones already in the ferns set up an answering volley. He was almost to the brake himself, another three long strides—

There was a sudden brutal jarring under his collarbone on the left side, as if somebody had hit him there with a hammer; it staggered him but it didn't knock him down. The whole front of his chest went numb. I'm shot, he thought, by God they shot me. Then the second and third bullets cut his legs out from under him, kicked him backward and rolled him the rest of the way into the fernbrake.

He came up on his back and lay there without moving, breath pumping in and out through his mouth, blood pumping out through the holes in his body. The .45 was still clenched in his right hand; he could feel it, hot and slick, in the tight grip of his fingers. There was still no pain. Just the numbness spreading through him, flowing and soothing like oil. The automatic weapon fire, the screams, the hiss and whine and pok-pok-pok of bullets went on and on—but they seemed far away now, happening somewhere else.

I'm dying, he thought.

And that was good because death was what he'd been after all along.

Not trying to knock himself off these days? The hell he wasn't. Time to own up to the truth now: that was the *real* reason why he'd made himself the first American to come back to Cambodia. If it hadn't happened on this mission, he'd have found a way to join another, and another, until it did happen. The book had only been an excuse, a kind of dust wrapper to cover his fear. He'd never have been able to finish writing it; he was empty inside, with Carol gone, and you can't write out of a vacuum. He wouldn't have been able to keep his promise to her . . . any of his promises to her, including the one about not drinking anymore. He couldn't write, he couldn't go on, he couldn't do anything but die. This way. It had to be *this* way.

So goddamn fitting and proper. The way a war correspondent ought to die, alongside soldiers on the front lines or guerrilla fighters in the jungle—like Ernie Pyle and Heinie Faust and the rest of the boys who had got theirs by enemy fire. The way Hemingway ought to have gotten his, in one of his wars, instead of the poor old bastard having to do it with a shotgun in a frigging Idaho kitchen. No kitchen for Peter Deighan; no hotel room or whorehouse. That had been the sticking point all along, that had been the reason he couldn't blow himself away in Phnom Penh. On a battlefield or nowhere. In the middle of the only war he had.

He realized dimly that the shooting had stopped. The sound of Khmer voices drifted to him; he heard faint rustlings in the ferns. Without thinking about it he lifted his hand, the one holding the .45. And laid the gun back alongside his head, with the muzzle up against his right ear.

More rustlings, louder now. Then a figure loomed out of the greenery, short and brown, with an M1 unslung in lean hands. Black-pajamaed figure, not one in combat fatigues. Khmer Rouge soldier. Grinning.

Oh no you don't, Deighan thought. It isn't up to you, you son of a bitch, the coup de grâce is *my* job. And the .45 felt huge in his hand, warm, comforting. Like a friend. Like the only friend he had ever had, in the only war he would ever know.

Now I've got the *cojones,* he thought.

And pulled the trigger.

PART FOUR

◆◇◆◇◆◇◆◇◆◇◆◇◆◇◆◇◆◇◆◇◆

April 1976

Kim

Kim spent the first two days after her escape at a war-damaged rice mill on the Mongkol Borei River, between Lovea and Phum Bavel.

The mill was a leaning yellow brick building, with part of one wall collapsed by an exploding bomb or mortar shell. The remains of a waterwheel lay along one side; a fire-blackened pier stretched out into the sluggish brown water on the other. A few hundred meters to the south, a partially destroyed bridge, planking gone and bare timbers exposed, sagged across the river and connected a dike road through acres of rice paddies with an overgrown cart track that disappeared into dense jungle to the west. It was along the dike road and several like it, under the cover of darkness, that Kim had made her way from the production cooperative near Lovea. She had reached the mill just before dawn, found it deserted, and decided it would serve as a hiding place during the daylight hours, when the fields teemed with workers and roaming Khmer Rouge patrols.

Inside, it was dim and hot and smelled of the rats and field mice that scurried among shattered wooden storage bins and other rubble. One of the millstones was cracked in three places, in such a way that a small dark pocket or cave had been formed at one end. Kim had spread the floor with handfuls of dry grass from outside, building a nest like that of a rodent. She had also found a fallen coconut beneath one of the palms that grew between the mill and the wrecked bridge, carried it back inside, and used a sharp stone to crack it open. The milk and the sweet meat mixed with rice had appeased her hunger, made it possible for her to fall into an exhausted sleep as soon as she crawled into the nest beneath the millstone.

She slept more than a dozen hours, so that darkness had fallen once again when she awoke. It had been her intention to leave the mill at that time and strike out south along the river toward Phum Bavel; the Mongkol Borei flowed in a south-westerly direction to Pailin, she knew, and for part of its course it paralleled the Thailand border within a few kilometers. Following the river would be dangerous, because of the villages which dotted it and presence of Khmer Rouge soldiers. But it would be no less dangerous than attempting to navigate the mountainous jungle terrain that spread out due west to the Thai frontier—twenty-five or thirty kilometers of dense vegetation, suffocating heat, poisonous snakes, and dozens of geographical menaces. Her chances of reaching Thailand safely were slim in either case, but she calculated them to be better if she followed the river. It would mean traveling by night and sleeping by day, which would keep her within the boundaries of Kampuchea longer than if she were able to traverse the jungle. On the other hand, it would also mean that she could rest and nourish her weakened body more easily. There would be much more food to forage along the river. The jungle, despite its surfeit of vegetation, yielded little that was both edible and available to someone without weapons or tools.

But she had not been able to continue her flight that first night. She had started out, only to come upon a Khmer Rouge patrol less than one kilometer from the mill. She had seen them in time to hide herself in a grove of trees; and from there she had watched them disappear along the river to the south. Yet she was afraid that if she followed after the patrol she would encounter it again, in a circumstance which might not allow her to remain unseen. It would be safer if she returned to the mill and waited until the following night, she decided, and so she had done this. And perhaps it had been for the best, because it permitted her to spend the rest of the dark hours foraging more food—another coconut, bark, crushed black beetles—and making other preparations. She had fashioned a knapsack from the cloth of one pajama leg and a length of creeper vine, and she had found a piece of stone that resembled a knife and honed its point against the millstone. The stone was no weapon against the guns of the Khmer Rouge, but at least it would serve her as a useful tool.

The daylight hours passed less quickly. Kim slept all of the morning and part of the afternoon, but the sun was still high when she awoke. Heat lay with her in the cave beneath the millstone like a hungry lover, draped over her body, caressing her with damp hands. She did not move for a time, her mind blank, listening to the whisper of the rats moving in the semidarkness. Then she roused torpidly, crawled out to where she could look through the hole in the mill's side wall. Beyond, the dry brown paddies shimmered with heat haze; in the far distance, like ant figures, *opakar* wearing checked head scarves moved in the same sluggish way as she, as the slender Mongkol Borei behind the mill.

Back in her nest, she drank a little coconut milk to ease the dryness in her throat and curled herself again into a sleep position. But sleep would not return. Only the heat, lusting over her, making her thoughts shift in dull random patterns—back to her childhood, to the temples of Angkor Wat, to Charoun, to Serey, to the *sahakoo toic* near Lovea.

To the woman who had been beaten to death publicly for eating the flesh of a dead man.

It was that incident, two days ago, which had given her the final impetus for her escape. There had been other executions, including one of a teen-age couple who had been discovered making love behind the livestock pen and who had been dragged away half naked, but none had been carried out for all eyes to witness. Even the teen-agers had been killed inside a screen of trees, their bodies buried in private and never seen by any of the *opakar*. It had been possible, with only a minimum of effort, to block out the fact of the executions, to pretend that they had no effect on her own existence. But the fatal beating of the woman, a once attractive fortune-teller from Phnom Penh, no older than her own thirty years, had ended that possibility and made her continued presence in the cooperative an impossibility.

The idea of cannibalism was abhorrent to her. And yet she could not blame the woman for what she had done. She had never been that hungry, even at the worst moments of her year under the yoke of the Angkar Leu, but who was to say that she might not become that hungry? Who was to say that if she had been out gathering wood for the blacksmith's forge and stumbled across the newly dead body of a suicide, as the fortune-teller had, she would not have found a stone and hacked away a piece of flesh from one arm? The Khmer Rouge had turned them all into animals, and animals had no compunction about eating their own kind, if it was the only means of their survival.

She had stood with the assembled others and listened to the *srok* intone the charges against the woman, who had been caught in her act of cannibalism by one of the soldiers. And she had looked at the woman's desolate face as she was made to kneel in the center of the commune, with a smaller ring of soldiers around her. And she had watched the soldiers use hoe handles and bamboo canes to beat the fortune-teller's head to a mash of white and red and gray, then take the body to the blacksmith's hut and burn it in the forge. And she had thought that she must not allow this same thing to happen to her. She must not be driven to cannibalism. She must not be beaten to death in front of a thousand other suffering animals. She must not let the Khmer Rouge destroy her. She must escape, she must survive, she must find freedom and then fight the Angkar, see *them* destroyed for all they had done.

It had not been difficult for her to slip out of her thatched hut shortly past midnight. Nor had it been difficult to avoid the Khmer Rouge guards stationed around the commune, to slip away into the dark paddies. There had been clouds that night, hiding the bright face of the moon; and she had moved swiftly, with the silence and cunning of purpose. All that she had taken with her was the last of her ration of cooked rice. Yes, and the image of the fortune-teller after the soldiers had battered her to death . . .

Shadows began to gather inside the mill as afternoon waned

toward evening. Kim dozed, awoke, ate a small portion of rice mixed with coconut. Once she heard a noise outside and lay rigid inside her cave, listening, her fingers tight around the knife-shaped stone. But it was only a stray pig, lean and half wild, rooting for food; she heard it squealing and had a glimpse of it through the ragged hole in the side wall.

When darkness came she crawled out and prepared to leave. But she did not step outside until she was certain that there were no lantern lights anywhere in the paddies, no boat lights visible on the river, and that a heavy rolling cloudbank obscured both moon and stars. Then, with her makeshift knapsack slung over one shoulder, the stone knife tucked inside the waistband of her pajamas, she left the mill and went south along the Mongkol Borei.

Traveling was not difficult along this section of the river. There were dike roads through the paddies, and cart paths where the paddies gave way to tobacco and maize fields and still-unreclaimed jungle. The road between Lovea and Phum Bavel was some distance away to the east, and occasionally she saw the flash of headlights in that direction; but there were no lights or vehicles on the dike roads or cart tracks. And she saw no sign of another Khmer Rouge patrol.

Long past midnight she stopped for her first rest in a marshy area thick with reeds and scattered purple hyacinths. But when she left there a short while later, her pace was slower and she could feel herself growing heavy with fatigue. The fibers of her body had become toughened by all the long hours in the fields, but the lack of proper diet and touches of dysentery and beriberi had robbed her of strength and stamina. She stopped twice more to rest, and in the hour before dawn, as she made her way through a thick patch of jungle, she considered stopping altogether and making a burrow in which to spend the day. Yet she was loath to sacrifice any of the dark hours. Each kilometer she traveled brought her closer to Thailand, to freedom, and the more ground she covered each night, the sooner she would reach the border.

The first light began, slowly, to creep across the sky. A thin mist rose off the river, eddying across the path she was on, giving the jungle a distorted, ghostly appearance. The heat was oppressive, and combined with her growing lassitude, it turned her thoughts and her perceptions sluggish again. She told herself that now she must find a safe place to pass the daylight hours; dawn was almost upon her.

The path curved away from the river through a long line of bamboo, so that the water became screened from her view. This seemed as good a place as she was likely to find. She plodded ahead for another few meters, looking for a break in the dense thickets. But before she found one, the path looped back to the west and she could see the river again. She could also see, some fifty meters distant, a single *paillote* standing heronlike at the water's edge. Beyond it, inland, where the bamboo thinned into a section of dusty elephant grass, another, wider path curled away toward the Lovea–Phum Bavel road.

Kim stopped, squinting at the rickety stilt house. There was no one visible anywhere around it, but she could see wisps of smoke coming up through an aperture in its thatched roof: a fire burning in the family cookstove. It was only a fisherman's *paillote,* but that did not mean its occupants were fishermen. Had those who fished the rivers for their livelihood been left alone or had they, like almost everyone else, been rounded up and put to work in the cooperatives? She had never been told and no one else had seemed to know. Secrecy and ignorance were two of the KC's strongest weapons. She backed off a few paces, started to turn back the way she had come.

A man stepped out of the thicket less than a dozen meters from her.

Kim stopped again, stiffening, her hand flat against her stomach where the stone knife was concealed beneath her blouse. The man was in his thirties, hawk-faced, with close-cropped black hair and thick lips, dressed in peasant pajamas similar to Kim's. Slung over his shoulder was a woven-grass sack filled with cassava roots. And in his right hand he carried a short, rusted, but sharp-looking jungle knife.

They stood looking at each other, neither of them speaking, Kim keeping her expression as neutral as the man's. Fifteen or twenty seconds of silence passed, broken only by the droning of insects and the rustle of an animal somewhere in the bamboo. Then the man's face broke into a smile and he came forward in a friendly way, without apparent wariness. Kim remained motionless, but her hand crept closer to the stone knife.

When the man reached her he stopped, holding the jungle knife pointed downward at his side, and said, *"Look mien barey tee?"* with the rough-edged inflection of a peasant. His teeth were stained reddish-black from betel juice and it made his smile look bloody.

"No," she said, "I have no cigarettes."

"Are you from Phum Bavel?"

"No. From Lovea."

"Ah."

"I'm looking for a woman who escaped from the *sahakoo toic* near Lovea," Kim said. "Have you seen any strangers in this vicinity in the past two days?"

"Only you, *mit.*"

"Are you a member of the Party?"

"No, *mit.* I am only Ney Narin, a humble fisherman."

"You are permitted to live here alone?"

"Not alone. With my wife."

"And you are not bothered?"

"By Angka? No, *mit.*" He paused. "Is it permitted to ask if you are alone in searching for this woman?"

"There are others in the area."

"Then perhaps you would like to wait for them in my *paillote,*" Ney Narin said. "My wife would be pleased to prepare rice and tea for you."

"That is not necessary."

"But I would be honored."

"No. I must continue my search."

There was a subtle shift in Ney Narin's countenance, a hardening; guile crawled into his eyes. The blade of the jungle knife tilted upward slightly, so that it was pointed at her lower body.

"I insist, *mit,*" he said. "To have a member of the revolutionary Angka in my humble house would be a rare privilege."

He suspects me, Kim thought with alarm belated by her fa-

344

tigue. He must be a Khmer Rouge *chhlop*. That is why he's permitted to live here instead of in one of the communes.

"Have you decided, *mit*?" Ney Narin said politely. But the point of the jungle knife raised higher as he spoke, glistening in the early-morning mist only a few centimeters from her abdomen.

There was nothing she could do; the advantage was all his. She placed a smile on her own mouth and said to him, "Of course, Ney Narin. I would not deprive you of your pleasure."

"You are most generous," he said—and held the knife close to her body at every step to the *paillote* on the river's edge.

Foxworth

He sat in a tearoom near the intersection of Ploenchit Road and Rajdamri, ten minutes early for his meeting with Natalie, and drank tea and stared out at the traffic. Six lanes of Ploenchit and eight lanes of Rajdamri swirled in front of him: horns, squealing tires, metallic glints of light and color under the blazing sun. But inside the nearly empty tearoom it was dim and quiet, the white-jacketed waiters hovering along one wall like ghosts.

There was more to look at outside than the traffic. Colorful signs, for instance, that said British Overseas Airways and Caesar Key Club, among other things. And a shrine to Brahma, the four-faced Hindu deity, creator of the world. The shrine held Foxworth's attention for a time. The creator of the world, he thought. But when was it created—four thousand years ago in seven days or a couple of million eons ago in a welter of confusion? When was Cambodia created? What about Angkor Wat? Or were they being created right now, with him and the rest of the world, as the Khmer Rouge broadcasts claimed, witness to that creation?

Cambodia, he thought. Everything comes down to Cambodia these days. And Kim. Cambodia and Kim.

He took up the teapot, inverted it to pour more tea into his cup. His hand was just the slightest bit unsteady. Without humor he smiled at the hand, and incidentally at the creator of the world out there, frozen in gilded metal. Scared? he asked himself. Damn right he was scared. He had made his big decision, he had quit the State Department, and now here he was afloat in Bangkok, living in the Victory Hotel, trying to get his act together so he could make the next big decision, so he could go ahead and do . . . what? Do what? It was the future that scared him, with all its uncertainties. It was his own uncertainty that scared him. And because Natalie was a part of that future, in the short run if not the long one, and a part of that uncertainty, she scared him too. What was he going to say to her? He hadn't had an answer to that question a week ago, and so he'd dealt with the problem by putting it off. But now he couldn't put off facing her any longer; now the problem loomed larger than ever. What was he going to say to her? What did he want from her, from their relationship?

Well, he had gotten through the phone call all right. But then, he'd been expecting her to contact him at any time, as soon as she found out, and it was almost a relief that she'd done it by phone last night instead of coming around in person. He'd been able to say, "I'll explain later, I'll explain tomorrow," and then made the appointment for this morning, cutting off even the possibility of questioning before it began. Her voice, hurt and distant over the wire, had fallen to a whisper, saying, "All right, David, tomorrow then," and that was all. So he'd ducked her again and bought himself one more day.

He'd become adept at ducking people during the past week. Coworkers at the embassy, Thai officials and acquaintances, Tom Boyd twice, once in his former office and once in his former villa on Sukhumvit Road—all by saying he was busy packing and making new arrangements and besides, he didn't feel like discussing the matter. His father, too, on three separate overseas telephone calls. The first one had come the day after he'd submitted his resignation. Benjamin Foxworth had been the one to call and tell him he'd been *appointed* to the foreign service; it wasn't surprising that the old man would have found out right away that he'd quit. That time, and the two following, he'd said the connection was bad as soon as he recognized his father's voice, hung up, and went away before the old man could ring back.

Oh, he'd ducked everybody very neatly, all right. But he couldn't go on ducking them indefinitely, that was the problem. You had to face people sooner or—

His waiter was there beside the table, asking if he wanted more tea. "Maybe later," Foxworth said. The waiter went away. "Maybe later," he said again, softly to himself.

Maybe later. Sure. Maybe later the mixture of relief and resolution would return, the one that had propelled him through his resignation and its immediate aftermath, with the feeling that for the first time in his life he had arrived at self-definition, that he had done something for himself, for David Foxworth. Where was that feeling now? He couldn't even remember when he'd lost it, when the fear and the uncertainty began to pile up inside him. Sometime in the past couple of days, when all the packing and moving and busywork was finished and he was alone again with his thoughts.

And maybe later he'd be able to face Boyd, his father, his future. But first he had to face Natalie. Not later, sooner.

Right now.

He saw her through the tearoom window, the refracted sun backlighting her image as she crossed Rajdamri Boulevard—a tall dark-haired woman with a splendid figure, moving with confidence and grace in his direction. She might have been some collegiate fantasy come to life, except that he felt the shaking begin again in his hands and had to suppress a mad urge to jump up and run out through a rear exit. Momentarily she passed in front of the shrine to Brahma and there was a juxtaposition of Brahma's four faces peering over Natalie's own, creator and created alike. Then the images split and she was moving toward the tearoom door, her hand reached out, the door opened, she came inside and saw him and crossed to the table. She avoided looking at him as she sat uncomfortably, put her pocketbook on her lap. Her cheeks were flushed from the heat, her eyes shrouded. She looked sealed off but he sensed that that was only on the surface; down inside she was open to him. Far too open.

"Have some tea?" he said tentatively.

"I don't seem to have a cup."

"I'll call the waiter—"

"I don't think I want any tea." Her hands moved over the surface of her pocketbook. "You look relieved," she said.

"Do I? I didn't think it showed."

"It shows."

Silence. But she was looking at him now, and after a time she said, "Why didn't you tell me, David?"

Well, that was the basic question, wasn't it? he thought. That was the first question she was bound to ask. And the answer? He didn't know the answer. No, that was a lie; he did know the answer. He just didn't want to face himself, either.

"About my decision to resign," he said.

"You know that's what I mean."

"All right." He took a breath. "I didn't tell you because I had to do something on my own for the first time in my life. If I'd told you it would have been like seeking prior approval or moral support, and I didn't want that."

"I see. Is that the only reason?"

"Yes."

"Are you sure, David?"

"Yes."

The waiter reappeared beside the table. He asked Natalie, in his precise English, if she cared for tea, sweetmeats, cakes? She shook her head, and he bowed and went away.

"You're disappointed in me," Foxworth said.

"Not at your decision to resign, no."

"Because I didn't tell you."

"Yes. I thought we had something, David—a better relationship, a deeper one. All those nights we've spent together . . . they weren't just physical for me."

"They weren't just physical for me, either," he said. "I care for you, Natalie, you know that. It's just . . ." He broke off, let the unfinished sentence hang in the air between them.

"Kim," Natalie said.

"Yes. Kim."

"You still feel the same way as before?"

"About her? I'm afraid so."

"Then why did you resign? If you'd stayed on at the embassy you'd be closer to what's going on in Cambodia, wouldn't you?"

He winced; the question seemed to lodge in his mind, like a splinter. "I don't want to be that close to it anymore. I need some distance, some perspective."

"And then what?"

He shook his head.

"Will distance and perspective change anything for us, David?"

"I can't answer that. Not now, not yet."

She looked away, out through the window at the teeming traffic beyond. Then, still not looking at him, she said, "I don't want to stay here any longer. I feel like walking, hot as it is. You can come along if you want."

"All right."

Foxworth left several baht on the table and they went out into the stifling humidity and walked for some time, along the Chao Phraya River. Neither of them said much. From time to time he would look at her or catch her looking at him, and there was an awkwardness, a distance between them. But at the same time there was an easy companionship, a kind of intimacy, as there had been between Kim and him among the parasols abloom in Le Phnom Park.

Kim.

But Kim might be dead. Kim was in Cambodia in any case, and her condition was as removed from his as was that of Pol Pot or Henry Kissinger. No matter how much he had loved her or how torn he was by guilt, no matter how much he might want it otherwise, Kim was starting to become an abstraction. Her existence had no effect upon his own. The thought unleashed another wave of guilt, but just as suddenly it receded, and he found a clarity that he had not had before. It was another way of considering the situation, wasn't it? Wasn't it?

After a while, walking, they found themselves on the huge

Pramane Ground near the Grand Palace, where children and adults were kite-fighting with star-shaped male and rhomboid-shaped female kites high above. They stopped to watch the spectacle—the twisting maneuvers, the sudden collisions, the random explosions of kites damaged by impact, falling.

"They're serious, aren't they?" Natalie said.

He nodded. "It's a sport they take as seriously as we take football. The male kites are called *chula,* you know. The females, the ones with the long tails, are *pakpao.*"

She gave him a sidelong look. "How come you're so knowledgeable on the subject?"

"Embassy guidebook."

"They made you memorize stuff like that?"

"There were some empty nights," he said.

They walked along the rim of the field, past the chattering kite flyers. Not talking again because they had used up all their small talk. Avoiding a return to the issue on both their minds, Natalie because she was afraid of the answers, him because he was afraid of the questions. Another urge began to work itself up inside him, small and perverse; he pushed it down. But it wouldn't stay pushed. It got a firm grip on his brain and made him stop walking, made him say, "Natalie."

She turned to him, her eyes questioning.

"I did work for the CIA. Low-level intelligence work—I wasn't a spook. But I *was* one of the Agency connections, and they weren't too happy to see me go."

She didn't react, didn't say anything.

"I believed it was the right thing," he said. "I wasn't ashamed of it."

"And now?"

"Now I've changed my mind about the Company—about their involvement in the Sihanouk coup, among other things. Now I guess I am ashamed."

"David," she said, "that's good to hear, I'm glad for you. But your former CIA connection isn't the main point here. The main point is what you're going to do now that you're out. About us. About the rest of your life."

He looked at her for a span of time, the shadows of kites casting flickers of intercepted light over her features.

"I don't know," he said. "I just . . . . I don't know."

Chey Han

The bonze would not let him alone.

"You're a fool, Chey Han," he said, juggling his crimson head. "Instead of chasing around the countryside this way, you should have returned to Sisophon. What will the Angkar say if you don't return as scheduled? What will the Angkar do?"

"It was you who insisted the hen Mey Yat is really Than Kim. You talked me into looking for her. Now you try to talk me out of looking for her."

"There is no need to look for her any longer."

"Why is there no need?"

"She has become a fugitive," the bonze said. "She will be captured and killed in any case. You don't have to worry about her now."

"What if she *is* Kim? What if she reveals this fact before she is butchered like the other chickens?"

"I thought you believed she was not Kim."

"She isn't," Chey said. "But what if she is?"

"She wouldn't reveal herself. Why would she? Besides, she might not be captured at all. She might escape across the frontier and never be seen in Kampuchea again."

"She will not escape."

"How do you know that?"

"I know it because I will find her first," Chey said. "I will find her and prove to you that she isn't my half-sister."

The bonze looked at him through eyes streaked with blood and laughter. "Oh Chey Han," he said. "Oh Chey Han. You're such a fool."

"I am not a fool. *You* are the fool."

"Such a fool. Such a fool."

The jeep bounced over a rut in the dike road, trailing a parachute of dust. Chey squinted through the heat-haze ahead, ignoring the bonze; a line of ox carts moved sluggishly on the Lovea–Phum Bavel road. He leaned toward his driver, ordered him to stop when they reached the intersection where the carts were. The sergeant gave him an uncertain look—the same sort of look the bonze kept giving him with his bright-red eyes—but he did not argue. Like the bonze, the sergeant did not think they should be out here canvassing the countryside for an escaped *opaka* named Mey Yat; he thought they should be back at the cooperative, preparing to escort the eighty or ninety chickens to their new roost at Mongkol Borei. But what did the driver know? What did the bonze know? He had come this far; he must pursue the matter to a conclusion. He must find out if Mey Yat was or was not Than Kim, and the only way he could do that was to first find Mey Yat.

If she was not Kim he would bring her back to be butchered. If she was Kim he would butcher her himself.

It was sad, it was terrible, but he would have no choice. She was a chicken, wasn't she? And he did not wish to become a chicken himself. No, he would have no choice.

The bonze winked at him, twirled his bloody head, and laughed like one who was mad.

When they stopped at the intersection Chey spoke to the KC guard who watched over the carts and the chickens attending them. But the guard, like the others he had questioned since leaving the cooperative, knew nothing of a hen named Mey Yat. To his knowledge, he said, no single hen had either been captured or killed by local troops in the past two days.

Chey ordered the driver to go on, down the road to Phum Bavel. The bonze, his laughter expended, had become silent; his head, balanced on the palm of his right hand, inclined to one side and his eyes were closed. Chey looked at the pitted road, at the tall elephant grass and the green wall of jungle flanking it. And a question came to him: Would this and similar roads one day be paved, filled with traffic and people carrying the goods of plenty, bringing husbands home to wives and headless bonzes to the graves where they belonged?

The bonze stirred, began giggling again. "If there are such roads, Chey Han," he said, "you won't live to travel on them."

They were approaching a place where a narrow trail curled in from the west, through the elephant grass, and joined the road. A man was bicycling rapidly along the trail, his head bent forward, his legs pumping in a blur. He seemed to become aware of the oncoming jeep at the same time Chey became aware of him; he raised his head, then made an urgent beckoning gesture. And when he came to the juncture with the road, seconds ahead of the jeep, he hopped off his bicycle and used both arms as semaphores.

Chey said to his sergeant, "Stop, but be alert," and put his hand on the butt of his sidearm. The jeep nosed to a stop just beyond the intersection; Chey sat swiveled around, facing the man as he hurried up with his bicycle. A peasant, in peasant dress, with thick lips in the face of a fat hawk. A fisherman: the odor of fish came from him faintly on the hot morning air.

"Good! You're a soldier of Angka," the fisherman said. His features were flushed; his eyes seemed filled with excitement. "I couldn't have wished for better fortune."

"Who are you?" Chey asked him. "What do you want?"

"I am Ney Narin. I live nearby, on the river; it is my privilege to serve the great and glorious Angkar."

A *chhlop*, Chey thought. He said, "State your purpose in flagging us, Ney Narin."

"Not one hour ago, near my home, I came upon a woman walking alone through the jungle. She claimed to be of Angka, but her clothing was that of a peasant and she offered no *laissez-passer* or other identification."

The bonze stirred again. "Oh Chey Han," he said.

"What is this woman's name?" Chey asked the fisherman.

"She calls herself Chan Sron."

"What have you done with her?"

"Nothing, *mit*. I took her to my *paillote*, instructed my wife to detain her, and came to report the incident."

"Than Kim," the bonze said. "Oh Chey Han, oh Chey Han."

Chey ordered the fisherman to abandon his bicycle and climb

into the jeep. Then he ordered his driver to follow the trail to Ney Narin's *paillote*.

"If I have done well to detain the woman," Ney said, "will there be credit for me from Angka?" There was both eagerness and pleasure in his voice. "Will I be rewarded?"

Chey said nothing.

The bonze said, *"Chhlop! Chhlop!"*

"Shut up, you fool."

"Oh Chey Han—"

"Silence!"

His driver looked at him; he felt the fisherman looking at him. He had spoken aloud again, even though he had warned himself against such outbursts. He must *not* do it again. How could he explain to anyone that a dead bonze lived inside his mind? How could he make them understand such a relationship as he possessed with the headless one?

"Can you keep it a secret?" the bonze asked him slyly. "Or will you expose me by accident? Or worse, will you cut off another part of me?"

"I did not cut off your head."

"No?"

"Ly Sokhon cut off your head."

"And you are not Ly Sokhon."

"No. Never."

"But you plan to cut off the head of Than Kim."

"If she is Than Kim."

"Still, you plan to cut off her head."

"That is different."

"Why is it different?"

"It is the will of Angka."

"There is no Angka," the bonze said, and laughed and laughed in the sun, the wrinkles in his face dribbling blood. "There is no God, there is no Angka, there is no Buddha, there is no Kampuchea. There is only blood. And chickens. Ah! And chickens!"

Jouncing, spinning up more clouds of dust, the jeep raced down the path through the tall stalks of elephant grass. Ahead, now, Chey could see the coffee-brown river, glinting with reflected sunlight, and the frail-looking *paillote* on its near bank. He did not feel excitement at the prospect of confronting Kim, if the hen was Kim; he felt only a sense of great sadness. Doremy's face floated into his consciousness, smiling, whispering, "You are my Great Ox, Chey Han, touch my body, Han, touch my breasts," but the laughter of the bonze drove Doremy away and he saw chickens instead, chickens without heads, running and flapping their wings, and then they too vanished, only to be replaced by more chickens, real chickens this time, scurrying out of the way, flapping and squawking, as the jeep skidded to a halt before the *paillote*.

Chey leaped out and ran to the bamboo ladder that led up to the entrance. From inside a woman's voice cried out, "Ney Narin! Ney Narin!" Chey drew his sidearm, clambered up the ladder ahead of his sergeant and the fisherman.

Chinks in the *paillote*'s bamboo walls let in crisscrossing shafts of sunlight, so that the floor had a webbed pattern of light and shadow. A low bamboo partition separated it into two rooms. The one in which Chey stood was empty except for the family cookstove, utensils, water jar; he ran to the partition, peered over it into the other room.

A lean hen with a gold front tooth lay on a raised platform below the partition, looking up at him with frightened eyes. Her hands were bound to her waist with a length of homemade rope; her ankles were bound as well. Chey had never seen her before.

"Ah!" the bonze said. "Ah ah ah!"

"The other woman—where is she?" Chey shouted at the gold-toothed hen. "Where is she?"

The hen shook her head and made a squawking noise. The fisherman, Ney Narin, was beside Chey now, rubbing his hands and looking anxious; he stepped around the partition, into the other room, and began to untie the hen's hands.

"*Where is she?*" Chey shouted again.

"She attacked me," the hen said, and clucked and squawked again.

"You permitted her to escape."

"Baat, cah! I didn't! She attacked me and tied my hands and ankles and ran away."

"Where?"

"I don't know. I was bound here, I couldn't see—"

"How long ago did this happen?"

"Fifteen minutes. Twenty."

Chey whirled, ran back to the ladder, slid down it to the ground. He went part way along the path through the bamboo to the north, saw nothing, heard nothing, and came back to stand at the river's edge. The narrow expanse of water was empty except for something floating on the far side downstream that might have been a log or a crocodile but was definitely not a chicken. He looked up at the sky. He looked into the elephant grass. He looked again into the bamboo. None of these told him anything.

The bonze laughed. The bonze told him nothing either.

I'll find her, he thought.

And put the thought into words, a shout that echoed through the heat and the stillness of morning: "I'll find her!"

Cambodia File: Excerpts from a Declaration by Prince Norodom Sihanouk, April 2, 1976

. . . It has been my great pride and honor from March 1970 to this day to accompany my most beloved Kampuchean people on the great and prestigious historical march that is now leading Kampuchea into a new era, in which the people are the only true masters of their destiny and of the nation and the fatherland, a new era which beyond all doubt will be the most radiant and glorious in the two thousand years of our national history.

When the *coup d'état* of Lon Nol and his clique took place in Phnom Penh on March 18, 1970, I swore to myself and to the Kampuchean people that after I had accompanied my countrymen to complete victory over U.S. imperialism and the traitorous clique, and after the opening of the new revolutionary era, I would retire completely and forever from the political scene, for my role would logically come to an end.

Today, my dream that Kampuchea would recover and strengthen forever its independence, sovereignty, territorial integrity, and neutrality, and acquire a system capable of giving the people and the nation true sovereignty and perfect social justice, and a national life that is absolutely clean (without stain, corruption, and other social ills), has been fulfilled beyond anything I could imagine, thanks to our fighting men and women, peasants, laborers, and other working people, under the enlightened leadership of our revolutionary Angkar.

Thus, all my fondest wishes have come true. Better yet, our Kampuchea has achieved, thanks to its heroic revolutionary men and women, splendid exploits of great significance, which are among the greatest in the history of all mankind, such as being the first to overcome completely the arrogant and allegedly invincible U.S. imperialism, the most powerful, cruel, and tenacious imperialism the world has ever known.

As for myself, shortly after the liberation of the fatherland, our people, our revolutionary Angkar, and revolutionary army solemnly honored me as a patriot and member of the resistance and spontaneously renewed my term of office as head of state of Kampuchea; they then invited me to return officially to Kampuchea and just as they had welcomed me in March 1973 during the war, gave me a solemn, extremely cordial and warm welcome and extended to me a hospitality filled with affection, respect, and consideration, and with understandably great pride they showed me their wonderful and innumerable achievements, most thrilling among them being the new irrigation systems which will assuredly make our country one of the most advanced and highly developed agricultural nations.

My content is therefore greater than can be imagined. . . .

It is with this sentiment and with the conviction that our people and revolutionary Angkar understand me as one of their fellows that I request them to permit me to retire today. I wish to assure you that everywhere and under all circumstances I shall remain a valiant supporter of the Kampuchean people, the revolution, the People's Representative Assembly, the government, the State Presidium, the revolutionary Angkar, and the revolutionary army of Democratic Kampuchea.

Long live the most heroic and glorious people of Kampuchea!

Long live Democratic Kampuchea!

Long live the Constitution of Democratic Kampuchea!

Ly Sokhon

In less than fifteen minutes, she thought, Sihanouk and the traitorous Pol Pot will be dead.

She knew great excitement as she sat listening to the monarchist dog give his prepared speech of capitulation over Radio Phnom Penh, the speakers carrying his lies throughout her cubicle at the radio station. Under her blouse, in a sheath she had fashioned last night of cloth and thin cord, the Vietnamese sword nestled tight against her body. She could feel it thick and hard along the flesh of her abdomen, and it seemed to throb there, warm and waiting and as eager as she to make the blood flow from the poisoned veins of the enemy. Soon, she whispered to it with her mind. Soon.

"Today, my dream that Kampuchea would recover and strengthen forever its independence, sovereignty, territorial integrity, and neutrality," the voice of Sihanouk was saying, "and acquire a system capable of giving the people and the nation true sovereignty and perfect social justice, and a national life that is absolutely clean . . ." Static crackled around his voice, obscuring it for a time. ". . . thanks to our fighting men and women, peasants, laborers, and other working people, under the enlightened leadership of our revolutionary Angkar. . . ."

Lies, Ly Sokhon thought. Corrupt lies. As was the official

statement already issued by Pol Pot and the remainder of his clique, in response to the written version of Sihanouk's retirement declaration: "The Council of Ministers considers that Samdech Norodom Sihanouk is an eminently patriotic prince who has actively contributed to the struggle for national liberation . . . in recognition of the services rendered to the Kampuchean nation by Samdech Norodom Sihanouk, who took an active part in the national liberation during the most barbarous war of aggression waged during the last five years by the American imperialists and the traitors of Lon Nol, the Council of Ministers unanimously wishes to confer upon Samdech Norodom Sihanouk the title of Great Patriot . . . at the same time the Council of Ministers proposes to build a monument in honor of these services . . . the Government of Democratic Kampuchea will fully guarantee and bear his living expenses of himself and his family in recognition of his honor and status as former Head of State. . . ."

Corruption.

Everywhere in the city—corruption!

She felt the rage welling within her, closed her eyes, and held it down. She must remain calm and controlled; she had worked toward this day for some time now, and at all costs she must not betray her plans by a loss of control. Listening to Sihanouk's smug lying voice, the flashes of static like cries of derision against the false words, she thought of how his blood would look when she made it flow. Red and hot and thick, like all the blood of all the other enemies she had spilled. Like the blood of Pol Pot, who had betrayed not only her, not only himself, but all the dreams of revolution and all the believers who had fought for those dreams and died for them. Sihanouk's blood and Pol Pot's blood, flowing together, flowing out hot and red and thick to bring the new cleansing, the new and purified revolution of the People.

The sword seemed to grow harder, to pulse more urgently, to lay a trail of fire along her skin.

It will not be long, she told it again. She reached down to caress its length through her blouse. The plan is a good one: in only a few short minutes the traitors will be dead. They *will* be dead.

She had evolved the plan with care. And she knew that it was a good one precisely because it had not come to her full-born. Before she had settled on it, she had rejected several other plans as too simple, too rash. She could have rushed into the main control room and assassinated Sihanouk as he spoke, but then the guards would have overpowered her and she would not have been able to destroy Pol Pot, who was in the building but not in the control room, nor would she live to lead the new revolution. She could have intercepted the two traitors on their way *into* the station and killed them before their lies could be disseminated, but that came to the same problem: they were heavily guarded, the guards would cut her down whether or not she accomplished her objective. The sacrifice of her own life must be avoided. The revolution must begin again in the jungles, sweep through this time to utterly consume the hateful cities; only she could lead it, only she truly understood the depth of the betrayal and how to set it right. She *had* to live. No one could replace her.

The plan that she had worked out was both feasible and cunning: both Sihanouk and Pol Pot would die, while she survived. She had a mind superior to any of these fools, they could not possibly react until it was too late; then she would be out of the building, and soon out of Phnom Penh, safe in the jungles, regrouping the forces of old and planning for her own assumption of power.

When Sihanouk's lying speech neared its conclusion she stood and went to the door of her cubicle, the sword heavy and warm against her. In the office next to hers the faceless young man who was her assistant sat behind his table, listening intently to the words of the monarchist. She stood for a moment in the doorway, considering him. He was about twenty-five years of age, his name was Cheng Seng, and he had formerly been an administrative assistant in Siem Reap Province. He had never fought in the jungles.

He sensed her presence and looked up at her. He had no features; he was but an unimportant cell in the body of the new revolution. "Yes, Mit Ly?" he said.

"Attend to the broadcast, Cheng Seng," she told him. "Listen to the words of the great Samdech."

His head revolved away from her, cocked once again toward the speakers. Ly Sokhon glided up behind him, taking out the sword as she moved, and in a single fluid motion she brought the blade slashing downward, saw it cut deep into the point where his neck and shoulder blades conjoined. He made no sound, only spilled forward to the floor, the blood spurting from him in lush arterial blossoms.

Her eyes glinting, she watched him die. But his blood was thinner than the rich blood which was soon to flow, for which his own purposeless life had been sacrificed. She dragged his body out of the cubicle and across to the entrance to the broadcast area. The door to the anteroom where Pol Pot and his guards waited was still closed, but through it she could hear the revolutionary music that meant Sihanouk's speech had reached its end.

She cleaned her sword on Cheng's clothing, then opened the door a crack. Sihanouk was just emerging from the main control room; Pol Pot and three cadres stood ready to greet him. The Prince's plump little face seemed to glow with satisfaction. Pol Pot's eyes were withdrawn and intense, but he was smiling. Dogs, she thought, they have brought this upon themselves. She widened the opening, assumed an expression of terror, and stumbled into the anteroom, the sword hidden in the hollow beneath her right arm, throbbing and swollen and hungry.

"An assassin!" she cried. "A CIA assassin is in the building! He has already killed Cheng Seng!"

The five men before her came as one to a standstill. There was a frozen moment as all of them stared at her, past her through the open door to where Cheng's bloody corpse could be seen in the hallway.

"Stop him!" she shrieked. "Destroy the assassin!"

The three cadres rushed forward, weapons appearing in their hands, voices babbling questions and confused commands. Sihanouk remained in position, staring, more bewildered than frightened in these first few seconds. But Pol Pot, his face reshaping itself into a mask of fear, retreated against one wall and ducked cravenly behind a piece of furniture.

There was a wild singing inside Ly Sokhon—a mixture of joy and hatred and desire. As soon as the guards were past her into the hallway, she moved forward as if to join and protect the two leaders. Sihanouk was nearest, but her eyes were fixed on Pol Pot, Saloth Sar, the cancerous head of the Angkar Leu, the primary betrayer. He had taught her passion, he had inflamed her loins with physical hunger and her mind with the ardor of revolution, but now he was corrupt and the passion he had instilled in her was for death, his death, because he had become that which he had always despised. He must be the first to die. Pol Pot, the great leader, the great pollutant, and then it would be the turn of the prince of treachery.

He did not know who she was. He watched her approach him and in his eyes there was no recognition, just as there had been none that day in his office at the Foreign Ministry. The corruption had wiped away his memory, along with all truth and all righteousness. Her hatred for him leaped, soared, spread through her as if on bird's wings. Make his blood flow, she thought, watch its redness flow and fill the room, fill all of Kampuchea, rivers of blood, running red and lighting the fires, burning . . .

And the sword was in her hand; it had been hidden and now, as if magically, it was in her hand, upraised. But she had drawn it too soon, too soon: the traitors saw it, both of them cried out, Sihanouk lunged to one side and Pol Pot fell to his knees behind a chair, threw his arms over his head like the cowardly dog he was. She ran to him, swung the sword, cleaved wood instead of flesh, saw splinters instead of blood. She raised the blade again—

Something struck her arm from behind, sent the sword arcing out of her fingers to clatter against the wall, to fall with a metallic ringing noise. Hands clutched at her, an unyielding hardness struck the side of her head and drove her to her knees. Then there were blows, many blows, thudding down on her like heavy rain, and she screamed, "Swine, dogs, you will all die, I will make your blood flow in rivers!" but the words were empty now, meaningless, because inside her there was no more joy and desire, there was only a great wrenching frustration and a pain far greater than that of the blows.

She had failed.

She had been too anxious, she had forgotten herself and become weak and lost control: she had failed. Now Pol Pot and Sihanouk and the Angkar Leu and all the cities would go on and on, the new revolution would not be born to sweep it all clean, she would not be the new broom, the new leader, she would not go back into the jungles, she would not, she would not, no blood, no red running fires lighting sword slashing no no

Nothing.

Kim

The sky and the river at sunrise were bathed in ocher-colored light. Wisps of early-morning mist still clung to the wall of jungle along the west bank, and where Kim was, inside the fisherman's pirogue hidden in one of the narrow side channels, clouds of mosquitoes swarmed around her as they had all during the night. But the shawl of nylon mosquito netting kept them from feeding on her as she fed herself on bits of coconut and a few grams of rice.

It had been twenty-four hours since her encounter with the *chhlop* Ney Narin and his wife at the stilt house two kilometers upstream. Ney had made the mistake of leaving her in the woman's care, instead of sending his *propôn* to alert the Khmer Rouge and watching over her himself, and for this she was grateful. Even though Ney Narin's wife had been armed with the jungle knife, she had not been wary enough or strong enough for the task of jailer; Kim had had little difficulty in overpowering her the instant the woman's vigilance relaxed, surprising herself with her own strength and savagery. She might have killed the woman if it had become necessary. It would have been good to kill one of the Khmer Rouge, even a lowly *chhlop*. Yes, good. It was regrettable that she had not done so.

Instead she had remained in the *paillote* just long enough to tie Ney's wife, to gather a tin of cooked rice and, as an afterthought, the roll of mosquito netting. At first she had thought to flee back into the bamboo to the south. But then she had seen the pirogue drawn up out of the Mongkol Borei behind the house. The boat was a more rapid means of travel, and it also provided her with a protective coloration, a form of camouflage, in that she could assume the role of a fisherwoman. There had been no poles or net in the pirogue, but she had found both in the storage area beneath the *paillote;* and found also a wide-brimmed straw hat to protect her from the sun and to partially conceal her face.

The river had been empty of other craft, and she had considered paddling the pirogue as far downstream as possible, past the villages of Phum Bavel and Khum Kdol; the alarm sounded by Ney Narin would surely increase KC patrol activity in this section. On the other hand, when Ney discovered his pirogue missing he would know she had taken it, and it was possible the Khmer Rouge further along the river would be alerted to the fact that she was traveling by water. It would be wiser, she had decided, if she hid during the daylight hours and either abandoned the boat and proceeded on foot, or proceed with the boat under cover of darkness. There was the problem of fatigue as well: she had traveled all the previous night and had not slept in sixteen hours. If her senses had not already been dulled, her thoughts muddied, she might not have been caught by Ney Narin in the first place.

She had paddled the pirogue through three long bends in the river, a matter of at least two kilometers, keeping in close to the east-bank jungle, when she found the entrance to the channel. It could not be seen more than a few meters distant, for it was choked and half obliterated by liana vines, giant ferns, the great gnarled roots of Banyan trees. She had slipped the pirogue through the tangle, made sure that the channel entrance was still hidden, and moored at the base of a tree. Then she had crawled under the mosquito netting and slept until an hour before dusk.

But the sky last night had been clear, cloudless, swollen and bright with moon, and she had changed her mind about trying to bypass the villages before or after midnight. There were certain to be KC patrols at or near each one; if they saw a lone person in a pirogue, traveling by moonlight, they would certainly become suspicious. And she was reluctant to give up the boat altogether, to revert to the longer and just-as-dangerous trek on foot. By day, even though the risk was considerable, there would be other pirogues, other rivercraft, and if she were cautious and the Lord Buddha heard her prayers, she would be able to pass unnoticed and unchallenged. Beyond Khum Kdol, the progress of the Mongkol Borei became twisting and torturous, flowing through dense and unoccupied jungle, and there was not another village until the river separated into two branches at Ta Krei. Once she reached that point, she would only be a few kilometers from the Thai frontier.

When she finished her *petit déjeuner* of rice and coconut she stowed the rest of her food and the mosquito netting in the stern, untied the mooring line, and pushed the pirogue along the channel to where she could look past the lianas and ferns at a full five hundred meters of the river in both directions. There were no other visible boats, no sign of activity along the opposite bank. She paddled quickly out of the channel, shipped the boat around until the prow pointed downriver. The sun, balanced on the edge of the horizon, gave off a fierce reddish glare; she pulled the brim of her straw hat low over her eyes. Then she readied Ney Narin's fishing equipment, dropped a line into the muddy water, and began a slow drifting progression toward Phum Bavel.

She came in sight of the village within the hour, just as the rising sun burned away the last of the mist. Four other boats dotted the river here, three of them fishermen's pirogues and one a small empty rice barge on its way upriver. Kim watched each of them covertly, but none of their occupants paid any attention to her. In the cleared fields around Phum Bavel, groups of *opakar* worked without enthusiasm. There did not seem to be any Khmer Rouge soldiers among them, nor anywhere else in the vicinity. The village itself appeared to have a good deal of activity as well, figures moving here and there, smoke rising from some of the houses, women herding water buffalo and oxen along the riverbank. Kim saw none of the communal longhouses of the new production cooperatives; all the buildings were traditional Khmer *paillotes,* with a pair of large structures at one end that would be the meetinghouse and the blacksmith's.

Phum Bavel was a perimeter village—one of those which had been in a government-held zone during most of the war and which had fallen to the Khmer Rouge only in the last months. Kim wondered if its original population had been displaced elsewhere and if the people she saw here were forced migrants from other parts of the country. Or if Old People from the KC villages had been mingled in with the New People to help control and govern them. It did not matter, she supposed, except that knowing the answer would give her a better understanding of Khmer Rouge methods. And the more she knew about the ways of the enemy, the better she would be able to fight them in the days to come.

Her drifting passage by the village seemed to go unnoticed. Beyond, where the road from Lovea passed close to the river and another road intersected it from the east, she saw two military trucks with the GKR insignia of the Black Cobra still intact on their sides, even though they had been in Khmer Rouge hands for at least a year. She also saw half a dozen armed KC soldiers, but they were too busy unloading some thirty *opakar* from the trucks, herding them out into the surrounding fields, to pay any attention to a fisherman's pirogue. None of the soldiers even glanced in her direction.

Khum Kdol was some five kilometers from Phum Bavel, around several bends in the river. The jungle growth between the two was thick and lush, with trees overhanging the water and narrow backwaters along which the knobby brown shapes of crocodiles sunned themselves on exposed landbars. The only other sign of life, the only carrying sounds, were chattering gibbons swinging acrobatically from vines among the rafterlike tree branches overhead.

When the jungle thinned out and the first *paillotes* of Khum Kdol appeared she saw that it was a somewhat larger village than Phum Bavel but similar in every other way: black-garbed peasants working in cultivated fields or inside the village proper, women tending livestock, a group of fishermen repairing nets on the small communal dock. If there were soldiers here, she saw no sign of them. And no one sought to challenge her as she drifted by.

Just south of Khum Kdol the river's course became snakelike, rippling through more dense jungle. Lines of fromager trees, their trunks gaunt and bone-white, stretched away like a procession of giant skeletons. Thickets of bamboo and groves of giant ferns were visible where the terrain rose upward in long slopes. It would be like this, Kim remembered from her geographical studies at the university, all the way to Ta Krei and the Thailand border.

She had traveled beyond sight of the last *paillote* when there was a sharp tugging on the trailing line, so sharp that it almost jerked the pole free of its anchorage inside the boat. In reflex Kim grabbed hold of it just in time; she had forgotten about putting out the line as part of her protective camouflage, and it was the first time a fish had struck at the bare hook. She managed to bring this one, fat and shining in the sunlight, into the pirogue. Raw fish would make a good meal, she thought as she removed the hook from its mouth, cut off the head with her stone knife. And add much-needed protein to her diet. Perhaps catching it was a sign, combined with her safe passage by Phum Bavel and Khum Kdol, that the Lord Buddha was watching over her and would guide her safely to freedom. Perhaps escaping from Kampuchea would not be so difficult after all.

But she was wrong.

The fish and the easy morning travel were false signs; the true sign was only minutes away, and it was not that of a fish but of dragons.

She paddled the pirogue into the first of the sharp bends, seeing nothing on either side, nothing ahead, except unrelieved jungle. But when she reached the point where she could look to what lay beyond the curve, the unexpected appeared and made her body go rigid, made her catch her breath. The path of the river narrowed there, into a short reach between two tiny peninsulas; and on the eastern side, less than fifty meters from where she was, were a pair of thatched huts, a pair of jeeps drawn up behind them, a motorized pirogue moored at the short arm of a nearby pier, at least three soldiers visible among them.

Khmer Rouge checkpoint.

There was nothing she could do. One of the soldiers was already looking toward her; if she tried to paddle around, reverse her course, he would know immediately that something was wrong and they would come after her in the motorboat. Her only hope was to let the pirogue drift toward them without any show of hesitation, to continue her masquerade as a fisherwoman. Perhaps they were used to fishers along this section of the river. Perhaps, if she did nothing to arouse their suspicion, they would simply watch her go by without challenge.

Paddling, she looked at the soldiers and did not look at them. I am a fisherwoman, she thought. I have every right to be here; there is no reason why they should accost me. Twenty-five meters to the checkpoint. Twenty. Two of the soldiers were watching her now. Fifteen meters. Paddle slowly—slowly. Put out the line again; adjust the pole. Ten meters . . .

One of the watching soldiers stepped over onto the pier and gestured for her to bring in the pirogue.

Panic clawed at her; she fought it down. Ignore him. Pretend not to have noticed his gesture. Five meters. If only she could get past the pier, past the checkpoint. The next bend was no more than twenty meters away—

The soldier cupped his hands at his mouth and shouted, "You there—fisherman! Bring your boat in here!"

She turned her head toward him, shaded her eyes, feigned an attitude of momentary deafness. The pirogue was almost abreast of the pier.

"You are not permitted to fish this section of river," the soldier called to her. The second one had come onto the pier too; this one carried a rifle at port arms.

"I have business at Ta Krei," she called back. It was the only thing she could think of to say. She was parallel to the pier now, the soldiers' young-old faces glistening in the sunlight, no more than a dozen meters separating her from them.

"Then come here and present your mission order or *laissez-passer*," the first soldier said. "You can't proceed without the proper papers."

She had no choice this time, either; there was only one thing for her to do, and it was not to approach the checkpoint without papers. She kept watching the two on the pier, the third one stirring around behind them, until the pirogue was seven or eight meters beyond. It took them that long to react decisively. And when she saw the second one lift his rifle, heard the first one shout something, she pitched her body forward, half draped over the port gunwale of the pirogue, and began to paddle furiously with her left hand.

Behind her the rifle cracked and water spouted up near the boat's prow. A second bullet droned above her head; a third made a *ploking* sound somewhere astern. There were more shouts, a fourth rifle shot, and then—most ominous of all—the heavy throbbing cough of the motorboat's engine.

Kim raised her head, still paddling, and saw that her pirogue was some distance past the checkpoint, just entering the next bend. When she looked back she saw two of the soldiers inside the motorized craft, the boat just swinging out away from the dock. The third soldier was on the pier, still shooting, still missing.

Roaring, spinning up foam, the motorboat started to arc around toward her.

Kim clambered up on one knee and threw herself across the starboard gunwale, out into the river.

The water was shallow here, warm from the sun and humidity, and she was only a few meters from the tip of the west-bank peninsula. She surfaced, shaking water out of her eyes, saw the motorboat just completing its swing, perhaps forty meters away, and immediately struck out for the bank. Ferns and dwarf palms and creepers made a tangle all along it, but there was a miniature cove almost directly in front of her, and beyond that a cleared space upward through the fromager trees. She swam half a dozen strokes, clawed a hold on one of the lianas trailing into the water, and dragged herself up onto the bank and into the undergrowth. Behind her, from the pier, or perhaps from the motorcraft, there were three more shots in rapid succession.

Stinging pain across the back of her right thigh; then, in the next instant, the whole leg seemed to go numb.

She stumbled, almost fell, knew if she fell she would die and half ran, half dragged herself through the ferns, into the denser marshy growth beyond the waterline. More shots; a voice yelling, fading. The roar of the pirogue's motor, then silence.

Sudden crashing sounds behind her, the sounds of pursuit.

She plunged deeper into the jungle, praying for it to swallow her before the Khmer Rouge found her and swallowed her life.

Natalie

Lying in the room she rented from the Thai family, Natalie replayed in her mind the events of the day with David. And decided that she didn't like them very much at all.

She was in bed, unable to sleep, looking at the cloud-streaked moon through the window; but what she was seeing was their relationship in a new and cheerless light. The fact was that David didn't know what he wanted, whether it had to do with her or Kim or anybody or anything else, and she might as well admit it to herself. He had gotten to this point in life through convenience, connection, and mimicry; he had never had to confront himself because he'd been shielded by easy circumstance. So when you looked at him that way, you began to see that Kim had become a kind of convenience for him: until her fate was determined he was spared of having to commit himself to another woman or to his own future. The State Department and the CIA had played the same role in his life for a time, giving him an excuse not to take a position on what had been done to the Cambodians. His resignation had been an act of revulsion, it was admirable, but it only indicated what he could *not* do; it didn't show what he thought he could. And it didn't solve the problem of Kim, or the problem of Natalie either; it only brought him up against the even larger and more confusing question of what he was going to do with the rest of his life.

"I don't know," she remembered him saying, shaking his head, his eyes sad and troubled, "I just don't know," and his irresolution had been moving in a way, there was no question about that. But had it really been sadness in his eyes or had it been fear? With whom—this was the final, basic question—had she fallen in love? A man, fallible and flawed, or merely an idealization?

An idealization who had worked for the CIA.

Why had he confessed his former connection to her, and why of all places while they were watching the kite-fighters? It was as if the process of confession was indivisible to him: having told her part of the truth, he now needed to tell her all, like an adulterous husband forcing his wife to the knowledge of other adulteries long undiscovered. There was an explanation for that; she didn't have to look too deeply. The blundering husband spewing out admissions might want to be thrown out of his marital relationship. David, piling the CIA atop his uncertainty about his future, about Kim, might have been looking to be thrown out of this relationship too, handing her the weapon—and the opportunity—for ending their affair.

Bitterness began to assail her as she lay in the darkness. She drew up her knees, stared out at the restless sky. The quiet sounds of night rustled around her; her Thai hosts made noises in their bed, audible through the thin walls, and night birds wickered in the trees. She found herself moving through corridors of recollection: other men, other relationships, all of which had either ended badly or simply ended because none of the men were what she had thought them to be. Maybe that had been her fault, not the fault of the men at all. Maybe she was looking for something which didn't exist in them, because it would enable her to be disappointed and enable her to get out. Maybe she didn't really want to be in love with anyone.

But she thought she did. She was sure she felt that way about David.

She closed her eyes and ran him across the screen of memory: his face, his voice, his body heavy against her in the darkness, then arching and light, the way he held her, the way it had been that first time on New Year's Eve, the way he had looked at her on the Pramane Ground today. It wasn't that he was a frivolous or a shallow man; she had heard him cry out in passion and in anguish, felt his pain, hurled her own cries against him. She couldn't doubt the legitimacy of his feelings of her own feeling for him. But did that alter the basic situation? Did it make him any less weak and irresolute?

I've got to be fair, she thought then. Maybe I'm not giving him the benefit of any doubt; maybe my own involvement, my own jealousy, is causing me to lose perspective. But no, she didn't believe that. She was seeing this clearly now, for the first time; she was seeing it the way it really was. And the way it really was was that David could leave Bangkok at any time, he was free of the State Department and the CIA, he could return to the States and leave her in the same equivocal position she was now . . . and if he did that, the way was open for him never to see her again. Without ever taking a position he would have taken one; he could slide right out of her life forever.

Her thoughts danced away from that, settled briefly on Kim— the woman she had met a lifetime ago in Phnom Penh, who might at this moment be suffering in Cambodia or lying in a mass grave somewhere, no longer a woman, just bones. The half-formed image was hideous; it filled her with revulsion. She wondered if it was similar to images that David saw, that he may even have seen while he was making love to her . . .

The thought flicked out like a light bulb, and she heard her father's voice saying, "You have to protect yourself, Natalie, you've got to stop feeling so much," and in that moment she came close to an understanding of her life. She couldn't use the feelings of others as a mask for the confrontation of self: she couldn't flee her own desires anymore, she couldn't be as irresolute as David. If she wanted him, then she was going to have to force the issue. No more equivocation on his part, no more on hers either.

So all right, she thought. All right, David. You're going to have to make up your mind one way or the other.

You're going to have to decide if you want me.

Chey Han

The hen, Mey Yat or Than Kim or someone else entirely, continued to elude him. She had eluded him at the cooperative near Lovea, she had eluded him at the *paillote* of the *chhlop* Ney Narin, and she had eluded him during the thirty-six hours he and his reluctant sergeant and the foolish bonze had been canvassing the countryside south along the Mongkol Borei River. He knew she was somewhere in the area, most likely on or near the river because Ney Narin's pirogue had been missing; that was how she had escaped the immediate vicinity yesterday morning. But he still could not find her or anyone who had seen her. She continued to elude him as if she were neither a woman nor a hen but a wraith, one of the spectral demons of ancient Kampuchea.

He had become obsessed with finding her, finding out who she really was. The bonze, cajoling and demanding and begging by turns, no longer laughing and no longer juggling his bloody head, wanted them to return to Sisophon before Angka classified him as a deserter; yet it was the headless one who had planted and nurtured the seed of this obsession. The headless one had to take the responsibility for the situation now as fully as Chey himself.

"I am going to find the woman," he told the bonze, "*then* I will return to Sisophon."

"You may never find her. And if you do it will be too late. You will lose everything."

"I have nothing to lose, bonze."

"Except your life."

"I have no life any longer."

"You're a fool, Chey Han," the bonze said remonstratively and shook his bloody head. "If you had listened to me, you wouldn't be in this position."

"I *did* listen to you. This is all your fault."

"Oh Chey Han. Oh Chey Han."

It was midafternoon now and they were on the dusty road that followed the river just south of Khum Kdol. Chey had spent all of the morning interrogating Party civilians, soldiers, and chickens in Phum Bavel and Khum Kdol. No one knew anything. But the *srok* at Khum Kdol had told him that, earlier today, there had been some sort of disturbance at the river checkpoint south of the village; gunfire had been heard in that vicinity, which usually meant, the chief said, an encounter with small bands of jungle-based guerrillas or attempted escapees. Perhaps this was the information Chey had been seeking. Perhaps the disturbance concerned the woman, the wraith, the demon, the half-sister. The chicken.

"And perhaps not," the bonze said. "Listen to me, Chey Han, before it's too late. You must give up this pointless quest; you must return to Sisophon . . ."

Chey pushed the bonze away, crowded him far back into a corridor and closed him up behind the door of perception.

When they reached the small river checkpoint Chey identified himself to the lieutenant in charge, an elder KC soldier of thirty-five or so whose face rippled with a series of small tics, as if he had seen something long ago which he still could not quite forget. "I have been told," Chey said to him, "that a disturbance took place here this morning."

The lieutenant nodded. "Yes, but it is of little import. A routine encounter with a fleeing *opaka.*"

"Male or female?"

"Female," the lieutenant said.

"On foot or traveling on the river?"

"Traveling by pirogue, in the guise of a fisherwoman."

Chey's blood quickened. "Tell me what happened."

"There is little to tell, Mit Chey. Fishers are not allowed in this sector; when she approached the checkpoint she was hailed and warned. She ignored the warning, and also ignored orders to bring in her pirogue and to present either a mission order or a *laissez-passer*. Our motorized pirogue was sent out immediately to intercept her. She was also fired upon."

"With what result? Was she killed?"

"No, *mit*."

"Captured, then?"

"Unfortunately not."

"Then she eluded your soldiers, escaped again."

"Possibly."

"Possibly? Did she or didn't she—which is it?"

"She jumped from her pirogue," the lieutenant said, "and swam to the far bank. Several more shots were fired at her. We are certain she was wounded before she vanished into the jungle."

"There was a search for her afterward?"

"Oh, yes. Scattered drops of blood were found; they could not be followed but they confirm that she was wounded. She may be dead by now."

"She may also not be dead by now," Chey said, and the prospect gave him an odd feeling of relief. To have come here and found the hen already dead would have ended the matter and allowed him to return to Sisophon, and yet Sisophon now would answer nothing. *Nothing.* He must find her himself, look upon her face and determine if she was Mey Yat or Than Kim or a spectral *absara* and then he would butcher her himself. The responsibility was his. "The jungle has many hiding places," he said, "for the wounded as well as the unwounded."

"That is true, of course." The lieutenant paused. "Is it a woman you seek, Mit Chey? A woman such as the one this morning?"

"Perhaps."

The lieutenant began to look uneasy; the tics in his face grew more pronounced. "Is she a traitor, a CIA spy? Someone of importance to Angka?"

"That is of no concern to you."

"You must understand, Mit Chey," the lieutenant said, nervously now, "I and my soldiers did everything possible to apprehend her. It is through no fault of ours that she managed to reach the jungle. It was only a matter of misfortune—"

"At what place did she disappear?" Chey asked him.

"*Mit?*"

"Where did she emerge from the river? Where did she vanish into the jungle? Point out the location to me."

The lieutenant pointed across the sun-dappled river, downstream at an angle to the end of the peninsula there, where fromager trees marched away into thick stands of bamboo. From this vantage point it looked impenetrable, but back away from the river it would not be; there would be the usual jungle network of half-visible paths and trails mapped by animals, there would be enough food to sustain human life, and it would be possible to walk all the way to the Thai border.

All the way to freedom? Chey thought.

The bonze opened the door behind which he had been shuttered, rushed through into the center of Chey's mind. He held up his severed head accusingly, and the expression in his blood-filmed eyes was one of terror. "No, Chey Han," he said. "Oh no, oh no."

The lieutenant said something to him; Chey did not listen to the words. He did not listen to the bonze either. He only stood on the checkpoint pier and stared across the Mongkol Borei at the green and brown jungle wall, thinking that she had eluded him again but that she could not elude him forever, the jungle could not always hide the chicken or the chicken's identity from the butcher.

No, Chey Han?

Yes, Chey Han, he thought, and smiled at the lieutenant, smiled at the horrified bonze.

Oh, yes.

Kim

From where she lay cradled in a hollow between two of the banyan tree's upper limbs, Kim could look down on the faint jungle path that had brought her here hours earlier. The path had remained empty ever since her struggling climb into the tree; she had not seen any sign of the Khmer Rouge soldiers from the checkpoint. For a while she had heard them in the distance, the directionless sound of their voices, but then they had given up the search for her and gone away.

It was not fear that they would come back which kept her hidden in the banyan; it was weakness and the sharp throbbing pain in her wounded leg. Not long after dragging herself clear of the river, she had had the presence of mind to staunch the blood flow by using part of her sodden blouse as a tourniquet. That had taken time and risk, but it had kept the soldiers from following a trail of blood that would lead straight to her. The wound—a deep trench through the back of her left thigh, just below the buttock—continued to bleed every time she removed the pressure of the tourniquet, though less heavily each time; the whole of her leg was caked and stiff with dried and still-sticky fluid. She was afraid that if she left the tree now, it would not close up at all and then become infected. It was better to stay where she was, to rest, for the remainder of the day and throughout the night. Tomorrow she could begin her trek west to the frontier. Tomorrow was soon enough.

She lay listening to the chattering of monkeys, the whistling call of birds, the faint rustling noises of animals burrowing or stalking through the undergrowth. Travel would not be easy through jungle such as this: limited visibility, suffocating heat, insects, snakes, tigers, the ground rocky in some places and marshy in others, barriers of sawgrass, fallen trees, root tangles, thickets of thorny leaves, nettles, and creepers. And she no longer had any food, nor even the stone knife and the mosquito netting. In spite of all this, however, the situation was not quite as overwhelming as it seemed. For one thing, the jungle was seldom so dense that a person could not walk through it and maintain a sense of direction; most of the trees stood straight, with distance between them, and the paths were numerous. For another thing, the Thai border could not be more than thirty kilometers due west or southwest along the path of the river. Farther along, the terrain would become mountainous, climbing to an elevation of two thousand feet at the escarpment along the perimeter, but the ascent would be gradual and the descent rapid. For someone who longed to survive as intensely as she, it was neither a great distance nor a great hardship.

Time passed. Once she heard a thrashing nearby that might have been a large animal and might also have been a man; she lay alert for several minutes, listening, watching, but nothing appeared within the range of her vision. Some time later, the faint but unmistakable odor of cat came to her on the moist air. Tiger? She did not like tigers; she had been afraid of them ever since her childhood in Rovieng, where stories of man-eaters had been rampant and there was much superstition. She wondered what she would do if she encountered one. Beat on the ground with a stick, as the peasant folklore instructed, wait for the tiger to roll himself into a ball, and then whistle shrilly to make him run away?

But she must not think of tigers. Or of dragons, for that matter. There would come a day when she was no longer afraid of either one, when she would fight like a tiger herself and all the dragons would be slain. Meanwhile she must think only of survival and escape. Survive to escape; escape to survive.

Evening came, and along with it swarms of mosquitoes that fed hungrily on her exposed flesh. There was nothing for her to do except to endure it. And endure the burning thirst, the hunger, the pains in her thigh and her cramped body. She slept, dreamed of dragons and tigers and Serey dying in her arms on the train, and woke when something made a slithering noise close to the banyan tree below. The jungle was alive with sounds in the darkness; she listened to them and found them soothing. And slept again, woke again, slept and dreamed and woke again in constant cycle until the first light of dawn tiger-striped the sky above the branches overhead.

The bullet groove in her leg had stopped bleeding during the night. Its edges felt puckered and sore to her exploring fingers, but touching it was not as painful as it had been yesterday. She tore off another piece of her blouse, tied it around the wound. Then, carefully, she pushed herself out of the hollow between the two limbs, keeping her wounded leg stiff and straight and scraping along on her right knee, and managed to climb down out of the tree.

There was a sharp cut of pain when she put weight on her left leg. But part of the reason for that, she judged, was the stiffness of her body, its cramped positioning over the past eighteen hours. She hobbled back and forth, flexing arms and both legs, reviving the circulation of her blood. The pain subsided after a time, as did most of her hobble: she found that she could move with only a slight favoring of her left leg.

The inside of her mouth was parched, so dry it made swallowing difficult. But there was no point in searching for water; this was the dry season and there would be no water anywhere except for what remained in stagnant pools. Nor could she risk trying to make her way back to the river, at least not until she was a full kilometer or more southwest of the Khmer Rouge checkpoint. Hunger was something she could appease more quickly, however. She foraged out away from the banyan tree, following a path which she reckoned wound away to the southwest, though she could not be sure until well past sunrise. Bark, leaves, and a single turtle's egg in an unattended nest were all she found to eat, but there was enough to ease the gnawing in her stomach.

The path connected with another, and another, and when the sun rose she realized that she had not been heading southwest at all but due west, away from the river. She found another path, rutted by the hooves and paws of countless animals, that took her in the right direction. And she walked. Through the heat, through the dank, alcohol-smelling humus that coated the jungle floor, across sharp-pointed and half-hidden rocks that cut at her sandals and bruised the soles of her feet. Not thinking, as she had not thought during all the hours in the fields and rice paddies and communes of the Khmer Rouge. Suppressing all emotion, all fear: making herself nothing more or less than a thing that moved through the jungle, a thing that if seen through the eye of the Lord Buddha might be nothing other than an insect crawling slowly but purposefully over the face of the unredeemed country.

The will of the caterpillar, the stone determination of the ant.

Foxworth

The White Orchid Restaurant, in the Amarin Hotel on Ploenchit Road, was two thirds full when Natalie and Foxworth entered a few minutes past eight o'clock. It was also dark and somber-looking, despite its elegant Chinese decor, and it made him think instantly of Le Royal Restaurant in Phnom Penh. Which made him think in turn of Peter Deighan, who seemed to have dropped out of sight since the night he'd come around asking for the name of someone in the Khmer resistance. Foxworth wondered what had happened to the man; whether he'd gotten involved with the resistance fighters, gotten what he was after or himself into some sort of trouble. He had ended up kind of liking Deighan, which was just one more indicator of how much he himself had changed in the past year. At the bottom line, though, what happened to Peter Deighan or anyone else was more or less irrelevant; it was what had happened and was going to happen to *him* that was the focus of his attention these days.

An obsequious maître d' ushered them to a corner table, somewhat more secluded than the others. They sat quietly, with a slight unease between them. The unease had been there from the moment he'd picked her up, and he understood, or thought he understood, why she seemed withdrawn; his failure to tell her about his resignation, compounded by his admission of having worked for the CIA, and the ghostly presence of Kim, had worked to put them, however subtly, at odds. He didn't want it to be this way, but he didn't quite know how to make it any better between them.

Well, that wasn't true—he *did* know how to make it better between them. It was obvious what Natalie wanted. The problem was that he wasn't sure yet, specifically, what *he* wanted. Oh, he had a pretty good idea what his next big decision was going to be. In fact, he had a very good idea. But it had only been two weeks since the submission of his resignation, less than ten days since he had cleaned out his desk at the embassy, given up his villa, and moved into the Victory Hotel; he simply was not ready to make a second life-changing resolution so soon. It had taken him weeks, months, to screw up the courage to make and follow through on the first. It might not take so long for the second, it damned well *wouldn't* if he could just go somewhere and get his head together, but he still needed a lot more time than he'd had so far.

At least he had been able to deal with his father, he thought. He might be in a state of schism, but the irresolution wasn't total; what was basic he could handle. Two days ago he'd rented a car—no more embassy-maintained sedans for ex-employees, with or without CIA connections—and driven up through the Chao Phraya lowlands to do some more solitary thinking; and one of the things he had thought about, the only significant decision he'd made, was how to get Benjamin Foxworth off his back. Overseas telephone calls from Grosse Pointe, cables, copies of cables to high-placed officials in Washington . . . it had all piled up and become unbearable. So what he'd done, he had written his father a carefully worded, businesslike letter in which he offered no explanation for his decision to resign but instead asked the old man to please stay out of his life, personal and professional, and assume no responsibility for him ever again. At the age of thirty-two, he'd said, this seemed to be a reasonable position for a man to take. Benjamin Foxworth wouldn't understand the letter, of course. He would probably interpret it as provocative and unfriendly, the act of an ungrateful and maybe traumatized son, and would do some sulking and complaining to his friends at the country club. But for all of that, the old man's stiff-necked pride would force him to put an end to his interference. From now on Benjamin Foxworth, vice-president of American Motors, bastion of conservatism, hater of commies and (although he would never admit it) most religious and ethnic minorities, would leave him the hell alone.

And so would everybody else, Foxworth thought sardonically, unless he took control of his life and got on with the business of living. You could only exist on emotion, on raw nerve ends, for so long. There came a time when everything had to settle back into an even, consistent pattern, a sort of remission, so that you could go on functioning in human society. Otherwise you would end up either dead of a cardiac arrest, as Boyd had warned him, or tucked away somewhere in a place with benches and trees and mattresses on the walls of your room.

A waiter appeared at the table, took their orders for drinks, offered menus, and glided away again. Foxworth looked at Natalie; she met his eyes for a moment, then looked down at the table, around at the other diners. It struck him in that moment, whether illusorily or not, that tonight, in these surroundings, she looked almost as she had that first night he'd seen her, in Le Royal in Phnom Penh. Wearing similar clothing, her hair combed the same way; the same dim lighting, the same restaurant noises, the same brown-faced and white-faced diners. He felt the pain and weariness come over him again and closed his eyes momentarily. But when he opened them he saw her solid and substantial, someone he knew well, someone he was with as he had been with Kim, someone he cared for in his own irresolute way, and he felt a little better. If nothing else, Natalie had offered him an alternate reality.

He said, "Aren't you going to say anything?"

Her gaze flicked up again, held on his. "I could ask you the same thing."

"I tried to make conversation when I first picked you up. You didn't seem to be interested."

"I don't want small talk, David."

"Then what do you want?"

"That's not the issue. The issue is what *you* want."

Looking at her, he saw that beneath her masking calm was an intensity, a profound seriousness. And he realized, with one of those belated insights that should have come long ago, that her life was much too important to her, every part of it, to allow any inconsequentiality. Particularly in her emotional relationships. If he hadn't been prepared to understand that, he should never have gotten involved. In her own way, maybe she had been trying to tell him that all along.

"Some peace," he said at length, "that's what I want."

"It's what we all want. But it's not enough, David, not for you and not for me. Besides, I'm not asking you for generalities; I'm asking you for specifics."

"Us," he said.

"Exactly. Us. And what you're going to do now that you've left the State Department. Are you going back to the States? Are you going to stay here? What are your career plans? Where do you and I stand? Those are the questions; you supply the answers."

"I can't supply them. Not just yet."

"You're going to have to, David."

"Can't you just—"

"Well, well," a new voice said, "look who's here. I thought you'd have quit Bangkok by now, Dave, just like you quit State."

Foxworth looked up, startled, at the man who had approached silently and who now stood alongside the table. Tom Boyd. He felt another shimmer of *déjà vu:* at first the voice had sounded like Peter Deighan's, that night in Le Royal—the same sort of wryness, edged and made husky with alcohol; the same sort of sudden interruption. Then the feeling gave way to a flare of resentment because—truth was truth, after all—he had never liked Boyd much, in all the time he'd known him, and he liked him even less right now for intruding, for his vaguely belligerent smile, for the snotty bureaucratic tone of his voice.

"What do you want, Tom?" he said.

"What do I want?" Boyd's eyes had a slight glassy sheen; he was just a little drunk, Foxworth thought, the way he'd gotten sometimes in Phnom Penh, just enough to take the edge off his rigid control. He made a sweeping gesture toward another part of the restaurant. "What do you think I want here? A little dinner, a little relaxation with my woman after a hard day's grind. But then you wouldn't know about that anymore, would you? You're out of the grind now. All that's behind you, right?"

"Would you mind leaving us alone? We're having a private discussion here—"

"Oh sure, right, a private discussion. I can see that. I could see that all the way across the room. But we've been friends a long time. Buddies. You don't mind if an old friend joins you for a drink, do you?" Boyd peered at Natalie with the same veiled hostility, as if she were an old adversary. "How about you, Natalie? Mind if I join you?"

"Yes," she said, "I do." With frost in her voice.

He gave her a mock bow and looked at Foxworth again. "I've got some news you ought to hear," he said. "Just came in this afternoon from Aranyaprathet. You'll love it, Dave."

"What news?"

"Can I join you or not?"

"Look, Tom—"

"Never mind. I'll tell you standing up. That leftist bastard Peter Deighan is dead. Got himself hooked up with a band of resistance fighters and went along on one of their raids across the border into Cambodia. A patrol of KC gooks ambushed them, blew him away along with eight Khmers." Boyd made a noise that might have been a snort and might have been an ironic laugh. Either way, it was loud enough to make some of the people at the nearby tables turn to look at him. "Now isn't that something?"

Natalie said, "My God," and seemed to shrink back from Boyd, from the callousness in his voice and the half-formed smirk on his mouth. There was a lurching in Foxworth's stomach; he could feel himself going cold all over, as if the temperature in the White Orchid had suddenly turned frigid.

"Isn't that something?" Boyd said again. "There were only two survivors and they just made it back into Thailand last night. Chuon Van got it too in the raid. You remember him, Dave—one of the camp leaders at Aranyaprathet."

Foxworth stared at him numbly. I put Deighan in touch with Chuon, he thought. But I didn't know he intended to go back across the border. Jesus, I didn't know that.

You may be a lot of things, Foxie, and I may be a lot of things, but the two of us are human beings. What separates us is nothing compared to what separates us from a whole legion of others—the liars, the thieves, the protected, the deluded, the power-mad who run wars from inside their electric bunkers and never give a single thought to the millions they condemn to die.

I know it, and you know it too. All I'm asking you is a small favor, not from a diplomat to a journalist—from one human being to another.

"That's awful," Natalie was saying to Boyd. "My God, that's terrible and you seem almost happy about it."

"Maybe I am," Boyd said. "And why not? It's the first bit of cheering official news I've had since we pulled out of Phnom Penh. That son of a bitch Deighan dedicated his life to discrediting the American mission; he was writing another lousy tract full of lies, trying to make fools of all of us by going back in there and eyeballing the commies so he could whitewash them in print. Well, they showed him. They showed him, all right. They blew his commie-loving head off and that's no less than he deserved."

Natalie looked angry, nervous, uncomfortable; she appealed to Foxworth across the table. But he barely noticed. There was a rage in him now so clean and deep that it was like a purgatory fire, consuming years of frustration, blindness, and half-truths. Boyd was in the foreground of that rage, the immediate focus of it, but there were other people, larger issues, in the background. Peter Deighan, alive, had unwittingly helped him make his first major decision; now Peter Deighan, dead, might just be helping him make his second.

"You're a cruel bastard, aren't you, Tom?" he said. His voice was calm, controlled, but he could feel the violence trembling beneath it. "Cruel and unfeeling and full of your own misguided self-importance."

Boyd squinted at him; his face was flushed. "Is that so? Well, I always suspected that you didn't have the guts for our kind of work and I knew it for sure when you handed in your resignation. But now I know just what kind of freak you really are. You're a—"

"Don't say it, Tom."

"The hell I won't say it. You're a weakling and a sell-out and a goddamn nascent bleeding-heart liberal; you're the same kind of freak Deighan was and I wouldn't shed one tear if you got it the way he did."

The violence in him came boiling up to the surface. Natalie

saw it happening and said, "David!" warningly, but by then it was too late. He stood with such suddenness that his chair toppled over backward and he almost ran into the waiter who was returning with their drinks. The waiter danced out of the way, managed to avoid dropping the tray, but some of the liquid in the glasses sloshed over. All of the other diners had stopped eating and were sitting motionless, waiting, like statues in a museum exhibit.

The odd feeling of *déjà vu* came to Foxworth again. This was the way it had been in Le Royal: up out of the chair, the waiter coming, facing off with an adversary who had stirred up his rage. One of those crazy but significant coincidences that happened now and then. But this time it was Boyd, not Deighan; and this time it was a different David Foxworth too. The other one, like Kim, had never made it out of Cambodia.

The only other difference was, he hadn't hit Deighan that night in Phnom Penh. The rockets had stopped him then, or maybe he had stopped himself, but in any case he hadn't hit him. And he *was* going to hit Boyd.

And he did, standing flat-footed with less than a foot separating them, Boyd with his jaw thrust out pugnaciously, Natalie saying, "David, please!" and the other patrons and the Chinese waiters staring: he threw up his right hand and watched his balled fist crack off that outthrust jaw, saw the head snap back and the neat waves of hair puff outward with the impact; felt the good stinging pain in his knuckles and the shock of the blow in the center of his armpit; saw Boyd stagger, go down on one knee, lift a hand to his chin and then stare up in amazement—all of that happening in a kind of slow motion, as if time had slowed down deliberately to let him savor the moment. But then there seemed to be a clicking in his mind and all at once he was aware of noise, movement, people getting up from tables, Thai and Chinese and English and French voices. And Boyd getting to his feet, looking bewildered and furious and embarrassed at the same time, pointing a finger that trembled and saying something inarticulate that might have been a threat. Come on, Foxworth thought, come on, Tom, I'll do it again, in here or outside or anyplace else you want. But there was no fight left in Boyd. He just stood there, pointing, until his attractive Thai mistress appeared beside him and tugged at his arm, pulled him around with hands and words and led him away through the restaurant, Boyd looking back over his shoulder the whole way, glaring.

All the fight went out of Foxworth, too. He righted his chair and slumped down in it, and only then did he realize that Natalie was gone. He looked around for her but she just wasn't there anymore. He shut his eyes. And saw Boyd's face, Boyd's head snapping back from the blow . . . but there was no longer any pleasure in it, not even any satisfaction. Because it had been an empty gesture.

Boyd was like U.S. foreign policy, like the State Department —no, he *was* the State Department: immutable, invulnerable, resilient, eternal. He had been in Vietnam and then in Cambodia and now he was in Thailand and later on he would get himself a secure slot in Japan or perhaps return Stateside. He had had a Vietnamese mistress, a Cambodian mistress, now a Thai mistress, and in Japan he would have a Japanese mistress or in Washington some nice little American summer intern to soothe his needs. He had been knocked on his ass, but he had gotten up again; he had gone away but he would come back. He and all the other Tom Boyds would go on and on in a thousand dusty offices, doing nothing, learning nothing, stoking their dim confusion with false assurance, their empty minds with assumed knowledge, flows of memos, reports, wrap-ups, native mistresses, drinks over the bars of a thousand hotels, hiding their feelings of superiority behind a façade of altruism, hating communism and hating anybody who disagreed with them and living forever because what they represented could never die. Like the British colonels in India, the Tom Boyds would survive the Empire itself. They were in for the duration.

So what good had it done to hit him? A child's act, a child's release. It was like hitting the Washington Monument or a cornerstone of the State Department building. All it had accomplished was to give him a bruised hand and a lot of reproachful looks. Not to mention making Natalie walk out on him.

No, the fight had been pointless. But just before the White

Orchid's manager came up and asked him politely but firmly to remove himself from the premises, he thought that the incident had produced at least one positive result. Or maybe it had just been the news of Peter Deighan's death.

He was now one step closer to making up his mind what he wanted to be when he grew up.

Ly Sokhon

Kneeling.

Waiting for the sword—

Again I imagine he has come to me as he did so long ago in Paris. In the darkness he lies beside me: hands touching my body, preparing me, giving me passion of the flesh as he has given me passion for the revolution of the future. I lift my hands to his face, hold him, hold his dreams, and there is no betrayal, there is no blood, there is only Saloth Sar and the Paris night.

Slowly I draw him inside me, feeling his need rise as the need of Kampuchea has arisen. His face, smooth in the moonlight, contracts to the torment of passion as he begins to move upon me, and I feel his power, my power, our desire, there is no betrayal, no corruption. His breath against me is the wind of revolution and I feel the wild singing within me.

But then there is a sound at the door, noise in the corridors, the heavy beat of footsteps—and I smell the festering city. People come through the door, moving toward the bed of our passion. I see Sihanouk and Im Chung and Chey Han and Cheng Seng and all those with whom I have moved in the jungles. They are city-dwellers now, one and all, and their faces are corrupt, their eyes bright, their mouths vengeful. I hear them as they turn toward me, saying the words of accusation, and I clutch Saloth Sar but it is too late, he is also corrupt, in terror he slides from me. Our connection is broken. He rolls away, his eyes going dead with maggots and I try to hold him but he is gone, he is hidden.

Then the laughter begins.

Then the laughter is overcome by screaming.

For there are others in the room now, others without heads wearing the robes of bonzes and children and men without flesh, all of the dead come back to haunt me crying the chant of death, and as they approach I curl in the bed, clutch myself, try to protect myself against them. But Sihanouk seizes an arm, Im Chung another arm, Chey Han a leg, Cheng Seng an ankle, and they drag me from the bed and through the room and out the door to the stairs, the dead and fleshless parting for me, screaming, and I am carried through the corridors and into the diseased city and taken to a place where at last their grip eases, but I cannot move; I cannot move—

Kneeling.

Waiting for the sword.

"Execute her," Pol Pot says. He has appeared now in the clothing of command, festooned with the symbols of corruption. "Let the beheading of the traitor be done."

And as my sword poised above all the others, so the sword of Angkar rises above me, poises to come down upon my neck with the speed of wind, the speed of blood, the speed of death

And the sword, oh Saloth Sar, and the sword

Comes slashing down

Cambodia File: Summary of Interview with Cambodian Refugee (Name Withheld), Conducted by U.S. Embassy Officer at Trat Refugee Camp, Thailand, April 1976 (Secret)

Subject is former warrant officer of the GKR government. When the Khmer Rouge seized control in April 1975 he was stationed in the Sisophon area, Battambang Province. He assumed the identity of a farmer and was sent with his family, which consisted of his wife and five children, to a newly constructed communal village called Anlong Kruos, east of Ta Krei. Work there was difficult and there was little food; the only days off to be given were the tenth, twentieth, and thirtieth of each month. At the end of 1975 all children over eight years old were separated from their families and taken away to be raised by the government. Subject's two sons, ages eleven and fifteen, were taken away. He occasionally heard that they were in this or that village, but he was never permitted to look for them. Subject became ill after about nine months and the Khmer Rouge began to suspect that he was not a farmer. Along with some twenty others, including his wife and his remaining children, he decided to escape to Thailand. Mass escape attempts were not uncommon, he says. He has heard of at least two cases where entire villages of seventy or more people located near the Laotian and Vietnamese borders attempted to escape in a body. A few of the people from each managed to cross the frontier, but most were killed outright by Khmer Rouge patrols, captured and probably executed, or died of starvation, disease, or other hardships en route. Subject's own wife was killed in a fall in the rugged, mountainous jungle west of the Mongkol Borei River, and his remaining daughter was shot by a sniper when she climbed a tree to pick fruit less than one kilometer from the Thai border. Only five of the original twenty survived the trek.

Kim

She had been in the jungle for seven days, or perhaps it was eight or nine, when she encountered the band of fleeing villagers.

Her time sense had become distorted. At first she had sought to keep track of the days by placing each period of light and dark in separate columns inside her memory; but after a while, as day blended into night, and night into day, and waking and sleeping commingled, she lost count. There was a sameness to the jungle that numbed the mind, a sameness to her actions that ritualized them and made them half forgotten even as she was living through them. By day she walked the network of animal trails, charting her course from the location of the sun, stopping now and then to eat leaves or tree bark or to dig up locusts. Twice the trails had led her to the river—and once to a narrow backwater that she had veered away from because it was rimmed with crocodiles—and she had drunk enough of the silt water on each occasion to keep the threat of dehydration at bay. When the curtain of night began to fall she either climbed a tree, if a scalable one was nearby, or fashioned a sleeping hollow by spreading brush over the upper swells of fromager roots. She did not sleep more than an hour or so at a time. Sounds would wake her, dreams would wake her, the false scent of danger would bring her instantly alert and trembling.

Not once during those first seven or eight or nine days did she see another human being. Nor any of the dragons. She had had a glimpse of a huge yellow-eyed tiger, and climbed a tree in terror, but it had not had any interest in her. She had seen an elephant across the river, wiggling its ears and trumpeting at the sky. A cobra had slithered out of a clump of grass, stopped long enough to swell its hood and flick the air in her direction, but then it, too, had vanished. The sounds of other creatures were all around her, but except for the gibbons swinging overhead, giant butterflies shining in random shafts of sunlight, they seldom revealed themselves. From time to time she could feel eyes on her, watching her. Particularly at night. Once she had come awake in her sleeping hollow to find a pair of luminous green eyes like those of a demon staring at her from a few feet away. They had disappeared at the noise she made, and she had not discovered what sort of beast they belonged to.

By that seventh or eighth or ninth day, her clothing was in tatters. A piece of her blouse had been ripped away by thorns, exposing her left breast; that night she had mended the cloth with a length of creeper vine, for no other reason than that a leech had dropped off one of the trees and fastened itself painfully near her nipple. Her face and arms and legs were covered with insect bites, leech marks, scratches, bruises. Her sandals had been flayed into strips by the rocky ground and the soles of her feet were raw. The bullet crease in the back of her thigh ached dully, constantly, but did not impair her ability to walk. She couldn't see it very well, even by twisting her body, but she could feel it with her fingers: it did not feel infected. She had cleansed it twice at the river, wrapped it with water-scrubbed pieces of her pajama bottoms. And each night she examined her leg for evidence of gangrene or blood-poisoning—that, too, a ritual, because if she had found such evidence there was nothing she could have done about it.

Early on that seventh or eighth or ninth day the terrain began to jumble upward in a gradual ascent. She judged that she must be near Ta Krei, where the Mongkol Borei hooked to the west, branched, and flowed into Thailand along its upper arm. If this was so, no more than fifteen kilometers separated her from freedom. The river would be straight ahead, and if she continued on the same course she was following now, she would encounter it sometime tomorrow. Which meant that she must be even more careful. The closer she came to Ta Krei, the more danger of being seen by KC patrols. Nor did she wish to stumble out of the jungle anywhere near the village itself.

Perhaps the wisest thing for her to do, she thought after a time, would be to change direction so as to parallel that of the river. And this she did by midday, trusting her instincts.

Late in the afternoon, when the sun vanished beyond the treetops and the clouds burned with gold and orange fire, she passed through a bamboo grove into a short reach of elephant grass that was bordered on one side by a deep ravine and on the other by patchy jungle strewn with rocks. The section of jungle seemed a good place to spend the night. She went into it, found nothing edible except leaves and bark. Then she spread brush over the lower branches of a small tree, whose foliage was like tufted wool, and lay down inside the hollow to eat her meager supper.

It was still light when she finished. She closed her eyes. Exhaustion took her to the edge of sleep, but she could not seem to fall away into its emptiness. The humidity was stifling and her sinus passages were clogged, turning each breath into an openmouthed gasp. It had been two days since her last drink at the river; her throat felt fiery, the inside of her mouth made even drier by the acidic leaves she had eaten. Her mind was empty of thoughts, and yet thoughts rippled and flowed like turbulent water just under the surface. She tugged loose a prayer to the Lord Buddha, filled the cavity with it, soothed herself with it.

She was still praying when she heard the movement and the voices in the elephant grass beyond. She lay rigid, her hands clenched, and peered out through the screen of brush. Twilight created dense blue shadows in the bamboo thicket, in the jungle surrounding the grassy reach, but she could see the shapes of half a dozen people moving along a different path than the one she had been on, coming from the southeast. At first she thought they were Khmer Rouge soldiers. But as they drew nearer she realized that two were women and none was armed and all wore clothing as tattered as hers; that she was looking at a band of other fleeing refugees.

Her fear gave way to relief, then to a sudden and overwhelming need for companionship, for a sharing of her misery. The ragged group, bunched together in single file, were forty or fifty meters away when she scrambled down out of the hollow and showed herself to them. They stopped as one, poised for flight until they recognized who she must be. Then they stood waiting for her, and welcomed her into their midst.

They were all from a production cooperative near Khum Sneng, southwest of Battambang City, she learned as she helped them make camp for the night. The leader, a man in his forties named Chhun Kaon, who had lost most of his teeth and who spoke in whispers because he had once been kicked in the throat by a KC soldier, told her this. He also told her that he and three of the others had been porridge cooks at the commune; their job had been to bring water, fetch and chop firewood, grow and tend vegetables, store rice and other foodstuffs, and prepare daily rations of porridge for seventy-five people each. Two porridge cooks before them, Chhun said, had complained that their duties were too strenuous and had subsequently been sent to the Angkar Leu. Chhun and the others had also feared execution, Chhun because he had stolen rice for himself and his wife, the others for various reasons, and had reached a joint decision to flee to Thailand. There had been eleven persons in their group when they left the cooperative nine days ago, but three had become separated and two others had been killed by snipers east of Ta Krei.

Kim explained her own circumstances, omitting only the fact of her collaboration with the Americans in Phnom Penh. When she had finished it was decided by Chhun and the others that she would be permitted to join them, to share whatever food they managed to find. She was grateful for this, but even more grateful for the offer of a drink from a small water jar one of the women carried, which had been filled at the river. The fire in her throat was not quenched by the drink, but it no longer raged quite so painfully.

Her good fortune in encountering these people, she discovered, extended still further: another man in the party, Koy Thuok, had heard of rendezvous points along the frontier, beyond the long escarpment, where refugees could contact members of the Khmer resistance forces. The guerrillas would lead them safely across the border, and would also provide clothing and bribe money to satisfy the Thai Border Patrol Police. Without these things, nearly everyone who escaped into Thailand these days was arrested and imprisoned; some women, it was rumored, had been raped or sold into slavery.

Kim asked, "Do you know how far it is to the escarpment?"

"Perhaps a dozen kilometers," Chhun said. "Another two beyond it to the border."

"It may even be less than that," Koy said. "We passed near Ta Krei two nights ago."

Kim said, "Then we must continue due west from here."

Chhun shook his head. "To the northwest. We have heard that Khmer Rouge patrols are heavy along the border between the river and Ta Sien, so we must make our crossing well above that village."

"You speak as one who knows this jungle well."

"No one knows it well except tigers and *koprei*," Chhun said. "But yes, I was born in Phum Siem and hunted here before the war. I can lead us across the escarpment, near one of the border rendezvous points."

Kim slept better that night than at any time since her escape: she woke only twice, inside her brush-covered hollow, and was not plagued by nightmares. At dawn she roused with the others, accepted a tiny portion of coconut and a swallow of water, and offered to carry the jar when they set out. She did not doubt Chhun's ability to lead them through the jungle, but one of the things she had been taught by the Khmer Rouge was that she must rely on no one but herself. She watched the angle of the sun carefully until she was satisfied that they were proceeding west by northwest, and checked it from time to time thereafter. She also maintained a sharp watch for snakes and predatory animals.

The terrain continued its gradual ascent throughout the morning and afternoon. They climbed over rocky ground snarled with fromager roots, past a scum-covered pool in a depression between mounds of rock, past ravines and small sections of flatland thick with reeds. The heat was worse than it had been during the past days, like the flame breath from an open furnace; it forced them to stop for rest several times, and wrung all the moisture from Kim until her skin felt leathery and brittle. The last of the water in the jar was gone by midday—one final swallow for each of them, the last they would drink, Koy said, in the independence-sovereignty of Democratic Kampuchea.

Now and then, over the flats behind them, Kim could smell the heavy odor of tiger, and each time she felt a return of her primitive fear. But no cat revealed itself. Across a grassy flat they saw a rhinoceros blundering through a colonnade of fromagers, but they were downwind of the beast and it offered no threat. In the late afternoon one of the other women stepped into a hole and fell on a sharp projection of rock, opening a gash in her side and twisting her ankle. Despite her own wounded leg, Kim helped support the woman, walking at a retarded pace a short distance behind the others, until the sun sank below the overhead canopy and sunset colors began to streak the sky. Then Chhun called a halt so they could make camp for the night.

They were in a section of medium-dense jungle near a narrow creek bed. On the far side of the bed was a bluff some ten meters high, with a sheer wall that curved away to the south; to the north the bluff broke up into jumbled rocks with a narrow defile cutting through them at an angle. Both the creek and the defile would be filled with water when the monsoons came, but now they were dry except for a stagnant greenish-brown trickle in the center of the stream bed.

While the men fashioned sleeping places in the trees, Kim and the other two women went foraging for food. By tacit consent the women, who were sisters and the wives of Koy Thuok and another man in the party, walked north toward the defile, and Kim followed the bluff wall in the opposite direction, looking for the air holes of locusts along the near bank. She did not find any, but beyond where the stream bed and the bluff wall curved, she came upon a nest of fat red ants. She caught several of them without being bitten, crushed them between her hands, and wrapped them in one of the hanging strips that had once been her blouse. Then, away from the bluff to the east, she saw a patch of smallish plants whose leaves were edible. She moved over there, bent to begin picking the leaves.

Sudden noise behind her.

She whirled, half crouching, thinking that it must be a tiger because it had been that kind of crashing sound. But it was not a tiger that came out from behind a tree directly in front of her. It was worse than a tiger, much worse.

It was a dragon.

And in the dragon's hand was that which breathed fire.

She stared at him, at the handgun leveled toward her, and poised to run. But something stayed her, froze her fear just short of panic. He was very close to her, only three or four meters away; she saw that his green khaki uniform was torn in several places, that his coarse features were blotchy with insect bites. His eyes, huge and black, seemed to want to devour her. His eyes—

She knew those eyes.

Yes, and that oxlike face . . . she knew that face too. It was not possible, it could not be, but the dragon was familiar, the dragon was someone from the dim past of that other Than Kim in that other Kampuchea, like a vision in a waking dream; the dragon was—

"Chey Han," she said.

Natalie

Dear David:

It's been almost a week, six and a half days, since that night in the White Orchid and I haven't heard from you. No telephone call, no note, nothing. For all I know you've already left Bangkok—I just called your hotel and they said you hadn't checked out but you hadn't been in for several days either—and by the time you get this letter you'll be in Washington or Grosse Pointe or God knows where. So writing it may be a sort of anticlimax. But I have to get it all said in any case, for my own sake.

I want you to know that I didn't walk out on you because of your fight with Boyd. I've never liked him and what he said about poor Peter Deighan made me want to hit him myself. I walked out because it all seemed so damned hopeless—you and me, your refusal to face our relationship or take control of your life. I just didn't want to be with you anymore that night.

Later I tried to tell myself that your loss of control with Boyd was healthy because all your life you'd played it the other way, *never* losing control, and it showed you were finally on your way to taking a position. I might have gone on thinking that if only you'd come by to see me. Or called. Or written. But you didn't. And that's been the hardest of all for me to take because it can only mean one thing.

David, if only you knew how much I wanted you to call. I think that's part of the reason I walked out after the fight—I wanted you to come to *me* for a change. Not to apologize, I never wanted an apology. I just wanted you to care enough about me, about us, to share your feelings. I just wanted you to need me.

Silly.

Now I'm admitting the truth. And throwing in the towel.

You may already have decided, or half decided anyhow, that our relationship is finished. That may be why I haven't heard from you. But if not, if you're still as indecisive as ever, then I've got to be the one to say it. It's finished, David. No more affair, no more relationship. It hurts too much and I don't want to be an easy lay anymore, or a surrogate for Kim or a warm body to help you ease your guilt. I hope we never see each other again. There's no point in even talking to each other again, so let's not let it happen.

I'm sorry things had to turn out this way. You'll never know how sorry I am.

Natalie

Chey Han

Facing the hen at last in the hot jungle twilight, he thought with a sense of wonder: It is Than Kim, it *is*.

"It is!" the bonze cried, tossing his head from one hand to the other, spraying droplets of blood in his excitement. "Oh Chey Han, it is it is it is!"

Even before she spoke his name, Chey could see his own perception reflected in her eyes: she recognized him, as he had recognized her. He could also see shock, terror, mirrored there. And confusion. Above all, confusion.

He understood this, for confusion gripped him as well. Wonder mingled with elation mingled with great sorrow mingled with the chattering, nattering voice of the bonze. He did not know what to say. He did not know what to do next. All during his quest he had thought often of this moment of confrontation, but only of this moment, not the ones which would come beyond it. The quest was not over. Confronting the hen, identifying her as his half-sister, little sister, did not put an end to it.

"Chey Han," she said.

It was her voice, and yet it was not. Cracked, brittle—not the musical voice of the child and the young woman he had known in Rovieng. Twelve years. Twelve lifetimes. He wanted to say to her: Remember when we played together along the banks of the Sen? Remember when we danced the *lamtong* and ate balls of sweet dough dusted with coconut? But he had no words, only the dim and fading memories. All gone now. Never again. Never again.

"Make up your mind, Chey Han," the bonze said to him. He had quieted himself and was standing now in the posture of a wise old chief. "What are you going to do? Are you going to butcher her or not?"

He did not want to listen to the bonze; if he had had the strength he would have driven the bonze away. The headless one had been his good friend and companion for a long time, but he had begun to wear out his welcome. The time had come for him to retreat, if only for a little while, so that Chey could be alone with Than Kim. Why did the bonze not understand this?

"I understand much," the bonze said. "I understand everything."

"You understand nothing."

"Everything. Everything!"

Foolish argument. Foolish bonze. If only he were not so weary, if only he could think more clearly. Eight days since he had left his sergeant and his jeep at the checkpoint below Khum Kdol and entered the jungle. Eight days of hard travel, little water, little food, following the Mongkol Borei because he sensed this was what the hen would do. Eight days of listening to the bonze tell him first that he must turn back, he must not do this, and then change his position abruptly, as the headless one seemed wont to do, and urge him onward, exhort him to find the hen and complete his quest and resolve this madness. Then, today, the glimpse of her with the other chickens, the certainty she was Kim even though he had been too far away to see her well, and the following, and the waiting, and now this moment, the two of them together at last, reunited, alone.

Except for the bonze. "*Are* you going to butcher her, Chey Han? Are you?"

"I don't know yet."

"Are you? Are you?"

"Leave me alone!"

He said these last words aloud, and the sharpness of his voice made the hen, the little sister, tense and look again for a place to run. She was like a bird, he thought, about to take wing. Wounded bird with tattered feathers. Poor bird. Always so pretty, always making music with her voice and her laughter. Poor bird. Poor hen.

"Poor hen," he said to her. "Poor bird."

She shook her head, and again he was aware of her confusion. "It is you, Chey Han," she said. "But I don't understand . . . why are you here like this, alone?"

"I'm not alone. The bonze is with me."

"What bonze?"

"The dead bonze who lives inside my mind."

Another headshake. She seemed to tremble.

"Be quiet, Chey Han," the bonze said. "Why do you want to tell her about me? She doesn't understand."

"But I want her to understand."

"She can't. She won't."

The hen, the little sister said, "Your clothing . . . you're one of them, one of the Khmer Rouge soldiers."

"Am I?" Chey said. "I was."

"Are you fleeing them now? Is that why you're here?"

"Ah!" the bonze said. "An important question. *Are* you fleeing them now?"

"I don't know."

"You don't know anything, do you?"

"I don't know," he said to the little sister. "I came looking for you. All the way from the cooperative near Lovea. No, all the way from Sisophon."

Still another headshake. "How could that be?"

"I saw you at the Sisophon train station in December. You and the other chickens from Pursat."

"That's not true," the bonze scolded him. "*I* saw her at the train station; *I* recognized her. You give me no credit, Chey Han. You must tell the truth."

"It was the bonze who recognized you," Chey said. "I didn't believe it, not for a long while. But then he convinced me that I must find out for certain. But when we went to the cooperative we learned the hen named Mey Yat had escaped. You kept eluding me after that. Twice you eluded me, but I knew I would find you. And now I have. The quest is almost over."

"Are you going to shoot me, brother?"

"Shoot you?"

"Why else do you point your weapon at me?"

Chey looked down at the gun in his hand and was surprised to see it there. He could not remember drawing it from its holster.

"I'm not sure," he said.

"You can't delay any longer," the bonze said. "You must decide now."

Sweat stung Chey's eyes and blurred the face of the little sister; he wiped it away with his free hand so that he could see her again. "Poor hen," he said. "I don't want to butcher you."

"Then let me have what remains of my life."

"I've butchered so many. So many. I've had enough of butchering, enough of death."

"Enough of chickens?" the bonze asked slyly.

"Yes. Enough of chickens."

"Perhaps Kim is not a chicken. Perhaps she is a woman."

"Little sister."

"Yes. And perhaps you are not a chicken either."

"No, I'm a man."

"Are you?"

"Yes."

"Do men butcher women? Do brothers butcher sisters?"

"They do not," he said to the bonze. Then, to Kim, "You're not a hen, you're a woman. I'm not a rooster, I'm a man."

She held out her hand—a gesture of appeal. "Let me go, Chey Han."

"The border is not far from here," he said.

"No, not far. You can escape too; you can be free."

"No," he said, "I can't escape."

"Why can't you?"

"There is no escape for me."

"No escape," the bonze agreed. "No escape."

Without thinking about it, Chey realized he had made his decision. "Turn away, little sister," he said. "Run. Run to the border."

She hesitated. "If you intend to shoot me, do it as I face you."

"I will not shoot you. Run. Run!"

She turned and ran, away toward the dry creek bed and the bluff wall beyond. Once, only once, did she look back, and then but for an instant. Moments later the trees swallowed her and it was as if he had never seen her at all.

"Oh Chey Han," the bonze said. He had placed his head back on his shoulders, and there was no longer any blood, and he was weeping. "Oh Chey Han. I salute you."

Chey said nothing. He turned into the jungle, in the opposite direction from where Than Kim had fled, and found a path that curled away to the south. But then he stopped again: there was a heavy weight in his right hand and he was aware that he still carried the unholstered American sidearm. He looked at it, frowning. It was an instrument of death, and he had had enough of guns, enough of death. Enough. He hurled it away into the trees.

He walked until darkness settled, then climbed a tree and fell into an exhausted sleep. He dreamed of his youth in Rovieng, of playing with the little sister along the banks of the Sen, of dancing the *lamtong* with her and listening to the music of her laughter. He dreamed of the day in Siem Reap during this past year, when he and several other officers had been served whiskey mixed with dried lizard meat, herbs, and the gall bladders of ten butchered chickens. This drink had not endowed him with courage, as it was supposed to do; it had only made him drunk. And the gall bladders, which he could see plainly in his dream, were not those of chickens but of prostitutes, of women, of dead Khmers. He dreamed of dead Khmers, thousands of them screaming on the killing fields, thousands of grinning skulls and bleached white bones, thousands of ghosts whispering his name. And he dreamed of Doremy and her voice whispering his name on nights when the moon shone full and bright and there was the scent of passion in the air.

In the morning, when he awoke, the bonze was gone.

He was not surprised. The bonze did not need him any longer; he did not need the bonze. Now the headless one could return to his grave and find peace in the lap of his Buddha. Now Chey could go on alone, contained within himself, given new strength by the end of his quest and by the bonze's blessing, the bonze's release: "Do men butcher women? Do brothers butcher sisters? You are a man, Chey Han. You are a man."

He walked all that day, south toward the Mongkol Borei, and his footsteps felt light and he was not bothered by the heat or the rugged terrain. In the middle of the afternoon he came to a rocky clearing and paused for a moment to rest. It would not be long, he thought, before he reached the river. And then? He had told the little sister that there was no escape for him, but perhaps this was not quite true. Perhaps he would cross the border after all and seek his future in Thailand. Perhaps he—

The first sniper's bullet caught him in the left shoulder, spun him half around and dropped him to the stony earth.

I'm not a chicken, he thought, bewildered. I'm a man.

The second bullet took him in the right side, flopped him over on his stomach.

I am a human being.

The third bullet struck him in the center of the back and exploded his heart, and he never heard the sniper come up to him out of the jungle ahead, never heard the young soldier sprinkle words over him as the bonzes of his youth had sprinkled incense.

"Another one," the sniper said. "Another traitorous pig to die by the hand of Angka."

Kim

Two days after her strange encounter with Chey Han, Kim and the other refugees crossed the escarpment above Ta Sien. And when they made their way to a point near the bottom of the steep western slope, they were within a single kilometer of freedom.

It had not been an easy two days. The heat and the mountainous terrain had retarded their pace, creating a constant need for rest and a constant struggle over sharp outcroppings, across water-eroded gullies and ravines, through dusty snake grass that beat at their faces with every stride. One of the men had stepped on a snake and been bitten; the fangs had only struck glancingly, injecting a small amount of venom, or he would not have been able to go on. Edible matter was more difficult to find in these higher elevations: they had eaten nothing on this final day except dry leaves. But they had survived it all, including the treacherous descent, and now, across the flats below, they could see the line of jungle beyond which, Chhun Kaon said, was Thailand.

Chhun and the other men held a brief discussion. It was agreed that the flats were likely to be full of KC traps—mines, pitfalls—and that it would be safer if only one of them made the crossing to the rendezvous point in the jungle beyond, while the others waited here; that one, which Koy Thuok insisted was to be him, would then return as soon as possible with members of the resistance, who would lead them all safely to the border two kilometers away. Koy wanted to leave right away so that he might reach the rendezvous point by nightfall. Chhun argued that it was too late in the day to attempt the crossing, that shadows had already begun to lengthen on the flats and it would be difficult to see, difficult to avoid the traps. Koy prevailed, however. The others were anxious to reach Thailand and supported his position. Kim agreed with Chhun but made no mention of her feelings. She was an outsider, a part of the group only by their good favor; and she was also a woman. They would not have listened to her.

Koy set out as soon as the discussion ended. With the others, hidden on a wide tree-screened ledge, Kim watched him vanish and reappear again through the lower jungle, then through the grass and scrub brush on the flats. No one spoke. The evening shadows deepened; Koy dwindled to an indistinct shadow among them. And disappeared for the last time . . .

The explosion made a dull thudding boom in the stillness; light erupted a third of the way across the flats, just beyond the point where Koy had last been visible. Something black, like a burnt and misshapen log, burst upward with the flare but was gone again in an instant.

Koy's wife cried out, a keening sound that cut over the last fading echo of the explosion. Kim clapped a hand over the woman's mouth, pulled her down and held her until she stopped struggling. Then, as she began to weep silently, Kim moved aside so that the woman's sister could enfold her in a tight embrace. No words passed among any of them during this time. There was nothing to be said.

Not long afterward there was movement on the flats, off to their left. Kim squinted through the purpling dusk, saw a line of shadow shapes approaching from the south. Khmer Rouge patrol: she could just make out their weapons in silhouette. They had no doubt been close enough to hear the explosion and had come to investigate.

She watched the soldiers stop in the vicinity of the mine, some of them visible and some not; the visible ones appeared to be reconnoitering. But then they continued on to the north, apparently satisfied that Koy had been alone—a single refugee caught by one of their traps, an occurrence that was perhaps not uncommon.

When the patrol had been swallowed by darkness Chhun turned to her and the others. "I'll be the next to attempt the crossing," he said. "At sunrise. If the Lord Buddha wills it, we will all be in Thailand two days from now."

No one argued with him and there was no further discussion.

They each built sleeping hollows, climbed into them for the night. Kim said her silent prayers, repeated over and over in her mind Buddha's mystical invocation against the forces of evil. Afterward, as sleep coiled around her, Chey Han entered her thoughts. During the past two days she had dwelt little on the meeting with him. In her memory it seemed surreal, almost as if he had appeared to her as an apparition. Or perhaps the entire incident had been imaginary, a product of her exhaustion and mental strain. If she had truly seen him, spoken with him, a great many perplexing questions presented themselves: Why had he searched for her all the way from the cooperative? Why alone? How had he followed her and found her? Why had he spoken so strangely of chickens and dead bonzes? Why had he allowed her to flee instead of shooting her or placing her under arrest? Too many questions; she was not equipped to deal with them now. Perhaps she would never be equipped to deal with them. Perhaps the incident *was* hallucination and for her own sake she must always consider it so . . .

Sleep claimed her, held her in fitful dozes broken by dreams lost to her the moment she awakened. She was up before the others, a full hour before dawn, foraging in darkness close to the camp. She found nothing, but the activity relieved her restlessness, eased the soreness in her injured leg.

Chhun left them just at sunrise, when the sky was aglow with light and the flats below were empty of shadow. As before, Kim and the others watched his progress from their hiding place along the ledge. Down through the lower jungle, out across the grassy and rock-strewn flatland. Visible part of the time, invisible most of the time. He went much more slowly than Koy, detouring twice to different paths, zigzagging out to the northwest instead of crossing in a straight line. Watching him as the minutes passed, Kim could feel tension climbing to the point where her hands began to tremble. It was the same for the others, she could see, and perhaps worst of all for Koy's wife.

The sun crawled higher, grew visible through the treetops behind them; the flats shimmered with its glare. Chhun disappeared altogether. Kim half expected to see another flash of light, hear another dull thudding explosion, but this did not happen. Noonday came and went, and nothing happened.

Some of the tension eased. But only some of it. Chhun had avoided the mines, yes, but they would not have heard his cries if he had fallen into a *punji* trap; nor would they know it if he was attacked by a Khmer Rouge patrol before he reached the rendezvous point. If something happened to him, they would know it only when he failed to return within a maximum of three days. There was nothing to do meanwhile except to wait.

The rest of that day passed quickly enough. Kim and the two sisters went foraging and came upon a breadfruit tree some distance from the camp; the fruit gave them the first moisture they had had in days and buoyed their spirits somewhat. They sat in a circle and talked to each other in low voices, mostly about what they would do after they reached Thailand. Kim listened but like Koy's wife spoke little of her own plans. They were clear and yet they were unclear; it was not time for them yet. Survive first, then plan for tomorrow.

The second day was more difficult. Up before dawn. Another forage, this time without finding food. Waiting. Dawn. Crashing sounds in the jungle: a dead tree falling somewhere nearby? Waiting. Sunrise. The distant cry of a tiger. A *koprei* moving sluggishly out on the flats. Waiting. Midmorning. The sun hotter than any day before, the humidity thicker and more unbreathable. Waiting, waiting. Noon. Wild peacocks on the flats now, close to the jungle on this side but too far away to be easily caught. Waiting. Early afternoon. Dark clouds rolling across the sky, breaking up the sunglare, laying quilted shadows over the landscape. Waiting, waiting, waiting—

And then, among the shadows to the northwest: men coming toward them.

Kim stood against the bole of a fromager tree, head craned forward, staring out to where the men were—eight of them, as near as she could tell. She could feel herself panting. They were not Khmer Rouge soldiers; they carried weapons, but as they drew closer she could also make out camouflage helmets and uniforms, knapsacks, heavy boots instead of sandals. Resistance fighters. And Chhun. One of the men must be Chhun.

The others clustered near her, and when they were certain of who was approaching, and that Chhun was among them, they broke into relieved smiles and embraced one another. Kim did not smile, nor take part in the embracing. She only stood against the tree, watching and waiting. The relief would come later. Everything would come later. There was still now to live through.

They left the ledge and went down through the jungle to meet Chhun and the other men. There was more embracing, but it did not last long; the leader of the guerrillas, a man named Song Sarun, said that they must hurry if they expected to complete the crossing before dusk. With the refugees in the

408

middle, they set out in single file, retracing the northwesterly course across the flats. Song Sarun and his men seemed to know the area well, where land mines and pitfalls had been laid; they were able to move rapidly along a half dozen different paths. The crossing took less than an hour and was made without incident.

When they reached the jungle on the far side they paused long enough for the refugees to change into peasant clothing from the knapsacks. They were also given a handful of Thai baht each. Then they plunged on again, skirting another flat grassy section, climbing over root tangles and barriers of rotting logs. Blue shadows formed around them; overhead the sky paled and began to bleed sunset colors. Darkness was only a few minutes away when Song Sarun called another halt in a small clearing.

"This is where we part," he said to the refugees. "You're safe now. From this point on you will have no more trouble with the Khmer Rouge."

"Then we've crossed the border?" Kim asked him.

"Yes. We're in Thailand."

It was only later that she learned the date: the seventeenth day of April, the first anniversary of the death of Kampuchea.

Cambodia File: Excerpt from a Report Prepared by the Refugee Section, U.S. Embassy, Bangkok, Thailand, April 1976

The selection process for inland camp refugees is a complex procedure involving the following steps before a refugee can depart for the United States (or, similarly, for any other nation involved in resettlement).

1. Interested refugees register with a Joint Voluntary

Agency (JVA) prescreening team. (JVA is under contract to the Department of State.) JVA representatives indicate on the registration form whether the refugees appear to qualify under existing criteria, and under which category they fall.

2. The JVA team sends or brings registration forms to Bangkok, where the JVA clerical staff opens dossiers on potential qualifiers. The staff prepares security clearance cables on all refugees, relative search and verification cables for Category I refugees, and employment verification cables for Category II refugees. The staff also files documents and correspondence, and, when necessary, requests additional information from the refugee's relatives in the U.S. or from former employers.

3. Refugee officers inspect dossiers to check the validity of documentation. The officers interview as many potentially qualified refugees as possible in order to determine whether they meet the qualifications for presentation to Immigration and Naturalization Service (INS) officers.

4. Refugee officers and JVA personnel accompany INS officers to the camps, where INS officers, during personal interviews, approve or disapprove refugees for entry into the United States.

5. JVA representatives send biographic information on all approved refugees to the American Council of Voluntary Agencies (ACVA), which then initiates the sponsorship search.

6. After ACVA confirms sponsorship, the Refugee Section contacts the Intergovernmental Committee for European Migration (ICEM), which asks the Bangkok Regional Office of the United Nations High Commissioner for Refugees to request the Thai Ministry of Interior to transfer sponsored refugees from the camps to Bangkok.

7. ICEM handles medical examinations for the refugees— sometimes in Bangkok and sometimes in the camps—and makes travel arrangements abroad.

8. After the refugees have received the required medical clearance, they are permitted to depart for the U.S.

There has been some criticism of this program. As many have observed, selection of refugees for resettlement can be slow. It can take from two to six months or more from original registration with a JVA representative to arrival in the United States. The slowness is attributable to several factors: the scope, particularly of the inland camp programs, where justice demands that virtually all potentially eligible refugees be interviewed before INS approvals take place; medical examinations and clearance; a necessity to insure that refugees who are selected meet U.S. legal requirements; and, because the refugee camps in the U.S. have been closed since December 1975, the time needed to find sponsors who will care for the refugees immediately upon their arrival in the United States.

Foxworth

When he came back from eight days alone at Pattaya Beach it was with the first true sense of purpose he'd ever known. He had gone there to finally get his head together, and that was what he'd done. He hadn't told anyone where he was going, not even Natalie. He'd felt that she wouldn't want to see him for a few days anyway, after the way she'd walked out of the White Orchid, and he hadn't wanted to see her, either, until he'd come to terms with things.

He had left for Pattaya Beach the morning after his one-punch knockdown of Tom Boyd. It was a popular resort ninety miles south of Bangkok on the Gulf of Thailand, one which was frequented by American embassy officials, among others; that was how he knew about it. He hadn't wanted to see any of his former coworkers, but then that wasn't a problem because he hadn't done any golfing or swimming or partying. Instead of taking a room at the Pattaya Palace Hotel, with its plastic Western poshness, he had rented a private bungalow just south of Ban Pattaya—a solitary place where he could look out over white sand and coral islands, watch water skiers and boaters, take in sunsets the color of polished bronze. Where he could sit and think and map out the new patterns of his life.

This time he had to be absolutely sure. Which wasn't to say

that he hadn't been absolutely sure about quitting the State Department; he had been and he still was—there was no question that it had been a decision both right and overdue. But getting out of something was not half as uncertain and difficult as getting into something else, particularly personal relationships and brand-new career directions. The decisions he made now, at this point in his life, age thirty-two, were ones he would have to live by for the next thirty or forty years. He'd made crucial mistakes before, both of omission and of commission; for his peace of mind, maybe even for his sanity, he couldn't afford to make the same mistakes, or even similar ones, a second time. This one was for all the marbles. This one *had* to be right.

He watched boats and people, he walked on the beach, he spoke to no one except the man who had rented him the bungalow and the maid/cook who came in every afternoon. On one level it was the first real vacation he'd had in years, since before joining the foreign service, and it relaxed him and gave him the first measure of peace he'd had in over a year. But most important was that somewhere during those eight days, at an hour or even a minute he couldn't pinpoint afterward, he had made his resolutions. And was sure of each of them.

On the morning of the ninth day he drove back up the coast on Highway 6. When he arrived in Bangkok he went straight to the Victory Hotel; his intention was to put away his luggage, shower off the sweat of the drive, and then call Natalie and make a date with her for dinner. But that wasn't the way it worked out. That wasn't the way *any* of it worked out.

Her letter was waiting for him at the hotel desk.

He read it in the elevator on the way up to the fourth floor, and his first reaction was emotional and childish: she had no right to do this to him, to recomplicate and add more *Angst* to his life just when he'd finally worked it into positive order. But that reaction was gone by the time he reached his room. He'd been a fool not to have told her he was going away, and why, if not where. She was a person, not an object, not a thing which could be tucked away and assumed to be ready and waiting whenever he wanted it. Or ignored if that was what suited him. That was how he'd treated her throughout their relationship, he realized, just as it was how the Americans had treated the Cambodians since at least 1970. For God's sake, the key to understanding himself was understanding his relationship with each of the women in his life—Andrea, Kim, *and* Natalie. He'd understood that at Pattaya. He should also have understood that her feelings were just as intense and just as important as his.

He thought of using the telephone, rejected the idea as too impersonal for the situation, and left the room and the hotel as soon as he'd put on a clean shirt. It was midafternoon and he thought that she would probably be at the Thai Relief Organization offices; he drove to Vorachak Road and entered the building where the TRO was housed. But she wasn't there. And she wasn't going to be there for some time, either, according to the polite young Thai with the slicked-down hair who greeted him.

"*Kha* Rosen is not in Bangkok at the present," the young man said. There was no inflection in his voice and there hadn't been any change in his expression when Foxworth gave his name, but Foxworth sensed a subtle hostility. If that wasn't just his imagination, it was obvious enough who had instilled the hostility and why.

"Where did she go?" he asked.

"I am afraid I can't say."

"Why can't you? Did she ask you not to tell me if I came looking for her?"

"I'm sorry," the young Thai said. "Perhaps you try again later. Next week, possibly."

"Is she at one of the camps? Aranyaprathet? Surin?"

"If you will excuse me, I must return to my work. *Sawat dee khrap,* Mr. Foxworth."

He went back to his rented car, drove around past Lumpini Park to the house of the Thai couple she roomed with. The woman had always seemed to like him in the past; now she was cool and distant, and gave him the same nonanswers as the young man at the TRO.

"Don't you understand?" he kept saying. "It's important that I see her—important for both of us. Can't you give me an idea where she is?"

"I know nothing, *khrap*."

"Will you at least tell me if she's coming back here?"

"I know nothing, *khrap*."

Frustrated, he had a momentary impulse to rush past the woman, go into Natalie's room, see if her clothing was still there, if there might be some clue to her whereabouts. But he couldn't blunder through Natalie's life anymore: he refused to be that kind of man, that was the kind of man he had spent a full year renouncing. Instead he went back to the car and sat in the sultry heat, shirt plastered to his skin, feeling humiliation crowd in on top of the frustration. But that was all right. Somewhere at the deep center he found an odd satisfaction in what was happening; if he paid for his attitudes toward Natalie with humiliation, then maybe at the end there would be a balance achieved, an expiation, and everything would work out as he had envisioned it at Pattaya.

After a time he started the car and drove back to the hotel. He ate a solitary dinner, went to bed early, slept badly, and was up at 6 A.M. At 7 A.M. he was back in the car, driving. And at seven-thirty he found himself heading out of Bangkok along the same Gulf road that he'd driven on the previous day.

When he reached the juncture with Highway 8, the road that led up through rice paddies and forestland to the west and eventually terminated in Aranyaprathet, he turned onto it without conscious selection. She must be at one of the camps, he told himself then. Where else could she be? If she had gone back home to New York, the young man at the TRO or the woman at the house would probably have told him so; they wouldn't have needed to keep her whereabouts a secret if she had already put several thousand miles between herself and David Foxworth. Going to Aranyaprathet at least gave him something to do, some positive approach to the situation. It was as good a place to start as any.

He was wrong about that, as it turned out. Aranyaprathet wasn't a good place to start, it was almost the best possible place. Natalie wasn't there, but she had been, only a couple of days ago, and one of the U.S. embassy officers told him she had gone on to Trat, 140 miles to the south. But that wasn't the news that turned his legs weak, sent a kind of wild relief bursting through him. That wasn't the news half the people in the embassy had known for two full days, according to the official, and that Foxworth would have known too if he hadn't put himself under wraps at Pattaya.

Natalie wasn't the only one at Trat.

Kim was alive, Kim had crossed the border—Kim was at Trat too.

Natalie

She was alone in Hall 1, Room 10 at the Trat Refugee Camp, going over the last of a series of prescreening forms filled out by the refugees, when David walked in. She heard the door open, she looked up, and there he was. A little rippling sensation passed under her breastbone, but that was all—no other reaction, physiological or emotional. She had known he would be coming to Trat as soon as he found out about Kim; in fact, that was why she had cut her own visit short and was scheduled to leave early that evening on a charter flight to Surin. She wouldn't have come here at all if she'd known about Kim beforehand, but she hadn't. She'd only found out yesterday, the day she arrived.

Another few hours, she thought, looking at him, and she would have been gone, she wouldn't have had to face him at all. But she should have known it wouldn't work out that way. Nothing seemed to work out the way she wanted it these days, whether it involved refugees or love affairs or anything else of consequence in her life; nothing seemed to be without a surfeit of pain. *You live with pain, Natalie, you make pain your profession and the motivating force in your life. How can you not get hurt sooner or later?* Oh, her father had been right. So right. For all the good it did him and all the good it did her . . . just two battered Rosens, survivors, refugees from one type of hell or another.

David said, "Hello, Natalie," as he shut the door behind him. And she said, "Hello, David," and stood from the table. She was conscious of the heat, the sound of voices and activity outside in the compound, the droning of flies, the smell of disinfectant. The slow steady rhythm of her breathing, like the susurration of the wind across a wasteland.

He came over to stand in front of her. There was beard stubble on his face, at least two days of it; he looked tired, but it was a physical kind of fatigue, not mental strain. No, she thought, it couldn't be mental strain, not now, not anymore. She made herself watch his eyes without blinking or glancing away—but just the eyes themselves, not what was reflected in them. There was no room in her now for his emotions; she had barely enough room for her own.

"How long have you been in camp?"

"Only a few minutes," he said. "I've been driving all day from Aranyaprathet."

"You know about Kim, of course."

"Yes."

"But you haven't seen her yet?"

"Not yet. I wanted to talk to you first."

She felt another twinge in her stomach. "Why, David? There's no need; you didn't have to see me."

"Yes I did. There are a lot of things we have to discuss, but not just yet, not until after I see Kim. The OIC said you were planning to leave this afternoon; I'm asking you not to. We can go somewhere later and talk."

"About what? You got my letter, didn't you? I think I said everything I had to say in there. And you said everything you had to say with your silence."

"No, you're wrong," he said. "I didn't get your letter until yesterday, when I returned to Bangkok; that's why I didn't respond to it." He reached out, took hold of her arms. She wanted to pull away, but there was a leaden feeling all through her body; she just stood still and let him hold her. "I went to Pattaya the morning after the Boyd incident," he said. "I felt I had to get away, to spend some time alone so I could work things out."

"And did you?" It was an effort at irony that did not come off.

"Yes. But I should have told you I was going; I had no right to leave you dangling the way I did, it was selfish and unfeeling and I'm sorry. That's not a superficial apology, Natalie. I mean every word of it. I was a fool and I was insensitive but you've got to understand that I never intended to hurt you, I never meant you to think I was running away from you."

She could feel her control starting to crumble. Wetness came into her eyes and made his face blurry, indistinct; she looked away from him for the first time and blinked until she could see again. But she couldn't speak. No words came to her; what could she say? What could she say?

"Do you believe me?" he said.

I don't know, she thought. "Yes," her voice said.

"Will you wait here for me? Will you let me take you somewhere later so we can talk?"

No, she thought. "All right," her voice said.

He held her arms a moment longer, eyes moving over her face; then he released her and stepped back and nodded once, as if he too had run out of words, and turned and went out, shutting the door softly behind him, leaving her there alone.

In her mind she pictured the thin ravaged empty-eyed woman who lay in one of the screened-off infirmary cubicles. Heard again the soft cracked voice that had spoken to her during their brief meeting this morning. Kim. Than Kim. Except that she didn't look anything like the Than Kim Natalie had met in Phnom Penh more than a year ago; she looked like every other refugee in this and every other camp, like just one more survivor from one more corner of hell. What did she need now? Was it David? Was it the company of other survivors of her own race? Was it anything any American, except perhaps her own father and those others in Abraham Rosen's scrapbook of photographs from Nazi Germany—and they, of course, were not native Americans at all—could even begin to understand?

Natalie went to the room's single dust-streaked window, looked out over the camp. It was the worst of them, the most squalid. Huts and administrative sheds with roofs made of plastic or thatch instead of tin, with walls of clapboard instead of solid timber boards. Pathetic little vegetable gardens along the perimeter fence. Men and women in small groups, some eating or doing small chores, most just sitting and looking at nothing, like figures transformed into stone by what their eyes had seen. Children running back and forth, wearing T-shirts that bore sayings in English—*Jesus Loves You,* that was one—which none of them would comprehend.

Jesus Loves You.

Jesus.

And yet, even with all of this, all the squalor, all the suffering, there *was* hope, wasn't there? Hope for the refugees, hope for Cambodia in spite of the Khmer Rouge; hope for the United States too, the America she had always believed in, the country that had been founded and built on hope. *Give me your tired, your poor, your huddled masses yearning to breathe free, the wretched refuse of your teeming shore.* Couldn't it be that way again, for the refugees, these refugees, the children out there starving in their Jesus Loves You T-shirts? Couldn't the mistake, the aberration, of Vietnam and Cambodia be rectified and abrogated? The United States would survive; couldn't Cambodia, couldn't the people, survive too?

Yes. And so would she. Hope for her too, with or without David. Hope for a time when there would be no mass pain to assault her, none of her own to absorb; hope for peace, her own and everyone else's.

Hope.

Kim

It was time for the meeting of strangers.

She had known for some while that this meeting must take place, and she had prepared herself for it. The man who stood at the foot of her cot had features she recognized, a way of standing and moving his head that recalled someone she had once known; but she did not know him. And in the way he looked at her, in what she saw in his eyes, she was a stranger to him as well. Perhaps he did not know this truly but he would. He would.

He said her name. "Kim," he said.

She did not speak. In her mind a faint voice whispered, "Hello, David," but it was the voice of someone she knew no better than this man before her. She raised her hands instead in formal greeting, let her fingertips rest against her lips for a moment, and returned her hands to her sides.

"How do you feel?" he asked awkwardly.

"I am well," she said.

"Well enough to talk for a few minutes?"

"Yes. It is good to see you again."

The formality echoed in her mind. *I am well. It is good to see you again. I am happy to be free.* These were the words of boatmen on the Tonle Sap, shopkeepers near the Marché Central, waiters in Le Royal Restaurant, peasants from the villages along the Mekong; these were the words of dead Khmers. There was no longer any formality in Kampuchea. As they had done with the Lord Buddha, the Khmer Rouge had decreed and rendered the past meaningless.

"They told me you were shot," he said.

"Yes."

"In the leg."

"Yes. It is not serious. It will heal."

He came closer, stood alongside and above her for a moment; then he knelt and placed his hand on the cot near her hand, left it there with the fingers upraised, in a manner which made it resemble a large white spider overturned on its back. She looked at it incuriously, trying to divine his purpose. Was she meant to touch it? But that would have been impolite. They were, after all, strangers.

"They also told me some of what you went through," he said. A shudder seemed to pass through him. "It must have been . . . God, I can't even imagine what it must have been."

"It is good that you can't imagine," she said. "You would not want to know."

"But I would. I *do* want to know."

"Why?"

"Because I was one of those who helped make it happen. I didn't understand that a year ago, in Phnom Penh, but I do now. I helped make it happen and I've got to know how it was so I can help keep it from happening again."

His breathing had become more rapid; his eyes were filmed with a moistness, and he was very intense, very agitated. This must be difficult for him, she thought. Such meetings were always difficult for Americans.

"I'm not the same person I was back then," he said. "You do understand that, don't you? I've changed . . . I'm still changing."

"We have all changed," she said.

His hand moved, as if to touch her; but he did not. "I'm not the same person," he said again. "I've quit the State Department, Kim. Did anyone tell you that? I don't work for the American government anymore."

"Yes," she said. "Miss Rosen told me."

"You spoke to her, then."

"Yes. This morning."

"I wish I'd had the insight and the courage to resign a long time ago," he said. "In Phnom Penh, before the fall. Kim . . . would you have come out with me if I'd resigned then?"

She sensed that he wanted desperately for her to say yes. She said, "Yes."

"Do you mean that?"

"Yes."

"It would have been different then, for both of us. It would have been so much better for you."

Would it? she wondered. It was true that she would not have experienced the past year, she would not have seen death and felt death and smelled death and held death in her arms, all of this was true, but she would also not have known what she now knew about the dragons, she would not have found purpose, she would only have lived in darkness and delusion and safety while so many others died in light and clarity and anguish.

"I loved you, Kim," he said. "You know that."

"I know it."

"But not enough. That was what I didn't understand until just a while ago. I never loved you enough."

This talk of love made her feel sad. Perhaps she, too, had once loved someone such as this stranger; she had certainly loved another stranger, whose name was Charoun and whose face had vanished from her memory, as he had vanished into the earth. But these passions had happened a long time ago, to a woman she barely knew. David and Kim? Charoun and Kim? No, no. No.

"But I thought I did," he said. "After you disappeared and I couldn't find you I thought I loved you with all my heart and soul. I didn't know how to love then but I *wanted* to love, I was changing and full of guilt and I made you into the focus of feelings I was just starting to learn. Like a new language, you see? I read the signs but I didn't quite know what they meant."

"I understand," she said.

He seemed to want to touch her again; and again he did not. "I couldn't stop thinking about you, I devoted myself to you after the fact. You were never out of my mind for more than a few minutes at a time."

She waited, not speaking.

"I deluded myself into believing I loved you deeply, so that I wouldn't have to face the truth. It took a long time for me to understand that and to admit it to myself. But now I have. And the truth is that I still love you but I still don't love you enough. I love someone else more."

"Natalie Rosen," she said.

He looked at her in surprise. "Did she tell you about us?"

"She did not have to tell me. It was in her eyes when she spoke your name."

"We've been together almost four months," he said. His face was mobile with emotion; the moistness in his eyes glistened like dew in the sunlight. "We would have been together long before that, I think, except that I felt I had to remain faithful to you. I didn't want to abandon you a second time, I wanted to be there waiting for you when you came out. In a way I guess I was afraid of being like Tom Boyd. He left *his* Khmer woman behind in Phnom Penh and didn't give it a second thought; used her and then just left her." He paused, looked down at his hand on the cot as if seeing it for the first time. He took it away and hid it from her sight. "And now you're here, safe, and I'm here, it's the kind of reunion I kept hoping for all those months. Except that it isn't, and it never could have been. Even if it weren't for Natalie, it just . . . it never could have been."

No, she thought, it never could have been. She would not tell him this, but there was little difference to her now between this stranger and the other one, Tom Boyd. Perhaps there never had been a difference. Because the Americans—how sad this was— the Americans were, after all, only a race of strangers.

She wanted to close her eyes, to rest; she had been feeling better with each passing day, but she was still weak, it would still be many days before she was strong enough to concern herself again with the dragons. But to close her eyes, even for a moment, would be impolite. She must be attentive to the man who knelt beside her, because he had been through much himself and because he cared for her and because she sensed he was a good man. She must make it as easy for him as possible. Then she could rest. When the meeting of strangers was ended —then she could rest.

"You will be happy with Natalie Rosen," she said.

"I think so, yes. I'm going to ask her to marry me."

"This is good. God will bless and keep you both."

"I'm glad you understand," he said. There was relief in his voice, as if he had been concerned that she might feel differently. What would he have done then? If she had wanted him for herself, if she were still the woman he had known and if such a thing were possible, would he have given himself to her? It seemed clear that he would have. Yes, she thought, a good man. A man who had learned many things, and profited by them, and found the companionship of strength and compassion.

"What will you do in the days to come?" It was the old voice inside her, the ghostly one that had whispered *Hello, David* when he first said her name, that asked this question and the next. "Will you return to America?"

"No," he said. "At least not permanently."

"You will work in Thailand?"

"Refugee work. With Natalie and her father, if they'll have me. Does that surprise you?"

Nothing surprises me, she thought. "No," she said.

"It did me at first. But it shouldn't have. I've known for a long time that politics don't matter, *people* matter. And yet it took me months to make up my mind, even with all the answers right there in front of me. Natalie. Refugee work. All the things you were to me and that you made me."

"I?"

"Yes. I'd be none of those things if it wasn't for you. And now that you're free and safe, I'm free too. That's a terrible thing to say, isn't it? That you had to suffer so much so that I could learn. But truth is truth; I have to be honest with you."

"We must all do what we must," she said.

"I was afraid you might hate me."

"No. I hate no one but the Khmer Rouge."

"Kim . . . what will *you* do after you're well?"

"I have not decided yet," she said, and this was, of course, a lie. She did not like telling a lie to the stranger, but it would make matters easier for him. And for her. If she told him the truth, about her plans for the dragons, he would only anguish and make words of argument, and she was very tired.

"You won't have to stay here at Trat. Or at any of the other camps. I'll see to that. I'll get you a visa to France or America, wherever you want to go."

"That is kind of you," she said, "but I do not want to leave Thailand."

"Then I'll help you get a Thai visa. And a job, if you want me to."

"Perhaps."

He seemed to sense her fatigue. He looked at her a moment longer; then he rose slowly to his feet, saying, "I think I'd better be going now. You need rest."

She nodded.

"I'll come back and see you tomorrow, if that's all right."

"If you wish." But then she thought: No, that is not quite

right. That does not show the proper respect for his concern. "Yes, of course," she said. "You may see me whenever you wish."

The moistness glistened in his eyes again. He leaned down and kissed her once, gently, on the forehead, and even though he was a stranger and such acts of familiarity were not proper, she made no protest.

"Kim," he whispered, "I love you, I do love you." And then he was gone.

She closed her eyes and waited for sleep to claim her again. And in the moments before it came, she thought of Charoun and Serey and Chey Han and some of the other strangers who had passed through her life and that of the other Than Kim. And of all the strangers who had passed through Kampuchea over the centuries: the Cham, the Thais, the Annamese, the Vietnamese, the French, the Americans. The plunderers of today, the dragons, had been spawned from among the Khmers themselves, from the dark side of the divine Naga's soul, but they were no different from the others. Once, on the night when she had first been raped, she had thought that Kampuchea would die, that the dragons would destroy it; now she knew that this was not so. They had come and pillaged, as the others had come and pillaged, but one day they too would be overthrown— by new conquerors who would come and pillage and be overthrown themselves in endless cycle—and in another time the ruins of the empire of Angkar Leu would be indistinguishable from the ruins of the empire of Angkor Wat: jungle-shrouded temples of death to be uncovered and studied and marveled upon, just as had the mystical temples of the God Kings. The land would remain, the Khmer people would survive. It was only those who came to shed blood who would be swept away in the tide of history.

In Kampuchea, she thought, all has changed and yet everything is still the same. The plunder, the pain, the dying. The fire of the dragons, the thunder of the guns.

It goes on and on and on . . .

Afterword

The story you have just read, of course, is fiction. But if the characters seemed real to you, it is because they have their counterparts in true life. The brutal events took place; the nightmare actually happened. Not only were the gentle people of Cambodia cruelly savaged, the horror is still going on.

For years, the appalling story was locked in secret U.S. government files. It was suppressed by Richard Nixon and Henry Kissinger, who had helped to precipitate the Cambodian tragedy. They were aided by other officials who had participated in the shameful decisions and had hoped to hide the terrible consequences.

But their secret was too monstrous to keep under cover. A few conscientious officials refused to be witnesses to genocide and remain silent. They began to slip me the secret documents —intelligence reports, eyewitness accounts, aerial photographs— which portrayed an episode in history so cataclysmic, an apocalypse so chilling that it cannot be hidden from the world. There has not been a story like it since the Nazis enslaved and exterminated millions in Adolf Hitler's Europe.

The classified accounts revealed how a band of Cambodian radicals, who had roomed together as students in Paris, returned to practice their mad politics upon an innocent nation. These revolutionary zealots, led by the terrible Pol Pot, imposed a reign of death and terror upon their own people.

Entire cities were forcibly evacuated, their hapless inhabitants driven into the countryside on death marches which left hundreds of thousands of bodies rotting by the roadsides. By mass shootings and clubbings, the new rulers sought to eliminate all vestiges of the past and to transform the populace into their own radical image. Every civilized value was systematically debased and debauched.

Five weeks after Pol Pot seized power, I was ready to begin the story, but my words were too weak to convey the utter horror of the Cambodian experience. I tried repeatedly to awaken the world to what was happening behind the sealed Cambodian borders, but my columns were ignored by a world preoccupied with other, more visible problems.

Then in May 1978, I recapitulated the story and told it all over again in five urgent, consecutive columns. Those who claimed membership in the human race, I pleaded, could not turn their backs on the slaughter in Cambodia. Millions had already died, I reported, from executions, starvation, disease, and overwork.

This time the response was heartening. Thousands of readers wrote to Congress, the White House, and the United Nations urging action. The Cambodian story at last was out; it could no longer be suppressed. But the concern of the American people was not shared at first by their government. Except for a few, the bureaucrats shuffled papers in their air-conditioned offices while the suffering Cambodians were beaten into the ground by the ruthless Pol Pot regime.

The facts that I had shaken loose, meanwhile, began to appear on the front pages. Eventually, a year after my five-column splash, President Carter belatedly sent his wife, Rosalynn, on an inspection trip to the scene. Then Congress appropriated funds to succor Cambodian refugees, and the immigration restrictions were eased to permit their entry into the United States.

Still, the news accounts had not captured the epic dimensions of the tragedy, the human anguish underlying the upheaval in Cambodia. Here was a story that had to be humanized, with blood and tears, so the world would not easily forget it. At a time of rampant terrorism, here was a grotesque account of what had happened when a band of terrorists won their revolution and imposed their radical philosophy upon a civilized nation.

I brought the project to Doubleday, the book publishers, who wanted the story to be written by one of the nation's best novelists. They put me in touch with Bill Pronzini. We agreed to collaborate on a novel that was to take two years to complete. I supplied the raw facts; he wove them into a human saga.

The novel ends in April 1976 on a note of hope. But for most Cambodians, there was little hope. Pol Pot and his Khmer Rouge fanatics continued to eradicate Cambodia's civilized past until nearly half of the seven-million population perished at their hands. Those who tried to escape across the Thai border were turned away by border guards or gunned down. The few who reached Thailand were thrown into wretched refugee compounds where more torment awaited them.

Some were beaten, robbed, and raped by Thai camp guards. Some were thrust back over the border to face certain death. Those who were allowed to stay in Thailand were confined in squalid internment camps. At one camp, a U.S. investigator found 1,055 Cambodians occupying five miserable acres. The only well had run dry, and the inhabitants had to barter their meager belongings to buy water and food from nearby villagers.

A few lucky refugees made it to America. One was Thach Minh Loi, who had all but abandoned hope in a Malaysian camp. Forlorn and malnourished, he had given up most of his scant food rations to his small daughter and pregnant wife. He ate rats and snakes to survive. Their situation was so hopeless, he wrote a sister in America, that he had decided to end their suffering by doing away with his family and then killing himself. The anguished sister appealed to me, and I intervened in time to prevent the family suicide. With bewildering speed, the Loi family found themselves on their way to the United States.

I sent an associate to the airport with Loi's sister to share the poignant reunion with them. The family straggled off the plane, fatigued and ill. Their Asian stoicism broke down at the sight of the awaiting sister. Smiles lit up the gaunt faces; tears began to stream. Choking on their first words, they fell into one another's arms.

Then a sudden calm, like a sigh of relief, settled over them. My associate drove the family to their new home in Veyo, Utah. As they piled out of the van, Loi could no longer suppress his emotion. He could speak no English, but suddenly he threw his fists into the air and jumped with joy, like a football player who had just scored a Super Bowl touchdown. With all his lungpower, Loi yelled at the nearby mountains: "America!"

Back in Cambodia, the cheerless survivors were suddenly engulfed by new violence in late 1978 when a Vietnamese military force rolled across the border. The attackers swiftly captured Phnom Penh and set up a puppet regime. Pol Pot escaped into the jungles, and once again innocent Cambodians were caught in the cross fire between rival forces.

But at least the dispossessed civilian population were liberated from the dread work camps. They limped back to the cities, which they found in shambles. All banking and private commerce had been eliminated by the Khmer Rouge extremists. The currency had been abolished, the transportation system wrecked, the stores emptied.

The returning inhabitants scrabbled out a bare existence at a starvation level under an inept puppet government and a military occupation by the Vietnamese soldiery. The Cambodians accepted the presence of the Vietnamese, despised for centuries, only because they were a lesser evil than the deposed Khmer Rouge killers.

The pathetic survivors were forced to kowtow to the Vietnamese, whose corrupt officials diverted scarce rice and other supplies to their own country. A usurious black market reduced the Cambodians to beggary.

At this writing, emergency food relief efforts have foundered. Confidential State Department cables warn that the country's starving rice farmers are consuming the seed rice for the next planting. The outlook is that an entire, weakened populace could die for lack of food.

The carnage might not have come upon Cambodia if Richard Nixon had not ordered American forces crashing across the border during the Vietnam War. Pol Pot might never have gained power if Nixon had not supported the corrupt and ineffectual Lon Nol. And the infamous Pol Pot government might have been discredited before the world if Jimmy Carter, playing three-handed international poker with the Chinese and the Russians, had not ordered the U.S. representative at the United Nations to vote to allow the Khmer Rouge to retain the Cambodian seat.

Thus we share in the horrible legacy that has befallen Cambodia. We must share in helping to prevent the death of a country, its culture, and its people. My hope is that someday Bill Pronzini and I can write a happy sequel to our novel.

—Jack Anderson